KAREN TOMLINSON

Join Karen's newsletter for a FREE fantasy book, release news, & writing updates,
and more.

❀ Created with Vellum

Editing Judi Soderberg
Hard Cover Art: Samaiya Beaumont
Character Arts: Lauren Ritchilieu
Couple Character Art: Mageonduty
Maps: Karen Tomlinson

Find all Karen's books & reading order:
www.karentomlinson.com/books

For special edition e-books/paperbacks, and hardbacks with colour maps, character art, exclusive formatting, hardcore art, foiled dustjackets, and optional sprayed edges, that are not available on retailers go to
www.karentomlinson.com/shop

FROZEN SEA
BORRON
KAMARAL
RIOU MILITARY CAMP
RIOU CITY
PADUR
CETRON
MOOREST
TETRIS
CAVE
MEDALLION ISLES
CORUSAH ISLES
PORTAL WORLD
MAP KEY
MAIN TRADE ROUTE
SEA TRADE ROUTE
SILK ROAD
BORDERS
N
E
W
S

VEIL OF SOULS

Aether is life, love, death, rebirth. But above all else, it is power.
I was born into a world of love, kindness, and pretty things...until it was brutally ripped away.
To survive I became a Viper. One of a violent gang of thieves and cutthroats who prowl the city of Tetris.
My only calling is vengeance. And it will be mine—it's only a matter of time.
Yet, vengeance must wait. The Aether, the Veil between our mortal world and the Netherworld, is sick. The souls of the dead are restless, and the souls of the living are being stolen, dragged without mercy into the darkness.
When I'm caught using magic to destroy the soul suckers who threaten my home, everything changes. I'm forced to work for the man I hate most in this world. He's dangerous. Ruthless. A liar who ripped apart my heart.
Well, he'll soon find out that I'm not the same love-sick fool he left behind. This time, Dexalion won't chew up my heart and spit it out. It doesn't matter how sexy his smile is, or how much I enjoy pushing his control; the only one in charge of my life is me.

*Warning! This book contains swearing/cursing, violence, hot & sometimes detailed sex scenes, plus major emotional feels that may leave a book hangover.

CHAPTER ONE

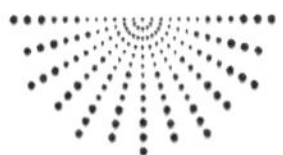

exalion

Icy fog wrapped its ghostly fingers around me, the wind breaching my too-thin clothes as the damp made them stick to my skinny body.

Only seconds ago, my mother had collapsed next to a huge boulder. I studied her pale face and blue lips, my heart racing. My hands trembled so much I could barely grasp my mother's boney shoulders to shake her.

"Momma?" I croaked, my mouth and throat so dry it was difficult to speak.

Her eyelids fluttered open. Deep green irises fringed with long, dark lashes that were so like mine, peered at me but without the spark of life, the defiance they normally held. My mother had always been beautiful. Even now, as death stalked her, she was the most beautiful thing in the Netherworld, and especially in my world. My heart hurt, my chest squeezing so hard I couldn't suck air into my lungs. Hot tears tipped from my eyes, cutting a trail through the dirt and dried blood on my cheeks.

Her eyes fluttered closed.

"Momma, please don't go! I don't know what to do." I shook her again, unable to hold back my sobs. If Father was here, he'd tell me crying was weak, that I was an embarrassment to myself and my bloodline. I sniffled loudly and tried to be strong, biting my lip so hard I tasted blood. "Momma? *Please.*"

Once again, she opened her eyes, her whispered voice barely strong enough to hear.

"You are so brave, so strong my beautiful son. Far stronger than your sire, which is why his hate knows no bounds. You have a long road ahead, but you were born to rule the shadows. And you will."

I swiped away my tears, snivelling hard as she dragged in a weary breath.

"No." I hiccoughed. "I *can't.* Not without you. *He* won't let me!"

I gripped her palm to my wet cheek, the iciness of her hand shocking me.

She smiled—the most serene smile I'd ever seen in my twelve years. I wanted to scream and shout and tell her to fight, but instinct told me not to. She *wanted* to go. She wanted the suffering that had been her life to end.

"Yes you can, Dexalion. Use your magic as I have taught you. The light of the Aether always shines brightest when surrounded by the darkness."

"What do you mean, Momma? What light?" I cried, my whole body trembling.

She placed her other hand upon my heart. "Find the Angel who will be the light to your darkness, my son. Save the Heart of our world and heal the Veil. Promise me, Dexalion, promise me you will become who you are meant to be."

Her emerald eyes briefly sharpened, but she needn't have worried. I would do anything for my mother. I would make any promise she wished, especially if it would bring her peace in her final moments.

The growls and snarls that had chased us for days grew closer. It built to a frightening crescendo, amplified in the strange still air that wreathed the outer reaches of Haldaag. Hiding my fear, I nodded and kissed my mother's pale cheek.

"Good boy," she whispered. "Take this."

She pressed a strange circular band into my hands. I stared at it, my stomach churning. It was the bone bracelet that my father wore on his arm. I had no idea what it was for, yet something inside my soul clicked as I touched it. All I knew was that Mother had been fiercely protective of it since we had run away. Through my tears, I managed to slide it over my bicep, jumping when it snapped closed. It fell down my skinny arm to my elbow. My nostrils flared. I promised myself that one day my muscles would be bigger than my father's, that no one I cared for would ever again be treated as he had treated her.

"This is the most precious possession you will ever have. Keep it safe until you find the light." She panted hard, each word an effort. "Do not sell it—or lose it. Ever." Her eyes shifted, widening at something over my shoulder.

The Barg skidded into the clearing, materialising through the mist like monstrous phantoms. She eyed the biggest one.

"He's the Alpha. The King. Kill him. Then you'll have them at your mercy. I know you are scared of your magic, but use it now or all will be lost." She coughed weakly. "Give my body to the pack. Make them yours." She blinked, and a tear ran down her cheek. "I love you. So much. Never forget that. Now go!" She pushed me backwards before her hands fell to rest limply at her sides, her head lolling to one side.

A loud growl rumbled through the air.

I spun on my knees, my legs shaking so much I toppled onto my side landing in the black mud. The Alpha Barg lowered his head and snarled, revealing huge yellowed fangs, though its endless black eyes rested upon my mother, not me.

Fury shoved at the grief in my heart. "No. Not you," I snarled. "You cannot have her. *You* are going to die." My mother was right. These were the fabled Hounds of Death, their Alpha the sovereign of these dark and dangerous lands. These shifters sensed death; they hunted it, feeding on the flesh of the dead to increase their power. From what I remember, Barg were shape-shifting demons. The hounds were their demon form.

I scuttled in front of my mother, whose chest was now still. My heart shattered, but my promise remained, burned into my soul for eternity; I was to use my darkness to find and free the Aether's light. I vowed then and there as I stared into the fathomless eyes of this ruthless killer that I would never give up. Once I found the light, I would do everything in my power to keep it safe.

The pack stalked forward, creating a semi-circle around my mother's body. I was aware of them all, but my eyes focused on the Alpha. The others wouldn't attack unless he ordered them to.

I opened my numb fingers, feeling the touch of magic race from my soul and into my bones. Pushing away my fear, I yanked on it. The Barg growled, lowering to its haunches as it stalked closer. My heart thudded against my chest wall, and my hands, though cold, were slick with sweat. Finding some courage, I held the Alpha's gaze, trying not to cry or cower as it bared its teeth. Knowing I would die if I showed any weakness, I snarled back and threw my magic with everything I had. Nothing happened. Threads of shadow stuttered across the muddy ground, stopping short of my target. A mewling sound escaped my lips, and I shook my head. *No! Not now!* My magic had always been erratic and untrustworthy, especially when I was anxious. I often tried to summon its full strength only to end up struggling to control it.

The Alpha leapt backwards, away from my pathetic attempt to end its life. Its eyes narrowed as it snapped its great jaws and growled at the rest of the pack. Clearly an order to stay back.

I gulped, my tongue sticking to the roof of my mouth, panic raging as I tried to grasp the magic that promised so much yet kept slipping away.

The Alpha dipped down on powerful haunches, then launched. I threw myself to the ground, screaming as pain exploded across my back. Its huge body passed over me, landing on the boulder above my mother. Claws, now dripping with my blood, clicked against the stone as it found purchase, its predatory gaze weighing me before completely disregarding me. Instead, it focused on my mother, its black eyes full of intent, saliva dripping from its fangs. Muscles rippled under its black scaly skin as it landed gracefully beside her body, intent only on its prize. It would wait until I was closer to my end before attacking again. It was the Barg's way. They were, after all, the legendary Hounds of Death.

Thick liquid trickled down my sides, seeping into the ground under my stomach. The smell of my own blood made me retch. No matter how much I cursed or prayed, immortality was not a given for a Shadow Demon like me, at least not until I reached adulthood.

"No!" I screamed as the Alpha nudged my mother's body with its nose.

Screaming against the pain that burned along my back, I grappled with my magic, tugging and cajoling, even praying to the Higher Powers to give me this one thing.

"Me! Come for me!" I hollered, hitting the sodden earth with my cold palms to get its attention. Dread took hold when it ignored me. Instead, it grabbed my mother's foot and dragged her flat to the ground.

In desperation, I pulled the small knife my mother always made me keep in my boot. I threw it with everything I had.

"No!" I half yelled and half sobbed.

With a dull thud, it landed in the Alpha's hind leg. Flinching, the powerful creature whipped its head towards me.

"That's right! Me!" I cried, hitting my chest now. My blood boiled and darkness, much like the inky fog that covered this land, grew from my fear and horror. It entwined my very soul. Horns sprouted from my head, and my body changed, growing taller and broader. *This. This* was the legacy of my birth. Pain. Destruction. Death. It was what I fought every day, what I feared most—this almost uncontrollable desire to kill and consume.

Bellowing my grief, I blasted a wave of obsidian magic across the ground, knocking the great beast into the air and sending the others sprawling. Ignoring the chorus of yelps and growls, I flew straight at it. My feet pounded the ground, and my heart thumped painfully against my ribs, my roar echoing through the fog.

The Alpha was still trying to get to his feet when I reached it. I yanked the small knife from its hind leg and thrust the blade through its ribs and into its heart. As I pulled the blade out, hot metallic blood showered my clothes and skin. Like a spectator looking on, I watched my hand reach out. Gore-covered fingers grasped the largest horn on the Alpha's head and heaved it back. The Barg didn't know it was dead. Its jaws snapped weakly, fury in its dark eyes as it tried to fight me. I cocked my head, newly detached from the horror as my blade sliced its throat open. Blood bubbled out, soaking my hands and arms. The Alpha's huge body became lax, the light fading from its eyes.

For a few seconds, I stared, unable to believe I had survived this creature. Trembling and panting against the pain blazing across my back, I let go and turned to face the pack. They bayed and howled, clearly confused. If I didn't cow them now, I was as dead as my mother—and I had a promise to keep.

I snarled and stood. This time my magic came easily. I sent a wave of power over them, not to harm but to warn.

As one, they laid down and rolled onto their sides, baring their throats.

"That's right. You're mine now."

My eyes drifted to my mother. I brushed my scraggly black hair from my face and stalked through the pack. The Alpha's blood dripped from my hands, and though I had never done it before, I instinctively dragged its soul into me. Its death nourished my magic, nourished me. Despite that, my strength was fading fast, and it was all I could do to stay upright. I stumbled, falling to my knees by my mother's side. She had suffered such pain and hopelessness because of my father. I swallowed my ever present hatred and guilt. I had been born of that pain, but not once had she let her anguish taint her love for me.

With reverent fingers, I brushed her dark hair from her bloodless face. She may have died wearing rags, but she would always be a Queen to me.

"I love you, Momma," I whispered, my voice breaking along with my heart. I didn't want to be alone. The thought of never again seeing her smile or feeling the comfort of her touch left a sorrow so deep it scarred my soul.

Tipping my head back, I wailed at the grey sky. The wind dropped, leaving the clearing disturbingly still, almost as if the gods themselves were watching.

I shuddered at that thought. The Higher Powers scared me.

A chorus of whines filled the eerie silence, the Barg watching me with unwavering focus.

Perhaps I wasn't alone...I had a pack.

I shuffled away from my mother's body, the cold wet mud mixing with my blood and soaking my already sodden breeches. Mother was right. This pack of predators would never respect me if I didn't abide by their laws. An Alpha, especially a new one, always fed his pack.

I looked down. This was no longer my mother but an empty shell of flesh and bone. My mother had gone, though her soul would not rest or be reborn until our world was safe. She had been the axis that kept the balance between the mortal world and our Netherworld. Now that she was gone, there was no one to decide whose soul would go to the Heart of the Aether for a chance at rebirth, and whose soul would feed the Veil. The Veil between our worlds would weaken, and all life would suffer. My mother had been the Angel of the Aether. Her life had lasted six hundred Heart cycles. Only she had suffered so much at my father's hands that, in recent years, her power had diminished to the point of being non-existent. The Veil was already weakened, and without an Angel it would disappear. The balance would be completely lost. It would take hundreds of heart cycles, but it *would* fail. And the journey to its inevitable end would lead this world into a darkness so thick and cold not even the worst of my kind would survive.

In the distance, the sound of hooves rumbled through the ground. The King's guards. I would stop my father, but not yet. I was a child, my magic untried and undisciplined; but it wouldn't always be so.

I swallowed back my tears as I looked down at my mother's face. It was the most peaceful I'd ever seen her. This was how I would remember her, not the broken, sad woman who was terrified of her own shadow.

I peered down at the nearest and biggest of the Barg. He laid in supplication, not meeting my gaze, yet somehow still seeming proud. Perhaps he had been the Alpha's Beta, his second in command. It didn't matter, I decided he would be mine. I ran my cold hand over his roughly scaled, hairless head, wrapping my fingers around one of his horns. He studied me warily.

"It's alright my friend, I have no interest in more killing."

He huffed, watching intently as I sat back and shoved my arm towards his mouth. Organising my thoughts and magic was hard with the beating of hooves getting louder and louder. The baying of the *Alzac*, the Netherworld's equivalent of the four-legged horses mortals used, was deafening.

"Feed," I commanded.

His predatory eyes narrowed, but he levered up onto his paws, his claws sinking into the mud. His head dipped, a snarl baring his teeth. And struck. There was no time for me to change my mind. Between his powerful jaws, my forearm snapped. He didn't try to feed on any more than the first blood I gave him. It was enough. It bound him to me. The bond between us snapped into place, painful at first but settling quickly.

"Stop." True to my command, he released me, sat back, and waited. Forcing myself to remain conscious, I curled my uninjured arm around his huge neck and used his vicious-looking horns to haul myself up from the ground.

"Feed," I snarled down at the rest of the pack.

I could not watch as they disposed of my mother's body. It didn't help to know, as she had, that I needed to feed them to gain their loyalty. Moreover, we couldn't risk her body being found.

My Beta allowed me to throw my leg over his ridged and scaled back. I dragged myself up until I was draped over his spine. It was uncomfortable, but there was no way I could even walk, let alone run from my father and his warriors. We managed to disappear into the fog. It wasn't long before the pack left my mother's corpse and closed in protectively around us. No matter my determination to stay on my Beta's back, my strength faltered, my shaking fingers slipped on his horns, and my legs weren't strong enough to grip to his sides. I fell from his back, landing with a thud on the sodden ground. Agony roared along my spine and through my wounds. I rolled onto my stomach, lifted myself to my hands and knees—and vomited.

Knowing I'd pass out very soon, I called on my shadow magic to search out and cover the mess of my mother's sacrifice, commanding it to drag her blood and remains into the earth, leaving no evidence that she had ever been there. My Beta dipped down, and two other Barg helped steady me with their heads as I hauled myself back up. There I stayed, clinging with my arms around his neck until, once again, I fell to the cold, wet ground. It seemed like an eternity that I lay there, surrounded by my pack of death hounds, drifting in and out of consciousness. In moments of wakefulness, tears burned my eyes, but I didn't let them fall. I was a boy no longer. Nothing remained of my mother except the love and memories I held in my heart and the promise I'd made, one I would strive to keep until my dying day. I would find the light and restore the Veil to its full glory. But to do that, I had to destroy my father and any who remained loyal to him. I'd take his damned crown and rip his heart from his chest. Never again would an Angel suffer at the hands of our bloodline.

ia

Disgust burned through me, though I resisted the urge to march into the dark and abandoned warehouse. A deep-chested growl vibrated right up my throat, my fingers curling into fists so tight that my nails scored my skin.

I wasn't some naive upper-caste maiden, so this situation didn't surprise me. I hadn't believed Garret when he'd told me I was special, that he'd never want anyone else; not a fucking word of it. Though I hadn't expected to feel so humiliated. Funny, since I didn't have great feelings for the arrogant bastard.

I snorted, unfurling my hands. Garret definitely wasn't worth any anger. Gods, I didn't even like him all that much. My capacity to care about any man that way had been numbed years ago. My long brown braid brushed my back, snagging in my cowl as I shook my head. I was twenty-four, and I'd found out when I was seventeen that I couldn't trust any man in my life, let alone a prick like Garret. It was just my pride that was hurt more than anything.

Lifting my chin, I inhaled deeply, then blew a determined breath from my nose. Willing the echo of my footsteps into the Aether, I stalked away from the soft groans and slap of skin against skin.

I squared my shoulders. I was too damned good for him, anyway.

Outside, the frigid winter air stung my skin. It was icy enough that my breath made small clouds of fog as sleet hit my face. Dala waited for me outside, her sympathetic look soothing me.

"I'm sorry, Zahlia." She rested her hands on the hilts of her daggers which were always fixed at her waist.

My friend looked like the fierce warrior she was. Tall and strong, she had been by my side since I was fifteen years old. Dala rarely shortened my name, and only to Zah, never to Lia. The only person I'd ever allowed to do that had broken my heart, and I hated it when anyone else used it. If they kept it up they soon figured out that they shouldn't, especially when my fist slammed in their gut, or my blade ended up at their throat.

I chuckled. "Honestly, I'm not all that bothered. Besides, it's not your fault he's a lying, cheating bog worm, is it? I should have known better. I just thought…" I swallowed the lump in my throat. It wasn't that I was hurt about Garret. It was more that I'd convinced myself I wanted him.

"He could at least have shown me some respect. And, you know, dumped me before he fucked someone else."

Irritation at my own vulnerability set in. I didn't do love, not anymore. People living as we did didn't care about anyone but themselves. Even my guardian didn't care about me enough to not lie, cheat, or sell me out to save his own skin.

Life on the streets of Tetris was tough; love didn't enter into it. I'd learnt that lesson as a child, and it had been reinforced when I was seventeen. Now, Dala was the only one I truly loved and trusted.

Dala pushed off the wall and wrapped her arms around me before I could stop her. She was a bit taller than me, so I rested my head on her shoulder. I wasn't a hugger with anyone else. Neither was she. In our world, showing affection made you vulnerable, but with Dala I could let myself relax and succumb to my friend's support. She was the only person I would ever show this sort of weakness. She pulled back and rested her forehead against mine, huffing at my reaction. Her message? I lived with liars, killers and thieves, what the hell did I expect?

"You know, this is as it should be. He's not good enough for you. And you *were* getting bored with him."

I smiled, she was right. "Yeah, but now it's just embarrassing. Everyone will know he's been cheating on me…"

"Not necessarily. I found out because I didn't trust the slimy bastard, so I followed him." She shrugged before her lips curved into a devious smile. "Who cares anyway? It won't be a surprise to anyone; he's a player. He'll do whoever is handy to get what he wants."

"Yeah, I know. A little bit of me just hoped…Ah, shit it doesn't matter."

She met my gaze. "I know you don't want to hear this, but he wants to humiliate you because you refused to let him use you to get closer to Hentus. He can only succeed in doing that if you let him." She paused, a slow smile stretching her dark lips. "You know, it's the gathering tonight, so break it off with him then, in front of the entire nest of Vipers. It'll be hard for him to save face with Hentus after that."

I gave a half-hearted chuckle. "Yeah, you're right. He can find another way to suck up to Hentus."

Dala grinned. "Yeah, so long as he doesn't try and hurt you for upsetting his plans." She gave me another hug before releasing me. "You're beautiful in every way, inside and out. He's a bastard, born of Haldaag. Being with that idiot was the worst thing you ever did."

I huffed a laugh at her reference to the most horrific place mentioned in all the books we'd read about the Netherworld. "Please, don't hold back. Tell me your thoughts, why don't you?"

She grinned. "Always. Besides, I love you; you don't need anyone else."

"I know you do," I replied, my mouth stretching in a wide smile. I took her hand in mine and squeezed. "I love you, too, but unless you're going to grow male parts, I will eventually need more than even you can give me."

Dala laughed out loud and shoved my shoulder. "Not even for you would I change my anatomy."

Giggling, we walked away.

Dala was my best friend, a sister in everything but blood. She was two years older than me, and we vastly differed in looks but not attitude. I was also tall but ridiculously pale-skinned with deep brown hair. At least, that's how everyone saw me. My hair was truly a bright silver blonde. My mother taught me how to use my magic to change my appearance when I was barely knee-high. Except I'd never been able to change the brightness of my blue eyes.

A familiar tightness spread through my chest. The image of my beautiful mother lying in a pool of blood, a sword speared through her chest, was as clear as if it had happened yesterday. She'd fought the red-eyed demon even with the sword sticking through her heart. Dark blood that looked almost black had covered her chest and dripped down her chin by the time my father had scooped me up and pushed me out through the basement window of our home. He'd rasped at me to *"run!"* just as that same sword had pierced his heart.

I had.

I'd run like the wind. Even though I was only six years old, I still remembered the cold rain soaking my hair and my fine silk dress. We'd been ready to go somewhere. Some kind of gathering. Mother had instructed me to behave, and to sit quietly once we were there. Her orders not to play on the ground and dirty my dress were still clear in my mind. I'd hidden in the darkness of a small alley, hoping the bad men wouldn't find me, too scared to move. The killer hadn't come. Instead, a boy had found me.

I swallowed the painful lump in my throat. Dexalion had taken my hand and led me away from the monster who'd killed my parents. We'd spent the night on the dirty streets, huddled together in the rain until Hentus had found us soaking wet and shivering outside an ale house. He'd offered us a place in the Vipers, and together we'd grown up among the thieves, liars and cutthroats who served Hentus. The Vipers ruled the Slopes, the slums of Tetris. We weren't an official caste, not like the other castes in the kingdom of Tetron, but we had laws, and a hierarchy of sorts—one that Hentus presided over.

I forced a smile. "Perhaps Hentus will kick Garret's arse for using me."

Dala raised her white brows, which were always stark against the darkness of her skin. Dala was half Riou, a race of ebony skinned warriors who lived on the northern borderlands of Tetron. She was also half human; or so she thought, and bald as a baby's bottom with tattoos adorning her scalp. Her mother belonged to a pleasure caste, one which served the lower levels of society. And since her mother didn't know who her father was, neither did Dala. They hadn't seen each other for years, not since the lord of the pleasure caste had tried to sell Dala to the highest bidder at the age of nine. Dala had been fierce even then. She'd stabbed the buyer in the groyne before running to the Slopes, surviving on her own for years before Hentus offered her a place in the Vipers.

My fierce and beautiful friend rolled her eyes. "That's not going to happen. You know the rules. You fight your own battles. Besides, if I know Garret cheated on you, it's guaranteed Hentus knows. That means he's waiting for you to work it out and leaving you to deal with it yourself."

I knew it was true. Hentus had always pushed me to stand up for myself. He wasn't my father, not by a long way, but he'd been in my life since he'd found me hiding on the streets with Dex.

"Yeah, you're right."

Dala nodded, her hazel eyes studying me. "You know, if he thought you really loved Garret, and that the two-timing shit would break your heart, he'd slice his dick off in his sleep."

"Yeah." I grinned, realising that was probably true. I pulled on my gloves. But Garret was Garret. He was a liar and a cheat. And I found I didn't really care.

The biting sleet turned to snow, sticking to my cold face, so I raised my thick cowl. Dala did the same, covering her tattooed head. Winter in the Slopes was no fun. The sea winds gusted, bringing freezing fog and snow, battering this part of the sprawling capital city of Tetron. At least those winds sent the stench of fish, old seaweed, and rotting flesh high into the city where the upper castes pretended there was nothing bad happening in the world. So long as it didn't affect them, they ignored the bodies in the streets, and the bloated corpses floating in the harbour.

I wrinkled my nose. That stink, mixed with the open sewers that ran through the streets of the lower levels, made our existence even more grim. This city had always had a dark side, but since the Aether, the Veil between the mortal world and the Netherworld, had become sick, it was even worse. Permeating the stink of the city was the bitter stench of fear. People were terrified of the approaching night and the creatures that arrived with it.

The sun was already low in the sky. "Come on, we need to find a mark and then get back. I don't want to be out here at dusk without more weapons."

Dala nodded, her face dour.

Our boots sloshed through a glutinous puddle, stirring up a foul stench. I cringed. How I longed to wrap my magic around me and run. It would take only seconds for me to reach our destination if I did, but I wouldn't leave Dala nor would I risk anyone seeing me disappear. They would sell that information to the Mad Prince's soldiers in a heartbeat. And the soldiers, along with their monstrous mage hounds, were only ever a step away. The prince was convinced magic was the cause of the sickness that thinned the Veil. Maybe he was right, but regardless, I couldn't allow him to find me. I wasn't ready to die and couldn't leave, not until I found my parents' killer. So I readjusted my daggers and the small dart blower I always kept in my pocket and stalked after Dala.

We kept our heads covered and smartened our pace, keeping our wits about us. The Vipers held a specific territory in the Slopes, but that didn't make this part of the city safe for us. Other gangs, thieves, and the dregs of society hunted here all the time for likely victims—even in the daytime. They killed members of the Vipers the same way we killed them if they tried to steal our marks or threatened us. Though, nighttime was always worse. That was when the Veil thinned and the darkness from the Nether seeped into the city. The monsters that pushed through the Veil every damned night took more and more mortal souls. It didn't matter what caste they were from, high or low born, innocent or corrupt, children or fully grown, they took until the light of dawn chased them away.

It hadn't always been this bad. When I was younger, the monsters that went bump in the night were only tales. Now they're folklore come to life. They had started away from the city by pushing through the Veil on the moors. I didn't know why the Veil was weakest out there, but it was. The King had taken his army out there and fought them until he died about eight years ago. Since then, the Mad Prince and his general had been holding them back—until they couldn't. Now the city was overrun with refugees trying to find safety within its walls.

Every night the creatures seemed hungrier, almost desperate. No one knew what it was about our souls that they hungered for, but every single person in Tetron knew that winter was fast approaching, so the nights were getting longer and the days shorter. The refugees that had flooded the city in the past months were the most vulnerable. They were homeless and casteless, their collective life energy seemingly a beacon to the monsters that hunted in the darkness.

My nostrils flared. I hated that so many died every night, and there was precious little any of us could do about it. Even predators like the Vipers were at risk of being dragged kicking and screaming from their mortal flesh and into the murkiness of whatever was beyond the Veil.

No, the Slopes were never safe—not even for criminals like us.

CHAPTER THREE

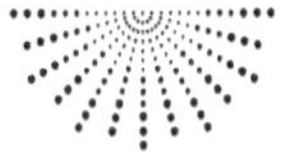

ia

Three hours later, my pocket was weighed down with the coins I'd lifted from a nobleman. The skinny, dark haired man hadn't begged for his life, though I'd been feeling generous and granted it to him anyway. In return, I'd emptied his pockets and taken his fine cloak and shoes. I rubbed my cheek against the soft material. I had no idea what it was made from, but it was a beautiful midnight fabric that shimmered when it moved. What an idiot, coming down near the Slopes wearing such a beautiful garment. It had made him a mark for every thief. I just got in there first.

I'd never owned anything like the soft black cloak, so I pushed my hands into its pockets, scrunching my fingers into the material and simply enjoyed the softness and smoothness of its fabric. My footsteps faltered as the tips of my fingers brushed against something in the right pocket. Creases furrowed my brow. I'd checked his pockets earlier and found nothing. *Strange.* I must have missed it.

I wrapped my fingers around the piece of soft leather and pulled it out. A quick glance told me there was an old faded image on it. A coat of arms and a name that I couldn't quite make out. Quickly, I shoved it in my tunic pocket. It didn't look expensive or important. I'd look at it later.

Reluctantly, I removed the cloak. It wasn't really mine; it belonged to Hentus now.

The noise in the dining room made me wince. It seemed more people than usual were here for the once a month gathering. The moon was at its highest tonight, so it was the night the Viper's captains came to give their ill-gotten gains to Hentus. It was also when Hentus would dole out punishment or praise to his minions.

The heavy smell of boiled beef and onions had saliva rushing into my mouth, and not in a good way. I swallowed hastily, glad I'd pocketed a couple of apples off a distracted market seller. Boiled beef, or what we were told was beef, onions and potatoes was our staple food. I should have been used to it, but I really wasn't.

I pushed past the crowd of kids and adults and headed to the vat of boiled potatoes. An earthy, damp steam laced the air. I shoved down my revulsion at tonight's fare, piled some of the bland white pulp onto a slate, and then held it out to the cook. He took it without looking at me and slopped some beef on top.

Thin gravy sloshed over my fingers, its heat scalding me. I winced. *"Ow,"* I muttered under my breath, already spying bits of meat I'd save for Dala. She'd eat anything. Me, not so much. I had suspicions about the meat's origins, and I *really* didn't fancy chewing on bits of the dock rats that feasted on sewage and dead bodies.

Spotting a table at the back of the room, I headed through the crowd and plonked myself on a stool, staring despondently at my food. Giving myself a mental slap, I picked up my fork. There were many others in this city that were starving. I had no cause for complaint. Determined, I speared a brown lump and clamped my lips around it. Holding back a grimace, I ground the rubbery substance between my teeth and then swallowed.

Beef, my arse.

I quickly picked up my cup of water and washed the lump down my gullet. I forced down another two bits of chewy meat hiding in the potatoes, swallowing against my inclination to gag. I hated the thought of eating dead things; rats, beef, it didn't matter what it was. It made me shudder, but I had to survive, and there was precious little else to eat.

Managing another mouthful of gravy and potatoes, I saved the rest of the meat for Dala. Closing my eyes, I pictured the lush green skin of the apples I had stolen. Each one was so big they didn't even fit in my palm. I didn't care that they had likely come on the black market vessels from overseas, probably from the warm Medallion Isles, or that I had robbed the seller of much-needed coins by stealing them. I could already taste that sweet yet tart juice as it washed across my tongue.

I groaned in anticipation.

"Hey, princess, where ya been?"

My eyes snapped open.

Garret grinned, his deep brown eyes grazing over my body. He sat his slim, toned body on the stool beside mine and put his arm around my shoulders. "Was that sexy groan for me?"

I considered elbowing him straight in his handsome face; instead I shrugged off his touch and glared at him.

"No," I hissed. "And you don't touch me—ever again." I pushed back my stool and stood just as his face shut down and his eyes narrowed.

"What's up your arse? You liked my touch well enough yesterday." His eyes flitted around the men who sat at the long table, and who were doing their best not to listen.

Well, all except Angus. Angus was wider and meaner than a bull. He was just over a year older than me at twenty-six, or, at least, that's how old Hentus guessed him to be. No one really knew stuff like that in the Vipers. I liked Angus. I always had. He was one of those quiet watchful types. He didn't favour a sword but was an expert with the meanest-looking double-headed axe I'd ever seen. He'd never liked me becoming another of Garret's lovers. He'd said I deserved more.

I cringed a bit as Angus's eyes met mine. His nostrils flared and he shook his head sadly.

My cheeks heated. He knew. Aether's balls, did they all know?

Perhaps I'd missed the signs because I just wasn't that bothered. Garret had been my only lover since Dex had left, and that was over seven years ago. I inhaled sharply. Had it really been that long? I rubbed my chest with my fist. It didn't feel like it.

Garret sat back, smirked and raised his voice. "So what d'you say, princess? You gonna moan like that for me tonight? Hmm? While I pound into that sweetness between your legs?" He brushed his fingers against my breast, before squeezing its softness.

Hentus strolled in. I froze. Angus froze. And the men at the table froze. Hentus's grey eyes narrowed on Garret's back. A predator sizing up its prey. Then they slid to me before his gaze rested on where Garret groped my right tit. His dark bushy brows rose.

Right. Fight your own battles. I knew that rule better than most. Hentus's favour meant jealousy followed me. I'd always had to fight my own battles. He'd never done it for me. Respect—and, to some degree, fear—had to be earned. No one had dared disrespect me while Dex had been my shadow, but I'd had to learn to stick up for myself when he'd disappeared.

I took a slow deep breath, feeling through the layers of air around me. The brush of magic against my body had my eyes fluttering shut. I wouldn't use it unless I was desperate. None of the Vipers, save Dala and Hentus, knew of it, but the knowledge it was there as back up gave me comfort.

Garret had a temper. Everyone knew it—especially Hentus. It was why he'd been raised to command his own faction of thieves. Even though the Vipers were full of the unwanted dregs of society, like the official castes of this city, we had a hierarchy as well as rules. Garret was a captain, but Hentus was the Lord of the Vipers. Hentus had always cut me some slack, but he could be cruel and expected me to be, too, when the need arose.

I looked down at the flat piece of slate that served as my plate. Garret had never been respectful of women, especially those he considered clingy after he tired of them. But he had treated me differently, or so I'd thought. He'd chased me, persistently seducing me, so I'd given in. I swallowed the bitter taste of reality as I saw Emily, the girl he'd been ramming into this afternoon, smirking at me.

Dala and Angus were right. I deserved better. The insult that sneered through his last words and his completely unwanted and degrading touch made my blood boil.

I exhaled in a swift rush as my muscles exploded into action. The slate disintegrated against the side of Garret's face, the impact vibrating up my arms.

Garret jerked sideways, almost falling from his stool, murder flashing in his eyes. Without giving him time to straighten, I spun on the ball of my foot and slammed my boot heel into his chest.

His stool toppled backwards, and he landed in a crumpled heap. I pulled one of my blades, resting its spine first along my forearm. If it had been anyone else, I would have been on them with the blade against their neck—but not Garret. I wasn't stupid enough to get that close. My nostrils flared, still feeling the violation of him grabbing my breast.

He looked up from his position on the wooden floor and chuckled before spitting out a mouthful of bright blood.

"So you found out, hmm? Wondered how long I'd keep you hooked" He shrugged and looked at Hentus, whose face was dark. Garret's gaze soon returned to me, though his smile didn't reach his eyes.

I was surprised by his lack of retaliation, though I wasn't stupid enough to think he'd forget about me knocking him on his arse in front of everyone.

"It's nothing personal, princess, I get bored easily..."

"Shut up," I demanded, despite the tickle of unease his cold gaze instilled in me. "You're just a piece of shit. Do not touch me again. If you try, I will do more than shut your smart mouth with a slate." I turned away, stalking up to Hentus. I might have to fight my own battles, but Hentus would not allow Garret to stick a knife in my back.

Angus crossed his massive arms over his chest and smirked, winking as I passed his table. I tried not to show my satisfaction at smashing Garret's face in, and kept my expression in a scowl.

"About time," was all Hentus said when I reached his side.

"You knew he was using me." It was a statement not a question.

Sorrow fleetingly shadowed his eyes. "Of course."

"Why didn't you tell me?" Perhaps I should sound less pissed off with my guardian, but I was angry with him, with myself, with Garret, but mostly with the man who had left me in this shithole city instead of following through on his promise to escape with me across the ocean to a new life.

Garret got up and brushed himself down. I stiffened at the malice in his eyes. Then he shrugged and fixed an apologetic look on his face. *Sorry,* he mouthed and grinned, his teeth blood-stained and his scalp dripping thick, dark blood down his face.

I just shook my head, then mirrored his movements, shrugging before I touched my head. *Sorry.* I mouthed back. Was I fuck. I wasn't even a little bit.

He nodded, spat on the floor, then went to get some food.

I guessed that was it—for now.

I caught Dala grinning at me from Angus's table. I smiled back, knowing she would have my back, too.

Hentus and I watched as Emily flounced over and draped herself over Garret.

"Don't turn your back on him," advised Hentus. "Doesn't matter if he deserved it, he won't forget. Now, tell me where you got that lovely cloak. It looks like the sort of cloak people in Kamarate wear. Did you get anything else with it?"

I rolled my eyes, wondering when he'd been to the capital city of Pa'dur, and got straight back to business. The sun was already set, and my magic thrummed in excitement. It was almost time to hunt.

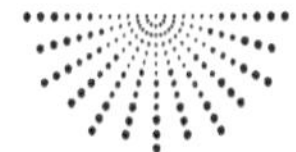

ex

Warm, despite the bitter cold, I smiled and kept my face upturned, letting the soft flakes caress my skin. I'd grown up learning to survive in the cold and darkness, but that bone-chilling cold had never looked like this white expanse of cottony powder. This kingdom, even this shithole of a city, looked beautiful as a winter wonderland, and it always got to me. I'd been in the city of Tetris for twenty-four years, and though it snowed every year, I still found it amazing. My world was swamped with night, so I loved how bright and ethereal the snow made everything; it disguised even the most grisly sights.

The crunch of our boots in the freshly fallen powder had that weird muffled sound that always accompanied a heavy snowfall.

"Dex!" Omeron snapped, his deep voice rumbling around us.

"What?" I asked, keeping my eyes shut. It was childish, but I loved to open my mouth and catch the flakes on my tongue.

"Open your eyes, or you'll fall flat on your face! Or worse, get a knife in the gut."

Several footfalls thudded on the snow behind us, slowing when we slowed. Even through the noise of the city, I heard them. *That* made me open my eyes. Someone was stalking us, though we looked neither weak nor well-off in the cloaks covering our armour. Then again, there were levels of squalor in these streets that hadn't existed when I'd last been here. Not even when I'd been one of the most dangerous predators in this city had the poverty and desperation been this bad.

I glanced around. Doorways and streets were crowded with the homeless and the wretched. Night was falling swiftly, and those desperate enough tried breaking in through the nearest doors to reach relative safety. Most were fought off by those inside. Win or lose, the violence was sickening—even to me. I knew why there was such a frantic need for an indoor space, and I couldn't do a damned thing about it—yet. My nostrils flared as the sole of my boot sank through the soft layer of snow, disturbing the stinking detritus of too many bodies and too little sanitation.

Most people ignored Omeron and me, too lost in their own misery to care about two more strangers on the crowded streets. That meant the stalkers were either exceptionally confident in their ability to take us, or they were desperate—and desperate meant extremely danger-ous. People did stupid things when they had nothing left to lose.

Magic danced under my skin, joyous at the prospect of a little free-dom, but I kept it locked down.

"Keep that magic of yours hidden, my friend. We're here to find *her*, not to draw attention to ourselves." Omeron's vivid amber eyes regarded me steadily. "We don't need it to kill a bunch of petty thieves. And we don't want to draw the attention of the mage hounds or their handlers." He pulled back his cowl while holding my gaze.

I frowned. "I wouldn't put us at risk like that. Besides, you shaved your hair off especially for this reunion of mine; why would I let you do that in this balls-freezing weather only to go and jeopardise our purpose?"

"Because you're an arse?" Omeron quipped.

I grinned and rubbed my gloved hand over his ebony head, which was minus the white, tightly-curled hair he normally had when in human form. There were plenty of Riou people in this shithole city who were closest in looks to my second in command, and most shaved their heads. We'd discovered years ago that a bare head was originally the mark of Riou warriors of the highest standing, but most did it now to stop the spread of lice, which infested many of the low castes.

Omeron flinched back and swatted my hand away. "I don't care if you're my…friend, Dex, do that again and I'll chop your hand off."

I chuckled. We both knew he couldn't harm me. Not when I was more than just his friend.

"It's bloody cold without hair—or armour. Especially in this fucking snow. Maybe I should hold you down and shave these ridiculous locks off." He tried to reach for my head, but I easily avoided him.

My grin was wide. "Hey! The ladies like to pull on my hair when I send them into fits of pleasure."

He rolled his eyes. "I don't want to know what you do with your women," he grumbled, looking mightily pissed off.

My mouth curled into a smirk. "I know. That's why I'm going to tell you about Veronica, oh, and Anna. Both of them were so soft, and felt sooo good." It was a lie of course. I fucked women when my body demanded it, but there was only one woman who would ever hold my interest for more than the time it took to bed her. Truth or not, teasing my friend like this was one of my favourite pastimes, a great distraction from the grim life we'd led for the past eight years.

Omeron scowled and turned away, his boots sliding around on the snow. My friend was saving himself for betrothal, as was his custom. His father had made it quite clear that no matter where Omeron lived, as a prince of the Haldaag, he was expected to follow their customs. We both thought it a ridiculous law and twisted it whenever we could. Omeron might technically be a virgin, but he was by no means ignorant of the delights of the flesh. In mortal terms, we both looked in our late twenties, but we were both ancient. Ome was younger than me at three hundred cycles of the Aether's heart to my four hundred. His father was my second in command and he'd quickly become my shadow.

I chuckled loudly and bumped his shoulder with my own, deliberately sending us both skidding on the snow. He cursed me as we stepped out into the market square, our stalkers somewhere behind us.

Omeron raised his brows in question.

I shrugged and shook my head, willing to give them a chance to live. "No, leave them. They'll lose interest in us in these crowds. It's unlikely they know who I am. Besides, it's getting dark. I doubt they'll think robbing us is worth risking their souls."

Omeron huffed. "Maybe. Let's watch our backs anyway. Perhaps they remember you and have a score to settle."

"They wouldn't be the first, but it's more likely because we're carrying so many weapons. They're worth a lot of orms."

Together we pushed through the small marketplace, one of many throughout the city. The narrow, cobbled streets closed in by the crooked buildings left little room for the refugees huddled on the ground, some waiting for their end. I frowned; that made this an ideal hunting ground for the thieves and rapists who prowled these streets. Those desperately trying to buy food or hurry to their next destination moved out of our way, eyeing us warily. We were both tall, packed with solid muscle, and carried a multitude of weapons. Even with our faces hidden by our cowls, those things gave us an air of menace. Most of the more dangerous thieves, let alone these wretched citizens, would have the sense to avoid us.

We walked past the few remaining traders who tossed their wares into their wagons, ready to retreat to the safety of their lamps and fires while their paid guards watched on. Voices intensified as despairing people begged for any remaining food. I breathed through my mouth, ignoring the multitude of foul smells that drifted up my nose. The familiar stench of terror and death was the same outside the city, especially on the moors. The time for fighting to keep the demons of the Netherworld from swamping this city had ended. As much as I wanted to protect Lia from her destiny, I couldn't, not anymore. All there was left to do was cure the Veil.

My lips pinched, I strode onwards, ignoring the fact that the very cure I sought would likely chop my balls off when I found her.

The light faded further as night drew in. With the darkness came demons. I wondered how much fuel the people of this city had left to keep them at bay. Certainly, the homeless and poor didn't have any.

I ground my teeth until it hurt. My home kingdom had been just like this one; the rich ignoring the plight of the poor, taking until there was very little left. It disgusted me.

No matter what direction we twisted, the streets were filled with people. Most just lay on the cold ground and waited for death, hopelessness in their eyes, though some tried to continue their daily lives. I ignored the men and women from the pleasure castes who catcalled and swayed their hips, displaying their wares, trying hard to seduce their next mark before the darkness drove them into the brothels.

A small baker's shop filled my nostrils with the heavenly scent of freshly baked Puchinella, a heavily spiced delicacy of Tetris. My stomach growled loudly. It had been over a day since we'd last eaten. If decent food was scarce out on the front line, freshly baked goods were nonexistent. Saliva flooded my mouth. I didn't really need food to survive. I could feed from the energy of souls, only not in daylight nor in front of so many people. Besides, being hungry when I got to the Viper's lair would not help my temper.

"Wait!" I tapped Omeron's arm and ducked into the shop. Dropping some coins on the counter, I bought us one of the mouth watering Puchinellas. I bit into the flakey pastry and groaned when the savoury, spicy flavours exploded across my tongue. Saliva rushed to my mouth as I chewed. There'd been nothing this tasty to eat on the battlegrounds. In fact, even the tough meat of a bog worm had become a delicacy. The creature ate our dead soldiers, and in return the soldiers ate them. We hadn't had proper food in the battle camps for months, despite my pointing out to the Mad Prince that if he didn't feed his soldiers, he would lose this war with the Nether creatures. It was irrelevant now; the weakness in the Veil was unmanageable. The reapers and demons were drawn to the souls of all the refugees who sought shelter in the city.

"This is good. Really good," I mumbled, my mouth full of pastry. The baker chuckled, his rotund belly wobbling up and down. His guard watched me closely from the door. I ignored him as he weighed me up while he eyed my weapons. I knew he was just doing his job.

All traders had to have guards of some kind now that the city was swamped with desperate and starving people, or the lawlessness would overwhelm those trying to make an honest living.

"That's good, son, feel free to come back and spend your orms with me anytime."

Grinning, I lifted my hand in acknowledgment. I hoped the food supply chains kept up for all our sakes. Supplies still came in from the other Kingdoms since they hadn't been as affected by the thinning Veil as us. I knew why, but I also knew it was only a matter of time before they were.

I glanced at the ocean as I stepped from the glorious warmth of the bakery into the bitter-cold dusk. The pale triangles of the ships' sails glowed in the fading light. Relief washed through me. The Veil hadn't thinned across the ocean since I was last in the city. If it did, no trade ships would risk coming here.

After passing Omeron his food, I stood shoulder-to-shoulder with him outside the shop as we leaned against the wall and ate. Omeron nudged my arm with his elbow and gave a minute nod. Four men stood in the entrance to an alleyway opposite and off to the right.

I hid my elation. I'd finally get a chance to release my darkness. They watched us but tried to make it as inconspicuous as possible by hiding amongst other people. Their clothes were scruffy, their skin dirty, but unlike many of the thieves hunting through the crowds, these men were not grossly undernourished nor were their eyes full of fear, just cunning and greed.

The tallest of them, a man with short, dark hair and handsome features, nodded at a boy who walked by the alley. Locals, then. I guessed they were the ones who'd been following us. My stomach tightened. The man could be part of the Vipers. I didn't recognise him, but that meant nothing. I'd been gone almost nine mortal years to give Zahlia some greatly needed space. She didn't realise it, but my magic had smothered hers until hiding what I was from her became too difficult. It had killed me to leave, and I had ensured Hentus wouldn't abandon her, yet I wasn't stupid enough to think that her life had been easy since I'd left.

Omeron grunted. "You had no choice. You had to leave. Keeping the Nether from consuming this city, and her with it, was your priority."

"Yeah, and now time is running out. Now *she* is my only priority."

"That's as it should be, though I doubt we'll get a warm welcome."

I couldn't help but chuckle. Zahlia had been a young girl by the time I'd tracked her down. I'd stayed by her side, protecting her, giving her the skills to survive, and watched her grow into a stunning and fierce young woman. But the threat to her life became too much, so when she was almost seventeen, I left her, making sure she hated me enough not to follow. Now I ached to see the woman she'd become.

Had she a lover? The fingers of my free hand grabbed my sword pommel, squeezing against the metal. I'd commanded Hentus to watch over her, or rather, threatened him. I had no guilt over that. The man was as much a liar as I was. At least in his sporadic updates, I'd gleaned she hadn't tried to leave, and wasn't interested in the other men who'd been sniffing around. Knowing she hadn't wanted anyone else since me made my heart stutter. Selfish? Maybe, especially since I hadn't remained celibate, but she was mine. She had been since the day she was born. And I was hers, even if she thought otherwise.

I swallowed another bite of pastry while watching our stalkers.

It was simple; if she had a lover, she would leave them behind or they would die.

The lead thief grinned and winked at a whore, flirting with her as he walked closer. His smile was pleasant enough, but his eyes were cold and constantly shifting from the woman to us. My nostrils flared, a memory slamming into my head. This close, I recognised the slimy fucker alright.

Omeron and I were now hidden behind our cowls, so I assumed he still had no idea who I was, although my size should have put the idiot off. Unless he did know and wanted to challenge me, either for the past or for who I was now. But I doubted it. Rumours of the prince's general might be rife, but my description had changed from person to person so it became entertaining to hear the differing opinions. No, Garret was too confident, too lacking in fear to be suspicious. He and his gang had seen me buy food, knew we had coin to steal, and clothes and weapons that would fetch a handsome reward on the black market. That was all he saw, not the man who had broken his arm for touching what didn't belong to him and knocked him out cold, before leaving.

"They've marked us, the stupid bastards," I told Omeron.

My friend grinned. "Good." He cracked his neck and rolled his heavily muscled shoulders. "I'm ready to make friends when you are."

I grinned back, happy he was by my side. He was my family, my true brother. Family by blood didn't mean loyalty or love. At least it didn't to me. The ache in my chest that had followed me since my vow to my mother and the memories of the vicious wars I'd fought since was a constant reminder of the cruelty of my bloodline.

"So where will we find Zahlia?" Omeron asked.

We marched further into the Slopes, leading the thieves on. Garret had been about Zahlia's age when I'd last seen him, but he'd lived in a different faction of the Vipers. I was pretty sure it was him, even if I'd only met him a handful of times.

I rolled my shoulders, my brows dipping.

The last time had been when he'd tried to charm Lia. I'd caught him running his fingers down her bare arms. Zahlia's cheeks had turned pink, and I'd seen red. Not just because of him, but because I'd realised that I'd have to leave her. My fury had been off the charts before he'd even touched her. Seeing that slippery bastard's hands on her only made it worse. I growled quietly, my nostrils flaring. But I hadn't been noble enough to leave her without my mark. Even now, I wasn't sorry. I'd taken her, made her mine, and held that knowledge in my heart ever since. No one could take that moment from either of us.

My stomach tensed as I remembered that night. I'd never forgotten the feel of her body wrapped around mine. I'd feel that again. It wouldn't matter if she fought her attraction to me. Ultimately, we'd be together.

I smirked. Lia had never been a delicate flower. She'd been fierce, and determined to find the demon who'd murdered her family. I'd encouraged it, even though I knew she'd never find him. I'd made certain of that.

Omeron and I both lowered our cowls, preferring the ability to see over keeping the frigid winds off our heads. I tilted my head, filtering out the street noise and picking out the footfalls that followed us.

"I honestly don't know. She hides her magic well. I can't feel her, except at night when she uses it, and when I get there she's always gone." I peered around at the squalor. "This part of Tetris is the most debased and violent part of this kingdom. There are so many damaged and corrupt souls for the reapers to steal. If I had to guess where she'd appear, it would be here, in the Slopes. Especially since she'd be drawn to fight the monsters of our world, to protect the souls of both the living and the dead, even if she didn't know why."

Omeron sighed. "I hope so, brother, because this adventure is about to get a whole lot more interesting. Hentus moved the Vipers and didn't tell you for a reason—to give her time to hide from you."

I growled as two of the thieves appeared from an alleyway in front of us. "Yeah, well, what he doesn't know is that I can track her anywhere. Even if it takes me a few days, I'll find her."

We halted. I loosened my muscles and glanced over my shoulder. Another two arseholes were sauntering up behind us. I opened my hands as if in supplication, and allowed a cold smile to curve my mouth.

"C'mon, boys, we don't want any trouble, we're just passing through."

"Really?" The leader grinned.

This close, it was easier to see it was Garret. His face had become leaner, his body brawny. His face, which had a huge bruise on one side, was a picture of amiability, though his eyes remained as cold as any predator from the Nether. He'd always had a false kind of charm that could suck in the unsuspecting. That was why I'd hated seeing him touch Lia. I noticed he wore the tattoo of a viper's captain. Clearly, he was vicious enough to earn Hentus's favour. The snake tattoo curled from his tear duct down across his cheek and disappeared under his earlobe.

"Well, you won't mind us relieving you of those heavy-looking boots and fine cloaks, then. Or those weapons that are strapped to your well-fed bodies, now will you?" he asked, almost conversationally, keeping his grin in place.

I grinned back, equally as friendly on the surface, but I knew my eyes were colder than his could ever be. Shadows gathered behind them. One command from me and Garret and his friends would be erased from this world.

"Easy," warned Omeron, quietly enough the thieves wouldn't hear.

I nodded and forced my magic to back down. Discovery wasn't an option. Not yet. I needed time to find Zahlia before the mage hounds and my men did.

"The thing is, I like my boots and my cloak—but here..." I unstrapped my daggers, those on show anyway, and dropped them to the ground. "You can have these. I can buy more."

Garret's eyes narrowed shrewdly. "Ah, we'll definitely be taking those. But..." he shrugged. "We'll also be taking those boots and your cloaks, along with the coin you have for buying more weapons. You'll not be needing any of it, you see—because you'll be dead." He cracked his neck and rolled his shoulders.

Beside me, Omeron shifted his weight. He'd take the men at our backs. I loosened my muscles and softened my knees. My daggers sat in the slush at my feet, but that was fine, I didn't need them.

"Look, I don't want any trouble. Like I said, we're just passing through." The lie slipped easily off my tongue.

Garret grinned, confidence oozing from him. "And like I said, you're going to die."

My fists curled, the leather of my gloves creaking.

Omeron spun, taking on the attackers that had crept up behind. I left my friend to it, not even turning my head. My trust in him and his skills was absolute.

"Now, that's not at all friendly," I commented darkly.

"Not meant to be," snarled Garret.

I raised my brows and cocked my head. "Well?"

Garret hesitated, only for a fraction of a second, but I didn't miss it. Thieves in this city were used to fear and weakness, not fighters. If Garret's men had more sense and less desperation, they would have noticed how we moved and realised their strength and skill wouldn't match ours. Even their viciousness wouldn't come close.

The man behind Garret threw a knife. There was some skill but little speed to the move. I allowed it to embed in my shoulder. The pain was nothing, merely a burn I could easily ignore, but I grunted anyway. Appearing strong but not invincible was an art I'd perfected through my years in the mortal world.

Garret threw his first strike into my gut. Still playing my part, I doubled over. At least he packed a reasonable punch. Fluidly, I straightened, clenching my right fist and loosening my shoulder. I swung, holding back my full strength, my soul singing as my fist connected with his jaw, knocking his head back.

I wanted to unleash myself upon these fools, consume them, and rip their souls to shreds. Quickly, I smothered those thoughts; that was my true nature talking, one that could not be released on this world. Yet Demonkind was flooding this world every night, which made pretending to be mortal harder and harder.

The other guy used the opening I deliberately gave him to punch my kidneys. I obligingly fell to one knee, icy water soaking through my leather breeches.

Grunts and the smack of fists against flesh told me Omeron was playing his part of being a mortal with his usual skill. A glint in the snow caught my eye. My daggers were right in front of me covered in mud and slush. I didn't want to kill these men, not really, but I needed them to be gone. Finding Zahlia was more important than saving their lives. My brother had been pushing more of his warriors through the weakest points of the Veil in an effort to find her. So her time for self-discovery was up.

I snaked my hand out. Icy slush covered my glove, soaking me right up to my wrist. Quickly, I grabbed the plaited leather of my dagger's handle. The blade glinted against the snow as I yanked it free of its sheath.

"Stop him!" Garret bellowed, kicking out at my head.

I blocked with my other arm and spun to my feet, driving my blade into the gut of the charging man. His eyes widened, his pupils dilated and his mouth opened. Curling my fingers into his filthy cloak, I forced his body down onto my blade. Warmth trickled over my fingers, the rusty stink of blood edging its way up my nostrils.

I heard a grunt and a heavy thud as a body splashed into the slush behind me. Omeron had subdued, if not killed, two of his opponents, but another had stepped into the mix.

The temperature plummeted, forming ice over the slush. It happened so quickly that it was hard to comprehend or would have been if I hadn't seen it thousands of times before. My attention moved from my kill to Garret.

"If you want to live, you need to run."

His eyes narrowed as a hideous creature with no eyes or nose and a wide mouth full of razor-sharp teeth pushed against the darkness. The Veil held the reaper back for a few more seconds before its large, grey head and gangly body pushed into the alley as if stepping through a shimmering curtain. Its tongue slithered out, tasting the air, searching for the energy of any nearby mortals. The last man fighting Omeron froze. The reaper had pushed through the Veil behind him. His eyes widened and the colour leached from his face. He was dead; we all knew it. Slowly, he twisted to look at his killer before bursting into a run. He didn't stand a chance. The creature opened its mouth wide, showing its rows of teeth. Its long, sticky tongue shot out and wrapped around his neck. It yanked him backwards and drove its long spindly fingers through his chest, then grabbed onto his soul and yanked the blue energy free, dropping his body in the filth before disappearing back through the Veil and into the Nether.

"Run!" I bellowed. There would be more reapers very soon, looking for the energy of those who were mortal. The Nether was steeped in darkness, a darkness that had spread since the day my mother had died. She'd been the life force for the Heart of the Aether, and it was so weak, it couldn't feed power into the Veil that separated the demon world from the mortal one. The only way to heal the Veil was to bring light back to our world. That's why my promise to her was so important, not just to me but to both worlds. The Veil was almost gone. At least, it was in Tetron.

When I first came to this world, I truly believed I would find the light and return home before things got this bad. I'd been wrong. Not only because I'd been arrogant enough to believe the Demon King was too young to wage war on this kingdom but because I'd left it too long to tell Zahlia who she really was.

Garret didn't look my way again. He ran, leaving his friends behind. Their mortal vessels would remain in the dirt and snow until they rotted. Maybe someone would heave them into the nearby harbour. Aether knew the ocean around this city was already defiled with bodies. Paying for a cremation wasn't something most people in Tetris could afford. Besides, even the Blackmaster castes responsible for burnings and burials were overwhelmed now that the city was heaving with refugees from the moorlands.

The reapers came nightly to hunt the energy of souls, but it was the light Zahlia carried that drew them here. She had no idea that using her magic was making things far worse for the people of this city. Reapers were neither good nor evil. Like many creatures, they had a purpose, but it had been missing for years. They were lost. To restore that purpose, the Heart needed to be saved. Without it, life on both worlds would cease to exist. We would become ghosts until, eventually, we faded into nothing. I couldn't let that happen.

"Come on. We need to find her. Time has run out."

Together, Omeron and I melted into the shadows.

ia

Dressed in dark clothes to blend with the dark, I forced open the small sash window of the room I shared with Dala. I didn't cringe when the old wood snagged and squeaked, especially since the roof guard was facing away from us. It was a shitty post, so I didn't blame him for his lack of vigilance. It was also blowing a gale and freezing cold. I snorted quietly, I probably wouldn't pay full attention either.

"Ready?" I whispered.

Grim faced, Dala nodded. The small window was only just big enough for us to slither through, but we were well practised at it. Icy air whipped around us as we crouched on the steep roof. The guard didn't even lift his head, just hunkered down near the corner where there was a small amount of protection from the weather.

Without hesitation, we stepped over the loose roof tiles of the dilapidated building. Both of us had done this often enough to know where to safely put our feet. Staying low, we headed to the edge of the roof. Hentus had chosen this place a few years earlier for the Viper's headquarters. I'd never understood why he'd moved us from the west side of the city to here, but I guess he had his reasons. Side by side, we leapt across the short distance to the next rooftop.

We repeated this process until we were far enough away not to be spotted by anyone we knew. It was easier than it used to be. Only the homeless and the stupid were out after dark. I didn't dwell on what that made us. Even Hentus kept his guards close to home, and any sign of the creatures from beyond the Veil meant they were to hightail it into the house.

We navigated our route over the buildings, jumping down onto lower roofs until we could easily drop to the street.

In silence, we jogged towards the harbour area where crowds of people cowered in terror. We hunted every night. Even though Dala couldn't kill the reapers, we made a good team. She'd distract the creatures until I was ready to ensnare them with my magic. Then I'd end them as quickly as possible. Yet, no matter how many I killed, their screams disturbed me far more than anyone else I'd ever killed. The devastation and sense of loss I felt were hard to explain, even to myself, so I hid it.

The demons from the Netherworld were easier to kill, though neither of us understood why they bled and the reapers didn't. Some looked mortal, others didn't, but from the first one we'd seen come through the Veil, we'd discovered that they were flesh and blood and could be killed. I've never enjoyed killing, but I learnt to do it to survive.

We worked quickly and efficiently. We only had a short window to end as many creatures as possible before the mage hounds sniffed out my magic.

The king of Tetris had hated magic. While he'd been fighting the creatures out on the moors, his mage hounds had been blessedly small in number. The creatures sniffed out anyone with magic and then hauled the poor souls back to the palace dungeons. The king had died about eight years ago, just months after Dex had left, and the Mad Prince ruled Tetron now. Recent rumours that the prince and his general had given up the fight in the moors and returned to protect the city had spread like wildfire, and with those rumours came even more mage hounds.

Even after so long, no one knew why the Aether's Veil was sick, but it had changed our world. Tetron was the worst affected kingdom, but I'd heard stories from the few traders who made it here that others were suffering too. Dex had taught me that the Veil was a pathway for the souls of the dead to reach the Heart of the Aether, where they would be reborn.

I spun and grabbed another creature, gritting my teeth against its squeal as I shoved magic down its throat and tossed it back through the Veil.

What would a world swamped by lost souls and monsters look like?

I ducked down a dark alley, trying to push Dex's face from my mind. Somehow, that was always harder when darkness fell. Probably because the shadows reminded me of him. It was where he'd always been the most comfortable—and most dangerous. We'd both hidden our magic when we were young. It had been necessary or those around us would have betrayed us and handed us over to the King's guards. Dex had taught me how to hide it, and I'd listened. He was older than me, and I'd had no clue how to survive on the streets. Between him, Hentus, and the viciousness of the kids in the Vipers, I'd quickly learnt how to survive, though Dex had taken on the role of my protector. He'd taught me how to fight and kill. He'd had some training as a boy before his parents had been killed, and he'd used that knowledge to grow into the meanest, most efficient assassin in the Vipers. He'd earned Hentus a lot of money before he'd just up and disappeared.

Only when we were alone did he show me his magic. It was like the darkest mist I'd ever seen, dangerous yet always gentle as it played with the iridescent colours of mine. I felt no malice when it touched me, only a great sense of belonging. Much like when Dex touched me.

I growled at the direction of my thoughts. Dex had promised to care for me, to always be there when I needed him, but he'd *lied*. He'd lied through his Aether damned teeth. Although I'd been tough on the outside, I'd given my heart to the boy who'd saved me, and he'd broken it. He'd used my body and then left.

Fucker...

If I ever saw him again, I'd stab him right through the heart as I'd always promised myself I'd do. Forcing away the all-too-familiar pain, I made myself concentrate.

We jogged through the night, stepping over prone bodies. I didn't know if they were alive or dead, and it didn't matter since there was nothing I could do for those helpless people. Nothing, except stop their souls from being dragged into the darkness beyond the Veil.

Since the prince and his general had returned, we'd had to be even more careful. Now that the general's attention was back on the city, he sent his soldiers out every night to hunt for people with magic, while the warrior caste who served the crown hunted the demons. No one knew why the royal family hated magic so much, only that they did, and it had been that way over many lifetimes. It didn't really matter why. My goal was to end as many creatures as I could and save as many lives as possible.

The screaming increased as the night got darker. Goosebumps peppered my skin. It wasn't just the people of Tetris who suffered. The lost souls who wandered back through the Veil from the Nether moaned and wailed. It was heartbreaking. I swore I could feel their anguish and confusion and it hurt my heart, especially as I was the only one who could actually see them. Others could hear their cries but not see them. Maybe it was my magic. I didn't know, nor did it matter. They didn't hurt anyone, but they did spread their melancholy and despair amongst the living.

Hounds bayed, getting closer. That meant the soldiers were hunting us.

I had no idea what the future held for all the homeless and caste-less people who'd come to Tetris hoping for safety, but that wasn't my concern; staying away from General Azaraah was.

I ran faster.

It was rumoured that those who were hauled to the castle by the magic hunters were never seen again. Perhaps if I got caught, I'd find my parents' killer in the castle dungeons. I had no idea if my parents had been magickers, but it seemed a sensible deduction, seeing as I was.

I glared up at the huge castle, my feet slowing. It was tempting to let the mage hounds and their handlers catch me. At least I'd have a chance to search that awful place for the bastard who'd ruined my life. Aether knew I'd not found him in the city. I tried not to think about the possibility that my parents' killer could be a world away. I wouldn't lose hope of finding him and getting justice for their deaths.

"Don't even think about it." Dala scowled at me from under her cowl.

"It would answer that question for me though, wouldn't it?" It wasn't a surprise that my friend knew what I was thinking. She knew me better than I knew myself sometimes.

"Yes, and it would likely end your life, too. Mine as well, 'cause I'd have to come and rescue your skinny arse."

Despite the heaviness that always invaded my chest when I thought of my parents, I smiled. "Cheeky bitch. You wouldn't need to rescue me. How insulting."

Dala just rolled her eyes, but didn't argue. My magic had grown strong these past few months, and I was grateful for it, especially when fighting the creatures from the Nether. But that strength also meant it was getting harder to hide it.

We slowed. A family huddling in the mouth of an alley shuffled out of our way, sending up the noxious fumes of sewage and rot as they disturbed the slime that coated the streets. I ignored them, sensing they were no threat. Beyond the alley, the harbour was seething with shadowy figures. Most were sitting on the disgusting ground. Those with any sense, leaning their backs up against a wall for the little protection that offered from the weather and the bastards that would snatch them and force them into labour of one kind or another. This area was overcrowded and stank of fish and the rotting bodies that bounced around the harbour.

I wrinkled my nose. Disease had already set in within the Slopes, and death was fast approaching for many of the weak and vulnerable. The number of people crowded the harbour walls and narrow streets of the Slopes made it a beacon for the Nether creatures.

I hated the bitter scent of fear that the night brought and frowned watching as the dead wandered amongst the living, begging for release from their in-between existence. No matter how loudly they cried and pleaded, no one could help them. I rubbed the ache in my chest, their grief weighing heavily on me. Until the Veil healed, they had no way to reach the Heart of the Aether and be reborn.

"Trossocks!" I cursed. "This is getting worse! There's almost more dead than living now."

It was true, and though I had no idea what to do, I'd find out. Somehow the Veil had to be healed. There had to be a way.

About twenty feet away, the darkness shimmered. I let magic dance across my fingers, and the monster whipped its attention from the small girl huddled against the wall to me.

"You ready for this?" Dala's eyes were fixed on the menacing form.

I exhaled and nodded. "Let's go."

Flicking my arms back to free them from my cloak, I jumped into the Veil, pulling a little of its energy my way. The creature shrieked, displaying its sharp teeth. Moving like the wind through the dull wall of energy, I grabbed the reaper and pushed it through the Veil towards Dala. As it became corporeal, she sliced it in two with her swords. Despite that, it wasn't dead. Demons could die, their souls sucked back into the Veil; reapers, not so much. Ignoring the lure of the dark curtain beyond it, I stepped from the Veil and became solid again.

Placing one hand on the reaper's severed head and one on its body, I sent my magic into it until it shrivelled, turning into a dark mist that was sucked back into the Veil. I had no idea if it would be reborn or not, but for now it wasn't a danger.

I straightened my spine and cocked my head, sensing more evil close by.

"More," was the only warning I had time to give Dala.

This had happened every night since my birthday two weeks ago.

Once my magic was free, the creatures flocked towards me. Except, tonight, there was more than ever.

"Run!" I bellowed at the people around me.

Some did, sprinting into the darkness, others physically couldn't, and some had the apathy of broken spirits. With dull eyes they watched as more and more creatures pushed through the Veil.

"Double trossocks!" Dala hissed.

There was no laughter at her use of the Riou swear word, not tonight.

"Double fucking trossocks, indeed," I muttered. "This might be too many, even for me."

"Dammit, Zah, don't you talk like that."

I shrugged and jumped into the Veil, reappearing to attack the monsters closest to me. The night became a blur of creatures screaming and me moving like the wind using the Veil's already weakened force. My guilt at taking its energy to boost my magic was secondary to survival. I'd never seen so many creatures in one place. My heart pounded and my limbs trembled. Every time I ended one, another pushed through the shimmering curtain. I cried out as one plucked the soul of a small boy and took him into the Nether; his body slumped to the ground, his mother screaming. My heart tore at her howls of grief.

Shit. We were overrun.

I fought and fought with magic and swords, taking down more and more creatures. Dala battled at the harbour's edge, trying desperately to protect the people who cowered there.

"Run! Find some light!" I screeched.

Her fierce gaze hit me, but I didn't have time to see if she complied. The baying of hounds and the stomping of booted feet drew my attention. The harbour erupted into a battleground. The Mad Prince's magic hunters joined the fight. My stomach squeezed as the huge, black mage hounds snarled and strained against their leashes, slobber spraying from their jaws. It was too late to hide. I glanced around, hoping their general wasn't with them. His reputation was enough to make my heart hammer and my palms sweat. I didn't want to be ripped to pieces by the hounds or imprisoned and tortured by the general.

These men were after me, but they'd have to get through the creatures first. For once I was actually glad there were an abundance of Nether creatures.

Above me a tall, dilapidated building loomed. It was an old warehouse of some kind. I could get up to its roof, but it would expose my magic. I'd be hunted without mercy. I dodged the spindly fingers of a reaper. It gave a haunting howl, and my stomach tightened at the loss in that sound.

There was no choice.

Taking a breath, I spun into the Aether's energy and used the Veil to lift me to the roof tops. Shouts echoed as the soldiers and bystanders looked on in disbelief. My magic burned the air, its silver glow shot through with iridescent ribbons of colour, rising high into the night. Once on the rooftop, I switched to the mortal plane to run. I wouldn't deplete the Veil anymore tonight. Sprinting over the flat roof, I leaped to the next one, leaving the sounds of the battle and the mage hounds behind. If I didn't use my magic again, they wouldn't be able to track me...at least not easily.

I jumped, and my feet slammed into the tiles of the next roof, its slant making it hard to keep my balance. My feet slipped as a couple of tiles cracked under my weight, and shards slithered to the ground below. My boots were unable to gain a purchase, and I slid towards the edge, gravity threatening to pull me over.

Aether dammit, saving myself with magic was my only option. It was that or break my damned legs.

From out of nowhere, a hand shot out and grabbed my wrist, halting my fall and yanking me back up. I stumbled against a large...and very hard...body, my palms landing flat against a leather-clad chest. The scent of midnight and danger hit my nostrils, filling my mind and rendering me immobile. Recognition jolted me and blood roared in my ears. I shook my head, pulling my arm free and stumbling backwards, away from the man who had deserted me. Shock took my voice, but my eyes feasted on him, even if my brain was telling me to kill him where he stood.

He wasn't as I remembered. His youthful looks were long gone, replaced by an older, hardened version. Dexalion had always been dangerous and alluring, even as a teenager, but now he stole my breath. It was hard to drag air into my lungs. This gorgeous man with his midnight hair and stunning green eyes had invaded my dreams every night for as long as I could remember, even before he'd abandoned me. Once, I would have blushed and smiled under his intense scrutiny—once.

"Hey, Angel." Dex's voice was as dark and delicious as him. It washed over my skin and through my senses until it touched my soul.

I shivered, heat blooming between my legs.

Oh, no, no way... I gave my body a stern talking-to. It was just a learned reaction to his closeness, just memories of my past, that was all. I resented him more than anyone else—except my parents' killer. Dex had been my rock as I'd grown up. He'd made me promises. Promises I'd believed. Then he used me and left me all alone in this shitty place. It had broken my seventeen-year-old heart.

My eyes narrowed. Still, it *had* taught me a valuable lesson about trust.

In a mirror of mine, his eyes narrowed and a small smirk played on his shapely lips. Since I'd started growing breasts and realised Dexalion was more gorgeous than any other boy around, he'd affected me. And it seemed my body didn't agree that it shouldn't react to him now. Bastard knew it too, judging by the glint in his eyes as he studied me, lifting one brow.

Cocky arsehole.

"What do you want?" I snapped, grabbing the handle of my sword.

He tracked my movements, his mouth losing that smirk. Yeah, I wasn't the same stupid, love struck girl he'd left behind. Gone were the days I'd throw myself into his arms when I'd not seen him for a while.

"Some thanks for saving you might be nice."

I cocked my head and scowled. "You didn't save me. I could have saved myself, and you know it."

The howls of the mage hounds grew closer. Dex held my stare.

"Sure you could, but then you'd have those ugly mutts hunting you down."

I shrugged. "Just another day...or night. I'd like to say it's nice to see you, Dex, but I'd be lying. I've no idea what you're doing back, and I don't want to know. But I do know I want you to fuck off."

A grin stretched his mouth revealing his perfectly white teeth, and he crossed his large arms over his equally large chest. "You sure about that, Angel?"

"Yes!" I snapped.

It had totally thrown me seeing my first, and only, love again, but he didn't need to know that. I turned to leave, only to find that someone blocked my way. I quickly studied the intruder. He was darker skinned than Dala, blending into the night, except for his weirdly glowing amber eyes. They were as sharp and disturbing as Dex's bright green ones, only somehow more animalistic.

The warrior studied me silently. "This her?" he asked.

I turned sideways so that I could watch them both.

"It is."

The dark warrior raised his white brows, and looked pointedly at Dex. "Well?"

Dex sighed and took a step towards me.

"Back off, Dex." I relaxed into a fighting stance and pulled my blade.

He lifted his hands in supplication. "I just want to talk, Lia."

"Stop with the nicknames, you betraying piece of shit."

"Fine, but I still need to talk with you."

"About what?" I wasn't really interested. At least that's what I told myself. But I was buying time as I weighed up my options.

"I need your help."

"Ha!" I barked a laugh, though he did look completely serious. "Me? I doubt that. You have more magic in your little finger than I have in my whole body. And you proved years ago that you don't give a shit about anyone but yourself, no matter what pretty words you spout."

The hounds were closer, their howls and barking closing in on the street below.

"Lia, I understand you don't trust me, but if you're caught by those men tonight, I can't help you. Come with me now and I can help you stay hidden."

Heat swamped my face, the fingers of my other hand curling on my dagger as I unsheathed a second weapon.

"You can't be for real," I whispered, shaking my head. "You left me, Dex. You fucked me, and then disappeared! You took my innocence and my trust, and turned it into something ugly. You LIED!" Hot tears blurred my vision, but I didn't let them fall.

I'd not allowed my pain or anger at Dex to colour my emotions for years, but seeing his stunning face, smelling his familiar scent, hearing his voice, it was all too much. I'd prayed over and over for him to come back. For years I'd been sure something bad had happened, that maybe the slavers had taken him, and that somehow he would find his way back to me. He never had. It had been about six months later that I'd learned he'd spent the night in a whore house after he'd taken my virginity.

His face hardened. "You were too young, Lia…"

I snarled. "It's Zahlia. And you'd better not finish that sentence. If you dare say I was too young to go with you, I will gut you where you stand. You knew I was saving myself for you. You took advantage of my naivety, and once you got what you wanted, you were history. You never had any intention of taking me with you when you left."

His gaze flicked to the blades I held before resting back on my face. His own softened, but I wasn't fooled.

"Lia…"

"Don't bother. I'm leaving now. If you or your friend try to stop me, I will kill you. Don't come near me again, Dex, or you'll find one of these blades embedded in your balls. The other I'll stick right in your heart."

Not caring that the mage hounds would track me, I leapt into the Veil and sprinted as fast as I could, away from that rooftop and the pain of my past.

As thrown as I was by seeing Dex, my mind was straight enough to know I couldn't return to the Viper's headquarters, not when there was a slim chance that he could use his magic to follow me. My heart raced at the thought of him hunting me down. He'd always been able to find me when we were younger, but now I could lock down my powers so tightly, not even the Mad Prince's mage hounds would sense it.

Breathing hard, I headed up past the Slopes and into the financial district. Once there, I jumped from the Veil. The creatures who watched me from the Nether howled but were too slow to keep up. They moved beyond the shadows that curtained the Netherworld, their haunting cries piercing my soul, and feeding my desire to help them, not hurt them.

I landed on the top of a temple and quickly ran to the edge. Fumbling, I found the hand-holds I knew were there and swung my legs over the parapet. Heights didn't bother me. I often used this tower to leave the Veil. This district was wealthy enough that most people would be indoors with some kind of light to keep them a bit safer.

Once at the base of the tower, I charged through the grounds and vaulted the iron fence into the street. From there, I jogged through the empty streets to the side of Tetris, furthest from the harbour. Regular guard patrols kept the refugees and the homeless of the Slopes from getting this far into the higher echelons of the city, so I ran unhindered.

A sense of awareness prickled the skin on the back of my neck. I turned swiftly, searching the darkness behind me. Even in the high-caste areas of the city, street lights were banned. Burning fuel was a precious commodity, and lighting the streets was not important. Keeping homes well lit was. No matter how hard I searched the shadows, I couldn't see any signs of life.

Ignoring the sense of being watched, I darted from the financial district and into the pleasure caste territory. Here more people lined the streets. I didn't stop, just kept moving down through the increasingly busy streets and alleys. No one gave me any trouble, yet my stomach only relaxed when I saw the familiar shadow of our run-down old mansion. My legs trembled with fatigue, so I climbed up the drain pipe using the last of my energy, until I hit the rooftop. From there, I ran forward, staying low just as I had when Dala and I had left earlier that evening.

I prayed to the goddess that Dala had survived and was warm in her bed. It had taken me hours to get down through the city levels, and I was exhausted and starving. There'd be no food, but at least I had a reasonably comfy bed waiting for me. Against the light of the moon, the silhouette of a guard came into view. I crouched low and waited until he started to walk the other way, then leapt onto the rooftop. I was soon swinging my body in through the window, landing with a soft thud on the floor boards.

"Bollocks and buggery, Zah," Dala whispered, rubbing her face as if she couldn't believe her eyes. "Where the Nether have you been? I thought you were dead." She jumped out of bed utterly naked, her dark flesh gleaming in the light from the window and flung her arms around me, hugging me close.

"Um, awkward," I mumbled into her throat.

She laughed. "Tough shit." But she pulled back and let me go.

I fell on my bed and covered my face with my arm, trying to get my head and my heart back under my control. Fucking, Dexalion. Why had he come back?

"What happened?" asked Dala, sitting on her bed, her brows drawn together.

"Dexalion is back."

"What? Your Dexalion? The one who broke your heart?"

"Yeah, that one," I muttered into my bicep.

"Oh."

I grunted in agreement.

"What does he want?"

I lowered my arm and turned my head to look at her. "I've no idea. I told him to stay away from me or I'd stab him in the balls."

Dala smirked. "Good girl. You look all done in. Want to tell me about it in the morning?"

Exhausted, I nodded. Dala climbed back under her blanket. It was always damned cold in our room as there were holes in the roof and walls, but Dala never seemed to feel it. She always slept naked, even when there was ice on the inside of the windows and walls. Checking that the door was locked, I slithered, fully clothed, under my own blanket, checking our lamp had enough burning oil to last until morning. The last thing I wanted was for the monsters of the Nether to find me as I slept. Not when I fought them every night to keep others safe. Pushing the image of Dexalion's face from my mind, I tried to sleep.

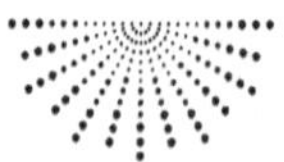

ex

The prince's hard grey eyes monitored my approach. He sat upon his golden throne, his square jaw resting on his hand. He looked physically strong, and most people would be intimidated by his presence. I wasn't most people, though. In fact, I wasn't a person at all. That didn't mean I wasn't wary of him. As his name suggested, he was unpredictable, and that was reflected in the dark circles under his eyes, and the overly bright light glinting in the hardness of his gaze. He couldn't hurt me, but a showdown with the royal family would delay my purpose, and would result in more innocent loss of life. He wasn't dubbed 'the Mad Prince' for nothing. We had fought side by side for eight years, yet I knew that wouldn't count if I angered him enough. His ability to reason, not to mention his temper, was tenuous at best.

"Where is the vigilante, General?"

I didn't deign to answer him while I walked across the marble floor of the throne room. I barely managed to hide the disgust I felt each time I had to face this cruel, weak-minded ruler. I'd deliberately saved him and not his father on the battlefield eight years ago, and I often wondered if I'd made the right choice. I'd wanted to rise in the ranks of the mortal army, and I had, but the longer the prince was regent and refused to take the crown, the more convinced I was I'd made the wrong choice. Even the cold-hearted king would have made better decisions than this cruel prince, who didn't care about the plight of his people or city. He only cared that the demons of the Netherworld and the magic that brought them here were expunged from the kingdom of Tetron.

No one knew why he refused to be crowned, but he had issued a decree that he would not accept the mantle of king until the Aether's Veil was restored to full health. I had to wonder whether his mental instability was a result of his anxiety and grief for his queen...

"She escaped my men..."

"Escaped!" His yell rattled my eardrums, and I bit down on the urge to roar back.

"Indeed," I said calmly.

"I want her found!" prince Escalon straightened, his eyes wild, and his hands gripping the gilded arms of the throne. "Every night she entices more of those creatures here. If she cannot be purified, they will overrun the city in a matter of weeks!"

Silently, I cursed the rumours of a silver haired witch that had reached the palace. "I am aware, prince. However, I need more time to hunt her down..."

"There is no more time!" he bellowed. "There is a whole army of those monsters surrounding this city. If the magickers aren't expunged from Tetris, we will all die!"

"I am aware of the gravity of the situation..."

"Oh, you are, are you? Then why did you lose the war against those things out on the moors? My army has been decimated thanks to your incompetence! I should never have listened to my father's dying wish to make you my general. You have lost my kingdom to the Nether demons, and soon my city will be swallowed by them. We will all die!"

I took a deep breath and shut out his rant, standing far enough away his spittle didn't land on me. In truth, I didn't give a shit about the city or the mortals here. There was a far bigger war going on than this idiot realised, and unless I could get Zahlia on my side, it would swallow more than this kingdom.

Once he'd exhausted his tirade about my incompetence, I took a steady breath. Before I could speak, a cough and a wheeze broke through the sound of Escalon's angry pants.

"I think what my brother is trying to say is that he thanks you..." Another wheezing breath. "For your service and loyalty. I'm sure you understand that this invasion is the very reason we abhor any mortal with the potential for magic. My mother, Aether rest her soul..." another wheeze. "...was always anxious over the possibility of an invasion from the Nether. I'm sure you have a plan..." Another breath.'"...to find the magickers who are enticing the creatures here."

I turned and nodded at the younger prince. His sallow skin looked worse than normal as he wrangled breath into his lungs. He'd always been a sickly one, yet, since I'd saved his brother and been given the post of general to the army of Tetris, I noticed he was the only one who could calm his brother.

Escalon's mental health had deteriorated more and more over the past three years. The Crown prince was stricken with grief over the worsening health of his young wife. She was rarely seen, even around the castle, and there were rumours she walked the grounds at night hoping to be taken by one of the reapers. I didn't enlighten those who gossiped that the reapers and demons avoided the castle. I had an idea why, but since my return to the city, I hadn't had the opportunity to investigate. Especially since I needed to search the very dungeons that I used to contain the magickers.

I inclined my head. "Thank you, prince Haruin. I do."

"That's good." prince Haruin took another breath, so I waited patiently until he was ready to speak again. His brother remained quiet, his eyes drifting to the door that led to his private quarters where his sickly wife resided.

"Would you share it with us?" Haruin asked in a wheezing sentence, an encouraging smile on his lips.

Haruin was a physically weak yet equally cold-hearted man, his only use being he could calm his volatile brother. I had no idea what having two compassionless heirs meant for Tetris, nor did I worry over it.

"Of course. I have a contact in the Slopes who will agree to help me track down the vigilante. She is a magicker herself, and one who knows the consequences if she disobeys me. I will use her knowledge to search the darkest, most hidden corners of Tetris. Once we have the witch and her magic is contained, there may be a chance we can discover how to heal the Veil."

I kept my face blank. Fixing the Veil relied on Zahlia's compliance. Her threat to chop my balls off made it clear she'd rather do anything else than work with me, but if I couldn't persuade her, we were all fucked.

Haruin nodded, his eyes alight with interest, yet he couldn't hide his underlying disgust at having a magicker in the castle. The dead King, and his Queen, had done a perfect job of prejudicing their sons against magic. In a way, it was true that the creatures of the Nether hunted magic, but it was one particular source of magic that drew the reapers and demons to Tetris. There was a sacred triad that maintained the balance between our worlds. The Heart of the Aether fed from the Angel's power, the Veil took power from the Heart, and the Angel replenished her magic from both the light and the dark sides of the Veil.

The absence of the Angel meant the Heart, the guiding beacon for the reapers, was dim, and because of that the Veil was weak. Now the light of *any* soul enticed the reapers to this world. The demons were a different story. They had far more sinister reasons for being here than souls, or at least, Baladon, the Demon King, did. His warriors came through the Veil where it was weakest. For years, that had been around the moors. With my help, the mortal troops had fought them. The city was rife with rumours of death hounds attacking demons and mortals alike. I hadn't corrected those tales, not when they were partly true. Omeron and the Barg were under strict orders to attack only the demon warriors and to stay out of sight using the shadows.

I ground my teeth. Since Lia's magic had reached maturity, she had weakened the Veil until the city was the easiest place for the demon army to push through. She didn't realise what she was doing, but if I didn't stop it, the mortal world would soon be overrun.

"Then, by all means, bring her here," muttered Escalon. "But keep her contained and under your control. If she uses magic in my home, I will have her killed, regardless of your plans for her."

I hid my rage at his threat.

"I assure you, she will be of great use and not a danger in any way."

Well, that was a lie.

Lia was as likely to assassinate me as them. Controlling her with threats against her own safety was pointless; she had very little fear of pain, or even death. I would need another way to persuade her to stay in line.

Haruin eyed his brother, catching his gaze.

Escalon sighed and waved his hand dismissively. "Fine, do what you must. But if I see no improvement in the situation of my city soon, it won't only be her head I want. Yours will roll too."

While he pushed to his feet, I grappled with my need to show him how dangerous it was to threaten me. Thankfully he glanced at his brother and missed the flash of bloodlust in my eyes.

"I'm going to see my queen," he muttered.

Haruin nodded. "Of course. I'll find you before dinner, brother."

The princes nodded at each other. As always there was an undercurrent of tension that I didn't understand, nor did I care to.

Haruin's attention came back to me, and he smiled tiredly. As he spoke, his words came interspersed with wheezing breaths. I listened patiently.

"It's in your best interests to find the magicker as soon as possible, General. We are running out of food and burning oil. Even the castle supplies are dwindling. We need to rid ourselves of all magickers. This cannot be allowed to continue nor...will I allow it to happen again." For a moment, his face dropped. "If there was a way to rid those sorry souls of magic without killing them, I would take it." He looked right at me, creases marring his brow, though his eyes remained cold. "I am sorry it falls to you to rid our kingdom of those unfortunate enough to be born with evil in their veins."

I hid my anger at his empty words. He wasn't at all sorry for the mass murder he encouraged. "It's no hardship," I answered, keeping my voice even, although my fingers twitched, itching to snap his neck, followed closely by his brother's.

Haruin nodded. "When you have the vigilante, we will, of course, want to meet her."

"Of course, prince Haruin." In truth, I didn't want either of the princes near Lia, but it was safer for her with me, under the castle roof than out in the city where the reapers could overwhelm her or the demons could drag her back to Baladon. Once she was by my side, I could use hunting magickers as a reason to keep her alive while I found a way back to Haldaag.

"Just one thing before you go," he said, as I turned away.

Unease tingled down my spine, but I forced myself to turn back.

"Escalon means what he said; if she uses magic anywhere in the castle, it will be seen as treason. Neither of you will be shown mercy. Find a way to contain it."

I met his steady gaze. "I know. And I vow neither of you will have cause to accuse me or her of treason."

Haruin huffed a small chuckle and pushed slowly to his feet. Leaning heavily on his cane, he shuffled up to me.

"Then all will be well, General," he said, continuing past me and disappearing through the same door as his brother.

Silence fell. I spun and walked out of the throne room, already constructing my plan to get Lia to work by my side until I could get us back to the relative safety of my home.

My footsteps echoed through the castle halls as I tried not to think about the night I'd left Lia. I'd known leaving would break her, but that had been the point. She'd always been brave and reckless. There were few in this world she cared about, but when she loved, it was with all her heart. She was fiercely protective and loyal to a fault. I'd needed to break that unfailing loyalty. And her delusion of perfection when it came to me also needed to crack. I was as far from perfect as anyone could get; I was a liar and a murderer, definitely no one's idea of a good guy. No matter what she'd seen me do, she still hadn't seemed capable of believing what her eyes had told her. So I'd used her heart against her. I'd wanted her to realise that if the person she trusted most could betray her, then anyone could. I'd needed her to hate me enough that I could justify staying away all these years.

The only way I could protect her from the creatures who threatened both the Netherworld and this one was to leave. I'd used the mortal army to hold them back for years, even though every damned day I stayed away from Lia had eaten at my soul. I'd been too selfish to leave without putting my mark on her and it was a night I would cherish and regret forever. I'd underestimated her effect on me to the point that walking away had been the hardest thing I'd ever done.

My fists curled and my magic roiled at the thought of her with anyone else. But, it didn't matter. She was mine now, even if she didn't know it yet. This close to her, I could feel the call of her magic. My soul and my shadows were screaming at me to find her, to make her mine again in every sense of the word, to protect her. But that wasn't what Lia needed nor would she ever tolerate that kind of base behaviour from me. She was a warrior. One who would chop off my balls and smile while she did it if I tried to force her into anything.

I smiled. Seeing the way she moved her lithe body, her skill and viciousness, the flash of wrath in her stunning gaze had been a gift. I'd felt more alive in her presence than I had for the past eight years.

I'd missed her.

It had been hard to breathe standing so close to her, forcing myself not to touch, not to pull her against me. She had become a stunning mix of beauty and strength. Her magic had immediately called to mine and it had taken every bit of willpower I possessed not to let them merge. We were opposite sides of power, we always had been, which meant we meshed perfectly when we were together.

I blinked and huffed out a heavy breath. The Higher Powers, the gods who had matched us, just hadn't figured on our fucked up situation. Part of me knew she would never agree to be mine, not even if I could persuade her to take her place at my side. Once she discovered my secrets, she would hate me with every fibre of her being. Some hatred was too much to come back from, and I don't mean a broken teenage heart. No, this hatred would be deep-seated, and one I didn't ever want to face.

I growled, the sound vibrating into the air. It was returned by another predatory rumble. From the shadows the amber eyes of my Beta glinted. Omeron morphed into his human form and fell in step with me.

"Are we to bring her here?"

"Yes."

"Then I hope for both your sakes that you can find a way back to the Nether before the Demon King completely destroys our world or the Heart withers and dies."

"Me too, my friend. Me too."

The stink of the city hit me as we walked to where our horses awaited in the frigid air. I swung up into my saddle and peered back over my shoulder at my soldiers. "You will maintain rank and formation unless I say otherwise. We are on an escort mission only. No mage hounds are needed."

The beast handlers immediately walked away, and the remaining soldiers quickly fell in line, with some in front and some behind Omeron and me. The massive keep gates opened and we urged our steeds forward. I straightened my spine, keeping my magic locked down, praying that the head of the Vipers would succumb to my threats. For all he had kept me informed of Zahlia's wellbeing, he'd moved the nest to somewhere it would take me time to discover. He was cunning. His spies would have informed him of my return before I appeared in his territory. He certainly wouldn't welcome me with open arms, not when it meant losing the girl he'd rescued and treated as a daughter for the past nineteen years.

CHAPTER SEVEN

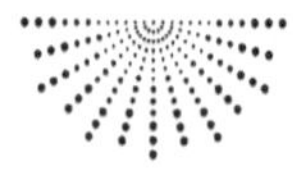

ia

Sunshine warmed my cold cheeks. I let a smile curl my lips. It was funny how such a simple thing could change my mood.

I'd slept badly. Dex's face had haunted me, the memory of his fingers trailing over my all too eager body, making my naked skin tingle, heating between my legs, and peaking my aching breasts. I'd tossed and turned all night until, eventually, I'd given up.

Leaving Dala asleep, I headed out. There was something I needed to do today, something I should have done a long time ago that would help me focus my resolve. I'd decided to get the flower Dex had given me when I was a frightened six-year-old tucked away in a locket. It would be a reminder not to care for anyone, especially him. And with it out of sight, Dex would never know I kept it.

Dex had been home to me. We'd fought side by side to survive in this shitty, violent world. I'd loved him, trusted him with every fibre of my being, and he'd betrayed me in the worst possible way. No matter what he wanted from me now, he couldn't undo his past actions. Anger wrapped me in a familiar blanket, but it was time to let it go.

Tipping my head back, I closed my eyes and, releasing a slow, steady breath, I absorbed the rare warmth of the winter sun. I listened as gulls screeched above me and waves crashed against the rocks below. I could sit here for hours and just let the wildness of this place absorb my turbulent thoughts.

The sun disappeared behind a cloud, and the temperature plummeted. I sighed and opened my eyes.

Oh well. All good things must end.

On the horizon, the sky was grey and heavy with rain. I pulled my threadbare jacket tighter around my shoulders. Pushing myself up, I balanced on the small ledge of rock that jutted from the cliff face, hundreds of feet above the ocean. Below, the water was a churning cauldron of blue and white foam, and above me the rock face led back to the cliff top. Staying on the cliff face wasn't an option. I'd freeze, and I needed to eat. My stomach rumbled in agreement. I decided to climb up and head back to the nest through the over-crowded streets rather than the rooftops. There was sure to be a vendor I could steal something from or an unsuspecting higher caste member whose guards were lax enough to not notice me picking a pocket or three.

Hentus had moved the Vipers' headquarters from where Dex and I had grown up, so I was sure I had at least today to devise a plan to evade my betrayer. I had no idea why he wanted to find me, but he could jump off this damned cliff if he thought he could waltz back into my life after what he'd done.

With my long braid flapping behind me in the frigid wind, I climbed the cliff face, my cold fingers gripping the edges of rocks as surely as ever. Turning my feet sideways so they were secure on the rock shelves I used as leverage, I pulled myself up, scrambling onto the grassy cliff edge.

No one but the warrior castes, who made up the city guards, patrolled the South-West cliffs of Tetris. Well, they had. Now they avoided the deadly cliffs, especially once the Veil became sick. Their only focus now was protecting the upper castes and the royal family and, for some unknown reason, hunting down magickers. Those outside the city walls were left to suffer.

I joined the column of exhausted people entering the city. Using my ability to jump into the Aether this close to the castle might set off any mage hounds nearby, so when I was almost to the gate, I magicked a farming caste mark on the inner part of my wrist. Casteless refugees were turned away, hence the throng of wretched souls sitting in clutches near the cobbled road, begging for scraps of food from those well-off enough to spare some.

Hate rippled through me. If the Mad Prince was so worried about his people, why did he allow anyone, casteless or not, to starve outside his city walls? Though I doubted it was any safer inside the city when darkness fell. The reapers didn't discriminate like the royal family did.

Eyes down and shoulders slumped like those around me, I showed my wrist. The guard was as exhausted as the refugees and only gave it a cursory glance. I passed him just as another guard raised his voice, denying entry to a young girl who was no more than eight. The girl's father raged and pointed to his own mark. A trade caste. He was built like an ox and had clearly kept himself and his family well-fed. The man's eyes sparked. I held my breath, willing him not to make things worse. He could fight the guards, but it would be useless; he'd get arrested and separated from his family. They'd starve. My stomach clenched as the man and his two girls were shoved back out through the gates. It didn't matter how well-fed they were; they'd eventually starve now all the farmland was barren, if the reapers didn't take them first.

I stared. The girl's face was dirty, and her eyes glinted with hatred. She grabbed her younger sister's hand and put her free one on her father's wrist, pulling it to get his attention.

"It's alright, Papa. We will go back home to the forest."

He closed his eyes and nodded. I understood his despair. The forest was in the far north, near the moors, where the General had been fighting the reapers, and it was well and truly dead according to the stories I'd heard. He took his daughters' hands and led them away, but not before I saw tears shine in his eyes. Fuck, I hated what was happening to our kingdom and its people. I felt so helpless. That's why

I went out every night to try and save at least one person. Even if I couldn't ultimately save them all, and even if attacking the reapers left me filled with a sadness I didn't understand, it didn't matter. They were killing people.

I melted into the throng of people but stood where I could watch the family retreat. I bit my bottom lip. Something about that little girl, and even the man, called to me. I couldn't let them all die.

I glanced around, checking the shadows for the tell-tale green reflection of the mage hounds' eyes. My scrutiny took in the guards on the wall, around the gate, and those patrolling the road into the city. No hounds. Not a surprise, really. They were needed to hunt the city for magickers.

Before my parents had been murdered they'd talked about leaving this place. I wish we'd gotten as far away from this city and its troubles as possible. Now I couldn't leave. I'd made them a promise to end the man who'd killed them. And I'd do it. *Then* I'd take Dala and leave. Hentus would understand. After all, he was the one who'd taught me never to rely on anyone but myself.

Except he didn't, did he? Dexalion taught you that. And it was a lesson I wouldn't ever let myself forget.

My eyes narrowed on the man and his girls. He'd be an asset to Hentus. At least, that was my reasoning for the plan forming in my head. Hentus would just have to accept it. If not, I'd look after them. Something about the determination in that little girl's eyes sparked a desire in me to at least try and give them a chance to survive. I waited until they were well down the road, then stepped into a dark alley to be certain I was alone before I jumped into the Aether. In no time, I was next to where the man walked. I waited until no one else was around, then stepped off the Aether right beside him. The girls squealed, and the man swore before he shoved them behind him.

I held up my hands. "Don't be afraid. I've come to help you."

The man's eyes narrowed. "What do you mean? I've got no orms. No food either." He pulled a huge wooden baton from under his cloak. "Leave us be, and I'll not hurt you, girl."

I refrained from rolling my eyes, not angry in the least. He was scared for his children and probably starving. The sheer size of him had to take some feeding every day. I opened my mouth to reassure him, but the oldest girl spoke first.

"You're a magicker."

I looked at her. There was no fear in her voice or in her eyes, merely curiosity. Searching with my magic, I touched something powerful...and gentle. Her magic was like the touch of mist on your skin—light and cool. I smiled then squatted down, trying to be unthreatening.

I tilted my head. "I am. So are you."

She nodded. "I am."

"Kayla! Enough! What have I told you?"

She eyed her father contritely, still holding her younger sister's hand. "To keep it a secret."

"Don't worry, Kayla, your secret is safe with me." I looked at her and winked before straightening and addressing my next words to her father. "I mean that."

He narrowed his eyes. "Yeah? And what do you want for your silence?"

"Nothing. I don't want the warrior caste after me any more than you do, but I can help you. I'm casteless, too. When I was six, someone helped me find shelter, food, and a way to survive in this city. I'm just paying that forward."

He tilted his head, his mouth flattening to a thin line. I kept my eyes on his face while keeping watch on the cudgel he gripped in his big hand. His gaze took me in, assessing me, but not with lust or deviousness. No, this was fighter to fighter. My instincts were right; he wasn't just a trade caste man.

"The Vipers?"

My brows dipped a little. "You know of them?"

He laughed, his whole demeanour relaxing. "I do. Hentus was once a friend of mine. We knew each other as kids. Hell, we even ran away from home together when we were young. We ended up in Tetris and started that gang of cut throats and thieves together."

I returned his smile but kept my guard up. If he was vicious enough to be a part of the Vipers and a friend to Hentus, there was ample reason to be wary. Hentus wasn't the type of guy to have friends. Then again, what did I truly know about him? Not much beyond what he let me see. And I'd never looked that deeply. That was on me, not Hentus. "Really? Then why'd you leave?"

He shrugged his massive soldiers. "Hentus was happy with that life. Being a king amongst thieves suited him. Me?" His gaze drifted to his girls. "I wanted a quieter life."

That I could understand. I remembered my father trying to persuade my mother to leave this city more than once. They'd argued about it a lot in the weeks before their deaths. I shook off those thoughts. "Fair enough. So what are you planning to do now?"

The man glanced at his children and his face fell. "Honestly? Find enough wood to make a fire tonight, and hope its light will keep the monsters away from my girls. From there, walk to the next town and see if we can seek refuge there."

"You could, but they're as rammed as Tetris. If anything, it's more violent in those places than in the city 'cause most don't have enough warriors to protect their own people, let alone refugees. "

His grip tightened on the handle of his weapon. "I can protect them."

"Maybe. But I can get you into Tetris, then you can come and see Hentus. He won't turn you away. You'd know that if you were his friend."

He huffed, running a hand through his hair. "Actually, friend might be pushing it."

"Papa stole Momma from Hentus," Kayla said matter of factly. "So Papa thinks he will still be angry."

My eyes widened, my gaze bouncing from the two young girls to the man. "You stole his woman? Damn, that's really brave—or really stupid." Hentus had a woman? I really needed to get to know my surrogate dad better.

The man squared his shoulders, his spine stiffening. "That was fifteen years ago. We were young." He glanced at his girls. "Though I'd do it again in a heartbeat for the time I had with my Arma."

I gave him a small smile. The conviction in his voice somehow hurt my heart. It reminded me that I'd loved someone like that. But he hadn't loved me back. It sounded like this man had sacrificed a lot to be with his wife. "Well, would you like to rekindle your friendship with Hentus? Or I can just get you into the city. I won't tell him I've seen you. Aether's hole, I don't even know your name so I can't tell him."

The man's grey eyes studied me before looking at Kayla. Her sister stood quietly watching. In a move that made me grin, the girls looked at each other, nodded and then looked at their papa together, and both nodded again. He blew out a steadying breath. "Okay, how are you going to get us in?"

I grinned, happy they'd at least have a chance, whatever they decided to do. A young soul like Kayla's with so much bright magic would bring the reapers like a beacon in the darkness. "I'm going to give her a caste mark."

"But the guard will still recognise us," he pointed out.

"He will, so we'll wait for the guard to change." I glanced up, checking the sun for an idea of the time. "That will only be about an hour, and by the time we get through the queue, no one at the gate will recognise you."

"Okay. Or we can wait until dark to make sure."

I shook my head. "No, that's not safe. It would take too long to reach the Viper's nest. It's down at the base of the Slopes. Darkness falls quickly in the city, and you'd be at risk, not just from the Nether monsters but the human ones too. They'd kill you to get to two young, untouched girls like these. They'd fetch a huge price from the slave ships and pleasure houses."

Anger flashed in his eyes. "Not if I kill those fuckers first."

I made a neutral noise. It didn't matter how good a fighter you were in Tetris. If a gang like ours set their sights on someone, that person was lost. I knew that, and so did this man if the look on his face was anything to go by.

"Fine. Then I guess once we get in the city, we should go find Hentus and see if he's forgiven me or not."

"Hm,' I answered, noncommittally, hoping for their sakes he had.

It took no time to pull a little energy from the air and give the girls a trade caste mark on their forearms that was identical to their papa's.

"Now let's see..."

I pushed their hoods back from their heads and ran my hands over their hair. Both girls had black hair with deep olive skin, more in keeping with the Medallion Isles or the kingdom of Pa'dur than Tetron. Kayla had light blue eyes, and her sister had grey eyes like her papa. It would cost me in magic and energy, but changing their hair colour to a common brown, even if I couldn't change their eyes, would protect them further.

I stepped back and grinned at their papa. "Well, would you look at that? They look like twins."

He raised his brows, mirroring my grin. "Yeah, if Daisy was another half-foot taller."

"True." I turned and looked at him. "Your turn, Mr."

"Mr?"

"Well, I don't know your name, so that's what you get called."

"Don't think I've ever been accused of being a Mr," he grumbled.

"So what's your name then?" I asked, laughing at his disgruntled expression while sending my magic to give him a short scruffy beard and longer hair.

"Edgar, but my friends call me Edge." He glowered, rubbing at his beard.

I raised a brow, the grin remaining on my face. For some reason I found such growly petulance funny in such a big man. "Why?"

"I used to have an axe as my favourite weapon. Because it was my favourite, I always kept the blade sharp. It gave me an edge over my enemies."

My grin widened.

"Hentus started it," he muttered.

I did laugh at that almost childish defensiveness. "Now *that* I can believe. C'mon, I have a friend who loves to play with a double headed axe. You'll like him. He looks a bit like you."

I guided them back to the city, trying to appear relaxed. They didn't need to know it was taking a huge amount of effort to maintain their disguises. We joined the back of the line. Rivulets of sweat ran down my spine. Changing an appearance for a short time wasn't taxing. Changing it for the four of us for the hours we stood in line, was torture. It took far longer than I expected, and by the time we were through the city gates, the sun was dropping, and I was exhausted. I stumbled over my own feet.

Edge caught my elbow. "Steady," he muttered, guiding us towards a small space next to a wall. I sank to the ground and panted. "Hide us," I said, tugging on the hem of his cloak. He understood, as did the girls. They helped him spread it out enough to hide us from prying eyes. When the magic fell away, we all reverted back to our original appearance. My head spun, and my stomach churned, but I hadn't gone back for this man and his girls just to have them lose their lives in the city.

"Come on. It'll take us a couple of hours to get down to the Viper's nest."

Edge and Kayla helped me up. Thanking them, I held Daisy's hand and led the little family through the throngs of people.

"You stay close and hold tight. Do you understand?" I asked, peering down at her angelic face.

She nodded solemnly, her eyes huge as the crowds closed in. The city gates were in the mid-echelon of the city, where markets and shops thrived. It was busy, the atmosphere aggressive and loud as people bartered for food while others tried to steal it. City guards patrolled the streets, their punishments brutal and swift. Thieving here was a death sentence—if you got caught. As we walked, my magic replenished enough that I had stopped shaking by the time the boom of the waves was audible beneath the noise of the city.

I turned down a familiar back street, past my favourite baker. The smell of puchinellas made saliva fill my mouth. I was so hungry. I saw Kayla's wide eyes and wondered how long it had been since they'd all eaten.

"This way, nearly there," I encouraged, smiling back over my shoulder at Edge. Breath exploded from my lungs as I walked into someone. Daisy's hand was pulled from mine.

"Hey, sugar plum, who's this you have for us?" said a familiar voice, one that sent shudders of revulsion down my spine. Urgh, how could I have ever let him touch me. Disgusting.

"Garret." My eyes went to Daisy's frightened face, and Edge's furious intake of breath didn't pass me by. "Let her go. They're friends of Hentus."

Garret smirked, raising a brow. "Really? Well how 'bout I don't believe you. These two'll fetch a pretty orm. Is that what you were doin'? Taking these sweet ones down to the docks to sell 'em for yourself?"

"Let her go right now, or I'll slice your balls off," I growled, pulling my knife.

Daisy's eyes widened further, and she looked at her papa.

"It's okay, baby girl. Just close your eyes for me. Like we practised. Okay?"

Daisy nodded and squeezed her eyes shut.

"Last chance, you little fucker. Let my girl go, or you lose your head." Edge's voice was utterly cold.

Garret laughed in Edge's face, and yanked Daisy backwards. "Oh, you're her daddy? Well, she's mine now. Boys, have at 'em." He eyed me coldly. "Don't worry about Hentus's bitch, have at her, too." He snarled at Edge. "When you take that fucker down, I want the other girl, too."

"Stand down," barked a familiar voice before any of Garret's cronies could follow his orders. Hentus stepped forward from behind Garret's shoulder and pulled Daisy's hand firmly into his own. He glanced down at her, and his face softened. "Hey, you can open your eyes now, little one."

Daisy shook her head.

"It's alright, baby girl. You can," said Edge, walking up to Hentus. He leaned down and scooped Daisy into his arms, hugging her while Kayla clung to his side.

The two men stared at each other for almost ten seconds. Something passed between them, then they both nodded. Edge surprised the crap out of me by passing Daisy to Hentus. Hentus took her and stood back, taking hold of Kayla's hand, too.

Edge moved almost too quickly to see. He slammed the baton into Garret's ribs, stepped sideways and cracked the wood down on his shoulders. Garret collapsed to the ground with a scream.

Wow, that had to hurt. I tried unsuccessfully to hide my smile.

"Touch my daughters again, and I'll smash your skull in and leave you for the city rats, you slimy piece of shit," Edge ground out, his eyes burning with fury. "The only reason you're still alive is because you work for Hentus. That won't save you a second time."

Still biting my lip, I watched the two men closely.

"Good to see you again, Edge. Glad you haven't completely lost your touch," Hentus drawled, completely ignoring Garret who had rolled into a ball to nurse his broken ribs and collar bone.

He'd be out of action for a while, but I'd have to warn Edge not to turn his back on Garret.

Edge smiled grimly at Hentus. "I'll never lose my touch. Now give me my girls."

"Of course."

Hentus handed over Daisy as Kayla scuttled behind the safety of her papa's big body. Edge placed Daisy down, and she took her sister's hand and hid, too.

"They look like her," Hentus said quietly enough that I nearly missed his words.

"They do. That a problem?" Edge asked, his eyes narrowed on Hentus, his stance relaxed but with enough tension to tell me he was ready to fight for their lives if needed.

Hentus shook his head. "Never. Now come and tell me where the fuck you've been."

"Are we safe with you, Hent?" Edge's question was cold, his eyes colder. He'd fight for his girls, and it surprised me that I would, too. Even against my surrogate father if needed. Hentus was not a good man—but neither was he totally bad. But money was money, and the girls would fetch a price. Then again, he'd never sold Dala or me, so I crossed my fingers.

"You and yours will always be safe with me. I owe you and Arma my life. That means your family is my family. I'll always protect them, even from my own, " Hentus vowed, glancing at Garret.

Edge relaxed and expelled a long breath. "Good. That means I don't have to kill you. Arma would haunt me from the Veil if I did."

A smile teased Hentus's lips. "That she would."

Edge turned to me. "Thank you. For everything."

I nodded and smiled, then knelt down in front of Kayla and Daisy. "I'll see you later. Be good for your papa, and do everything he says." I eyed Garret. Kayla followed my gaze. "Bad men live in this city."

She nodded gravely.

"You going somewhere?" Hentus raised a brow as I stood.

"Yeah, something I gotta do."

"Then my blood brother can explain how you found him," he said, aiming his demand at Edge.

Blood brothers? Only warriors became blood brothers; it was a bond that was taken when they'd fought together for years. Edge grinned at me, but there was a question and a warning in his eyes. *Don't tell them about my girl's magic, and I won't tell anyone about yours.* I understood completely, so I nodded.

Hentus laughed, misconstruing my silence for confusion. "His caste mark isn't real, Zahlia. Surely you realise a mark can be magicked onto someone's skin? If the magic is powerful enough, it can be permanent."

"Oh." Of course I knew that caste marks could be magicked, but I didn't know they could be permanent. I kept my face neutral and shrugged, but I was already working out how to discover what else magic could do. There must be so much that I didn't know.

The crowds of people made the going rough as I made my way through the city. They weren't deliberately stopping me. There was just nowhere for them to go to get out of my way. The city was full to bursting. I tried to ignore the stink of dead bodies as I wound my way through the small streets.

The sound of horses reached my ears above the din of the city, making my breath catch. That meant only one thing-soldiers. Moving quickly, I barely managed to duck into the shadows before the mounted warriors rounded a corner onto the steep, cobbled street. Pulling my hood up, I shrank back against a building, staying in the shadows. I wouldn't use magic to hide, not so close to anyone on horseback. Only the higher warrior castes, royal guards and the General used horses.

My eyes widened as the silhouette of a huge male came into view. He was impressive in his battle armour, sitting tall upon a huge war horse. Another silhouette followed, equally as imposing as the first, but dressed in different armour. My attention zoned in on the first man. All I could see was a perfect profile. A square jaw, sculpted lips and a straight and prominent nose. The line of it led up to a heavy brow and a broad forehead.

My heart sped up. I had no doubt who this was. The General was far more intimidating in real life than stories gave him credit for. He had to be at least six and a half feet if not more. His body was protected by metal plates and leather, and he had a huge sword down his back in addition to the weapons adorning his wide chest and thick thighs. Metal gauntlets protected hands that confidently guided his mount. The animal snorted gently as it pushed through the throng of people.

Something tugged deep inside me, and I had an insane urge to run towards that imposing figure. Pushing the palm of my hand against my chest, I shook my head to clear it. The only person who had drawn me to him like that was Dexalion. But this wasn't him. The General was taller, bigger—yet, he was also familiar.

Impossible! I'd seen Dex, and he was the same as ever, tall, but not that tall, handsome and as arrogant as always, but this wasn't him.

The General suddenly stiffened, reining in his horse. His head turned my way. My breathing hitched, and though his face was in shadow, I was sure he looked right at me. Shit. There were stories of him having a sixth sense when it came to hunting magickers.

I kept completely still, hoping the darkness of the alley was thick enough to disguise me. My whole body locked up as I felt the presence of powerful energy. It was like the charged air right before a thunderstorm. Shivers ran down my spine, and even the hairs on my arms stood up. In the blink of an eye, I'd pulled my magic so deep inside me no one could sense it, especially not this dangerous general. Someone who locked innocent people away because the mage hounds sensed magic in their blood. My heart hammered faster, anger bubbling through my veins. The General was a hypocrite. A magicker in disguise. There was something familiar about the feel of his energy, yet not. It felt like Dex's, but this was colder, more powerful—and it felt...ancient.

"General?" The other man reined his horse alongside the General's. "Is something wrong?"

For a beat there was silence. The General tilted his head as if listening. I held my breath, keeping utterly still, my fingers hovering over my blades.

"No, my friend. For a moment I thought I felt...something, but it's gone now."

A moment later they moved on. I waited until the sound of their horses had disappeared before I expelled the breath I'd been holding.

Damn, that was close. I wondered why the general and his men were out during the day, and without their mage hounds. But it wasn't my concern. All I had to do was stay away from them so I could do what I'd planned, which was to reinforce my promise to my parents. Shaking off a deep feeling of disquiet, I hurried through the streets and to the jeweller that I'd picked for my project.

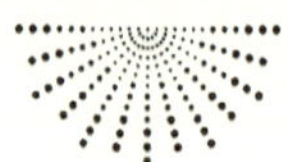

ex

Omeron urged his horse up beside mine. "What did you feel, my King?"

I shot him a warning look.

He looked back steadily, not cowed in the least. "There's no one close enough to hear."

"Walls have ears, my friend, you know that."

He nodded his acquiescence, though remained quiet. He would never ask me a question twice. If I wanted to answer, I would.

"I felt Lia's magic. Then it was gone. She was hiding in the shadows." I couldn't help the twitch of my lips. "She doesn't know the shadows belong to me. They will protect her, or betray her, as I command."

"Why didn't you go after her? It would save us this trip."

"You forget, brother, she doesn't know me in this form; she knows me only as the boy who grew up beside her, the thief and murderer who would kill to protect her, but then used her and broke her heart.

She would have fought me—or run. And the only way to subdue her would be to use magic."

"And that would expose us," agreed Omeron. His amber gaze swung my way. "So we visit the Viper?"

I nodded. I'd stayed away from my Angel for as long as I could. I shifted in my saddle. She was mine, and I needed her back in my own kingdom, needed her back with me. Her power was too much for this world. Soon she wouldn't be able to hide or contain it. And once she was in my homeland, she needed to be within touching distance of shadow magic, the only magic that could temper her light—mine.

We reined in our horses outside a merchant's mansion that had seen better days. It would once have been grand, especially for the trade caste that had owned it. Now it was run down, its walls cracked, plants and moss growing from its gutters and roof. I eyed the broken windows.

"Reaper's teeth, Hentus really hasn't gone up in the world," Omeron muttered under his breath.

I huffed a chuckle. "He hasn't. But that's the whole idea, isn't it? He doesn't want to. Being the king of his own castle is safer, especially with the Vipers as his own small army. Anonymity, protection, and profit. Plus he moved them to slow me down once I was back here. He wants to protect Zahlia, to give her time to escape if she wants to."

Omeron grunted his agreement. "That's a good thing, right?" Omeron hadn't been adopted by Hentus like Lia and me. He'd hidden outside the city with my other warriors, fighting the demons and reapers alone until I'd been ready to join him.

We dismounted, and I gave the order to my men to hold their position. They had no idea, but they were already surrounded by Vipers. It was time to call Hentus on his bullshit disguise and take back what was mine.

"Be ready for anything, but don't shift unless I give you the order."

Omeron nodded, his gaze taking in everything, his nose lifted to inhale nearby scents.

The time for lies and deceit was over, so I strode into the Vipers' nest. Inside smelled of dampness and the sickening stench of old cooking. Rat, if I wasn't mistaken. I swallowed my distaste. I'd been forced to eat that shit on the battlefield for years, along with the bitter flesh of bog worms. This city had food, but only for the privileged few. The whole caste system in this kingdom sickened me. Hierarchy, or at least, leadership, was necessary for all societies, but the highborn of this city, no matter their caste, took and took from those lower down. None of those privileged tossers gave a shit about the casteless. Still, this place was no better or worse than any other kingdom. Or, for that matter, the one of my birth. The rich and powerful took what they could while the lesser born gave and gave, sometimes until they paid the ultimate price. I clenched my jaw. My world hadn't always mirrored the mortal one in such greed, but it had for so long now that the land of harmony and plenty my mother had described seemed an impossible dream.

"Brave of you to come here, General."

I turned to face Hentus. He didn't look much different, still broad shouldered and tall. His jaw was square, his eyes sharp, and he moved with the strength and grace of someone who could end most men in the blink of an eye. The only tell-tale sign of the passage of time were the grey streaks in his hair and the small lines around his eyes and mouth.

I faced him, and met his cold gaze. "Hentus. We need to talk."

His eyes narrowed. "We do."

"Get rid of your Vipers. I wish to speak with you alone."

He gave a humourless smirk. "You're in my house without an invitation. I think I'll let them stay."

"I give you my word you won't be harmed."

"You'll forgive me if your word means fuck-all to me, *General*."

I hid my irritation at the sneer in his voice. He didn't trust me after what I'd done to Lia. I understood. But he had also agreed to my terms before I'd left.

Omeron released a low growl.

I glanced at him and shook my head. "Leave us," I commanded.

He scowled at me, his eyes flashing. I raised my brows and waited.

"I'll be outside." His amber gaze landed on Hentus before sizing up the group of men and women at his back. They all clutched weapons of one kind or another. I noticed a huge man standing side by side with someone I recognised. Angus. He held his axe in a deceptively relaxed grip, but I knew how lethal he was with it. The other man held an axe too, and looked just as relaxed. They were the ones to watch if this turned ugly. *They* were the ones guarding Hentus. The others would just be an annoyance.

"Any act of violence against him, and I will end you all," Omeron warned chillingly. These mortals had no way of knowing they'd been marked by this predator. Moving fluidly, he walked out.

I caught Hentus's gaze and raised my brows. "I need to discuss our mutual guardianship with you."

Hentus kept his face neutral, but the slight lift in his chin and tick in his jaw gave him away. It was another heartbeat while he weighed up his options. I was glad when he came to the conclusion that he had none.

"All of you. Out."

"You sure, Hent?" the bigger man asked after Angus had left. His gaze bounced between me and Hentus.

"Yeah, Edge, you go. But if I don't come out in a few minutes, kill all of his men."

I grinned. "That won't be necessary. I just want to talk. I think we can both agree this conversation should be done in private."

I watched Edge leave. I knew exactly who he was now that I had his name. I knew everything about Hentus and his blood brother. I walked across the wooden floor to a table and sat down. The old chair creaked under my weight, so I reinforced it with a bit of magic.

Hentus sat opposite me. "Talk," he demanded.

I raised my brows but nodded. "I want Zahlia. And you're going to give her to me."

"Fuck you! Why would I do that? She's as good as my daughter. I agreed to give you updates on her for your silence about us, but I'm not going to just hand her over." He laughed. "If she would even let me. Reaper's teeth, Dexalion, she has no idea you are the Mad Prince's general. You don't even look the same!"

"She's mine, Hentus, and I want her back."

"Are you kidding me? You were her world. You could have taken her from this place like I've always hoped you would. Instead, you took her body, broke her fucking heart, and left her behind." He cocked his head, his eyes colder than I'd ever seen. "I should kill you where you stand for that alone."

My nostrils flared. Part of me didn't blame Hentus for his fury. He loved Zahlia more than he'd ever allowed himself to show any of his Vipers. He'd fight and die for her if he had to. I didn't want to hurt him. He deserved more from me. He'd believed that I was a child, like Lia, when I'd let him discover us. He'd given us a home and some semblance of safety. He'd taught us to fight and survive. I hadn't needed that tuition, but he hadn't known that.

"You cannot kill me, Hentus Nzira. Like you, I've been protecting Zahlia since the night you found us. She means more to me than you, or she understands. But it will soon become clear how important she is to this world. All you need to know, for now, is that for her to fulfil her destiny, she has to stay by my side."

He huffed a laugh. "By your side? Good luck with that because she sure as shit won't go anywhere with you, not as Dexalion, the boy she once loved, and definitely not as the general who hunts and kills her kind. When she finds out you are such a hypocrite that you murder your own kind, I won't have to lift a finger; she'll kill you herself."

"She *will* come with me because you are going to make her. If she doesn't agree, I'll ruin all you have built here. If you want to stay hidden in this nest of yours, play at being king of your own little kingdom, then don't fight me or help her evade me."

Hentus looked at me coldly. "You hunt magickers for the Mad Prince, yet you hide your own from him and deceive the people of this city. It's you who should leave here before she returns and drives a knife through your lying heart." He nodded towards the door. "Go, and I will keep your hypocrisy and treason to myself. Stay and know, if Lia doesn't kill you, I will."

I grinned. Holding his gaze, I lifted my right hand, grabbed the shadows at the far side of the room and pulled. The large warrior, Edge, slammed into the floor before I threw him across the room and through one of the old interior walls. He'd crept quietly back into the room while we'd talked. My shadows had immediately whispered in my ear about his return.

Hentus watched, his face betraying nothing.

I shrugged. "I expected no less of a threat from you, old man. But you cannot beat me. I am not mortal. His axe will not kill me, only slow me down. And you are not strong enough. Not even with that magic you keep hidden." I propped my elbows on the table top, studying the Viper. I respected him. He was a hard but fair man. He was not good, but neither was he wholly bad. Like most living souls in this world and the Netherworld, there was a lot of grey area. We all did morally questionable things to survive. "I have another proposition for you. Help me, and not only will I let you and your Vipers live, I won't inform your nephew where you are."

Blood drained from his face before fury lit his eyes. "You fucking bastard."

I sat back and shrugged. "I never pretended to be otherwise. Now. Let's talk business."

"Who *are* you?" he breathed.

"I'll tell you when you need to know. Swear allegiance to me, and I'll keep your secrets. Betray me, and I'll destroy you."

Seconds passed. I remained quiet. He needed time to think. I wanted him on my side, not for me, but for Zahlia, who would need all the allies she could find in this world and mine.

"Fine. But when she finds out you've lied to her all these years, she'll kill you."

I grinned widely. "She'll try."

CHAPTER NINE

ia

The sun was low in the sky by the time I was done at the silver-smith's. The package I clutched inside my coat pocket was about as big as my palm. I assessed the people around me with care. No matter how much I wanted to put the necklace on, it would be stupid to do so with so many desperate people around. It would be like dangling a steak before a starving dog and expecting it not to bite.

I'd given up my paltry supply of burning oil and a significant portion of my orms stash to get this locket made. I told myself it was necessary, over and over. I needed a reminder of my purpose. Seeing Dex again was messing with my head. And this would help me stop obsessing over him and remember my promise. Once I'd found my parents' killer and avenged their deaths, I'd leave this shithole of a city behind and head out over the ocean. I had enough orms hidden to buy Dala and me passage on a trade ship to the Medallion Isles. The sun shone almost all day over there. Every single day. That meant if the

Nether creatures reached through the Veil, they wouldn't totally decimate the cities.

A large shoulder barged into me, shoving me against the wall of a building. I reflexively clutched my prize. I needed to get away from the crowds. Ducking down the next alley, I stepped over the prone bodies and searched for cracks in the brickwork. With practised movements, I used them as hand holds and climbed up to the rooftop. Once there, I found a sheltered corner and sank down.

Carefully, I pulled the box from my pocket and flipped the lid open. The silver locket nestled in a cushion of velvet. My eyes burned. It was the prettiest thing I'd ever seen. The etchings were exquisite and the flower Dex gave me was placed flawlessly. Dex had said it was from his home kingdom, though he'd never shared where that was. I'd often gotten angry with him, hurt that he'd never share his past with me. It was the thing we'd argued about most. He'd apologised once, saying that when I was older he would tell me. That day had never come. I'd trusted him, but he'd never shown me the same. I huffed. Of course, he hadn't because he'd never intended to stay. With my foolish young heart, I'd loved him, but he'd never felt the same.

My eyes blurred, so I impatiently blinked away my tears. Under my fingertips, the metal was cool, the glass smooth. The flower always seemed to glow, especially in the dark. It was so unusual, it was hard to look away. I'd never heard of or seen anything like it. The silversmith that I'd used had seemed as fascinated by it as me. It was still beautiful even after all of these years. Even now, its petals glowed a bright white. I'd never understood why it hadn't gone yellow or withered like other flowers did. Its vibrancy was untainted by age, its delicate petals shot through with veins of rainbow colours like someone had drawn on it in tiny threads of coloured ink. The main veins were utterly black, as were the stalk and leaves. It remained the most stunning thing I'd ever seen, yet that wasn't why I'd had it enclosed and preserved in silver and glass. No, this trinket reminded me to stay strong and not deviate from my purpose. Getting distracted, even by a gorgeous face attached to an even more gorgeous body, was not going to happen. Revenge first, a new life somewhere else if I survived.

The locket hung on a long chain so the flower would sit next to my heart. And though it was encased, I would feel it there every day and not be swayed from my purpose to find the monster who'd slain my parents. It was a promise I'd made to myself and my father as I'd climbed out of the basement window that night. I still had nightmares about the sword piercing my father's heart, instantly ending his life, a look of utter shock fixed on his face.

Dex had given me the flower after one particularly bad nightmare. He'd told me it had been his mother's favourite flower; that she'd loved it because it was the perfect mix of darkness and light.

Thinking about Dex was not what I wanted to do, so I shoved my memories of that night away and fixed the pendant around my neck, making sure it was hidden under my clothes. Moving quickly, I ran across the slippery rooftops until I hit a street too wide to jump. Using the cracks and holes in the brickwork, I climbed down and dropped to the cobbles. Ignoring the desperate glances and begging words from those around me was hard. Homeless people grabbed at my coat from where they sat on the frozen ground. I didn't react. They weren't a threat; there was no need for violence.

The sun was low on the horizon by the time I'd made it back to the nest. I wondered where Dala was. She would often wait for me on the rooftops of the Slopes, dropping down to my side as silently and gracefully as a cat. I was doubly unsettled after Dex's surprise return and seeing the General out in daylight. My gaze shifted, taking in the whole area. The atmosphere was heavy, prickling the hairs on my neck .

Something wasn't right.

I palmed my blades, resting them along my forearms out of sight. Remaining aware of the people moving around me, I hurried home. Three streets away, I bolted, running down an alley and leaping from one broken-down wall to another to get off the street until I was jogging low on the rooftops. The light was fading when I carefully peered at the rooftop near my window. A familiar guard stood with his back to me, watching the street below. I vaulted over the wall and ran to my window, prying it open.

Without a sound, I dropped inside and landed in a crouch, ready to defend myself. On the outside, everything looked normal, but something was definitely off. I couldn't put my finger on what, but my instincts were screaming to run. Yet I wouldn't leave without Dala or run without checking on Hentus. As gnarly and outwardly cold as he was, I knew he cared about me. If he didn't, he'd have handed me over to the General's men or sold me to slave traders years ago.

Light-footed, I made my way down the stairs, my hackles rising further when there was no one else around. This place was always full of people coming and going. It was never this quiet. My heart pounded, and I worked to control my fear. Could the General have raided this place while I was out? But why would there still be a guard on the roof? No, something else was up.

I stepped off the bottom stair and crept silently to the large common room. If it was empty, then I was out of here. I'd hunt one of Garret's mob down and get them to tell me what had happened. Then I'd find Dala and Hentus and free them from whoever had them.

Back flat to the wall, I peered into the large room. From my vantage point, I could see down into the dining area. The mismatched tables and chairs were neatly placed, not broken or tossed around as they would be after a fight. The area was empty, except for Dala—and Hentus, who sat pouring over a ledger. Dala's skin gleamed with a sheen of sweat, but it was the deep furrows on her brow along with the fury glinting in her eyes that stopped me short. If she could leave, she would.

Taking a deep breath, I steeled my nerves. If Hentus was up to something, I'd need to run, but not before Dala was safe. Hentus was the most skilled and vicious fighter I'd ever seen—except for Dex, who had surpassed his teacher while still a teenager.

Had Hentus betrayed me? I swallowed hard, shoving my hurt deep down inside. I needed to find out why he was holding Dala and where the fuck the rest of the Vipers were. I didn't believe for a moment that this place was as empty as it seemed. Dala was the kind of warrior you only threatened once. There would be no more because you'd be dead. So why was she sitting at a table looking majorly pissed, yet not tied to her damned chair? How was Hentus keeping her there?

Shifting my stance, I sent my magic out, searching the rest of the room for any other presence.

The light outside the window had dimmed, flames from the paltry fire the only light in the big room. They were enough to keep the monsters at bay. Just. Shadows danced along the walls. I tensed, knowing they could betray me, too.

"You gonna come out, girl? Or do I need to come over there and get you?" Hentus drawled, his gaze homing in on my hiding place.

I huffed. "How d'you do that?" I stepped out and moved forward.

Dala looked at me, her eyes full of warning.

I nodded, and let my magic come closer to the surface.

Hentus grinned, though there was no humour in his eyes. "I always know when someone is close by. It's what's kept me alive all these years when I'm surrounded by people I can't trust." His gaze locked on mine.

My heart banged in my chest as I held that heavy gaze. He was warning me I couldn't trust him. Who in the Nether Hell was powerful enough to control Hentus Nzira? I moved to see both of them better but kept my back to the wall. "Trust isn't a luxury I allow myself."

"Then I taught you well." He still held my gaze.

I couldn't help my bitter huff. "It wasn't you who taught me that, Hentus."

"No, it was me."

My traitorous heart skipped erratically. Dex's voice was deeper than ever and far richer. It sent goosebumps skittering over my skin as that sexy rumble settled in my chest. I turned toward his voice, slowing my breathing and heart, even as my magic reached for his. An ache bloomed in my chest at the familiar feeling, one I'd once associated with comfort and safety. It didn't last long before anger replaced that memory.

The shadows clung to him, almost as if they didn't want to let him go. But that was something I'd gotten used to a long time ago. I'd watched them bond to him since the night he'd protected me from the rain and cold with his young body. I'd never shared that Dex had magic. I knew, even as a child, that the king took people with magic, and I wasn't ever going to lose Dex, nor would I let any of the Vipers find out we had it. Someone would have sold us out as surely as the sun would rise.

Dex was far taller than he'd appeared on the rooftop, his shoulders were larger and his chest wider. I blinked. His face! He looked different, too—yet not. It was still him, though more beautiful than ever. His brow was heavier, his lips fuller, his jaw squarer, but it was his eyes that told me this really was Dexalion.

"Angel?" he stepped forward, a small smirk curling his damned sexy mouth.

I ignored his pet name for me. Instead my gaze narrowed on his armour, my grip tightening on my daggers when I recognised it. My heart thudded against my ribs, my stomach tightening. "Why are you wearing the General's armour, Dexalion?"

He stepped forward and tilted his head, tutting. "Don't pretend you don't understand. You're better than that."

I shook my head. My breathing hitched. He'd left me—to fight alongside the very people who tried to kill magickers? "*You're* General Azaraah? The Mad Prince's attack dog? The one who hunts magickers?" I couldn't keep the disbelief or anger from my voice. "You bastard."

"For reasons I will explain—eventually—that statement is completely untrue. For now, all you need to know is that I'm back for you."

I glared at him. "Are you for real? You disappeared without a word, and now you expect me to...what? Fall at your feet like the love struck teenager I once was?" I leaned forward and injected every bit of hatred I'd carried for eight years into my words. "You send men to hunt and kill my—no, *our* kind, and then have the audacity to turn up and tell me you've come back for me? You're as mad as that prince you serve." I spat at his feet.

His jaw muscles popped like he was clenching his teeth, his eyes flashing dangerously. "I *do* hunt magickers, and if you believe I kill them, you should probably consider your next words and actions very carefully, Zahlia."

A sneer curled my lips. "Oh please, you can't hurt me, you know that."

His face relaxed and he smiled, but for the first time in my life, I was suddenly unsure. *Could* he hurt me, even if I used magic to defend myself? I didn't know him anymore, if I ever had. This wasn't the boy I'd grown up with, or even the man who'd used me and then left. This was a different being altogether. He'd been killing creatures of the Nether for eight long years, he'd sworn allegiance to the royal family, and he hunted, even killed, magickers. No. I didn't know him—at all.

"I could. But I am not here to hurt you. You should just consider before you try and escape that even with your magic, you cannot beat me, and you cannot outrun me." His chin lifted slightly. "I'm here because I need your help."

I cocked a brow. "Well that must suck, because you're not getting it."

I felt another presence nearby. It was definitely magical, but not like I'd felt before. I glanced sideways. The man was as tall as Dex and his dark skin gleamed. It seemed this was the other rider, and now I could see him, it was clear it was the same man that had been on the roof. Like Dex, he looked as if a veil had been lifted from the way he'd looked before. His head was free from hair and tattooed, much like Dala's, though the markings weren't writing but unfamiliar symbols. I had no idea what they meant. Vivid amber eyes moved from me to Dex. Dex dipped his chin, an order of some kind.

Dex sighed. "Lia, you will come with me. I don't want to hurt you, but that doesn't extend to the others in this house. I'll ruin Hentus, and Dala will become a guest in the castle dungeon. Is that what you want? For them to suffer because of you?"

Fucker! Dex knew how much they both meant to me. I stared at this new version of the man I'd once loved. Not only did he look different, he'd never threatened the people I loved before.

"Touch either of them, and I'll kill you."

His eyes narrowed, his gaze sparking, right before he disappeared; only to reappear right in front of me. I didn't allow my surprise to show. He'd never moved like that either—like I did, vanishing into the Veil and reappearing where he willed.

His guard leapt fluidly towards my friend. Dala shot to her feet. She had no weapons, but still managed to smash her fist into his face before she'd even straightened. She was as tall as him and a warrior through and through. She wouldn't go easily. He grunted, and his eyes flashed with something like respect before he blocked her next attack.

"Eyes on me, Angel." Dex's fingers slid along my cheek, making me look at him again. I inhaled sharply at his proximity. His midnight scent hit me, rendering me useless. I hated myself for it, but there it was. He was my weakness; he always had been. I jerked back. Then again, weaknesses were meant to be overcome. His pull on me deepened, his emerald eyes holding mine captive. I felt myself getting lost in them, just as I always had. Until he spoke.

"Dala cannot win. No matter how good she has become."

Well, that was bullshit.

I kept my gaze locked on his, keeping a soft expression as if I was lost there—and drove my dagger into the gap between his chest plate and his back plate. It sliced right through the thick leather beneath and into the space between his ribs.

His eyes widened, his mouth becoming slack.

"Heed your own lessons, Dex."

I spun away, jumping into the Aether to get to Dala. I didn't get far. Air exploded from my chest as I hit a wall of muscle and metal. Once again Dex's scent wrapped around me, his shadows grasping my body and pulling me down.

I landed on my back with Hentus and Dex staring down at me. Hentus looked from me to Dex with wide eyes.

Oh shit.

Shadows filled Dex's eyes obscuring the emerald glow. I swallowed hard as he grabbed the dagger that stuck out from his side and pulled. He grimaced, blood spurting from the open wound, but it quickly stopped.

"Like I said, you can't kill me or him," he said, pointing with my bloodied dagger at his guard. "For reasons you'll understand in time, you need to be by my side, Angel, and I'm done asking."

Darkness closed in, shadows pushing into the air around me, stealing my ability to move. I panicked, fighting to drag up my power, but it was weak from helping Edge earlier. The harder I tried to escape, the more he drowned me in darkness. I thrashed, kicking and fighting until my limbs became too heavy. I'd seen him do this to others, but I'd never thought I'd be on the receiving end of his shadows. Tears burned my eyes. His treatment of me hurt, though I shouldn't have expected anything else from the Mad Prince's general.

I remained conscious, the shadows thick enough to muffle my hearing but not enough to block Dala's furious screech. There was a thump, and the sound of a scuffle. I screamed and raged at the warrior to leave her alone, but the shadows stole my voice. For the first time in years, fear skittered through me, not for me but for my friend. While I was helpless as a newborn, my wrists were pulled behind my back and tied. My weapons were taken, and Dex's shadows pushed my magic down so deep I had no hope of using it against him.

Slowly, the shadows released me.

Dex stared down at me. His eyes were back to their vivid emerald, apology in them though his face remained blank. I had no strength to rage at him when he put his hand under my arm and hoisted me to my feet.

I looked over at Dala. She wasn't any better off, her hands secured behind her back and her chest heaving. The warrior, whose handsome face was as neutral as Dex's, lifted her to her feet. She struggled, kicking back and catching him on his knee. He barely flinched, but I saw the surprise on his face at her fire.

A snarl curled my lip. If they thought we'd be good little prisoners, they both had another thing coming.

Dex spun me to fully face my friend.

"Dala!" he snapped. "Don't struggle. You don't know me well, but know that I *will not* tolerate you being a problem." He leaned down, his lips brushing my ear, whether by design or accident I had no idea, but it was impossible to hide my shiver as sparks of energy travelled down my neck from his touch. "Dala and Hentus will not be harmed if you do as I say."

His large body was pressed up against me and it was messing with my mind. I wanted to lean back into him as much as I wanted to kick him in the balls and run. I yanked my head away from his mouth. "Why should I believe a word you say? It's clear you lied about who and what you are well before you ever fucked me and ran away from what we shared."

He tensed and pulled back. Ah, I'd struck a nerve. He didn't like being called out.

"This isn't about me, Lia. It's about your safety and the safety of all the innocent people in this kingdom and mine. No matter what you think of me, I will not let you or them die needlessly."

"What makes you think I'm in danger? I can look after myself!" I snapped.

His lips twitched. A sexy brow lifted. "Clearly."

I wanted to slap that amused look off his arrogant face. "Oh, piss off! You cheated!"

"And so will every creature who hunts you because you have magic —strong magic—and you use it every night. It's become a beacon for the reapers and demons who push through the Veil. The prince knows there's a vigilante who attracts monsters. He wants you dead. I'm the only reason you're still alive. I sent my men to other parts of the city while I searched for you. But that can change in an instant if you don't obey me."

My nostrils flared. He was right. I'd tried to kid myself that I was doing good by fighting the Nether creatures, but even I couldn't deny that the monsters flocked to me, just as the ghostly, lost souls always followed me.

Nonetheless, he didn't get to push back into my life and take away my freedom. "How have you hidden what you are from the prince, Dex?" I snarled. "I've kept your secret for years, even after you abandoned me. Maybe it's time the Mad Prince and the people of Tetris know that their revered general is a hypocrite and a damned liar?"

Dex spun me towards the door. "You won't out me, Lia, because if you do, the people you care about most will suffer. Understand that I'm the only one who can keep you alive *and* stop the Nether creatures from consuming this world. Because they're only just getting started. Once this kingdom is gone, they'll move on to the next, and the next until there is no one left. Unless we stop them."

I glanced at Hentus. He looked steadily back at me, though I could see the frustration on his face. He wanted to help, but whatever Dex had threatened had to be really good because he just stood there, hands fisted and jaw tight. My mentor couldn't help me. As usual, I would fight this battle on my own.

Forcing my body to obey, I relaxed in Dex's hold. He knew me too well. I wouldn't put Dala or Hentus at risk. Besides, he was clearly more than he'd ever let me see. I needed to find out what he knew about the Nether creatures, and why the Veil was sick.

"You can hate me all you want for this, but once the Veil is healed, you'll thank me."

"I doubt I'm going to thank you for taking me prisoner or threatening my best friend and the man who has been my father since that red-eyed fucker killed my parents."

He guided me towards the door. "You will. But not yet. Before that day comes, you're going to help me hunt down more magickers."

"Fuck you, Dex. I won't hunt them just so that you can kill them."

"Then you may as well say goodbye to your friends. Omeron!" he barked.

"No! Wait!" I yelled, fear for Dala making me fight his hold. It was useless. His strength far outmatched mine.

"Stop." His command to Omeron was soft, yet the warrior nodded.

I breathed heavily, blood roaring in my ears. "Fine. I'll do as you say, just don't hurt her."

"I won't, as long as you behave. Just remember, Angel, my men hunt magickers every night because that's what the prince requires. I will not leave you here to be found. If you're by my side, I can keep you safe from them." He paused and took a breath. "And from the creatures."

It was ridiculous, not to mention annoying as hell, but my heart flip-flopped at those words. Still…"I don't need you to keep me safe from the creatures, or anything else. I've survived without you all this time; I don't need you."

It was true. I'd learnt not to rely on anyone but myself—and he was the one who'd taught me that.

CHAPTER TEN

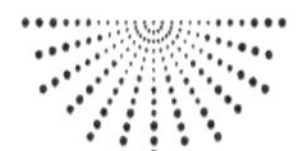

ex

Outside the nest, night was closing in. I hurried Lia forward as a small group of people surrounded my warriors. I recognised Garret immediately. It was clear by the way he moved that he was in pain, and he had dark purple bruises on his face. I guess he wasn't as good at fighting as he wanted to believe. He'd obviously been outmatched again.

My protective instincts fired when he eyed Lia with a sneer on his face.

"Always knew there was something off about you. 'Bout time someone kicked your uptight arse."

Lia's gaze rose, eyes meeting his as she smirked. "Yeah, because you never could," she retorted.

Garret's eyes darkened, his nostrils flaring. "Maybe, but I fucked you instead, didn't I?"

Lia paled before colour bloomed on her cheeks.

My blood boiled. She'd let that piece of shit touch her? I growled and glared at her, but she didn't look at me; she kept her eyes on Garret.

"Did you? I can't remember. Must have been pretty forgettable." And she turned away from him.

I unclenched my jaw, my lips twitching. Score one for my girl.

Normally I would charge my men with any prisoners we took, but I guided Lia to my horse. I couldn't appear to be too soft on her, not when word had surely gotten around about my presence in the Slopes. I didn't fully trust anyone who worked for the prince, my men included.

She yelped as I lifted her and threw her over my saddle. She landed on her belly and grunted. Mounting quickly before she could fight enough to fall off and injure herself, I grabbed onto her waist.

"You, fucker! I'm going to rip your balls off when I get free. You can't treat me like this!" She kicked out, nearly toppling head-first off the horse. Heat flashed through my blood. I loved her fire. She'd never been scared of me, not like everyone else. I didn't bother to hide my grin. Damn, she could rip my balls off, and I'd still forgive her, though I couldn't let her know that, not yet. She had a long journey of discovery before we got to that point. Besides, I had to be able to trust her, and she had to learn to trust me again. I tried not to think about that or the future too hard. The consequences of her rejecting my home—or me—when she learned my secrets, were too high. If that happened, it wouldn't just end my world, but hers too.

I caught Omeron's eyes. My brother scowled at me and eyed Lia pointedly. Shame stirred in my gut. He was right, she deserved better. Fuck the princes, and their spies. Sliding my hands around her waist, I easily lifted her and sat her so her back was to my front. It was still a little awkward with her hands being bound behind her back but she wouldn't fall. I wouldn't allow it.

"Guess you want to keep your balls then." Her profile was tense, her jaw tight and stubborn.

I grinned.

"Well, they can be useful at times."

"I'll bet," she muttered, flashing me a dark look.

Deliberately I leaned in so that my lips brushed the shell of her ear. "Don't worry, Lia. If you ever want them, they're yours."

Her whole body tensed. "No. Been there, done that, *never* doing it again."

Her words stung, but I didn't let it show. I'd been a bastard to her, so she was entitled to those feelings. Then again, I'd never pretended to be a good man. In fact, I wasn't a man at all. Lia just hadn't figured that out—yet. Revealing what I really was wouldn't happen until I could count on her loyalty and, hopefully, her trust.

Omeron gestured at Dala to get up on the horse. She gave him a murderous look, but put her foot in the stirrup. He steadied her while she swung onto the saddle before he mounted behind her and leaned forward to take the reins. Her whole demeanour stiffened at his proximity. In turn, Omeron looked so uncomfortable being up close and personal with Dala that I had to smirk at him. He scowled back.

Lia coughed, hunching forward slightly so I relaxed my arms a little to give her room, totally unprepared for her to throw herself backwards and slam her head into my nose.

Pain exploded over my face, and blood burst from my nostrils. Before I could put my thoughts back together, Lia had flicked her leg over the saddle and slid under my arm to the ground.

"Fuck!" I jumped off the horse. My men surrounded us in a heartbeat, drawing their swords and bows on Lia. She was already running. Sure-footed, she leapt onto a wall, then a roof.

"Hold!" I bellowed before one of my men could hurt her. Ignoring the throbbing in my face, I launched into a run. I glanced back and saw Omeron hadn't allowed Dala to pull the same move. She looked furious, but he was as calm as ever. He raised his brows and inclined his head in the direction Lia had run.

Yeah, I'm going.

Once out of sight of anyone else, I dissolved into the shadows and searched. She wasn't far away, heading straight across the rickety rooftops. I grinned, despite the drying blood on my face. I healed quickly enough, but I couldn't clean myself. It didn't hurt to let her think she could damage me. I knew Lia well. She needed to feel like she had a chance to control her fate, even if it was small. Until she accepted everything I had to tell her, if she needed some hope that she could escape, or even just make my life difficult, I'd give it to her.

Glad that she hadn't risked using her magic, I reached her quickly, stepping out of the Veil just as she turned to look back over her shoulder. She slammed right into my chest. A gasp of air exploded from her lungs. Her head snapped up, and her gaze met mine. I stared down at her, taking advantage of her shock. Holding her upper arms, I quickly bound her feet with ties of shadow.

"Let me go, you bastard!"

"No." I didn't bother wasting my breath trying to reason with her. She was mad. Well, so was I. She'd made a spectacle of herself and me when she didn't need to. I was trying to keep her presence low-key, not start damned rumours about how she almost escaped the infamous general. Flinging her over my shoulder, I headed back. When we were close, I jumped down onto the cobbled street and strode to where Omeron and my men waited.

Dala glared at me as Lia screeched her fury. Ignoring that venomous glare, I carefully slid Lia down my body until her feet hit the floor.

"Behave this time, or you will go back over my saddle, not on it."

Her eyes sparked, her lips pressing together into a thin line.

"Remember our discussion, Lia," I warned. "Your safety is my concern, and if you escape my men will be forced to hunt you down. I will not allow you to be hauled in by them or ripped apart by mage hounds. And if that isn't argument enough, think of Dala and Hentus." I glanced at Angus, and an angry looking Edge. "And the rest of your friends. Now get on."

Her chest heaved. If looks could kill, I'd be dead ten times over. I held her gaze, raising my brows. She narrowed her eyes, her lips thinning. My patience ran out, and I took a step forward ready to haul her over my saddle.

"Fine," she hissed and turned to face my horse.

There was no way she could mount safely without the use of her hands. My horse was a war horse and far too large for that. Once again, I spread my hands around her slim waist and released the shadow tie from her feet, all while feeling the heat of her skin through the leather she wore. I remembered how she'd felt naked beneath my touch, all silky smooth and soft skin. I took a deep breath, glad I was facing my horse as my arousal grew, pumping blood south until my leather breeches were strangling a hard-on I'd be proud of at any other time.

Aether damn it! Now was *not* a good time for those memories, though truth be told, I'd thought of nothing else every night since she'd given me her body. No matter who I'd taken to my bed since, no one came close to her. I'd been scratching an itch and that was it.

Keeping my face neutral, I settled her on the saddle and easily swung up behind her.

"Don't test me," I warned.

Without looking at Omeron, who would surely give me shit for allowing her to escape, I lifted my hand and indicated for us to move out.

Hentus watched us with a dark look on his face. I should feel some remorse for taking Lia from him, except I didn't. Lia didn't belong to him, she never had. He'd provided a roof over our heads, and had given her some skills, but it had been me who'd protected her, who'd truly taught her how to fight, to hunt, and to survive. I'd spent every day with her, only leaving her to find Omeron and hunt the reapers. In my need to protect her, I'd let her rely on me too much. Leaving her had ripped open my heart, but it had taught her to be self-sufficient and, yes, wary. I was immortal, not indestructible. I could still die.

As we made our way up through the city, I could feel the warmth from Lia's body seeping into my front each time her body swayed against mine. She held herself rigid, her hands tightly fisted against her lower back. I hid a smile. It looked like she was getting ready to grab my balls if I got too close. And not in a good way. Still, her nearness was a distraction that was hard to ignore. By the time we made it to the upper reaches, my self-control was ready to break. I just wanted to wrap my arms around her and pull her against me.

Urging my horse on, our progress sped up. We'd already passed through two checkpoints, so the streets here were clear of refugees. My top lip curled. Another royal decree—keep the upper reaches of the city and its elite caste members free from the reality of refugees, not to mention the demons and reapers who hunted them. The devastation wasn't happening if they couldn't see it. In this part of the city, more burning oil was available for the rich: more food, more firewood, more everything. But what the elite refused to acknowledge was if the Veil couldn't be fixed, then no matter the orms they had hoarded away, their lives would end.

Thankfully, the castle gates finally came into view. I needed to get Lia into her own rooms and decide how to approach this situation with her. I could get away with her 'working' for me for a short time, but eventually the royal brothers would want her gone.

"Your rooms will be in my quarters."

Her body stiffened even more.

"Why?" she snapped. "I don't want to be anywhere near you."

"Because you either stay where I can keep an eye on you, or you go to the dungeons where you cannot run, and no one but me will have a key to your cell. Which would you prefer?"

There was a beat of silence. I honestly had no idea if she would think the dungeons preferable to being near me. I guess I couldn't blame her if she did.

"Rooms in your quarters." The tightness in her voice conveyed how she loathed that idea.

"Wise choice. Let me make it perfectly clear, though. The princes don't want you in the castle. If you use magic we'll both be killed, so don't. Dala is here as an incentive. If you choose to disobey me, you'll put her at risk. There are no second chances and no takebacks. If you try to run, use your magic, or hurt anyone, she will die first, then Hentus and the others."

"Then why in Aether's name have you brought me here? You said you wanted to keep me safe, which by the way, doesn't make any sense considering you've completely ignored me for eight years. Besides, you know I can't abide being held back from my purpose."

I sighed. "You haven't found any sign of this red-eyed demon you saw kill your family. Not in all these years. Do you honestly think that will change now?"

"I don't know, but I feel it in my bones. He's here. That means I'll find him, and when I do, his life is mine."

I closed my eyes briefly before meeting her vivid blue gaze. "I know, Angel."

We remained in silence until we'd crossed the castle bridge and passed under the heavy portcullis.

"Help me hunt down magickers and I'll use my resources to help you find your parents' killer."

Her face twisted in disgust. "I can't help you hunt or hurt the magickers. They were born with their magic and should never be punished for it. I don't understand how you can do what you do. You're a filthy hypocrite, Dex. Or is that even your real name?"

I ground my molars, wishing I could make her understand my true purpose. "Yes, Dexalion is the name my mother gave me. I'd rather you worked with me willingly on this, but remember that you don't have a choice. We hunt magickers together, or you'll be relegated to the dungeons to await your fate like all the other magickers. Dala will die, followed soon after by Hentus." I hardened my voice. "Protection by my side and a chance to keep hunting the Nether demons, or imprisonment for you and death to those you love. Choose."

I remained silent until we reached the courtyard and dismounted. I pulled her down ensuring she landed safely.

"Dungeons or rooms?" I asked once more, praying to the Higher Powers that she would see sense.

"Rooms," she bit out like it was a curse. "But, just so we're clear, when this is over, I will kill you for what you have done to all those innocent people."

I nodded, my expression grim. "I know you will." I cut her wrists free. Omeron took my lead and freed Dala's arms. The Riou warrior rubbed her wrists and glared at Omeron.

"Dala!" I barked before she could attack him. "Talk to Lia before you do anything rash."

Dala lifted her chin and shot me a hard look but nodded. She exchanged another look with Lia. I waited, realising they knew each other so well that they didn't need speech. My stomach twisted at that show of intimacy, but I refused to let my jealousy show.

"This way."

I led them through a small entrance to the castle. The barracks for the warrior caste was built into the main corner tower of the castle keep. The building was as indestructible as the keep itself, made of heavy stone blocks with small windows. Lia kept pace behind me, followed by Dala and then Omeron. I was glad he was there. My feelings for Lia were complicated, and she meant more to me than I could ever express, but I still didn't trust her not to stab me in the back and run.

I hoped I could gain her loyalty back, at least enough to save our kingdoms. After that, if she hated me for my actions, I would accept it, but either way I'd never let her go.

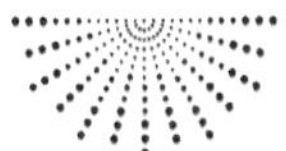

ia

Walking side by side with Dala, I followed Dex through a thick metal reinforced door. I'd never seen anything like it—or this castle. The place was huge. I'd only ever seen it from a distance as I'd never been in the city's upper level and never had reason to go into a building bigger than the old house the Vipers lived in.

We entered a dim corridor sparsely lit with torches. I shivered, unsure what was going on. Dex had never followed anyone's rule, not even Hentus'. He'd done his own thing, picked his own targets, and only handed over his spoils after he'd made sure he had enough to get us food, clothes and weapons.

He'd protected me, made sure I was fed, and that I had everything I needed to survive. I frowned, bitterness invading my heart. Despite his words, he wasn't protecting me now; he was threatening to end Dala and Hentus and to lock me up if I didn't cooperate. I stared at his ridiculously broad shoulders and back, my eyes dropping to his perfectly contoured behind, which I'd drooled over many times when I'd been a hormonal teen.

"Stop staring at my arse, Lia," he drawled, amusement in his voice.

I flushed at getting caught, my attention shooting up to his head where his blue black hair gleamed in the flickering light. "I wasn't," I lied when I saw he hadn't turned to look at me.

His deep chuckle did funny things to me. "If you say so. But remember the shadows belong to me, and there are many here. They tell me your every move."

I rolled my eyes and extended my middle finger at his back. "Tell him that," I muttered under my breath. He just laughed more. I even heard Dala huff. When I turned, she smirked at me.

Dex led us through the maze of corridors. I noted all of the exits and where guards were stationed, except there were no guards inside the building, only at the exits. A group of four warriors stood aside and saluted respectfully as we approached. They lowered their eyes from Dex, but I felt their attention bore into my back as we passed.

I figured magickers weren't their favourite people, so I ignored that uncomfortable sensation. I hated the prejudice Tetron had against magickers. Especially since I didn't know anyone who used their magic against others. In this kingdom, any magic was weak and pretty much useless. Perhaps it had something to do with magickers having been hunted for generations until it was practically bred out of our blood. I was an exception. As soon as I'd discovered mine, I was able to use it.

Dismissing their hatred, I took in my surroundings. We passed more doors but only three had guards. They had to be entrances to the castle. I didn't have to glance back at Dala to know she would remember every detail; she always did.

Dex led us past a set of stairs. "That's where the warrior caste is based."

"The barracks?" I clarified, wondering if there was another entrance to it.

"Indeed. Though it's more of a tower. You have no cause to go up there. You'll be in my house. Dala, you'll be staying with Omeron."

"What?"

"My liege?"

They both responded at the same time. I turned, almost laughing out loud at the horror on Omeron's face. Dala on the other hand looked enraged.

"You cannot keep me from her. I watch her back when we hunt," she snapped at Dex.

He just kept on walking.

"You still can, Dala. Just not when she's with me. Have no fear. I'll keep her safe."

"For Aether's sake! I don't need anyone to keep me safe!"

"Yes, you do. You're reckless," Dex said.

"I am not!"

Dala shot me a sheepish grin. "You kind of are."

"Hey! Loyalty, girl!" I groused.

She chuckled. "I am loyal, and you know it."

Dex stopped and looked over his shoulder at us. "You are, which is the only reason you're here; well, that, and Lia loves you. So don't give me cause to lock you away. Work with me, both of you, and know that I will not hurt you—unless you give me cause."

"And what do you call a cause?" I asked coldly.

He sighed. "We've been over this."

"Yeah, but Dala hasn't. Besides, I want to make sure it's clear in my head. You know...so you don't stick a blade in my chest before I get to stick one in yours," I said overly sweetly.

It could have been the shadows playing across his face, but I was sure his lips twitched. As a teenager I'd been reserved and watchful, even with him. I wondered what he made of my sass.

"Fine. In here."

I hadn't noticed we'd stopped outside the last door on this corridor. He unlocked it and then stepped through. I gasped. It wasn't grand in a palatial way, but the entrance hall we'd entered was large and lined with oak. About twenty feet away was a double door. Glass etched with the royal coat of arms let light flood the hallway.

We'd obviously come around the back way through the barracks to the general's quarters.

"Wow," I breathed, taking in the huge chandeliers and marble floor.

"I guess being a hypocritical, lying traitor of a general gets you some nice things. I can see why you do it."

Dex's jaw clenched, but he didn't respond. Instead, he turned, opened a large, carved oak door, and led us into a library.

"Oh...my." I stood in the centre of the room and gazed up at the books that neatly lined the oak shelving. Gold lettering on the spines of leather bound books gleamed in the light coming through the large windows. As I slowly turned to take it all in, the books became older, and the lettering faded. There was a ladder on a roller system perched on one side. The roller system followed the shelves along each side of the large room, even curving around the huge fireplace.

Warm fingers touched my chin, closing my mouth. "I knew you'd love it." Dex's voice was warmer, doing funny things to my insides.

"I do," I admitted a little breathlessly as I looked up at his beautiful face. He was standing so close I could feel his body heat; his eyes were so bright they ensnared me. The air between us heated. I watched, fascinated, as his pupils expanded and that brightness turned dark and stormy. My stomach tightened, and my heart sped up. I inhaled his deep scent, which reminded me of wildness and midnight, taking it deep into my chest. It scared me how right it felt to be so close to him, his huge body dwarfing mine. It was strange. He was Dex, yet not. I should be mad that he'd lied to me about who he was. After all, he'd changed his appearance and hidden his true self. I couldn't deny that it hurt, but I already accepted that everyone in life lied, not just Dex. I doubted I even knew everything about Dala; we all had secrets.

A throat cleared.

I started. Flushing guiltily, I dropped my hands from where I'd curled my fingers around his forearms. When had I done that?

Dex shot a dark look at Omeron, who just shrugged. Slowly, his warm touch left my skin, but not before he brushed his fingers gently over my jaw. Dala shot me a questioning look so I shook my head. She knew how broken I'd been after Dex had left, but she also knew no matter how hard I worked to hide it, he was still the only one who could affect me enough that I'd let him touch me without permission.

"Please, take a seat."

He waved his hand at two chairs he'd positioned in front of an overly large desk. I didn't argue. I'd had nothing to eat all day, my magic was still recovering, and I was so tired my legs shook. Dex took a seat behind the desk, and Omeron lingered behind us. Probably to make sure we didn't run.

Dex drummed his fingers on the desk, the skin between his brows creasing. I didn't push. I wasn't going anywhere, and neither was Dala. Yet.

Taking advantage of this moment of silence, I peered out of the large window behind him. There was a landscaped garden, criss-crossed with perfectly straight pathways. White winter roses bloomed in the flower beds. They reminded me of the flower Dex had given me, which made me feel the warmth and weight of the pendant between my breasts. It reminded me of my purpose. To find my parents' killer, though recently that purpose had become less urgent than helping the people of this city. Maybe while I was here I could do both. My attention went back to Dex.

"Would you like some food?" Dex asked, staring at me intently. "You're too thin."

I raised a brow at him, both irritated and embarrassed. He was right, but food was hardly plentiful. "Gee, thanks. And you're too damn big." I smiled sweetly. "Would you like me to amputate your feet?"

He scowled. "I didn't mean it as an insult, only that now you're with me, I can provide enough food to nourish you."

I opened my mouth to make another snarky remark when Dala kicked my foot and tilted her head in warning.

"Yes—please," I answered instead. She was right, he was being gracious, so I could be too.

He reached out, grabbed a cord of rope hanging down one side of the window and pulled.

I quirked a brow. "Really? Servants?"

He grinned. "Well, you didn't think I was going to cook for you, did you? In my culture, that is an honour reserved only for the soul-bonded."

"Soulmates? Not wives?" I asked, immediately curious, just as I'd always been about him.

"Yes.Where I come from, we pledge ourselves to others. But that union, like your marriages, is often for building alliances and wealth. Soul-bonded unions are rare, and many of my people are not blessed with one. When we are, we protect them with everything we have—even our lives."

That weird feeling was back in my belly. Did Dex have someone out there who perfectly matched his soul? That thought had me curling my fingers into my palms until my nails cut the skin.

"What if they don't want your protection?"

The small smile he gave me made me squirm. "Then we do it anyway, just in different ways. You forget. We—I—am not from Tetron."

"Yeah, no, I didn't forget. Though you haven't specifically said where you're from or what you are."

"No, I don't suppose I have. All you need to know for now is that your rules and social expectations are not mine. Now," he said, making it clear that the subject was closed. "We have other things to discuss." He waved his hand towards the door, and the brass key turned, locking it. I gaped as a shroud of shadow surrounded all four of us. "You will remain in this house for the foreseeable future. When darkness falls, my men will continue to hunt down magickers with the mage hounds. We will not go with them."

"What?" My interruption wasn't planned. The question just slipped from my lips. No way was I sitting in this luxury while people died. His brows rose. "Sorry," I muttered. Despite my snark, I didn't really want to end up in the dungeons.

Dex's face relaxed, and he nodded. "Make no mistake, the princes want magickers eradicated from these lands, which includes you and, should they find out, me. On the face of it, you're here to find what the prince's call 'the witch'. That's obviously not going to happen. What we'll actually be doing is going out every night to save as many souls as we can. I know you've been doing this anyway, so it should be no hardship for either of you. We're also going to scour every inch of this castle to see if we can find out why the Nether demons and reapers don't come here."

"They don't?" I asked, my curiosity piqued.

"No. It could be the iron in the rock that repels them, or it could be something else entirely."

"Surely you can figure that out without me?"

"I can, but I won't. You're here because you're in danger, and the safest place is by my side. I mean that. Once I can trust you not to run, I may give you more freedom, but until then, you'll stay safe either by my side or within the walls of my house."

I rolled my eyes and scowled. Dex had never been possessive or irrational before. Then again, he wasn't really the person I remember. He was something far more dangerous. Part of me wanted to believe he'd come for me just to keep me safe, but another, more rational part knew there was another reason. I gave him a small smile, willing to play his game—until I found out what that reason was—because another bitter and damaged part of me knew I wouldn't like whatever he was hiding. "Careful there, General, you're sounding a little over-protective—like a lover." I couldn't help the sneer in my voice because we both knew he was nothing of the sort. No matter how my heart pounded or how right it felt to be near him, he'd left me alone for eight cold and lonely years, and the damage was done.

His eyes glinted, his hands flexing where they rested on the edge of his desk. "Heed my warning; you need to stay inside my house. It's safe here. If the princes find you wandering the corridors, they will not ask why, they will have you imprisoned or killed. The hatred they carry is born of personal loss. That makes them dangerous. They believe every magicker is a threat."

I went with the change of subject. "So it's true then? A magicker did kill their mother?"

Dex nodded. "Yes. And they were never found."

"But why would anyone kill the queen? It was the king who enforced the law ending magickers. The queen always seemed a quiet and submissive high-born lady, not someone with influence who could change anything." I'd always sneered at her. She'd been in such a position of power and done nothing but follow her husband around, wear pretty clothes, and remain silent.

A dark expression passed over his face. "Being a queen is not as easy as you might think. And quiet doesn't mean useless. It often means observant and, in my experience, astute. Perhaps the attack was to exact revenge on the king by taking his wife rather than anything the queen ever did."

I latched onto three of his words. "In my experience? What experience do you have with queens, Dex?" My heart squeezed so tight I struggled to breathe. "Are you the queen's lover?" I couldn't think when or where he would have experience with any queen otherwise.

He laughed out loud. Godsdamn he was beautiful when joy lit up his face. I couldn't drag my eyes off him, even as my cheeks flushed.

"No, Angel, I'm not."

Relief flooded through me, though I narrowed my eyes, another sudden and unwelcome thought entering my head. "If you can change your appearance, were you actually young when you met me? Or was that a lie too?"

His face shuttered, his smile disappearing. I was almost sorry I'd asked—almost, though a familiar burn of anger heated my chest. He studied me for a moment before answering. "Yes, I was young, but I did make myself appear younger to make you feel more comfortable with me." His lips curved back into that gorgeous smirk. "I am still young compared to some old warriors I know. I'm just a little bigger and definitely more handsome than the version of me you were used to."

I raised my brows, then lied to his face. After all, I'm fairly certain he'd just lied right to mine. "Fine, I'll do as you ask and hunt with you. I'll even agree to stay here. But I want Dala with me."

"Dala can be here when I'm not. I still have duties to fulfil and an army to run. Omeron, please show Dala to your quarters. The same rules apply. They're in these rooms during the day unless we're training, and we hunt at night." He looked back at me. "We'll start hunting demons tomorrow night. Today you'll both rest and eat."

"Demons?" My curiosity flared. "Is that what you call the ones with no eyes and loads of teeth?" Dala and I had named the creatures demons or reapers based on legends we'd heard.

"No, those are reapers…"

"So we were right," I exclaimed and slapped Dala's arm.

Dex and Omeron exchanged a look. "You named them based on stories?"

"Yeah." I gestured to the shelves. "In case you forgot, we don't have access to knowledge like this. We guessed. We haven't named any of the others, though."

"Any beings from the Nether who come through the Veil are demons, at least those that become flesh and bone. Lost souls are ghosts and will remain that way until they find a way to the Heart. Demons all look different because there are different species, and kingdoms vary vastly in temperature and terrain. Just as there are variations in this world, it is the same in the Netherworld."

"How do you know so much about them?" I asked, my suspicions about his heritage only solidifying. I'd always known that his skin and hair were too dark to be from Tetron, but his magic had sealed it. I'd wondered if he was from Pa'dur where magickers had once been welcomed and revered. That was before he'd rolled up here looking different and spouting off about me being unable to kill him. That dagger in his side would have ended anyone else. He'd just pulled it out. My attention dropped to his blood-stained armour. The wound wasn't even bleeding anymore.

He smirked as he gestured around the room. "You're right. I have lifetimes of mortal knowledge at my fingertips. That's how I know."

"Of course it is," I muttered. "So why is it you can't discover what will fix the Veil, or why the monsters can't get through the Veil inside the castle grounds?"

He pushed to a standing position, looming over us both, yet not meeting my eyes.

"I've been through all these books, but there's nothing here. I haven't had time to read through all the books in the castle library since I just returned from the front line. Even if we had little access to books when you were younger, I know how much you love knowledge, so that's your job. It'll keep you out of mischief while I work."

"I doubt that," muttered Dala.

I shot her a dark look. She just laughed at me.

The shadow disappeared and daylight swamped my eyes, bright enough I had to blinked to clear my vision.

There was a knock at the door. Dex gestured for us to stay where we were and went to open it. A servant walked in, a tray loaded with ham, bread, cheese and apples held steadily in her grasp. A carafe of wine sat at the edge of the silver tray. My eyes widened, and my mouth watered. Such food wasn't available in the Slopes. I glanced at Dex and tried to hide my guilt at having access to such food when my friends were living off boiled rats and potatoes.

His jaw clenched. "Eat, Lia. It helps no one for you to be weak. Once you've eaten your fill, Omeron will show you around. I have somewhere to be. The only room out of bounds is mine."

Omeron nodded.

Dex walked towards me as the servant placed the tray down on a small side table. His fingers circled my forearm, his grip firm.

"Don't run from here. It may not be me who chases you down. The princes know what you are. They haven't worked out that you're the one they seek, but they will still want you gone." His gaze darkened, yet somehow sparked. "One of us seeking vengeance is enough."

What? Did he mean he'd seek vengeance if I was hurt? I was about to ask when he touched my cheek with his warm fingers and my brain stopped working. Magic stirred in my soul, and desire warmed my core. His face softened, even as I scowled and pulled my cheek from his touch.

"It's good to have you by my side again, Angel."

His breath brushed my cheek, and then he was gone.

I had no idea what to do with those words or his almost soft expression, so I did what I always did when emotions threatened to suck me under. I straightened my spine and ignored them.

"Come on, let's eat." I grabbed Dala's hand. My gaze hit hers and I chewed my lower lip as I thought of all the kids in the Vipers that would never taste this kind of fresh food. But no matter my guilt, my stomach growled loudly.

"Eat it. Like Dex said, you going without won't help them," Dala grouched.

I hated that they were both right. Even if I took this food to the little ones right now, it wouldn't be enough to make a difference.

Reaching out, I picked up some of the fluffy white, crusted bread and sniffed it. My groan was almost obscene.

"It smells divine."

"Eat it, don't smell it," Omeron rumbled.

Dala joined me in glaring at him. "Shut it. You've no idea what it's like to exist on sewage-stinking rat flesh and air."

His eyes glinted, something sparking in their depths. The big warrior bowed his head very slightly, and I nearly choked on the mouthful of bread I was chewing.

"You are right, I don't. I apologise."

Dala grabbed a bright green apple and bit into it, groaning at the sweet taste. Out of the corner of my eye I saw Omeron shift on his feet. Looking surreptitiously at him, I bit back a smile. He was riveted by my friend, and though she might seem oblivious, I knew she wasn't.

CHAPTER TWELVE

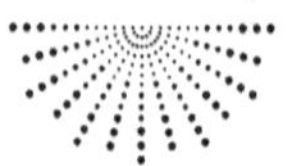

ex

Sleep completely eluded me the first night Lia slept in the room next to mine. My skin itched, and all I wanted was to be with her, to make sure she wasn't hungry, or thirsty, or too hot, or too cold. I rubbed a hand over my face. Reaper's teeth, since she'd come into her magic, mine had pulled me back towards her with a vengeance. I'd given her time to grow without my shadow or influence, but enough was enough. My soul was drawn to hers, and the need to tell her was like a living breathing thing under my skin, but so was the reality that she would eventually hate me.

"So how does this work?" Lia's voice washed over me, raising my awareness of her to the point where I wanted to pull her close and kiss the hell out of her. We were standing on the rooftop of the bakery where I'd purchased the puchinella. Weak light shone out from the upper floor window, telling me the baker had enough burning oil to last the night.

"We'll hunt down the demons while Omeron and Dala work to suppress the reapers."

"You mean they'll kill them?"

Her voice held a hint of sadness. I wondered if she felt her affinity to them, even if she didn't know why. She turned and looked at me, her head tilted.

My heart squeezed. It was getting harder and harder to hold onto my secrets, though hold I would—for now. I could at least reassure her. "No, Omeron can't kill them any more than Dala can. He'll show Dala how to send them back through the Veil without harming them."

"Is that possible? I-I always kill them."

I ground my teeth at the hurt on her face, wishing I could tell her the truth. Keeping secrets from her had always felt wrong, but it was worse now that she was an adult and had come into her magic. I was on borrowed time, and I knew it. The truth would destroy any kind of friendship we had, and selfish bastard that I was, I didn't want that to happen. Not when I'd just gotten her back. For now, it was enough that I knew our magic could end the enemy at our door. Most of the demons that came here were not lost souls but soldiers from beyond the Veil who served the King of Demons. In the Netherworld the throne of Aetris was the seat of ultimate power. And he sat upon it—for now.

"Reapers can be sent back, yes, but it's hard to do. Omeron has a special skill set that means he can be very effective at getting them beyond the Veil, where they should be. He cannot kill them, not as you or I can." I tilted my head and studied her. "When you've killed them, what happens to their bodies?"

She shrugged, but there were shadows in her eyes. I wondered at the things she'd seen—or done—these last few years. Killing the Netherworld creatures night after night was enough to scar even me.

"If I leave them where they've fallen, they come back to life. Some quicker than others. That's why I make sure to throw their remains back into the Nether. There's some sort of darkness there that grabs them and takes them somewhere else."

"There is. That's the dark side of the Veil."

"What's that? I thought the Veil was made of a curtain of light?"

"It is, but the light has always needed darkness to balance it or it would burn too brightly and destroy everything."

A line appeared on her brow. I wanted to smooth it with my finger, yet there was so much more for Lia to understand. And I doubted any of it would soothe her. As always, it would be me who had to push her out of her comfort zone and towards the harsh reality of who she really was.

"What about the demons?" I asked.

"I know they become flesh and blood when they enter this world. That means I can kill them."

"That's true. Yet, they can be reborn."

"Reborn where? In this world or in the Nether?"

"In the Nether. Normally when a demon dies, their soul would travel to the Aether's Heart, unless their master has already claimed it. That master can then grant them another body, take their energy for themselves, or send them into the Heart."

Lia's face darkened. "Like a god? No one should have that power."

I kept my face blank. "There are few who do. But the Demon King is one of them. Baladon is not a god, but he is powerful." I took a breath. "His kind of magic allows him to form flesh and blood out of magic, or pull a soul from the Veil. All he has to do is command them."

More lines appeared on Lia's brow. "You mean all of those demons that I've killed, that you've killed, over the last eight years were brought back to life by him?"

"Some, maybe. The King of Demons is powerful enough to command those who have pledged him their loyalty." I clenched and unclenched my jaw. "The Angel of Aether is the only being that can guide souls from the Veil into the Heart to be reborn. That's why some mortals are born with magic. It stays attached to the soul that may once have been a demon. But since the Aether's been sick, no souls have been reborn. That means any demons you've killed would wander with the rest of the lost souls—unless they were called back to their master." I released a steady breath wondering if she would really register my next words. "Or were absorbed by another demon."

"What type of demon can absorb another's soul? It felt wrong to even try and use my magic to do that."

Her voice dropped and her shoulders slumped. I wondered how much of a toll killing so many Nether creatures had taken on her. I couldn't help but move closer. Warmth bloomed in my chest when she leaned toward me.

"Reapers are drawn here by magic, then become confused by the sheer amount of souls in this city. They don't mean to kill indiscriminately. The demons are here for a different reason. They're here to hunt."

"Hunt what?"

I met her gaze and held it. "You already know the answer to that."

Her eyes widened. "Me? Why would they do that?"

I slid my arms around her, wanting to give her comfort, glad when she didn't pull away. I rested my chin on her head. "It's your light. It burns so brightly that in the darkness, you're a beacon. The King of Demons covets the light. It's the one thing he desires above all else. It can make him invincible, and now that yours has bloomed, he will send his most powerful soldiers to hunt you down."

If there was one thing I was good at, it was bending the truth and hiding behind my words and magic. I didn't elaborate. Instead, I released her, stepped onto some of my shadows, and dropped in a controlled movement down onto the street. As surefooted as a cat, Lia climbed down from the roof, following me like I hoped she would. There was no attempt to run.

"So Omeron and Dala are going deeper into the Slopes?"

"They are."

"Where are we going?"

I glanced sideways at her profile. "Not far. How's your magic today?"

"It's fine."

Her words were clipped. I sighed, already knowing it wasn't fine at all. Then again, how could I expect her to be honest when I was the master of lies? My belly tightened, a small snarl curling my top lip. Guilt had no place in my heart, not when the only way to keep her safe was to keep her with me, no matter what it took. And I was definitely no angel. My soul was as dark as my magic. I was born of darkness and would die surrounded by it.

There was silence as we walked down the gloomy streets. I welcomed the shadows that curled around me. They would whisper if anyone stalked us or if danger was nearby.

We headed towards the marketplace, which I knew was crowded with refugees. The reapers would be drawn there, and the demons would follow. Killing demons wouldn't win this war, no matter how many we ended, but that wasn't the point. I needed to know Lia could fight, and knew how to kill them, for her own safety.

The snow had melted into a thick slush that covered our boots, which caused our footsteps to stir the detritus and sewage trapped beneath. I kept the disgust off my face. The Mad Prince may want to keep his citizens safe and his city protected, but since we'd returned from the moors, he seemed more concerned with finding magickers than doling out the food and burning oil he hoarded in the castle and the cellars of the upper reaches.

I glanced at Lia, making sure she looked warm enough. Her face had a better colour now that she'd had a decent meal and some rest. She wore fitted leather armour that only covered only her vital organs and knee-high boots. Her weapon was a fine double blade that I'd seen her twirl skilfully before we set out. I had no idea if she'd mastered her magic enough to keep warm, but the temperatures would drop soon. I eyed the tantalising skin visible at the neck of her armour. A silver chain glinted and I wondered where it had come from. Jealousy stirred. If it had come from a former lover, I'd destroy it. My gaze fell to the soft curve of her breasts and heat unfurled in my lower belly, spearing right down to my balls. I bit back a groan. I'd been away from her too long. Her scent messed with my self-control, and my fingers burned with the need to touch her. My breathing quickened as my hands balled up into fists. She had no idea of the effect she had on me.

"How do you know when a demon's close?" She asked in hushed tones as we walked. "Are you like me? Do you feel it in your magic?"

I cleared my throat. "I do." My mind was still filled with thoughts of touching her.

"Oh." Her gaze met mine, and her face flushed prettily. The air between us sizzled, heavy with unspoken words. Her pupils expanded, her breath hitching. I couldn't stop myself from stepping closer until I was close enough to see the colours swirling in her stunning eyes. Her lips parted, and I leaned down, craving the taste of her soft mouth.

The brush of shadows against my skin sent a shiver down my neck. A warning. I growled and straightened, immediately on alert. Rolling my shoulders, I stood slightly in front of Lia, though I didn't draw my sword. I would happily kill whoever had interrupted that kiss.

"Demons," she stated.

"Can you tell how many?" I asked curiously.

Her brows drew down. "Most of the time, yes, unless there are too many, or too many lost souls wandering around, confusing my magic. The ghosts make me feel...sad, I suppose, as if they want me to help them. I find it hard to focus on the reapers and the demons when they do that."

I grunted, hating that I couldn't tell her why she felt such sadness for those confused souls. In their frustration, they wailed, their loss of direction and bewilderment undeniable. I ignored them; they were harmless. It was the small group of demons who had pushed their way through the Veil that got my attention.

I cocked my head. These were no ordinary soldiers; they wore the metal and leather armour of the royal house. My stomach turned. If the king's guard was here, he was getting close. I cursed my stupidity for bringing Lia out of the castle. They would feel her presence just as any other demon or creature of the dark would. Their death had to be swift before they could send word back that they had found her.

"Who in Aether's balls are they? I've never seen demons dressed like that before. They look like warriors."

"Let's not worry about who they are. They came through the Veil so they need to die." I ignored her bemused stare, took a deep breath, and ordered my shadows to protect her. "You ready, Angel?"

"Let's do it." Thankfully, she focused on our enemy. She was too clever to accept my non-answer to her question. I knew avoiding her curiosity was only a temporary fix, but I had to keep her on my side for as long as possible.

The demons stilled to a preternatural stillness that had me tensing, ready to strike. These were not an enemy to be taken lightly. I had a sudden urge to grab Lia and whisk her back to the castle, where she'd be safe. But she was a weapon herself. I had to remember that.

"You take the three on the right, and I'll take the rest. Do not spare them, Angel, for they will not spare you."

She nodded and was gone. My shadows danced, drawn to her light as she stepped into the Aether. I allowed them to trail her. She was safer if they were there to protect her. The Veil shimmered as she moved along it, leaving behind a beautiful aura of rainbow colours that were so stunning they stole my attention. Her magic was breathtaking. She materialised on my far right and punched a hole in the chest of one of the warriors, using her blade to slice off the head of another. Snapping out of my awe, I jumped through the shadows to reach my three targets. They'd seen me move and were expecting me when I materialised next to them. The first one spun away from my magic just as the one furthest away threw a blade. I grunted as it struck my shoulder. The Netherworld blade easily pierced the mortal armour I wore. Ignoring the discomfort, I pulled the blade from my flesh.

Moving quicker this time, I used my magic to step right behind the fucker. With no remorse, I slit his throat and stole his soul. The demons remained silent. They didn't communicate with words; they were a unit, battle-trained and honed to work together. They spread out, one on either side of me, their metal masks and hoods hiding any identifying features. Like many demons, they had completely black eyes that glittered like obsidian. To one side of me, I heard Lia fighting, but I didn't turn to look. These were no ordinary warriors; taking my eyes off them would be foolish. I had already underestimated them once. A snarl curled my lips.

My shoulder wound stung, but my flesh was already healing. I wouldn't die from any injury, but those weapons could still slow me down. I trusted Lia to hold her own, though knowing my shadows lingered near her eased my worry. They would shield her from the demons' blades. These warriors could get past my magic while I was in this world, but it would take time and energy. By then, they'd be dead.

I spun around my opponent in a blur of movement. Nearby,

mortals screamed and began to run, creating chaos among the hoard of people, but I ignored them. Taking my focus off my enemy wasn't an option.

The warrior was quick and agile, but so was I. I spun around him. As my shadows created a wall around the second warrior, I pulled my weapon, a double-bladed Onta axe that had served me well for many years. The blade remained sharp despite its age, the skull in the carved bone handle worn to fit my grip. It was bound to me, and contained enough of my magic that I could hide it with my shadows and call it from the darkness whenever I needed it.

The Onta were demons, small in stature at only three feet tall, but what they lacked in height they made up for in viciousness and skill. Working together in groups, they manipulated fire and metal to forge each weapon. There were few warriors strong enough beyond the confines of the Nether to wield the type of metal they crafted, but I had both strength and skill enough to use it just fine.

I grunted, swinging with enough speed to sever the warrior's neck, sending his head rolling. His soul tried to escape. I inhaled deeply and pulled it back towards me, absorbing every particle. My vision changed as I faced my final enemy, turning everything into shades of red and black.

I took the time to glance at Lia. She had her hand pressed against a warrior's chest, pulling the energy of his soul from him. She grunted with effort, yanking it free before throwing it back through the Veil. I needed to teach her how to feed on their energy. I faced my remaining foe, knowing she would resist taking her enemy's soul for herself. It went against the very nature of her purpose.

But making sure she survived was my priority.

"Do you serve the false king?" I asked.

It chuckled, a hollow, eerie sound. "He comes." He lifted his hand and pointed at my angel. "For her. She belongs to him. Nothing you do can prevent her destiny. She is not yours."

Cold fury blasted through me. Before the warrior could lower his arm, it was lying at his feet, followed by his head. I absorbed his energy and relished every second of it.

I strode over to the remaining warriors who fought to break

through the shadows protecting Lia. They pulled at my magic, trying to weaken my shadows. I snarled. By the time I'd ended my next victim, Lia had sent the last warrior to the Nether.

My heart slammed against my chest as I marched up to her. She was breathing hard and staring at the Veil. I hated that she'd been in danger, that I'd put her there. My clenched jaw muscles ached. Learning about her magic wasn't worth risking her, not when the king was so close.

An angry rumble left my chest. Unable to help myself, I stepped closer. Her eyes darted to mine—and narrowed, though she didn't step away. All the need I'd harboured for years boiled over, desire slamming into me. I sent my axe into the shadows, thrust a hand into her hair, and wrapped the other around her lower back. Her own hand speared into my hair and gripped—hard. Lust barrelled through me.

"You don't need to protect me anymore, Dex. I can protect myself."

"Make no mistake, Angel. Whether you want it or not, I *will* keep you safe." And I claimed her mouth, done waiting to devour those soft lips that had called to me since I'd seen her perfect face again.

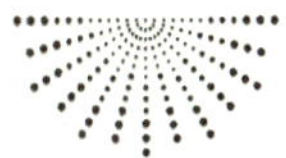

ia

Dex's kiss wasn't gentle. He devoured my mouth. He'd ruined me for kissing years ago. No one else's mouth had ever touched mine.

The whimper that escaped my throat wasn't one I wanted him to hear, but I couldn't contain it. His tongue dominated mine, taking everything and leaving no part of my mouth untouched. My hands grasped his shoulders, knowing all I could do was hold on and kiss him back. My body sang, coming alive like he was the air I needed to breathe, to function. I felt my magic spark through my veins. Foggy with lust, it was hard to remember the danger we'd just faced. He'd ended the demons with ease, and he'd commanded the shadows, pulling his weapon from them. *He'd become them.*

I stiffened. He'd spent years lying to me. I wasn't so far under his spell that I didn't remember that or the pain of his abandonment. He'd abused my trust and broken my heart. In fact, what the hell was I doing?

I yanked my mouth from his and pulled away.

Dex's eyes locked on mine. The big hand gripping my hair loosened, but he didn't release me fully. His gaze was darker than ever, glittering in the shadowy night.

I glared at him, though his taste lingered in my mouth. "Let me go." My memory didn't do the feel of his mouth on mine justice. Without meaning to, I licked my lips and almost groaned. He tasted divine.

"Angel, *you're* still holding onto *me*," he drawled, that sinful mouth tilting into an upward curve.

Flushing, I unfurled my fingers from the leather I'd grasped, dropped my hands to my sides, and took two steps away, coughing to clear my throat.

Aether's balls, I needed to keep my distance—for so many reasons. Dex was dangerous enough without my heart getting involved again. Hidden under my clothes, I felt the warmth of the moonflower pendant in the hollow between my breasts. Taking a deep breath, I concentrated on it, calming my breathing down, though getting a handle on the surge of lust he'd ignited wasn't as easy.

I spun away. "What now? Do you have a plan?"

Someone as powerful as Dex had a reason for everything, so I didn't believe his whole purpose for taking me from the Viper's nest was to keep me safe. Bitterness flowed through my veins like acid. He'd had eight years to come back, and chose not to. Why now? I sucked in a deep breath. It didn't matter. If I was going to get away from him and find my parents' murderer, falling for him couldn't happen. I walked away, not sure where I was going. I just needed a bit of space.

His footsteps kept pace with mine. "Yes, we need to return to the castle."

I glowered at him. "What? Why? We haven't been out here long enough to achieve anything yet."

"They know you're here, Lia. The souls you threw back into the Aether will return to their king and inform him of your whereabouts. Being on the streets of this city is no longer safe for you."

"I can't just go back." I stared at the helpless people, so at risk from the reapers. "I haven't done enough. Besides, I want to fight alongside Dala. I don't know your man, so I don't trust him with her safety."

"Omeron is more than capable of protecting your friend. And something tells me he will do that with every bit of viciousness in his soul."

I wasn't stupid. I could feel there was chemistry between my friend and his. Maybe he was right. If the reapers and demons were after me, Dala would be far safer if I stayed away.

I wondered if Omeron had magic. The warrior moved with the control of a predator, and his focus and stillness could be disturbing at times. He was just as tall as Dex and exuded power and strength. I'd never seen amber eyes or markings like Omeron's before, but then again, I'd never left this city. He could pass for a Riou warrior, but that didn't mean he was one.

I had a sinking feeling Dex and his friend were far more than they let me see.

I carried on walking into the filth-laden streets of the Slopes. "You know? I meant it. About your balls. If you try to stop me from seeing Dala, I'll chop them off." I thought about it, then added. "And if you surround me with a shadow shield to protect me again, I'll do the same." Childish? Maybe, but I could survive alone. I didn't need Dex.

"At least if I drag you back to the castle, you'll be alive to chop my balls off," he pointed out, sounding amused.

I huffed and walked away. I couldn't argue with that, so I didn't.

After a few minutes of walking in silence, the slimy feel of demon energy brushed my magic. "You feel them?"

"I do." Dex stepped up to my side as three demons pushed through the Veil. "Have at them, Angel," Dex murmured. "But when you're done, we return to the castle."

I scowled at him.

He raised a brow and made a grand gesture with his hand. "You don't want protection, remember? That means you can do the work while I analyse your fighting skills."

"Are you kidding me?"

"Nope," he said, crossing his arms over his chest and dipping his chin at them as they made a bee line for me. "Best hurry, they're almost on you."

"Fine!" I blustered, shooting a ribbon of energy into the nearest demon's chest, wrapping around its centre and pulling hard. *Analyse me, indeed! Arrogant son-of-a-bitch.* "But when the sun rises, I'm going to see Hentus and my friends."

"No, you're not."

"Yes. I am." I met his gaze as I balled the demon's energy between my hands and launched it back through the Veil. His body thudded to the ground. "If you want me to stay in that Aether damned castle, I need to know they're okay."

His head tilted, his look uncompromising. My heart lurched, I'd never asked for anything in my life, not since my parents had died, but I'd swallow my pride, give up every little bit of freedom to make sure the only family I had was safe. "Please. You know how much they mean to me."

His face softened. "I do. But it isn't safe for you anymore outside the castle. Not without me. I'll get word to Hentus and the others, and perhaps I can arrange for them to come to the castle soon. Dala, you'll see at sunrise."

My chest hurt and my eyes stung. It was a compromise, one I hadn't expected.

"You'd bring the Viper into the castle—for me?"

His finger traced down my cheek. "I'd do far more than that for you, Angel."

Before I could answer, his face hardened, his gaze fixing over my shoulder as his shadows shot forward. I spun, watching as his magic forced its way through the eyes, mouth and ears of the demon who'd crept up behind us. My mouth dropped open, and I blinked. It was as if it was drying up, shrivelling to almost nothing, before it exploded into darkness, the dagger it'd held in its hand clattering as it fell to the cobbles.

I swallowed hard, the slightly sulphurous smell of Dex's magic tickling my nose. He was far more powerful than I'd ever realised.

"I thought you didn't need protection?" he drawled, grinning.

I pressed my lips together and forced myself to roll my eyes, gesturing with my middle finger, all while trying to stop shaking from my close call. "I was distracted."

Dex laughed, transforming his normally hard face into something breathtakingly beautiful. I tore my eyes away and concentrated on dispatching my next foe.

By morning, we'd only made it halfway back to the castle. At every corner we turned, more demons came at us. I was exhausted and actually relieved to see the castle towers come into view as we made our way back through the city towards the upper reaches. Dex had let me fight without his interference—to a point. Mainly until I was overwhelmed by numbers. It was strange to fight without my best friend by my side, and I was anxious to see Dala, but I couldn't deny having Dex by my side made me feel...I frowned, trying to find a way to describe the alien feeling inside my chest. Safe. I curled my hands into fists. How did he make me feel that way when he'd lied and basically forced me to fight by his side. I didn't know, but there was no point in denying it. He wouldn't let anything harm me. He may have watched me fight, but it was clear he'd take out anything too powerful or any groups too large for me to fight alone. I didn't want to admit it, but that sense of protection filled me with warmth. I scowled, refusing to meet Dex's gaze when I felt his attention on me.

The gate opened as soon as the guards recognised their general. If they thought it strange he'd returned with just me by his side and none of his men, they hid it well. In the distance, I heard the baying of the mage hounds. I shivered, guilt souring my belly. I had no desire to see the poor wretches those men were dragging in.

"What happens to the magickers you catch? Do you kill them all?"

Dex's eyes met mine, his gaze intense. "They are taken to the dungeons, where they will await a trial at the prince's pleasure."

Anger and guilt coloured my next words. "How can you be so hypocritical? You've spent all night using magic, yet you condemn innocent people for just being born with it. Aether's balls, Dex, I've never met another person who knows how to access, let alone use their magic."

Even merchants from the neighbouring kingdoms hid their gifts when in Tetris. The law was the law. If caught using magic, they would be arrested and tried. The sentence for using magic in Tetris was death, regardless of where you were from.

"Surely you can't justify what you do, not when you know innocent people who have never accessed their magic are condemned?" I glared at him, that feeling of safety dissipating with my words. In its place was a fury I couldn't hide. "Does he kill them?"

Dex clenched his jaw. "Some."

"Fuck, I can't even look at you right now. How can you sleep at night?"

He stepped forward, his face cold, his eyes colder. I didn't step back. No matter how angry he was, I knew he wouldn't hurt me.

"One day you'll understand why I do what I do. Until then, do not judge me, not unless you're going to judge yourself. Especially when you've spent years being a thief and a murderer."

"That's not my fault. I've done what I needed to do; what *you* taught me to do, to stay alive."

"And what makes you think I'm not doing the same?"

As implacable as his expression was, there was pain in his eyes, a muscle twitching in his jaw. My heart stuttered. I'd never noticed those tell tale signs of emotion before. But then again, had I ever taken the time to look? I'd been young, in love with him, and in many ways, ignorant of the burden of responsibility he took on for others. Dex had been the only person I'd truly cared for, yet I hadn't really taken the time to know him. I'd taken him for granted—until he was no longer there.

Dex stopped walking. So did I.

"The prince believes that magickers are a threat to the safety of his kingdom, his family, and his life. It's hard to argue with those in power, no matter what your opinions are. You have to be willing to sacrifice everything for your goals and beliefs, Lia. Are you ready to give up your own freedom, maybe even your life, for your beliefs?"

I remained quiet. It was a hard truth, but we both knew I wasn't. I was a survivor. Yes, I'd sacrifice myself to fight for people I didn't know, magickers included, but ultimately, my goal had never changed. Find my parents' murderer and end him.

Dex grunted. "You are now a part of my deception. If you want to live, you need to pray that the princes don't discover my magic, because if they do, many, many more people will die."

He stormed ahead, his legs eating up the distance to his home. If I hadn't seen Dala standing on the steps to his front door, I'd have asked him what he meant. Did he really think the princes would kill him? And me? Or did he mean that he would kill whoever came for him? My friend's face reminded me of the cost if I caused too much trouble. Dex was right; I needed to stay with him for now. The city wasn't safe, but nothing lasts forever, no matter who you are. Even generals could fall.

CHAPTER FOURTEEN

ex

It was getting harder every day to ignore my feelings for Lia. I poured some ale into a tankard and drank deeply. The water in this city was stained with pestilence, spreading disease quicker than ever, and though it wouldn't harm me long term, the short term effects would incapacitate me, so ale it was.

I sank into my chair. My body wasn't weary, but my mind was churning with thoughts and emotions I couldn't control. Lia was tying me in knots. Her judgement had hurt, but didn't I deserve it? I'd lied to her for years and was still keeping secrets. I sighed. Secrets never ended well, but so much relied on her help that they were necessary. No matter my reasons, I was damned if I told her everything and damned if I didn't.

I rubbed my face. It was only midday, and I was already emotionally exhausted with the weight of my guilt. Outside the window snow fell heavily, large flakes whispering against the glass.

Omeron poured some ale and dropped into a chair opposite me.

"Will she stay in the castle while Dala fights alongside me?"

I scowled. "My shadows will...encourage her to."

His face pulled tight and he raised his brows. "You will imprison her?"

Every instinct in me baulked at taking her freedom, but her safety came first. "We fought the king's warriors last night."

Omeron's eyes flashed, his hound close to the surface. "I see."

My friend was silent for a while.

"I do not think the king will come for her—not yet. He has too much to lose if he passes through the Veil and cannot return with his prize. Even if he finds the gate, he could end up in another kingdom, and it will cause a war. Baladon won't risk that."

I gulped down a mouthful of ale and pondered Omeron's words. It was true.

"So if he's sent his best warriors after her, he either already has access to a gate or he'll bring a portal demon with him to get them back to Cimeria."

"Would that be your plan?"

I nodded. "Yes."

"Then don't you have even more reason to keep her by your side? If he comes for her, you are the only one who can protect her. The princes also expect you to deliver the magicker bringing creatures to this city. If they discover how powerful Lia's magic is, they'll put the pieces of the puzzle together and she'll be in danger from them, too."

I ground my teeth. "I know."

Omeron stood. "So maybe rethink the prisoner for protection idea? You know she'll fight you, and it will make things worse."

I took a deep breath and released it slowly. "Yes, I know."

Omeron left me to ruminate on my thoughts. I spent a few hours holding meetings with my senior officers, and when the late afternoon sun grew weak, I returned to my house. My body still buzzed with energy despite my lack of sleep. But then, I didn't need much sleep; I never had. Absorbing energy was all my body required. I enjoyed food and ate when I desired, but it wasn't necessary for my survival. What I needed to actually *live* was very different. To truly feel alive, I needed the light. I needed my angel's light. My shadows were darker, stronger, in her light. She was the centre of my world, the one focus that drowned out everything else.

My house was quiet, yet Lia's presence gave it an energy that hadn't been there before. It was an old building. Not quite as ancient as the castle, but still old. A few days ago, I'd found the ancient passages that led down under its foundations. It had been accidental. I'd wanted to explore the castle for many years but hadn't been able to find a way to do that undetected. I'd been at the frontline on the Moors until recently, and using shadow magic to disguise myself here was dangerous as I'd found out in the past. There were too many mage hounds around who would scent it. I'd accepted that I needed to wait, to be patient, but I couldn't wait any longer. I'd gotten myself promoted to general, fought to keep the Nether creatures away from Lia, and now I had free run of the castle.

I'd found the tunnels while choosing a room for Lia. Something about the room had given me pause, the feel of my magic dimming a little. Curious, I'd sent my shadows to explore. They'd shown me a door hidden behind a dusty old wall tapestry. I'd descended into the dark without hesitation, the cobwebs brushing my face and dust crunching under my feet. The roughly hewn stone steps had gone down and down until I knew I was in the rock under the castle. The deeper I went the more my magic was muted. Not gone, just...contained. It was a disconcerting feeling and not one I enjoyed. Once I'd hit the last step, I probed the entrances to the three tunnels with my bare hands. I could still see reasonably well in the pitch black, but without my magic, I couldn't see further than a few feet into the tunnels. The air was frigid and was laced with a mix of the sea, stale bodies, and fear. One tunnel obviously led out to the ocean, another to the dungeons, but the last one was a mystery.

I'd decided it would be safer to explore when I was better armed. There was a familiar energy down one of the tunnels that made my chest tighten. If it was what I thought it was, then my plans for Lia and my return home would need to be in place as quickly as possible. My magic was my main weapon, but I never went into battle without physical weapons. And whatever was down that tunnel was powerful enough to dampen my magic.

I tilted my head, listening to the sounds of the house. Perhaps I'd take Lia with me. If I wanted her trust, I needed to give it first. Omeron was right. She'd fight me if I tried to keep her locked in the castle.

After kicking snow off my boots, I walked purposefully towards her room. My shadows told me she was safe and sleeping. Good. She deserved a day of rest. I wondered how long it had been since she'd felt truly safe, able to just let her body and mind relax. Not wanting to wake her, I went to my library. Sighing, I eyed the paperwork on my desk. One of my least favourite parts of the day. Still it wouldn't be for much longer. I huffed a breath, at least in this realm.

The next morning, I walked past Lia's room and chuckled. She was still sleeping. The morning passed quickly, what with meetings, training, and inspecting the mage hounds. I stomped through the snow to my front door. I'd let Lia sleep enough. When she was younger, she'd always thrown something at the door and told me to fuck off when I woke her. But I worried about her need to sleep. Her magic should sustain her, but without the dark side of the Veil to balance it, she would burn through her power and be unable to replenish it. I'd have to be the one to explain that to her. I needed to make sure she knew all the different ways to feed.

Grinning, I made a fist and banged on Lia's door.

There was a muffled curse followed by rustling and the solid sound of something hitting the door. A boot at a guess.

"Come on, princess, time to get your lazy arse up!" I raised my voice enough to annoy her, then waited, laughing when there was a moment of silence followed by a *thud, thud, thud,* as she stomped to the door.

The door swung open, and I couldn't help but grin. Her hair was wild, her eyes sleepy, and she looked furious.

"I am not a damned princess, you jerk!" she groused.

I caught the pillow she threw at me, chuckling as I shoved it back at her, sandwiching it between us as I walked her backwards. "No you're not, but you are a warrior, and warriors have to get their arses up, wash, eat, and then learn how to fight."

"I know how to fight," she snapped, her eyes narrowing as I walked her further back.

I loved it when her focus was wholly on me. Using dirty underhand tactics like insults wasn't beyond me to get her full attention. My grin widened at her indignant look.

"And if I don't, that's your fault as you're mostly the one who taught me."

"I am, and I take responsibility for the fact that you are still alive after being alone all these years."

"I was not alone! I had…have…Dala, and Hentus, and Angus…"

I felt a bubble of amusement roll up my chest at her instant defence, unable to hold back my chuckle. "You do. And I'm glad you did when I wasn't there for you."

Her face fell and I wanted to kick myself. I'd wounded her badly, and bringing it up now was a bad idea. She shoved at the pillow, giving herself room to turn away, but not before I saw the hurt festering in her eyes.

"You should leave. I need to get dressed."

My heart thudded. I wasn't used to apologising, but I had a chance to make amends. If I wanted whatever feelings were still between us to grow, for her to trust me again, I needed to grab this opportunity and use it.

I didn't move away. Decisions warred in me. I couldn't give her the whole truth, but maybe I could give her some. Only my feet were stuck to the floor and I couldn't move away or give her space. My mind was in turmoil, and my focus was captured by the perfection of her curves and how the scrap of silk she wore barely covered her smooth skin. The garment was just one of the many items I'd bought for her. It looked far sexier than I'd imagined, and blood rushed through my ears, warming my face. That heat travelled south until my dick began to swell. I gritted my teeth. This wasn't the time for desire. But appropriate or not, my gaze travelled down the creamy expanse of her neck to the soft swell of her breasts. I wanted to grab that silk and tear it apart for hindering my vision of what lay beneath.

She cocked her head but didn't try to cover herself. Her cheeks pinked, and beneath that silk, her nipples hardened.

Damn, she was killing me. Unable to stay even a few feet from her, I stepped closer. I wanted her badly, more than I ever had, but…. Hesitantly, I lifted my hands, resting them on her shoulders. "Lia… I had to leave. You needed time to grow."

She tensed under my touch, but didn't pull away. I swallowed as energy zipped between us, tingling under my skin and travelling straight to my balls. I wanted her so much, I couldn't think. I forced my desire aside, fighting to control my need. I owed her some truths.

"Needed time to grow? What does that even mean?" Her question was bitter. She stared over my shoulder, but at least she didn't pull away.

I took a breath, exhaling slowly. Truth. "You needed time without me by your side so you could become the woman you are now; to know you didn't, and don't, need me by your side to survive. You also needed time for your magic to grow without the influence of mine. You are unique. A bright shining star in the darkness." Soft skin met my touch as I cupped her cheek and lifted her face so she would look at me. "The night I found you I was drawn by your magic. Even as a little girl you called to me. I wanted to protect you, and the only way to do that was to change my appearance so that you would trust me enough to stay by my side."

"But why?" she almost pleaded.

I ran my thumb over the creases on her brow. This was not the conversation I'd planned for, but it was long overdue. "Come, let's sit down."

She nodded and let me guide her to the bed. We sat shoulder to shoulder on the edge. "When I was a boy, my mother ran away from my father. He was controlling and abusive. My mother…" I swallowed the lump in my throat and dropped my head back as painful memories assaulted me. A gentle weight descended on the fist I'd clenched against my thigh. I looked down. Lia's hand covered mine. My heart squeezed. I'd lied to her for years, left her, and she still had the capacity to show me compassion.

"Go on," she encouraged softly.

I took a breath and nodded. "My mother was full of life. She smiled brightly enough to light the world… at least, that's what people who knew her said, but that was before she'd bonded with my father." I focused on the cracks in the bedroom wall, unable to look at Lia while I laid out my past. "It had been an arranged pairing, one in which my mother had no say. They'd never been soulmates. I was about four when I realised something was very wrong between them. My father was a cold man. He'd never shown affection or given praise. In fact, I rarely saw him. I hadn't understood what he was like until one day I went to see my mother and he was there. I was excited because I'd found her the perfect flower and knew it would make her smile. She'd rarely smiled, and I'd really wanted her to. The only time she ever did was when I brought her one of the moonflowers I gave you. She always said it was her favourite thing in the world other than me."

I swallowed the ache in my throat. No matter how long I lived, thoughts of my mother always evoked emotions I found it difficult to deal with. Emotions were something I fought against because they made me feel out of control, but I'd embrace them for Lia.

"Moonflowers only bloom at night and only in one place in our world, at the Heart of the Aether."

I heard Lia's sharp intake of breath, yet she remained quiet, giving me the time to talk. "It was a beautiful night. I remember the stars shining brightly and the moon's glow on my face. I'd run home, so happy, and barged into her room without a thought. My father held my mother around her neck. She had bruises on her face and blood running from a cut lip." I swallowed my anger and disgust. I'd never told anyone what I'd seen that day.

Lia squeezed my hand again, her eyes soft and full of support. Strength flowed from her into me.

"She was half naked, and he was rutting on her like an animal, slapping her face with his other hand. He raped her," I whispered hoarsely. "He was saying such terrible things. How he 'hated having to keep her as his whore'. How he had 'never wanted her, only her magic'; that she was 'just a shackle around his neck', and that now her magic had dwindled, she was 'useless for anything other than to fuck'." I squeezed my eyes shut. Why did talking about this hurt so much? It was hundreds of Heart cycles ago.

"Because things like that scar us for life, Dex."

Warmth bloomed on my cheek as she cupped my jaw and turned my face to her. I stiffened. I hadn't meant to say that out loud.

"They do," I responded gruffly. "That was when I fully understood he was the reason she didn't smile or laugh, why she was always so sad." I met her gaze. "He ordered me to stay in the room while he finished, and then he took my hand, crushed the flower and walked out, leaving her half-dressed and bleeding."

"I'm so sorry, Dex."

I couldn't speak, my heart hurt so much, but I nodded. After a few minutes, I continued.

"He'd visited often after that day. Almost like he was trying to destroy her. Each day he'd leave fresh bruises and wounds until my mother was nothing but a shadow of herself. I vowed to kill my father. Eventually, I snapped. I hid in her room, waited until he came for her, and attacked him. I'd wanted to kill him, to rip him apart for what he'd done to her. I didn't manage it, of course, I was only a boy. From that day on, he'd locked me up with my mother." I swallowed hard. "I had to sit and watch every time he raped her. "

"Angel's heart, Dex, I'm so sorry…"

I shook my head, locking all the hate and shame—so much shame —away deep inside. "I don't want your pity. I just want you to understand why I was near you that night." *Or most of it at least…* Guilt twisted my stomach as I spouted half-truths at her.

"In our lands, the Higher Powers set the destiny of everyone. Our laws and rules are based on following our destiny. My mother's bonding was more than just an arrangement between powerful families, it was an expectation because she had magic that could save souls. Her magic was connected irrevocably to the Aether's heart—like yours should be."

"Mine?"

"Yes." I knew I'd have to elaborate on that statement, but it wasn't something I wanted to tackle yet. "But my mother's magic faded with her despair. The more my father destroyed her spirit, the closer to death she became." I met her eyes. "I'm from the Nether, and there, when your magic fades, so does your life. Just like mortals, when demons die, our souls are called by the Aether's Heart to be reborn.

My father wanted my mother to die so he could find another with magic like hers."

"He wanted a new wife?" she asked.

"In a way. A demon with as much power as him could have as many partners as he wished. He didn't marry my mother, he already had a wife, one who eventually gave him another son, but she could never give him the power of her magic because she had very little."

Lia licked her lips and angled her head. "You're a demon, aren't you?"

I gave her a small smile. "I am. But you already suspected that, didn't you?"

She smiled back. "Not when I was younger. But changing your appearance? Your ability to move through shadows? Your knowledge about demons and the Nether? Yeah, it kind of made me suspicious. What happened next?" she prompted, though I knew she'd want more answers about who and what I was.

"To keep my mother safe, we had to leave, so I'd planned an escape. My magic was unpredictable and weak at such a young age, but I knew I could use it to get the keys from the guard who brought our food. He didn't think we were a threat. That was his first and last mistake."

"You killed him?"

"I did. We escaped with our lives but nothing else. It was hard to evade my father's warriors and even harder to find enough food to survive. My father was ancient, he knew all the places and people we might go to for support, so instead, we ran as far into Haldaag as we could. It's a harsh place and little grows in its inner lands."

"Is Haldaag where you're from?"

I hesitated. "That's where my home is, yes." It wasn't an outright lie. The kingdom *was* my home and had been since the night I'd killed their ruler, and they'd taken me to the seat of their power. I quickly moved on with my story.

"When we ran, my father and his men hunted us. We survived for weeks, but my mother knew as well as me that we couldn't escape him. She was too weak, and so was I. In the last few days of her life, we were hunted by Barg as well as my father."

"Barg?"

I smiled at her confusion. "Yes, the Barg. They're much like the mage hounds in this world. Only they sense death, not magic. Sometimes, they're called death hounds. They're also shape-shifting demons who turn into men."

A perplexed look lined her brow. "They shift into men? From hounds?"

"Yes," I answered with a smile. She was silent, thinking it over. I happily gave her the time to process that revelation, smiling when she nodded to herself, accepting it.

"Okay. They were after your mother?"

"Yes. And me. They sensed our weakness, our imminent death."

Her other hand went to her mouth. "They sound hideous."

I sighed. "They aren't. Remember, the Nether is not like the mortal world, which is why a veil separates us. What you consider barbaric, demon kind accept as the way things are. Besides, this was many, many Heart cycles ago, and a Heart cycle is far longer than a mortal year. Things have changed since then."

She didn't look convinced. "If you say so."

I smiled. "I do. My mother made her own choice. She survived long enough to ensure I had a chance, and she knew giving up her life and sacrificing her body would ultimately help me. She died in my arms before they attacked."

"And you let them have her?"

I tried not to sound defensive. It would take some time before Lia understood the ways of our world. "She'd wanted to die. The way my father had treated her...she had nothing left. No energy to fight for life. Before she died, she made me promise to give her body to the pack so my father would only find a few remains and think that we'd both perished."

"You fed your mother's body to a pack of hounds?" she murmured, her eyes wide and horror in her voice.

Despite her not fully understanding the ways of our world, my spine immediately snapped straight and I yanked my arm from her grasp. "I do not need your judgement. I had to. It was her dying wish."

Lia shook her head. "Oh, no, I'm not judging you. I was just thinking how hard that must have been."

Remorse flooded me when she took my hand again. I swallowed down the knot in my throat and stared at her hand laying on mine, lending me her strength. "I'm sorry, Angel. I...just..." I swallowed again, shaking my head. Of course, she wouldn't judge me, not when she'd lived her life among the Vipers. "It was hard. Other than leaving you, it was the hardest thing I've ever done."

A heavy silence fell between us, and I cursed myself for revealing how much she meant to me. I hoped that knowledge wouldn't drive her away. Her beautiful gaze met mine, and light sparked in their blue depths. With my free hand, I gently tucked some silver strands behind her ear. Goosebumps appeared over her skin, and I fought my desire, wanting so much to lean in and kiss her.

Lia coughed, her voice low and husky. "So how did you end up here, in a world that isn't your own?"

"When my mother died, I fought the Alpha of the death hounds and killed him. That gave me dominion over the pack. That's when I discovered that the Barg are shifters. They have a hidden city. It's cloaked in the mist and darkness, which is why they're so mysterious to our kind—or they were. I've lived with them for hundreds of Heart cycles. I grew up hidden there, doing my best to stay below the notice of my father's spies while I searched for a way to destroy him. He was a powerful demon, but his weakness was always his quest for power. To become the most powerful demon in existence, he needed another bonded with as much magic as my mother once had. Hundreds of Heart cycles later, I discovered that he'd found one, but that she was still a baby. A little girl who had no idea that she was a beacon of light in a world of dark magic and shadows. I knew how much danger she was in but couldn't get to her before he snatched her."

I heard her breath hitch and saw her tremble. My heart thudded, and though I dreaded her reaction, I wanted her to know where she was from.

"Go on," she whispered.

I turned to face her, my heart racing. "I disguised my appearance and got into his home. Omeron was with me. We managed to find her room, but she wasn't there. He was. Waiting for us with his men. He laughed as we fought, taunting me with insults, telling me we would never find the child, that he'd sent her somewhere she would never be found until she was old enough to become his bonded. He truly believed that I would lose that fight and leave her to her fate."

I held her gaze as she swallowed. "You didn't leave her though, did you?"

"No, I didn't. I fought my father that night and escaped with my life. I couldn't let the child go. Gut instinct told me my father would hide her where no demon could find her—the mortal world. So I hunted down a portal demon and came to this world, but it took me another five mortal years to track her down. I found her on a storm-riddled night, covered with blood and terrified."

Her face paled, understanding dawning in her eyes. "It's me, isn't it? That baby?"

"It is."

I caught her as she sagged forward and pulled her into my chest.

"Oh gods, I'm a demon?"

"You are, of a sort."

"But I don't want to be," she breathed.

I couldn't help but smile. "We are all what the Higher Powers and the Heart decided we would be. Being a demon doesn't make you bad, Lia. You're still you."

For a moment, she was quiet. I tightened my arms around her and stroked her hair, happy she seemed content to be in my arms. After a while, she pushed away and sat up.

"If I'm that girl, and it was your father who hunted me, why is the King of Demons searching for me?"

I stared at the floor, trying to hide the anger that tightened my chest at the thought of Baladon taking her. I'd rip him limb from limb if he laid a finger on her. My voice was deep when I had calmed myself enough to talk.

"He searches for the kind of magic you have with the same obsessive passion my father did."

"Did the king kill my parents?"

Her voice shook, and I wished this moment could be different, that

I could share everything, but she was already dealing with so much new information it would be too much. Once she'd worked through the knowledge that she came from the Nether, and I'd found a way to take her home and keep her safe, I'd tell her the rest. So I told her the truth and chose not to answer her question directly.

I shook my head. "I didn't see him near you, or feel any other demons nearby. It was just you and me that night—until Hentus found us."

CHAPTER FIFTEEN

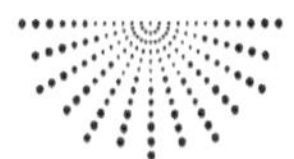

ia

My heart hammered and my chest squeezed tight. Trying to process what Dex had told me was overwhelming. I wasn't mortal, and I was from the damned Netherworld! Just like the monsters that came through the Veil, the ones I killed. Shit! I rubbed my face with my hands and shook my head. No, I still saved souls; it didn't matter where they, or I, was from....

My breath caught in my throat.Struggling, I tried to suck in more air. It wouldn't go into my lungs fast enough. My fingers started to tingle, the edges of my vision blurring. I leaned into Dex, resting my forehead on his shirt, taking comfort in the solid muscle of his chest. I was strong. I could survive alone, had done so for years, but it was nice to take strength and comfort from someone else for a change.

Especially him, a small voice said.

Reflexively, I inhaled, filling my nose with his deep midnight and musk male scent. My heart beat faster, and I nestled closer, my eyes burning. I'd missed him so much. Even when I'd hated and resented him for leaving, I'd wished he would return for me. Well, he was here now, and it might take time to trust him, but he was my only connection to who I really was. His big hands slowly rubbed circles on my back, warming and comforting me.

"So I really am a demon?" I mumbled into his chest.

Dex gently grabbed my upper arms and put me from him. He cocked his head, and I could almost hear the wheels turning in his mind. I wasn't stupid. I knew there were big holes in his story. There were things he hadn't shared with me—yet. Would he tell me, or was this just the start of another lie? I didn't think so. Yet even though I wanted to believe him, I was wary. We had a long way to go before I could trust him completely. Besides, my whole world had just crumbled; now, I didn't know who or even what I was. Panic tightened my chest again.

"Slowly, Lia. Just breathe with me for a moment. In...Out..."

I mirrored him, trying to take hold of that tumbling feeling. Control. I needed to take it back. I took slow, deep breaths and focused on Dex's beautiful eyes. Light sparked in them as I kept my focus on him, taking strength from his touch, from the dark magic that was caressing me, giving me support and comfort. He'd always done that, used his shadows to help comfort me.

"Being a demon isn't all bad, Lia."

"I'm not evil...am I?" Folklore painted life beyond the Veil as evil and dark. I'd seen that malevolence with my own eyes, reapers and demons of all kinds coming for innocent and broken souls. I'd killed people in the past. I'd stolen and manipulated, threatened and flirted to get what I wanted, but did that make me evil?

Now it was Dex's turn to cup my cheek. "No, you're not. Thinking of the Nether as a dark, violent, and pain-filled place results from mortals trying to explain what they sometimes see, but what they don't understand."

"But I've ended so many of our kind." My stomach churned at that thought.

"Angel, you fight demons to try and save mortal souls, not for pleasure." His eyes lasered into mine with such intensity it felt like he was seeing into my soul. "Those demons and reapers shouldn't be here.

Both of our worlds are unbalanced because of the sickness in the Veil. This situation isn't your fault. Circumstance and the Higher Powers made you who and what you are. Like mortals, there are demon kind who are good, some who are bad, and many who are a bit of both. And let's face it, most of us are in that grey area in between. Besides, whose right is it to decide what's good or evil?" He brushed the back of his finger down my cheek. "Stay with me. I can protect you from Baladon. He's as powerful as me and has an army of demons. You can't fight him alone or even run from him because he'll find you."

I fisted my hands in his shirt to stop them from shaking. I was tough, but even for me, the thought of being hunted by a callous, power-hungry king was terrifying. My heart rate skyrocketed as something occurred to me. "Is the king your father? Are you a *prince?*"

Dex's mouth quirked. "I'm no prince, and no, the Demon King is not my father. I killed my father for taking you on that night almost twenty-five mortal years ago."

"Oh." I couldn't help the disappointment in my voice. Dex had always seemed—more. I could imagine his imposing muscular body sitting on a throne, lording over others, demanding respect and fealty.

Dex chuckled. "Sorry, I can't be your prince, princess."

I cocked an eyebrow at him. "I don't need a prince. I need a master of shadows. Someone who will help me burn bright enough to annihilate an evil king."

His gaze darkened, hunger clear in his eyes, his voice low and gravelly. "I'll always help you burn brighter than any sun, Lia." His mouth tilted up at the corners. "I'll also be your master of shadows. I'll protect you forever. I won't let anything hurt you."

Did he mean that? Forever? My chest squeezed tight. I wanted him to, and that scared me more than anything. He was so close that his body heat warmed me, his scent stealing my ability to think. And my master, of anything I asked? I gulped. Flashes of him wrapping a big hand in my hair, of his other grabbing me to him as he whispered in my ear, all the sexy, hot things he would do to me had heat searing my cheeks.

My tongue flicked out to wet my dry lips. His pupils enlarged. I might crave his touch and his glorious body, but he wanted me, too.

That knowledge made me feel powerful. Of course I wanted him, I always had, but he'd have to work for my trust and, ultimately, my submission. Dex was never going to be a romantic lover who asked for what he wanted. He'd demand and conquer, but that didn't mean I'd make it easy for him. The thought of fighting him and proving to him that I could resist—until he made me surrender, of course, turned me on more than anything ever had. I squirmed in my seat, and his lips curved into a knowing smile.

"You like the thought of that, don't you, Angel?" he purred. "Me mastering you—in the bedroom."

I shrugged and tilted my head. No matter how right he was, he could wait to know for sure how much I wanted him, so I changed the subject. "If you used a portal demon to get here, why can't you use one to get back?"

His eyes narrowed, but he smiled, and after a moment's silence, he accepted that I wanted to continue our original conversation.

"Portal demons live in the Aether. They're elusive. Even if you strike a bargain to make a portal, it's only ever temporary. There are permanent gates between this world and ours, but I've never managed to find one." He pressed his lips together and seemed to think for a moment before nodding to himself. "In fact, maybe you can help. I found some ancient tunnels under my home that need exploring. You can do that, as it's not safe for you outside the castle."

"Why will that help?" I didn't fancy exploring dark tunnels on my own.

"The Nether creatures don't push through the Veil here, and something down there was powerful enough to dampen my magic. I don't know what it is, but perhaps a natural portal gives off some kind of energy."

I raised my brows. "You want me to go down there alone, with no magic and explore? Isn't that more dangerous than being on the streets of this city?"

He smiled. "I don't think there's any demons down there, but I do think there might be a gate. I've suspected for a long time that there was one at this castle but haven't had the chance to explore until now."

His eyes didn't leave mine, and with his hands on my cheeks, his thumb brushed my skin.

"I wouldn't send you if I thought you'd be in danger. Besides, my shadows will be with you. I'll not leave you alone ever again."

I felt my throat tighten and closed my eyes. I believed him. I sighed and met his gaze. "Even if we find a gate, I can't just leave this world. What about my friends?"

His eyes softened. "Dala can come with us. Hentus and the others will be fine. They are survivors, all of them. Right now, the king is hunting for you. It's more important that we get you away from this city. If demons sense you near Hentus, it will put him in danger. In the Nether, you can be safe in my home. It's well guarded and protected by Haldaag's mist and darkness." His thumb brushed back across my lips. "I can teach you more about your true heritage, about who you are, and how your magic works."

He was right. I knew that. Yet, as violent and beyond the law as my Viper family was, the thought of leaving them hurt. I shook myself. Missing them was something I could come to terms with; their deaths weren't. I bit my lip. I also wanted to know more about who I was and what my capabilities were. And the best person to teach me was Dex. I felt the warmth of my pendant resting against my skin. But what of the red-eyed demon and my promise to my parents?

"Dex…"

He pressed his thumb against my lips. "I know what you're going to say. I promise you that eventually, you will face their killer."

I narrowed my eyes and pulled back a little. "Do you mean that?"

"I do. Here." Letting go of my face, he pulled a small knife from his baldric. Then he made a small cut on his thumb. A drop of dark blood bloomed. He whispered some words I didn't understand, and the drop left his skin, hovering mid-air. "This is my promise. It's a vow, one I can't break."

"What happens if you do?"

"I won't. But broken vows cause great pain and suffering until they are fulfilled."

I eyed the drop. "What do I do?"

Dex's smile was sinful. "You open your mouth, let it hit your tongue, and swallow."

I flushed, not missing the heat in his eyes as I did what he said. Coldness rushed through my veins. I shivered, goosebumps rising on my skin. My magic sang, escaping my body. It whirled around me, mixing with the Dex's shadow. My skin flushed at the contact, getting hotter and hotter, desire running through me and gathering between my legs.

Dex's nostrils flared. "I will keep my vow, Lia. You belong in my world, by my side, where you can shine the brightest."

I blinked, trying to ignore the reaction of my body. Even so, my belly tightened at his promise. Maybe he would stay by my side; maybe it was another lie. But what did I know of the Nether world, *his* world? Surviving in this one was hard enough.

"I'll do everything in my power to ensure you're safe there. We'll be together, and the king will not sense your magic when it's hidden behind the walls of Haldaag city."

CHAPTER SIXTEEN

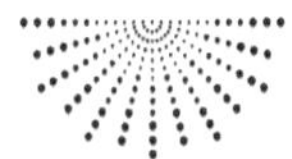

ex

I was so close that Lia's breath fanned my lips. She nodded, and relief hit me like a storm. She'd come with me. To Haldaag.

Risking her wrath, I stroked my fingers along her jaw, trailing them down and around the back of her neck under the wild tumble of silver hair. She was the most beautiful woman I'd ever seen. My mother had been stunning, but Zahlia was beyond words. She shivered under my touch, her iridescent eyes darkening. My restraint snapped. I leaned in and took her plump lips in a kiss that consumed me. Our tongues duelled, our teeth clashed, and her taste mingled with mine. It was heaven, and I didn't want it to stop. A whimper escaped her. That desperate noise had my balls tightening as my erection grew. I groaned when she grabbed my shirt, pulled me closer and nipped my bottom lip with her teeth.

My fingers curled, holding her to me, but she bit me again, harder this time, while she pushed on my chest.

"You left me, Dex. I-I can't do this. Not yet. I just don't trust you. Not after everything you've done. I'm sorry."

The pain in her voice made my heart clench. I could hunt and kill with no remorse, but causing Lia pain made it hard to breathe. I'd thought I was doing the right thing by leaving her to grow independently. I'd been wrong. I'd done irrevocable damage.

I sighed and leaned my forehead against hers. "You were too young to be tied into a relationship with someone like me, Angel."

A slight frown creased the bridge of her nose. "That was my choice. You promised you'd take care of me, that we'd leave Tetris together. That I'd be your wife," she whispered, colour highlighting her cheekbones. "And you broke every promise, along with my heart."

"I know. But I won't apologise for leaving. You weren't powerful enough back then to fight like you do now. I had to protect you, and the best way to do that was to defend this city, to fight the monsters where the Veil was weakest. I had to leave, but I wanted you to remember me, to leave my mark on you so that you never forgot who you belonged to." I leant closer again, my fingers still entwined in her hair. "I am not one of your mortals. I'm a demon. We fight for what we want, and sometimes we fight dirty. I wanted you. I still do. We are destined to be together. I'm yours as much as you're mine. I won't ever apologise for that."

"Bullshit!" she hissed, hitting my hand away. I released her, and she stomped across the room, grabbing her clothes. I couldn't keep my eyes from wandering down to her delectable rear and onto the long, shapely legs the silk nightgown showcased.

"I grew up among thieves, whores, and fucking murderers. I knew exactly what I wanted. And that was you! You took my virginity and left, you bastard. No explanation, not even an Aether damned note!"

I was across the room before she'd drawn her next breath. "You're mine. That night made you mine forever. It doesn't matter where you've lived, who you've been with, or what you've done since."

"Fucking me didn't make me belong to you, you arrogant arse! This isn't some archaic society where you claim me, and I swoon at your damned feet. It was sex, pure and simple. Then you left because you didn't want me enough to stay. And what? You've changed your mind, so I'm supposed to just forgive the fact that you lied for years about who you are *before* you even broke my fucking heart!" She shook her head and gave a small chuckle. "You're still lying. You've told me where I'm from, yet you're still holding things back, aren't you?"

I ground my teeth together, watching her chest as her breathing heaved. She was right, I was. I just needed a little more time. Once she was in my home, she would be safe. I'd tell her everything she needed to know and give her all the time in the world to process it—and if she needed to, to hate me before she accepted she was stuck with me for eternity.

Inhaling her unique scent, I cupped her face between my palms. "Make no mistake, Lia, you *are* mine. I can feel it every time we touch."

"Feel what?" she croaked, trying to hide her reaction as I entwined my shadows through the wisps of colourful magic that escaped her hold.

"The way your body reacts. I see the desire on your face and the lust in your eyes. You hate me for what I did, yet you still feel drawn to me. Your magic melts into mine. That's because mine is its perfect match. My darkness makes you shine brighter, and your light makes the darkness in me more powerful than it has ever been." I gently brushed my thumbs across her cheeks. "I can't promise never to hurt you again—here." And I placed a hand over her heart. "But I can promise I'll do everything in my power to stop anyone from this world or beyond the Veil from harming you." I leaned in and brushed a kiss over her soft lips, making myself pull away as her eyes fluttered shut and little shocks of energy zipped between us. "The best way to do that is to teach you how to control the power you hold."

Her eyes snapped open, flashing with iridescent colour. "I *can* control it."

I smiled and inclined my head. "You can, but there is much more you can learn to do with it." I dropped my hands and stepped away to give us both some breathing room. "How did you learn to hide it so well?" She'd been able to hide it while we were young, partly with my help but also because it hadn't been as powerful.

Her nostrils flared. "I've learnt many things without you."

There was a loud knock, and the door swung wider.

"There you are." Dala looked at me, not Lia. "Your faithful hound wants you," she drawled, her astute gaze bouncing from Lia to me.

Dala was a formidable woman—tall, strong, and clever. Her eyes missed nothing as she took in how close I was to her friend.

"Why?" I asked, raising a brow. I wouldn't put it past her to lie to get me away from Lia.

She smirked and crossed her arms over her chest. "I don't know, General. It might be because I just broke his nose in training practice, and he needs his master to fix it for him."

I raised my brows, wondering what Omeron was up to. He was hundreds of cycles old, so no matter how good a warrior Dala was, Omeron could easily avoid a strike like that. Besides, my friend was perfectly capable of healing himself, which made me suspicious that he needed to talk to me about something in private. I glanced over my shoulder at Lia, who grinned at her friend.

"You broke his nose?" she asked.

Dala shrugged, her white teeth flashing. "I did." She strode in, and they slapped palms high in the air.

"That's my friend you're talking about," I pointed out, trying to suppress my smile.

"Oh, you can heal him, Dex. We all know that. Dala was just showing him she's already a good fighter."

Dala shrugged, smirking. "It's true I am."

I refrained from pointing out that Omeron was the best warrior I'd ever known, as a man and a beast. They didn't need to know that, not when they both looked so pleased with themselves at her victory. I hid my grin, having my suspicions about why Omeron had let Dala injure him.

"I'll see you down by the training ground in thirty minutes. Ensure you eat first; you'll need plenty of energy for the training I have in mind."

Lia rolled her eyes at me, but I let her sass slide. Grin still in place, I left them behind.

Omeron was sharpening his sword when I found him. He was shirtless and completely oblivious to the cold. I grunted. Barg didn't feel the cold. I pulled the edges of my cloak closer. No matter my immortal heritage, I liked to be warm. Haldaag was always frigid. It had been for hundreds of Heart cycles, as had the rest of the Nether. The light that bathed and warmed our lands had faded as the Aether's power waned. The Aether drew its power from the Angel, which meant when my mother had died, its power became weaker until it was almost gone. The Angel fed the heart, the Heart fed the Veil, and the Veil fed the Angel. It was a cycle that should never be broken. Angels were immortal just as powerful shadow demons were, yet if one died, another was only born at the behest of the Higher Powers. They had not seen fit to gift another angel to the Nether after my mother died—until Lia.

"You let her win, then?" Sitting myself down next to my friend, I smirked.

Omeron kept on with his task, his long fingers sure and precise. His mouth curled into a smile, his yellow eyes meeting mine. "I don't know what you mean, General." His innocent look was totally contrived, and we both knew it.

I chuckled. "So it's like that, is it?"

He shrugged his big shoulders and wiped the blade with a rag, cleaning the tiny shards of metal away. Satisfied, he placed the whetstone down on the frozen ground.

"She is..." My friend frowned as if he couldn't find the right words. "Confusing." Then he grinned. "And a good warrior—for a mortal."

Slapping his shoulder, I smiled widely. "Say no more. I know exactly how you feel. But perhaps you shouldn't wait too long to explore why she confuses you."

Omeron stared at his pristine blade, twisting it to catch the light. "I cannot. You know that. I am a prince; she is...mortal. My father would never allow it."

I met his gaze, the corner of my mouth twitching up. "I think he will—if his king bids him to."

Omeron's mouth split into a wide grin, his eyes shining. "My Barg feels a connection with her, as do I. He wants to claim her."

The smile stayed on my face, pleased my friend had found his fated match. "Do you?" I wiggled my brows.

He chuckled deeply. "Of course. I have waited a long time for her."

"Then we'll work together on her accepting who and what you are, as well as getting Lia to accept me."

"Hm, let us hope the Higher Powers favour us both in that regard."

"Indeed. Though my priority is to teach Lia more about her magic."

"Hm." Omeron stood and swung his sword experimentally. "Are you going to teach her while we hunt for a way home?"

I sighed and rubbed my face. "Yes. Passing through the Veil like other demons isn't possible for us. We've been here too long. The Veil would strip our souls, and we'd be lost."

Omeron shuddered. "I know."

I nodded. "We'll find a way back very soon, I promise. In the meantime, I must keep Lia safe, especially now that Baladon has sent his personal guard after her. It's imperative she be able to defend herself against them—and him."

"If she doesn't want to go with him, he isn't powerful enough to take her."

"True, but she doesn't know that, nor does she understand what her magic can do. He can also be—persuasive. If he finds her, he'll poison her against me. I could lose everything, brother."

Omeron cocked his head, his eyes vivid in the dull winter light. "So don't let him. Do as he would do, gain her trust. Eventually, you'll have to tell her where we're from—where *she* is from. Why not make it now?"

"I already told her where she's from, but she needs to trust me before I can tell her the full story."

"My Liege, she *doesn't* trust you and likely won't because you offer no explanation or reasons behind your actions for now or from so long ago."

"That's not true. I told her this morning why I left her,"

He raised a brow. "Really? All of it?"

I chose to look away from my friend's all too assessing stare. "Enough. I don't want to discuss it anymore."

Omeron's sigh was loud. "Don't you? If you don't tell her and she finds out another way, her thoughts will be coloured by anger and pain. If you want her to trust you, then you need to trust in her and the bond the Higher Powers gave you."

My boots squelched in the mud as I stood and paced, fisting my hands. The problem was, my angel was the only one who had ever scared me. She had so much power over me it was terrifying. If she rejected our destiny, my whole purpose was gone: the promise to my mother, healing our world, freeing our people, none of it would happen. But Omeron was right. I needed to start trusting in her and repairing her trust in me.

"You're right, as always. Walk with me."

Omeron nodded and glanced at the soldiers and hound handlers who trained around us. They were far enough away to respect our space but still too close for us to have a potentially treasonous discussion.

He threw on a loose linen shirt, and we walked to the far side of the castle where there was no wall. The ground merely fell away into a massive cliff face. The sea boomed against the rocks below, sending huge swirls of foam and sea spray into the air.

Omeron stood staring out at the ocean. He remained silent, giving me time to speak. I stood by his side and followed his gaze over the vast expanse of water. Ships of all sizes sailed close, but few headed towards the harbour of Tetris. It was too risky for trade ships to dock. They could be swamped by people desperate to escape the nightmare of this city. Even with the warrior castes guarding the harbour, it was too dangerous. A few smaller boats braved the rough ocean to collect goods from the ships that anchored offshore and bring them back to the city. It was never going to be enough to feed so many, though.

"I found some old tunnels below the castle. Through a hidden door in Lia's room."

"Tunnels?" Omeron looked over at me.

"Yes. Two were nothing remarkable. I believe one led to the ocean, probably exiting somewhere on this cliff face under our feet." I peered down the sheer drop, grimacing at the bodies being tossed around against the rocks below. It was grim, but there was little else that could be done with the dead other than throw them into the sea. The ground was too rocky and frozen to dig hundreds of graves, and there was no fuel for burning other than the wooden buildings. Even I wouldn't tear them down to burn bodies, not when each dilapidated place provided shelter for refugees. They had precious little else. So, if I could give them a roof over their heads, I would.

Omeron grimaced. Unlike me, he did not relish heights.

"I'll take your word for it. What about the other tunnels?"

"One stank of iron ore and the stench of the dungeons." I paused for a moment. "Speaking of dungeons, we'll need to deal with the prisoners soon if we are to appease the princes and keep them off our backs."

Omeron nodded, his face grave. "I'll await your guidance on when the time is right. They're both distracted. prince Escalon tries to appear in control, but it's Haruin who's keeping this kingdom together."

"Which is good. I need time and no interference to find the gate. Escalon's occupation with his queen is more than helpful."

The young queen was sickly, but she was also why Escalon's attention stayed away from Omeron and me. We usually dealt with the magickers with little interference from the royals, though they always viewed the poor bastards in the dungeons before passing a death sentence on them all. There had never been any sign of the dark magic they sought, not in any prisoner. There wouldn't be because the only one with dark magic in this kingdom was me, and I hid it deep enough while I was in this castle that even the mage hounds couldn't sense it. The princes would never find their mother's killer.

I scowled out at the ocean. Murdering unarmed, innocent people made me sick. I was a killer. I had ended the lives of hundreds, probably thousands, of demons over my lifetime. I had fought numerous wars against my father before I'd managed to kill him. But the magickers had done nothing but be born into this mortal life with an echo of magic they had once possessed as a demon.

The princes always watched the first execution, then left. In Haruin's words, they 'trusted' me to do the job quickly and efficiently.

"What about the third tunnel?" Omeron asked quietly.

I frowned. "That's the one that makes me hopeful. It was a void. No air movement, no smells, even my magic was dampened by whatever is down there."

Omeron's expression became grim. "Well, at least that means it's not of this world."

"True."

We stood in companionable silence for a few more minutes, watching the ships and boats on the ocean.

"I should go. It's time to teach Lia how to feed from magic and control hers better. I don't think it will take her long to learn." I smiled, warmth spreading through my chest as I thought of how much she'd achieved alone. "She's already powerful."

Omeron stared at me, mirroring my smile. "I haven't seen that look on your face in far too long."

"What look?"

"Happiness."

He was right. No matter the danger we were all in, I was happy to be back by Lia's side.

I shrugged, my smile spreading. "She's my light." My brother would understand better than anyone what that meant.

"Then we must keep that light burning and find a way back to the Netherworld, where she will burn the brightest."

I nodded my agreement. "We'll explore the third tunnel tomorrow while our future bonded sleep."

"*Our* future bonded?" Omeron raised his brows.

I grinned. "That's right. You can try and deny your connection to Dala if you wish, but your kind does not become protective of a female unless you intend to bond with her. You protected Dala from even the slightest bruise and willingly took an injury yourself."

Omeron grinned back, his shoulders rising and falling. "Like you, I will do everything possible to persuade her that she belongs to me, but only when she knows the truth. I won't tell her who or what I am until you tell Lia who and what you are." He met my gaze and cocked his head, his white teeth gleaming. "Females talk too much."

I chuckled. "That's very true, they do." I slapped his shoulder and turned back to the training ground. "I'll tell Lia as soon as we return to the Nether or if the demons force my hand. In the meantime, we need to find that gateway."

CHAPTER SEVENTEEN

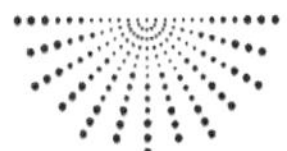

ia

I groaned. Reaper's teeth, my muscles had aches that had aches. I'd spent all of yesterday under Dex's tutelage. He taught me the correct technique for bows, daggers, and sword work. He'd corrected my stances, holds, and form until my muscles shook. And then, while the rest of the castle slept, he'd surrounded us in shadow, his voice low and seductive as he explained that I could feed from his magic enough to survive for a short time. I shivered, heat licking between my thighs. He'd let me feed from him. I still felt the remnants of his magic swirling seductively through my system.

I groaned, my fingers wandering between my legs as desire surged through me, the memory of his velvet voice rumbling through my mind.

"You can take sustenance from the Veil and heal that cut," he said, gently directing my gaze towards him with the touch of his forefinger on my chin while the fingers of his other hand brushed the tender skin around a gash on my arm.

I shook my head, trying not to get lost in the green of his eyes. Damn. Jade had fast become my favourite colour. I'd always found his eyes so beautiful, but I'd never noticed the specks of russet in them or how bright they were against his olive skin and blue-black hair. It was as if they were seeing into my soul.

"It's fine. It'll heal on its own. It was my fault for not moving out of the way quickly enough. I won't use the magic of the Veil any more than I need to."

His heavy brow drew down, and he stroked my lips with his thumb. "The amount of magic you need to heal won't make any difference to what's happening to the Aether."

"No, I won't weaken the Veil."

I tried to pull away from his hold, but he didn't allow it. His full lips quirked into a sexy half-smile.

"You're so stubborn. But it's okay, you don't need to take from Veil, you can use mine."

My heart thrummed as hard now as it had done then.

"How?" I'd whispered.

I pictured how he'd softly coaxed me to push my magic through his skin and into his body, his sinful voice encouraging me to wind it through his magic before syphoning it into mine. Pleasure at that connection had radiated through me, my legs almost buckling, it had felt so good. He'd given a deep, throaty moan, his eyes hooded and burning with hunger. We'd not touched, but it had been the single most erotic experience of my life.

My fingers slid through the folds between my legs, a moan escaping me. I shoved my free hand over my mouth, biting on the soft skin to keep from crying out. My fingers circled my sensitive nub before dipping lower, then dragging my moisture higher. I whimpered against my palm, imagining his hand between my legs, calloused fingers working my most sensitive flesh, his other hand palming my breasts and squeezing my nipple as his velvet voice encouraged me to climax for him.

"Dex..." I moaned, pleasure exploding through me, leaving me breathless and shaking. I worked my fingers slower and slower, bringing myself down until my arm flopped against the sheets. I lay there spent, wishing I knew where things were going between us. He'd been quiet as he'd walked me back to my room, and I'd had no idea what to say. What we'd shared had been intimate beyond anything I'd experienced, yet I was still processing all he had told me. I knew I'd forgive him for his lies, especially now I knew why he'd done it, but I also knew it would take time to trust him again.

A banging on the door made me jump. A deep flush stained my cheeks as I bolted upright, clutching the sheet to my chest. Shit! Was it Dex? Did he somehow know I'd gotten off on thoughts of his touch, his voice? Could he sense my lust, my pleasure…?

"Hey! You awake?" Dala yelled, the thick oak door muffling her voice.

I flopped back against my pillows. "No!" I yelled back, relief barrelling through me.

The door flew open. Dala strode in dressed in battle leathers and with her head cleanly shaved. "Good. Come on, it's time to train. You've been asleep nearly the whole day. If we want to get any practice in, we need to go while there's still some daylight left. Dex said to preserve your energy for the same training as last night and that we should both go to the library at some point and learn about the Nether."

She bounced up and down on the balls of her feet, looking so pent up and full of energy I had to grin, ignoring the flush of heat through my body at the thought of feeding from him again. There was no doubt I felt stronger than I had in a long time—and more turned on than ever despite my recent orgasm. Dala didn't need to know that, though.

"The library? With you?" I scoffed.

Dala was as likely as me to go and sit in a library for hours on end. We were both too wired for that kind of inaction. Dala and I had been raised on violence and blades. Except, after what Dex had told me, I saw the value of knowledge more than I ever had. Dala looked at me expectantly. I smiled. Tomorrow was soon enough for libraries and shit like that. "I don't think so."

"Right? He has no idea who we are, does he? Bloody library." Her voice was so indignant that I giggled.

But then, remembering, I sobered. "Seems he has more of an idea who I am than I do."

Dala cocked her head, her gaze assessing. "How?"

Propping myself up on a nest of pillows, I told Dala everything Dex had said.

"Will you go with him when he finds a gate?" Her question was quiet, pensive.

"I don't see what choice I've got. Besides…" I gave her a cheeky grin. "I'd get to look at him almost everyday. That's got to be a reason to go, especially when he's dressed in that form-fitting battle armour he wears." I fanned myself. "That's too fine a sight to refuse."

Dala laughed. "Okay, but don't leave without me. No matter how fuckable Omeron is, we…" She gestured between us. "…stay together. I've got your back. If that demon king comes for you, I want to be there to kick his scaly arse. Besides, I don't need to think about leaving this shit-hole city. I only stay for you."

Love for my best friend warmed my chest. She may not have my blood, but she was my sister, my family. Someone who was there for me through thick and thin with no judgement, ever.

Dala gave me a bright smile, then jumped off the bed, beginning to bounce on the balls of her feet again. "Come on, let's stop thinking about how awful this city is or even how fuckable our captors are. I want to train. I have too much energy to go to a damned library."

I narrowed my eyes at Dala. "You need to get laid, not fight." I knew her as well as she knew me.

She shrugged elegantly. "Fuck or fight, they're the same."

"Ha! No, they really aren't."

She shrugged, walking impatiently to the door. "Depends on who your partner is. Come on. Come on. I need to get rid of some energy."

"So what's stopping you? You love sex. And you've already said how Omeron makes your lady bits tingle."

A dark look crossed Dala's features.

I jumped up, my mouth dropping open. "Holy shit! He said no, didn't he?"

"No need to shout it from the rooftops, *Angel*," she snarled Dex's pet name at me.

I put my hands up. "I'm sorry. It's just...wow. I mean, no one's ever turned you down before, have they?"

"Nope." She yanked open the door, her nostrils flaring.

"Hey! Naked here!" I launched off the bed, grabbing some clothes. Dala watched me with an impatient scowl as I rushed through my morning routine. She marched out of the room as soon as I was ready, leaving me to catch up.

"Why d'you think he turned you down?" It was obviously bothering my friend. She must like him far more than she let on.

"No idea. Maybe he prefers men—or I'm just not attractive to him."

"Dala, you're attractive to everyone, male and female alike."

She stretched her neck. "Listen, can we just forget it, him, them... urgh..." She threw her hands in the air. "...whatever...for a while? I need to go get rid of this...this frustration."

"Sure, sorry." I linked arms with her, trying not to smile. My friend was a physical being. She loved to use her body for pleasure and fighting, and being denied was something she wasn't used to. We walked in silence down to the field of mud and gravel that served as a training ground. In small groups, soldiers practised with various weapons and hand-to-hand techniques. I stiffened. In one corner, a group of men stood. They were dressed in different uniforms than the others, mage hounds leashed by their sides.

I nodded towards a quieter area, which was off to one side, not to mention as far from those horrid beasts as possible. We had to walk past the hounds to get to it, and even though we gave them a wild berth, they went wild, snarling and gnashing their teeth. The whole training ground went quiet, the soldiers staring darkly at us. I felt my face flush but refused to lower my head out of embarrassment or fear. Not to them, not to anybody. Their prejudices were a result of this society and its rulers, especially when most magickers didn't even realise they had any latent power, let alone knew what to do with it.

"Will they let the hounds attack us?" Dala asked, her voice full of tension.

I tried to appear relaxed, though I was ready to defend us with magic if needed. Normally, my magic was well hidden. I kept my face neutral, but my heart drummed against my ribs. Had taking Dex's magic made mine too powerful to hide?

"No. We're here as allies of their general. They'll not defy his orders. I hope," I finished on a mumble. *Please let that be true.*

"Probably not, but will they follow his instead?" Her gaze rested on a sickly-looking man who sat under a canopy wrapped in large wolf furs. His skin was stretched tightly over his angled cheekbones and so pale it was almost translucent. He looked unwell, yet his eyes were sharp and flitted around the men before resting briefly on me. His hair was auburn, and he wore a single circlet of metal upon his head, marking him as one of the princes. Haruin. I'd heard of the younger prince but never seen him. It seemed he was as sickly as the rumours suggested. His body might be weak, but his mind was another story. There was something astute, almost cruel, in his gaze.

Dex's words about their mother being killed by a magicker came back to me. Was I in danger from the sickly prince, or was it only his brother who held enough power to order me killed? I glanced back at Dex's house. I knew how consuming the need for revenge could be. Did their rage simmer beneath their skin like mine? Hunting down my parents' killer was something I'd never give up on. The difference between them and me was that I didn't hurt people indiscriminately. I'd never hurt anyone just because they had a slight glimmer of red in their irises like I'd noticed some magickers did—including Dex.

"Should we go?" Dala's question was quiet, her fingers extending and then flexing. We had no weapons; Dex had made sure of that. I'd shield us and even escape using the energy of the Veil if I had to, though that would paint an even bigger target on my back. It didn't matter; I'd do whatever was necessary to save our lives.

"No."

Despite Dex's warning to stay away from the princes, running wasn't in my nature. Instead, I took her hand, turned my back to the prince and quickly hurried to where we could practise alone.

We worked hard for the next hour or so, drilling the way we always had: no-holds-barred punches, kicks—grappling. I was covered in scrapes and mud and was freezing when Dex came for us. The atmosphere on the training ground had stayed hostile, but now there were barked greetings, and men stood aside, letting their general and his personal guard walk through. I was glad to see prince Haruin had disappeared.

Dala and I stood panting, watching them approach. My stomach fizzed with nerves and something else…anticipation, maybe? Last night, as well as my imaginings this morning were fresh in my mind.

Both Netherworld warriors were tall, with broad shoulders, flat stomachs and muscular thighs, and were wrapped in form-fitting armour. Dex wore a cloak with a fur collar, but Omeron didn't. Dex's expression went from hard and unforgiving general to amused, a sexy little smirk curving his lips when he noticed me studying him.

I grinned. He was so damned confident and handsome it was ridiculous. Part of me knew I should be scowling and angry with him for his lies and taking away my freedom, but I wasn't. I was looking forward to spending more time by his side. Returning that sexy little smile wasn't something I could help—until I saw Dala's dark expression as she looked at Omeron. I swiftly elbowed her.

"Smile at him," I murmured out the side of my mouth.

Her eyes slid my way, a dark scowl in place. "Why should I?"

I rolled my eyes. "So he knows you aren't as scary as you look."

"But I am."

Higher Powers, but my friend was impossible. I didn't get a chance to say anything else.

"Angel," greeted Dex, coming to a stop before me, that smirk still on his lips. "Are you hungry?"

I crossed my arms over my chest, lifting a brow though my cheeks heated and my heart pounded. "Why? You offering to feed me?" I shot back.

His grin was full of sin and promise. "Always." But then, all levity fell from his expression. "Unfortunately, you need to learn to feed from other demons, just in case I'm not on the menu."

Dala's gaze darted between us. I almost laughed at her confused expression, though I shuddered at the thought of feeding from any demon except Dex. Catching her look, I wiggled my brows. That was all it took for her to realise I'd held out on her. She rolled her eyes, flattening her lips. I'd told her Dex had shown me how to take energy from another being, but I hadn't shared how erotic the night before had been. I don't know why, other than it felt private, something special between Dex and me.

Omeron's mouth twitched into a smile, his eyes sparkling as he watched her.

"That would be a shame." I lifted a shoulder but held Dex's gaze as I pouted. Was I flirting with him? I bit my bottom lip to hide my smile. Yes, I was.

"Dala, go with Omeron," Dex ordered without taking his eyes off me.

"What? Why?" My friend growled, her brows drawn down.

"Because I said so."

"Come on, you heard the General, so unless you prefer the library —or the dungeon, I wouldn't argue," advised Omeron, grinning now. "Don't worry, my lady. I'll protect you from the creatures of the night."

"Oh, fuck off, I'm not a lady, nor do I need your protection, and you know it," Dala snapped, straightening her spine, her chin jutting out.

Omeron barked a loud laugh. "Well then, by all means…" He made a grand gesture with his hand. "After you, *not a lady*. I shall enjoy your protection instead. First, you need food, clean attire, and a warm cape. More snow is on its way."

"How do you know?" she groused.

Omeron winked and touched the side of his nose. "Let's just say I have a nose for these things."

Dala looked down at herself with a frown. "And why do I need clean clothes? What's wrong with these?"

Omeron chuckled patiently. "They're damp and dirty. They'll freeze on you. Unless you want to get hypothermia and be forever indebted to me when I'm required to warm you up and save your life?"

That caused a spark in my friend's eyes. "You can warm me up anytime, but no debts will be owed."

Still grinning, Omeron turned away. "Let's go. Dex and Lia have their own business to attend to."

Dex's eyes glittered as he watched them leave. Dala shot me a look over her shoulder as she stalked across the training ground towards the stables. She didn't like being parted from me, so I waved her away, mouthing,

I'll be fine. Stay safe.

You, too.

At least she was with someone who could watch her back. I might not know Omeron, but I knew Dex, and he'd only have the best by his side. He'd also only work so closely with another if he trusted them.

"Come on." Dex gestured back towards his house. "Like Omeron said, it's going to snow. You need a cape."

I followed him, enjoying the view of his body as he moved until it dawned on me what I was going to do. All joking aside, I didn't want to share the feeling I'd had with Dex with some slimy demon.

It didn't take long to get togged up, and soon, we were standing on the very top of his roof looking beyond the castle walls and down over the east side of Tetris.

"You're very quiet. What's wrong?"

"Nothing," I denied a little too quickly, fiddling with the clasp of my new cloak. "You're quiet, too," I pointed out.

Dark eyes bored into me, sparkling in the moonlight. He ignored my comment and stepped closer, his lips curling in a little smile. "You can ask, you know."

"Ask what," I muttered, feeling my cheeks heat.

"If feeding from a demon will turn you on like feeding from me did."

"That's not…that wasn't what I…" My stuttered words trailed off.

"Really?" His finger brushed my hot cheek, his gentle touch sending bolts of lust through me.

"N-no…"

"Liar," he whispered and slanted his mouth across mine, kissing me languidly as if he had all the time in the world. His tongue lazily stroked against mine, tasting and exploring every part of my mouth with a dominance that left me weak at the knees. I lost the ability to think as his hand curled around the small of my back, the other sliding through my hair and cupping the back of my head. Firmly, he urged me closer until there was no space between us. I was cocooned in strength, hard muscle, and shadow.

It was pure reflex to hold onto him. With a whimper, I sank against his chest while tentatively stroking his tongue with my own. Desire rolled through me. I demanded more, exploring his mouth as deeply as he had mine. His taste was addictive. I kissed him desperately, our teeth clashing and tongues duelling. My fingers curled into his hair, gripping the soft strands and keeping him close. I didn't want to stop or let go—ever. A guttural growl escaped his throat, vibrating through me before he slowly pulled away, nipping my bottom lip. That tiny nip sent a jolt of pain and desire straight to my centre.

"No, it won't feel anything like it did with me." His breath came in heavy pants, just like mine. We stared at each other. "Our...connection makes feeding from each other special." His face darkened, and he ground his teeth, his shadows swirling around us.

"What connection?"

He turned his face away from me, remaining silent.

"Dex? What's wrong?"

The fury in his shadows didn't scare me, but they thickened until it seemed they were devouring even the small sliver of moonlight that had broken through the clouds. Still, he said nothing, but the light-heartedness from earlier had disappeared.

"Dex?" I unclenched my fingers from his cloak and cupped his cheek.

He jerked his attention to me, though he didn't pull away.

"Tell me what's wrong, please. Is feeding from a demon dangerous?"

"Only for the demon," he ground out.

"Why? Will I kill it?"

"Not unless you want to."

"Then why are you angry?"

"Because I don't want anyone else's energy inside you. Only mine. You are mine to feed. Mine to protect. Our connection is...special." He looked down, and what I saw in his eyes stole my breath. Possession, frustration, worry...need. "I don't want you to feed from anyone but me."

"Then why do this? Last night was…." I felt my throat close.

A small growl escaped his chest. "Angel, I know. It was…" He released a slow breath. "…amazing. But if we make it back to the Nether, you will need every bit of knowledge and skill to survive. If I could guarantee that we would always be together, I wouldn't even entertain this, but I can't."

That truth settled like a lead weight in my belly. He'd left me before. Was he trying to tell me he would do it again? I shook my head in denial.

"I don't want to do it."

It was stupid to deny my need to replenish the power in my veins by some other means than depleting the Veil further or using Dex's energy. I knew that, but the thought of doing anything so carnal with any other being sent my stomach churning despite Dex's assurance it wouldn't feel the same.

His jaw clenched. "It's safer this way."

"For who?"

"You. It means you can survive if anything happens to me."

With that, he firmly grabbed my wrist. His hold didn't hurt nor did it give me room to refuse. Before I knew it, we were travelling through darkness. I swallowed hard, trying not to panic. It was a darkness that had always beckoned to me. It was seductive, its touch silky, its midnight allure as difficult to resist as Dex. Up until now, I'd studiously refused to come into contact with it.

I peered at Dex as shadows curled around us, caressing my skin. I blinked. My magic allowed me to travel through the light. It seemed his allowed him to do the same through shadow. But just like me, he couldn't pass through to the Nether. I couldn't pass through the dark side any more than Dex could push through the light.

He stepped out of the shadows and onto the rickety rooftop of a run-down fish market on the harbour's edge. The smell of brine, old fish, and rotting bodies permeated the frigid wind. I pulled a face. After the relatively clean air in the castle, I was going soft. It had never smelt this bad before.

"Time to hunt. We'll be here long enough for me to teach you how to do this, no more. If any of the king's warriors come, we immediately jump on the Aether and high tail it back to the castle." His eyes bored into mine. "Do you understand? I won't risk your safety."

I nodded, that ridiculous warm feeling back in my chest. "I do." I had no intention of being caught by some mad demon king and used for the Powers only knew what.

Dex crossed his arms over his chest, making his biceps pop under the leather of his armour. I swallowed, my mouth dry. I wanted to run my fingers over them, to touch him. I swayed forward and managed to stop myself by digging my fingers into my palms, the sting grounding me. I cocked my head and stared, mesmerised as shadow played across the planes of his face. He'd come from another world to find me, to save me from his father. For years, he'd fought back hundreds of reapers and demons where the Veil was weakest to give me time, and now he'd returned—for me.

I reached out and took his hands. "I promise."

"Good. Then, let's get on with this. Taking a soul's energy is different than..." He clenched his jaw again. "Me sharing my magic with you."

"Taking a soul?" I shuddered and shook my head. "Oh no, nope, I'm not eating souls..." Another thought occurred to me, and my eyes widened. "I didn't eat your soul last night, did I?"

Dex shook his head. "No, I shared the energy of my magic with you, not my soul."

"Oh, okay. Shared it?"

"Yes, I allowed you to connect to my power because I want to give you sustenance, protection—and pleasure."

"Oh." I cocked my head and slipped my fingers around his. "So you were telling the truth? It won't feel like that with another demon?"

His jaw muscles popped. "No, even if you're both willing. It was so intense because we are matched." There was a short pause, then he added. "I was truthful with you, Lia."

I nodded and gave him a small smile but then wrinkled my nose. "I'm still not eating souls." The thought of absorbing what essentially was something's life force made me shudder, yet feeding from Dex wouldn't help me keep my heart distanced, and I didn't want to deplete the Veil of even more power.

Dex stepped closer, his midnight scent and warmth enveloping me. "Lia, I know this makes you uncomfortable. No matter what you have been forced to do over the years, I know you don't like to hurt or kill without cause. Remember that you can't erase these souls by taking a little of their energy. It takes dark magic to do that, not light. Your power is there to guide and to bring forth life, while mine is the opposite. Food will keep your body healthy to a point, but if your magic is left to wither, you'll become sick and weak—and eventually, you'll die —like my mother did." His voice caught on those last words. He cleared his throat and continued without looking at me as if he wasn't sure how I would react to his next words.

"I can absorb the energy of a soul and erase them from existence completely. I never do it lightly, mainly in battle, to give me strength, but the King's warriors will be reborn if I don't. Their purpose is to serve him. They'll follow his orders without fail, which means they'll hunt you down and kill anyone who gets in their way."

I released a steady breath. He was telling the truth. I could feel it. Could I really do this? I'd learnt how to take energy from the Veil to feed my magic without help. It had been difficult and took months. Would this be the same? No, it wouldn't because I had Dex to help me, and as much as my lingering distrust told me to refuse his help, I wouldn't. Deep down, I wanted it. I wanted him to be here to fight by my side, to protect me if I needed it, and to be proud of me when I succeeded in doing as he asked. It scared me how quickly I'd fallen back under his spell.

"What do I do first?" I asked, trying to keep my voice steady.

"First, you learn to let the energy of the dead pass through you. As it does, you can absorb what you need. If enough of their energy remains after you have fed, you can release them, and they'll go to the Aether and search out their King. If you take too much, they will become lost, just as all other souls. They'll remain like that until an Angel reconnects with the Heart."

"So I'm damned if I do, and damned if I don't. I can't let them be sent back as warriors, but I also don't wish them to become lost and confused." Dex's gaze didn't waver from mine. I bit my lip. What choice did I have? Fighting them again was better than condemning them to wander lost and confused until the Aether was cured. I doubted those warriors had much choice in searching for me. After all, soldiers couldn't easily rebel against the orders of a powerful ruler, demon or not.

"Am I likely to take too much?"

Taking Dex's energy had been easy, but I knew now that was because he'd allowed me to use him as a magical buffet. That must be why it had seemed like a walk in the park compared to learning to take energy from the Veil.

Dex's voice was husky when he spoke. "Not if you allow my magic to help you."

"How does that work?" My cheeks heated at the look in his eyes.

He stepped closer, gazing down at me, lowering his head enough that his lips almost touched mine. "I need to be close enough to touch you this time because I'm not giving you my magic," he whispered against my lips. "Then I'll need to slip my arms around you. Like this."

Slowly, deliberately, his large hands smoothed from my shoulders down my arms, which hung at my sides, trailing over my fingers before he gently urged me to turn, and then he stepped up close behind me. My breathing hitched, his touch burning my skin even though it wasn't exposed. His hot palms slipped over my hips and across the flat plane of my stomach until I was engulfed by his warmth, the smell of his leather armour, and the seductive scent of midnight. I inhaled deeply. I loved his unique scent. It affected me like none other. It was safety and sin in equal measure.

"What are you doing?" I asked breathlessly.

"I'm going to guide you through this." His voice was husky, gravelly. My heart hammered. He didn't even try to hide that our closeness was affecting him, too.

"O-okay," I stammered. My mind returned to the night when he'd taken me to his bed and afterwards when he'd held me close like nothing would ever come between us. I pulled my bottom lip between my teeth, remembering the mind blowing pleasure he'd given me that night. My centre throbbed at the memory. I tried pulling away, but he held me fast against him. Aether, forgive me, but I didn't fight. I loved, no, *craved*, this feeling of being close to him. I'd dreamed of it every night for so long, and now that I was in his arms, I didn't want to move. My breathing hitched when I felt a hard steel length pressing into my lower back. I whimpered. I couldn't help it any more than I could help pushing back against him.

He smiled against my skin, and I could sense his smugness when he angled his hips back. I growled in frustration at that loss of contact.

"Sweet, sweet Angel, now is not the time for that, no matter how much I want to. There's a demon coming. Let me show you how to take what you need." His words rumbled through me, his warm breath on my ear making me shiver.

He could get me to do anything when he spoke to me like that. I couldn't suppress a small groan when his lips brushed the skin just under my ear lobe. I felt him smile against my skin and instinctively tilted my head to give him access to my neck, but I kept my eyes open, searching the darkness.

"A demon? Where?"

Unlike reapers, demons couldn't come through the veil high in the air; it was as if the Aether grounded them. I'd seen all kinds of monstrous, sometimes strangely beautiful, creatures walk this city, but all of them were called back to the darkness when the sun rose, their physical forms disintegrating to dust and their energy sucked back through the Veil. I wondered if the Demon King recalled them all or if the Aether itself pulled them back, knowing they weren't meant to be in this world.

Dex dropped another small kiss against my skin. "Any second now..." A nip this time.

"Dex..." I breathed, desire washing through me, making my whole body tremble.

"Hm?" His tongue flicked out, tasting me before he nipped again, this time at my neck.

I hissed, the slight sting sending bolts of pleasure through me and making my core tighten. "Dex, you have to stop."

"Why?"

"Can't think straight..." I groaned as he sucked my ear lobe between his teeth before he gave a distinctly inhuman snarl and let go. I expected him to release me, but he didn't.

"Bring him to us, Angel."

I frowned, searching for my target and trying to clear the fog of need from my mind. "How?"

"Throw your magic out like a spear. To feed, you don't need to kill his physical form first. Once he's impaled, you need to compel your power to break down his, take the molecules apart and merge them with your own. Or, if you don't need to feed, you can drag the soul from his body and throw it back into the Veil, like you've been doing."

I'd lost focus, and now the demon was too close.

Dex's magic darted forward, ribbons of darkness slithering to do his bidding. The demon, a spindly creature with an emaciated, hairless body, glowing orange eyes, yellow hair, and black razor-like teeth in a large mouth, snarled before it turned tail and ran. It didn't get far. Those dark ribbons shot him through in several places.

Dex kept his cheek pressed against mine as he pulled. The creature thrashed and screeched, caught in those ribbons until Dex yanked. The demon's physical body fell to the ground, disappearing into ash.

"You ready? This is going to hurt a little, but the pain will fade." Dex's voice was seductive despite what we were doing. His magic brushed my face. "Let your power out, baby."

My skin heated at his endearment, though I did as he said. Immediately, a dark ribbon intertwined with my magic. With no idea what I was doing, I allowed him to guide me. It felt natural. I already knew how to kill and throw my prey back into the Veil; this was just the next step, and I trusted Dex to show me.

"Take hold of the demon's soul."

I contemplated the dark cloud caught in Dex's magic before wrapping my own around it. It trembled in my hold, its fear a palpable thing, and though it couldn't talk, I felt it begging me to release it, to save its life. I shuddered.

"It's alright, Angel. Remember, this won't kill it." Dex wrapped dark ribbons of shadow through my light but made no further move.

It screamed, the sound grating against my bones. I wondered who it had killed that night and my resolve hardened. It was one less demon to attack the helpless souls of this world.

"Unlike when you want to end them, you must pull the soul

through your body. Once you have absorbed the energy you need, you can cast it into the Veil. The Demon King will be unable to reincarnate it again because it isn't whole, but it will survive to await judgement."

"Await judgement by whom?" I asked, my eyes not straying from the trembling entity.

"From the Heart of Aether."

"The Heart?" I frowned. There had been very few books for me to read about the Nether, but all folklore and tales of the afterlife mentioned the Heart of the Aether. I had no idea what it actually was, whether it was a living entity or one of those unexplainable things you just had to accept or go insane thinking about.

Dex brushed another kiss against my skin.

"Yes. The Angel guides our souls through the Veil to the Heart. Souls can then be reborn as the Heart and the Higher Powers see fit."

"Is that why so many souls are lost? Because the Angel can't guide them anymore? Not since your mother died?"

Dex pressed his lips together. "That's right. It's taken hundreds of Heart cycles for the energy to become so weak, but only the Higher Powers can gift our worlds an Angel. The Heart needs one to survive so it can feed the Veil. Like I said before, the Heart, the Angel, and the Veil all rely on each other to exist. I'm hoping that once we return to the Netherworld, we can align with my allies and find a way to heal the Veil."

I contemplated the shaking cloud of demon energy. I was starting to understand what Dex meant without him actually voicing who I really was. I didn't understand why he held back, but I wasn't stupid. I didn't like to run from my problems either, but facing the discovery that I wasn't mortal or even from this world was enough for now. More responsibility could wait.

"If we force our way through both sides of the Veil, what will happen? Do we really need to hunt down a gate?"

"We do. The Veil will not allow demons who have dared to cross over to this world through a weakness to get back into the Nether. A gate is the only safe way to travel, or we'll lose our souls, and our bodies will end up like his—ash."

"Then I need to learn to replenish my magic while we search for a way to the Nether." Carefully, yet with a firm grasp, I pulled the trembling demon's soul into my body. Dex was right; there was nothing sensual or erotic about the experience. It was horrible. I could feel the soul's terror of being consumed and fading into nothing. Yet, I needed to know how to survive in a world I knew nothing about. My magic did my bidding. I pulled apart his energy, taking as little as possible while working out this awful process. When I judged I'd taken enough, I stopped. My magic sparked gently under my skin.

"That's not enough," Dex insisted.

"It is," I hissed. "I will not cause it pain."

"Sweetheart, it cannot feel pain, and cannot be reborn now unless the Heart judges it worthy."

"I know," I whispered, regret weighing me down. "But it's terrified of never existing again. I will not rob it of that chance."

I understood that Dex fed on souls to stop the Demon King from reincarnating his soldiers, but it felt wrong to me, so I urged the entity from my body and gently pushed what was left into the Veil. I felt a wave of relief, which I was sure came from the soul, not me, but I couldn't be sure. At least it couldn't be remade as one of the king's soldiers.

For a moment, we stood and watched the colours of the Veil dance in front of our eyes. Reluctantly pushing Dex's hands away, I put enough distance between us to turn and face him. "Let's go back to the castle. I don't want to do that again."

"But you've only fed once. That's not enough." His mouth pressed into a tight line as if he wanted to say more but changed his mind.

"I'll be fine. I can replenish from the Veil if I get desperate." I gave him a coy look. "Besides, I can feed from you."

"As much as I'd love that, feeding from me isn't the point of this exercise. You can only feed from the Veil while in this world. When we go to the Nether, the Veil becomes darkness and shadow. It's sick, Lia, which means there is very little light for you to feed on. The Heart will need to feed from your magic, too. It will be impossible for you to survive without feeding from demons—or me. If the Higher Powers allow it, I'll be by your side all the time, but the gods of our world are often fickle, and there are no guarantees."

I shook my head. "No. I-I can't. It felt—wrong. If you can't—or won't feed me, I'll find another way to sustain my magic. There has to be one."

A little puff of air escaped Dex, and he ground his jaw like he was trying not to say something. Instead, he turned and marched away. My eyes narrowed on the vee of his back, my stomach dropping. I was so out of my depth with him. Relying on only him to keep my magic strong was foolish, but I couldn't take the energy from another's soul, terrify them, and then leave them confused and wandering through the Nether with no purpose.

I narrowed my gaze on him. If he was trying to tell me he would walk away again at some point, I'd find another way to survive. I hated how much that thought hurt, but I'd learned not to rely on anyone else. Maybe visiting the library wasn't such a bad idea. All I knew about the Netherworld was from folktales, fables, and Dex. The Demon King, the monsters, who I was, how I needed to feed my magic, all of it came from him. He'd lied before. I frowned. Was he lying again?

Hunching against the frigid wind, I strode after Dex. Had I been stupid to start trusting him? Especially when my heart was involved? After all, I didn't know him, not really. Unless I managed to get to the Netherworld, I wouldn't find out if he was being truthful, nor would I discover how my parents found me and managed to keep me hidden from the Demon King. I swallowed hard. Or had the king found me, and it was him who'd killed them? It would explain why I couldn't find the red-eyed demon.

Dex turned to face me, his face blank, his eyes stormy with an emotion I couldn't name. He held out his hand. "Come here."

Instinctively, I bristled at the command, but Aether, forgive me, I wanted to touch him. He used the dark side of the Veil to transport us, and we arrived back at the castle in moments. I'd always been wary of the dark curtain, but I wasn't now. I couldn't access it alone, but it seemed almost welcoming when I was with Dex. His grip fell away before he said he had some paperwork to do, and strode away without another word.

I huffed out a breath. I got that he wanted me to have options, but I couldn't take another's soul. It was...wrong. I rubbed my arms. If he wouldn't tell me what I wanted to know, I'd find out myself.

CHAPTER EIGHTEEN

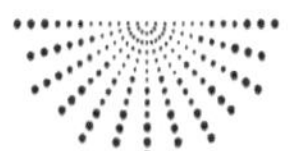

ia

After hours of studying in the castle library, my neck ached, and my eyes stung. The table in front of me was strewn with books, mainly folklore and legends. I was tired, and no matter how much I'd fed on that demon or Dex, my magic felt weak. Even my muscles ached like they hadn't in years. I frowned. Maybe I'd trained harder with Dala than I realised. I let light dance between my fingers, but even that seemed an effort.

I closed the tome I was studying, silently thanking Dex for teaching me to read when I was younger. Some words were still difficult for me, but I managed to sound them out, and the lexicon by my right elbow helped me understand the meaning of new words. The Vipers was not a place for learning classic languages or mathematics, but I'd learnt other things like how to skin a rat or pick a pocket. I rolled my eyes at myself as I sounded out another word.

"Sym-bi-o-n-t." I carefully pronounced each letter before repeating them slightly faster. I had no idea what it meant, so I reached for the lexicon. The moment I did, I heard a soft sound. It sounded like shuf-fled footsteps. I stiffened, listening hard. Nothing. I stood, grasping the letter opener I'd found lying randomly on a desk, and crept silently into the main library. I'd not heard the door, and I didn't sense anyone in the shadows. After a few minutes, I relaxed again. I'd been caught up in reading about reapers and how, in the legends, they were benevolent beings who helped guide souls through the Veil to the Heart of the Aether, where they were met by what the stories portrayed as an angelic being: a woman with wings wider than she was tall and a crown of light upon her head. She appeared to be blessing the souls who prostrated themselves before her. I glanced at the artist's rendering of the Netherworld. It was drawn in faded ink, and with such expertise, it looked almost real. Had the artist been there? Yet, this was a place of light and beauty, not one of darkness like Dex had explained. Behind the Angel, a large hole in the ground disappeared into the earth. Shadows and light swirled in the centre, and a huge column of rainbow-coloured light reached into the sky and spread over the land. Ribbons of that same light reached out for the souls, guiding them into the Heart.

Beneath the drawing were runes. I had no idea what they meant, but I'd seen similar runes before. Omeron had them over his scalp. I took a shaky breath. Beneath the beautiful piece of art were two words.

Aether's Heart.

"Darkness and light," I murmured, running my finger over the page, where the edge of the Heart was covered in blooms. Their white and pearlescent-coloured petals glowed, made even more vibrant by the gleaming black leaves and stems. I touched my pendant. They looked like my flower. My throat tightened. Dex was telling the truth. It was from the Nether, just like him. I stroked my forefinger over the depiction of the Angel.

Was this Dex's mother?

Another soft sound echoed. I stood, closing the tome with enough care not to make a noise. Silently, I moved into the shadows, leaving my lamp burning. As a magicker in a castle of magic haters, I was a target. With that in mind, I moved over to where they would need to pass between two large bookcases to get to me. Managing my magic reserves was important, but so was staying alive.

It was easy to keep my breathing calm and quiet. I was well-practised at playing a waiting game for my victims. It was one that I always won.

A few moments later, a woman's face appeared, barely illuminated by the soft lamplight. Shadows danced across the planes of her face before they moved away, almost as if they were assessing her, or at least the threat she posed, before deciding she was safe. My breath caught. It was as if Dex was here, but he wasn't; I'd feel him.

The woman peered around my little corner of the library.

"H-Hello?" she said, her voice barely more than a whisper.

I remained quiet, watching as the young woman approached the table, peering closely at the tomes.

"Netherworld legends and tall tales," she murmured, her small hand brushing the faded gold lettering.

My nose twitched as she stepped closer to my hiding place. She smelled...wrong. The sweet, sickly smell of death lingered in her wake, but another scent hovered beneath it. One that was familiar, only I couldn't place it.

Did she have some kind of disease? She was so pale; her skin was almost translucent, and the whites of her eyes were yellowed. She was terribly thin, more so than me, and I'd not had a good meal for years. Her silk robe hung loosely on her frame, the belt tied around a tiny waist. I blinked. There was such an air of sadness about her that it made my chest ache.

"Hello?" she called again a little louder, though her voice shook. It could be from fear or just that she was so weak. My heart went out to her. She looked so frail. I'd never considered myself kind; my life didn't allow for it. But I couldn't deny I wanted to sit her down before she fell and ask her if she was alright.

How often did she wander around the huge castle library at night? It was a creepy place, full of ancient information and an almost sentient atmosphere as if the books were filling the space with energy and warning us that they'd protect themselves at all costs. Then again,

Hentus had always said nothing was more powerful than knowledge and information.

Shadows curled closer, holding me in a careful embrace. It was hard to ignore the pang of longing in my chest. I wanted to see Dex, to find out why he'd become so remote that afternoon; it was like a switch had flipped, and he'd just closed off. I understood he wanted me to be able to feed, but surely he understood that taking another's soul and leaving it to wander lost and confused was too damned much, even for me. I'd throw those beings back into the Veil to save mortal lives but not drain them from a purely selfish need to feed.

I rubbed my arms and brushed thoughts of his gorgeous face from my mind. If he was angry that I wouldn't feed from another being, that was on him, not me. Right now, I needed to find out who this woman was. She wasn't staff, that was for sure. Her night clothes were far too expensive.

"Hello," I echoed, stepping from the darkness.

"Ah!" the woman screeched.

I grinned. Maybe Dex was rubbing off on me a little too much. Making someone jump almost out of their skin was something he'd do.

I put my hands up, palms out, my smile still in place. The woman had no weapons and looked more likely to damage herself than hurt me if she tried to attack. That sickly sweet odour persisted, yet I kept the distaste off my face, instinct telling me she didn't talk to many people.

"Sorry, I didn't mean to startle you. I honestly didn't think anyone else would visit here at this time of night."

She shrugged. "They don't—usually. That's why I come here."

Silence fell for a few uncomfortable moments.

I smiled. "Well, why don't you sit with me for a while? It feels creepy in this big space when you're alone." I wasn't bothered by the silence in the library, but I was trying to put her at ease.

The light caught her face, showing me how young she was, late teens, early twenties at best. The air of pain and desperation around her pushed against my magic. Her gaze darted to the library door, but she didn't run. Instead, she crossed her arms over her chest and stared warily at me then nodded and sat down.

I smiled encouragingly and sat across the table from her. "My name's Zahlia, what's yours?"

"Marianna," she whispered as though she shouldn't even give me that.

I kept my smile gentle and my voice calm in case she got spooked and ran. Whatever it was she feared, it didn't seem to be the darkness and shadows of the library or the solitude it offered. Instinct told me it was something far more tangible.

"It's nice to meet you." I leaned forward a little and lowered my voice, even though no one else was in the library. "Are you okay? Are you hiding from someone?"

She tensed and dropped eye contact, looking instead at the embossed cover of the folklore tome.

"I've always loved books. When I was younger, they were my everything. My papa always kept me locked in the confines of our… house. He said it was to protect me, yet I was always lonely. Only my uncle ever spent time with me, and he often found me in the library." Her expression turned wistful. "Books made the world beyond my home look exciting and beautiful."

I had no idea who Marianna was, but I wasn't about to stop her from talking. If she wanted to share her innermost thoughts with me, then I'd listen. I'd heard that it sometimes helped to share your problems with a stranger, where there was no judgement, only an ear to listen. I could do that for this sickly woman, who appeared not much more than a girl yet looked like she carried the weight of the world on her shoulders.

"Oh? Did your uncle like to read, too?"

She smiled, albeit sadly. It softened her too-thin face, though. She must have cared for him very much. "Not really. He was a warrior. Feared and respected. But when he returned from the army camps he'd always come and find me to make sure I was okay…" Her words drifted off, her gaze filling with sorrow.

"Do you still see him?"

Her fingers plucked at the silk belt of her robe, her eyes downcast, her shoulders slumped. "No. My father was killed by my brother, and my whole life changed. I haven't seen my uncle since then." She twiddled the material harder and glanced up at me, biting her upper lip as if deciding whether or not to trust me.

I gave her an encouraging smile.

"My father was King Alaman of Pa'dur."

My eyes widened. "You're a princess? Wait. So, what are you doing in Tetris? Did you have to run away?"

"No, I-I didn't have a chance. I thought maybe my uncle would return and save me, save us all. My brother is a cruel man. He hates anyone who has more power than him. He especially hated the power my uncle Hentasian had. He sent men after my uncle at the same time that he killed my father. Uncle Hentus never came home. I think my brother killed him, too," she whispered.

"Hentus?" I murmured, my heart skipping a beat. "Um, what does, I mean, what did your uncle look like?"

She smiled, her eyes softening. "A big man, huge, with arms like tree trunks. At least, it seemed that way to me when I was young. Maybe he wasn't really that big, but people always seemed scared of him. Except me, I always felt safe when he was around." Tears glinted in her eyes, and she huffed a bitter laugh. "I used to dream that I'd marry a prince as strong as my uncle and become a queen who loved and was loved back by her people. I should have listened to Uncle Hentus when he told me dreams like that were destructive, that I'd soon find out what the real world was like, that it was dangerous and cruel. And I did. Only I never thought it would be my brother who taught me that lesson."

I held my tongue. I could have told her at six years old that life was cruel, that it was about survival by whatever means necessary, including pain and violence when needed.

"So this castle isn't your home?" I asked gently.

She gave a small bitter laugh. "No, it isn't. It could have been, but not any more." She met my eyes. "I'm dying, you see."

It wasn't a surprise, but my heart still went out to her. "What's wrong?"

She shrugged her bony shoulders. "No one knows. Not even my

husband's physicians. Escalon tries his best to help me." She flushed a little. "My uncle was wrong in that respect. I found my prince. He loves me dearly, and I worry that he neglects his people to be by my side. At the same time, he is quite overbearing. He wants to protect me from...everything." She peered across the table at me, shrugging and giving me a weak smile. "That's why I walk through the castle at night. Some nights I come here. Sometimes, I go outside in the darkness. There's a beautiful rose garden that is hidden behind a wall. The guards can't see into it. It's my escape while my husband sleeps. I just need some time alone. If he isn't by my side, his brother or one of their guards is. I know they don't mean it, but I feel more of a prisoner now than I did with my brother. Escalon is influenced by Haruin, you see. It was Haruin who said it was best I stay out of the public eye, or the people would see how weak I am, and it could cause unrest." Her words dried up, and her breath hitched.

It was hard to come up with words when I was still trying to wrap my mind around the fact that this was the young queen everyone spoke about. Too young, even for an arranged marriage, they'd said. Just a girl. Too fragile. Not strong enough to birth an heir. Mad. A magicker whose own people cast her out after the new king of Pa'dur had renounced magic; and so many other derogatory comments, I'd given up listening to the tittle-tattle of those voices. The politics of the neighbouring kingdoms, or even my own, had never interested me, only fighting to keep myself and others alive. Maybe some of those things were right. She *was* dying; I could smell it on her. But, no question, she wasn't mad. I wondered how she felt so kindly towards her husband and brother-in-law when they hated magickers. Maybe she didn't have magic of her own. That rumour could be a lie. There was also that familiar odour clinging to her. I couldn't place it, but it lingered under the ominous smell of death. I contemplated her as she sat, twisting her hands together. It was unlike me to care about a stranger, but lately I'd found myself thinking more and more about those who touched my life.

"You won't tell anyone, will you—about meeting me? They'd lock the doors to my room at night, too. I'd never get out. I..."

Pushing to my feet, I walked around the table and squatted in front of her, placing my hand over hers. Her panicked words ceased.

I met her gaze. "I honestly won't. Your secret is safe with me." I contemplated her, biting the skin of my upper lip. Should I say anything about Hentus? I could be wrong about my suspicions of him being her uncle. After all, the timeline was wrong.Then again, I'd learnt that nothing was ever as it seemed.

"So, what are you looking for?" Marianne asked, her eyes drifting to the books and sparking with interest.

It was nice to see some of her anxiety melt away. I had very few friends, and it seemed Dala would be fighting by Omeron's side every night. It would be nice to have another person to bounce ideas off. Could I trust her? She was married to one of the magic-hating princes, after all. Yet I didn't sense any malice in her, and it would be nice to have company. Maybe trusting Marianne would be good for us both.

"I'm looking for information about the Aether—the Veil."

Her eyes widened. I understood. The Aether was revered as the beginning and end of all life in this world; to try and unravel the mystery of it was thought sacrilegious, even though it was dying.

She swallowed. "Am I allowed to ask why?"

I smiled. "You are. But just as you're trusting me, I'm trusting you. Your husband and prince Haruin can never know about me visiting this library or what I'm looking for."

Marianne's eyes narrowed. She might be ill, but she wasn't stupid.

"You're the magicker I've heard people talking about. The one working with the General to find out who those creatures from the Nether are searching for."

There was no question in her words. I nodded. "I am." I almost expected her to run screaming from the room. Her husband hated magickers, and she'd been portrayed as a girl who was timid at best. I wondered at his devotion to her if the rumours of her having magic were true.

She gave me a rueful smile. "Don't worry. I'm not frightened of you. My father revered the magickers in our kingdom. They were rare and becoming rarer. He used to encourage them to make themselves known to him so that records could be kept of their gifts. He always paid them well when the crown required their help. My brother changed all that. Ultimately, the records my father kept got those poor people killed. I had magic once, too. It's why my brother locked me away." Her face fell. "Since I've been sick, my magic has all but gone."

I tilted my head and studied her."I'm sorry, Marianne. Or should I address you as my queen?"

"Mari," she said without hesitation, which relaxed me. My question had been a test of sorts. If she was so self-absorbed as to insist on a title when we were alone, then in my mind, I couldn't trust her.

"I'm no one's queen, not really. There's no point in pretending I am. I'm here in this world for a limited time, and I know it." She shrugged, a small smile curling her lips. "All of my life, men have told me what I can do, how to behave, where I'm allowed to go, who to talk to, so working with you is my choice. I hope we can become friends for the time I have left."

A kernel of warmth spread in my chest. No one had ever accepted me so readily. "I hope so, too."

"Good, so what am I helping you with?" She looked almost excited as she eyed the tome that sat between us on the table.

I grinned. "You're helping me discover how to find a way into the Netherworld." I wouldn't expose Dex's magic, not even to Mari. He had a false warrior caste mark, and the royals thought him a descendant of an old warrior caste. The man he'd copied it from had died and had no family, so using his name and history was safe.

I wondered how Mari had gotten to the library without being followed or seen. I'd used the shadows in the traditional fashion until it came to getting through the guarded door from the General's quarters into the castle. I'd jumped on the Aether just briefly. Enough to get through the particles of the door, but I didn't stay there. The risk of someone sensing my energy trail was too great.

"Will you tell me why you want to get into the Nether? Isn't that where all those hideous monsters that are killing people come from?" Goosebumps rose on her exposed skin.

"It is. If I can find a way to fix the Veil, maybe I can stop so many from dying. Something tells me it needs to be fixed from that side." I shrugged, knowing full well it did. "But I need to find a way into the Netherworld first. "

Mari contemplated me for a moment, then pulled a book towards herself, a determined tilt to her chin. "Well, we'd better get researching then."

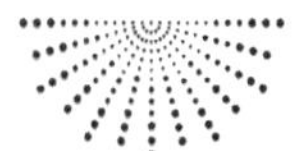

ex

Squaring my shoulders, I took the stairs two at a time. My shadows were weak, fatigue tugged at me, and the simmering worry I'd held all night had me itching to get to Lia.

I'd spent hours after leaving her last night going through paperwork before finally giving up. Concentration was impossible with all the frustration and concern for Lia eating at me. Commanding obedience, ruling through respect and sometimes fear, was what I was used to. I'd become Alpha and King of the darkest kingdom in the Nether when I'd killed the Alpha of the Barg, though I hadn't known it until I'd awoken from my injuries after my mother had died. Boy or not, I suddenly had power and more responsibility than I'd ever known existed.

I'd made Wraith, Omeron's father, and the Beta of the pack, the Lord of Haldaag and my right hand. When Omeron was born, I'd watched him grow into the kingdom's best warrior and strongest shifter. Omeron and I had trained together, and when he was a teenager, he'd pledged his loyalty and life as my personal guard. I gladly accepted.

I wasn't used to anyone refusing my orders, especially not Lia. She'd always listened to me and done as I'd said. Part of me loved her defiance; it excited me that she wasn't afraid to challenge me, but part of me was furious. Her magic would be her downfall. As soon as she set foot back in the Nether, the Heart would drain her of it—unless she agreed to our bond. My nostrils flared as I inhaled sharply, then blew air out through pursed lips. The chances of that happening were low once she knew everything about me .

I'd just have to persuade her. Or come up with another way to protect her—until she admitted we were meant to be together.

When I'd found her gone last night, fear had turned my blood to ice, panic slamming through me. Jumping on the shadows had taken seconds. If she'd run, she'd go straight to her friends. Lia might think herself tough and uncaring, but she wasn't, not at all. Her makeshift family was everything, and if hurt or upset, she'd head right back to them. They were one of the reasons she hadn't left the city behind. Even though she denied it, that was the truth.

From the shadows, I'd watched Hentus sitting around a table with Angus and Edge, but no Lia. Wondering if she'd run to find her friend, I'd materialised near Omeron, who fought next to Dala.

An insidious, heavy feeling ate at my heart. Lia missed Dala more than she'd ever admit, and relied on her for support. That thought bothered me. I'd kept them apart for selfish reasons; I'd wanted her to rely on only me as she once had, but it was clear I'd destroyed that trust a long time ago. Swallowing the bitter taste in my mouth, I suddenly knew where she was. Finding a solution to the question I'd refused to answer.

The library had been as eerie as only those spaces could be. I'd hidden among my shadows before searching for Lia, relaxing when they reassured me she was safe and well. The guards I'd drifted past were none the wiser to her having left my house. Nor were they aware of the young woman who sat with her. My shadows assured me she was no threat, so I stayed hidden.

Learning that this was the young queen Escalon protected to the point of madness made sense. She was delicate...and dying. I wondered how she'd got into the library unseen. Still, it didn't really matter. There were many secret passages in the castle, and I had no desire to stop what little freedom she'd found. I could imagine Escalon's obsession was suffocating. Besides, it was gratifying to see Lia make a new friend. I wasn't about to stop her, not when I'd kept her apart from everyone else who meant something to her.

I stretched my neck trying to loosen my tight muscles. I needed to do better. Trust was earned, and I was beginning to realise no matter how much control I was used to, Lia was too wild to keep contained. Keeping her separated from those she loved wouldn't earn me her respect—only her resentment. I had to give her my respect and trust if I wanted it in return. Leaving her to research her true home was one way to start, though I would show her much more than these books could once I was able. For now, I'd give her privacy.

It was hard to tear myself away from my Angel, especially when she was with a stranger, no matter that my shadows sensed the young queen was no threat.

I'd been unable to settle. Instead, I'd tried to work all night until my self-restraint had snapped. My long strides ate up the distance from the top of the stairs to Lia's door. I smirked, anticipating her grumpy yet endearing wrath. I didn't bother to knock. Courting her irritation and sass lit a fire in me that I was coming to crave. I loved her spirit. Since she'd come back into my life as a living, breathing flame, I'd been like a moth; I couldn't stay away.

She didn't even twitch as I entered her room. My heart clenched, and desire flowed through my blood. Her naked body was wrapped in the sheet, giving me a tantalising view of the smooth skin of her back and the long length of her legs, her silver hair cascading across the pillow.

I bit back a groan and fisted my hands. Every instinct in me urged me to touch her, to lower myself onto the bed and explore her body with my tongue, my teeth, my hands...

My gaze narrowed as she stirred. I could be her enemy, a demon sent to harm her or take her away, and she had no clue I was there. Breathing slowly through my nostrils to calm myself, I stalked to the bed. As I did, she lifted her head, her eyes snapping open. Her brow furrowed.

My gaze lowered to the alluring swell of her breasts.

"Dex? What the fuck? What are you doing in my room? Knock first, you arrogant bastard!"

Her snark fired my lust and my anger. "What would you do if I was one of the Demon King's warriors? Hm?" I gestured to her naked form. "They'd take you before you even knew they were here. Lock your damned door, Lia!"

I was being irrational, and I knew it, but I couldn't stop. The castle was safe—to a point. But Baladon was powerful enough to raze this place if he found a way into this world.

Her gaze narrowed, and in the blink of an eye, she stood naked in front of me with a blade pressed to my throat; not hard enough to cut my windpipe, but enough to cause rivulets of blood to course down my neck. I grabbed her loose hair, twisting it into a rope and yanking her head back.

Desire slammed through me, making me hard enough that I ached, my erection pressing against the confines of my trousers. "You think cutting my throat will stop me? You know better than that, sweetness."

"I'm not fucking sweet," she purred back, using the doubled-bladed scythe she held in her other hand to slash at my side. My blood roared at her fierceness. She'd kept her weapons close. Thank the Higher Powers. Anger was replaced with a burning need. She'd not hesitate to kill if needed, but she wouldn't kill me, even if she could. Her cheeks were flushed, and she was breathing as hard as me. I wrapped my shadows around her weapons, pulling them from her grasp and sending them skittering across the room.

I grinned. "No, you're not. You're like the flames of a fire, bright and beautiful and deadly to anyone who gets too close. Anyone but me." I slammed my mouth down on hers in a brutal and consuming kiss. Our teeth clashed as I held her to me, our tongues duelling. She bit my lower lip, and I couldn't stop a groan from escaping. That meagre sting of pain lit a fuse, and even if she hadn't been gripping my hair and holding me to her, I wasn't going anywhere. This had been building between us since I'd seen her fighting so fiercely on the docks. In all the years I was away, my need for her had never faded, only grown.

"I need to be inside you, Lia."

My balls tightened, my heart slamming against my ribs at her answering moan. I slipped my hands down the silky skin of her back and palmed her round buttocks, lifting her. Swearing at the heat of her centre pressing on my stomach, I walked to the bed, lowering her down without breaking our kiss. I was desperate to have her, to show her what she meant to me. She might not understand it yet, but she would. I'd make sure of it. I'd show her everything.

I blocked out the guilt of my duplicity and trailed my tongue over her lips, using my lips and teeth to drive her wild. Her moans and whimpers urged me on. Trailing kisses along her jaw and down her throat, I swirled my tongue around one rosy nipple before sucking the hard nub into my mouth, teasing and biting until she breathed my name. My heart squeezed. I wanted to hear more. I wanted her begging for my touch, for release. Gently, I blew over her damp skin, and she whimpered, her eyes meeting mine.

Wrapping her fingers in my shirt, she tugged hard. "Get this off, now."

I raised my brows at her demand, but she snarled, light flashing in her eyes. I sent my shadows to wrap around her wrists.

"No, Angel, not yet. If my skin touches yours, I'll lose control, and I want you screaming with pleasure; I want you wet and ready to take me before I undress."

Her breathing hitched, and I sat back, studying her face. Her eyes were dark and stormy, her lips, swollen from our kisses, open in anticipation. I wound the other end of my shadow around the head of the bed, stretching her arms high.

Her nipples puckered under my gaze, and she writhed as I ran my fingers teasingly from neck to navel and lower.

"Open your legs."

She did, mewling when I trailed a fingertip through the dampness that waited there. She gasped as I slid a finger inside her. Tight, silky, enticing...

"Fuck," I whispered, gritting my teeth. I was so hard, it was painful.

I added another finger, and her hips undulated, her internal muscles trying to suck me in harder and faster.

"So ready for me," I murmured, giving her what she wanted, pumping my fingers against her movements until she was gasping.

"Need you," she panted. Her gaze met mine. "Please..."

My control nearly snapped at that yearning plea, but I wanted her begging for release, to explode with pleasure, and to *know* that she wanted me as much as I wanted her...

I lowered myself onto my stomach, lying between her legs, and kissed up her warm thigh, stopping at her apex, where her sweet scent drove me to the edge of my control. Her body trembled, her movements desperate. I gave the other silky thigh as much attention, trailing open-mouthed kisses towards her soft folds before slowly swiping my tongue through her slick flesh. I groaned, unable to hold back as her taste filled my mouth and rolled down my throat.

I was lost. Completely enraptured. At that moment, nothing else existed except her. I kept my fingers moving, perhaps too hard, too desperate, but she encouraged me, rolling her hips in time to my plunging fingers. I curled them forward and rubbed just as I sucked the bundle of nerves at her apex between my teeth, still flicking it with the tip of my tongue.

"Dex, Dex. Please...I...oh, shit..."

She screamed and exploded, her internal muscles gripping my fingers and pulsing hard. her juices coating my hand. Gods, I needed her, but holding her gaze, I carefully withdrew my fingers.

Keeping her restrained with my shadow, I stood. My nostrils flared as she writhed, watching me, her face flushed. With a snarl, she opened her legs, challenge in her lust-filled eyes.

"Aether, you look beautiful, tied to that bed by my shadows, demanding I fuck you."

I pulled off my clothes. Within moments, I was naked. With hooded eyes, she raked her gaze over me, making my skin itch. I was on fire with need, but I let her look at my body, allowing her to drink her fill. When her gaze met mine again, I moved between her legs.

I lowered myself until I covered her body, goosebumps rolling across my skin at the contact. Her magic seeped out of her control, mixing with my shadows. I groaned but held back my hips even as she arched to reach me. Releasing her hands from my shadows, I entwined our fingers, my heart thudding against my ribs. I lifted enough to look down at her curves, my gaze snagging where my hardness reached for her softness. I pushed the tip in, gritting my teeth against my need to ram into her, to make her mine again. I teased her with shallow strokes until she was bucking her hips up.

"Stop making me wait. Fuck me, you bastard…" Her eyes flashed with magic, sending a fresh wave of need roaring through me. My control snapped, and I plunged forward. In one single hard thrust, I was seated inside her. She was slick and tight and felt so fucking good my head swam.

"Goddess…" I whispered, completely overwhelmed.

"Dex…" She moaned at the same time.

It took every bit of control that I had, but I held still, allowing her time to adjust to my size.

She fought my hold on her hands, so I released her, craving her touch. Her fingernails raked down my back. The sting only made me more feral, my baser side fighting to be released.

"Move," she demanded, rolling her hips against me. "Don't you fucking dare hold back. I'm not a virgin this time."

I grinned. "No, you're not. That gift was mine, and mine alone."

As arrogant as some might consider it, satisfaction slammed through me. She'd had one lover since me, but that piece of shit didn't count. She was never his, only ever mine. Nothing would keep me from her again. I'd never again willingly leave her.

I pulled my hips back and slammed forward. Her gratified sounds were music to my ears.

"That's it, Angel. Let me hear every single sound from that beautiful mouth, every moan and whimper. They're all mine and only mine."

"Gods, that's so…hot."

I slammed against her. "Glad you think so. Because I mean every word of it."

Every cell in my body ached for more: more connection, more pleasure, more of everything that was her.

She arched into me, her fingers gripping my hips, urging me to go harder, faster. I lifted my body and rammed home, over and over. My warrior goddess met me thrust for thrust, demanding more. Neither of us wanted soft. This connection between us was too wild and burned too hot for that.

With each drive into her slick heat, I watched her face. "You're mine, Zahlia. And I'm yours. I always will be."

Her eyes widened at my admission, and a look of awe crossed her stunning face before her eyes rolled back in her head.

"Look at me. I want to see it in your eyes when you fall apart." I changed my angle, hitting that perfect spot inside her. "I want you to see what you do to me, too."

"Oh gods..." she whimpered, her eyes huge, her skin flushed and shining with sweat.

"That's it," I encouraged, working my hips faster and faster, my balls tightening and tingles running up my spine. "Let go, Angel," I commanded, desperately holding on to that edge of pleasure before I fell.

Her eyes rolled. "Dex!" she cried, her muscles clamping down on me, milking me. It was too much. Her spasms triggered my climax, and I rammed home as wave after wave of pleasure erupted through me. I roared, my heart utterly lost, and deep in my soul, I knew I could never let her go.

CHAPTER TWENTY

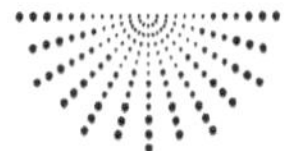

ia

I smirked, enjoying the way the leather of Dex's armour moved with his body. He was a sight to behold, from his broad shoulders to his perfect arse and thick thighs. And I enjoyed every minute of it.

"So I thought, if you wanted, Dala could move in with you. If that's what you want." He stopped and looked over his shoulder, an amused look on his too-handsome face.

"Um…what?" I asked vaguely, not registering his words, not when I was busy remembering what that leather-clad body had done to mine. Heat swelled between my legs, and I flushed.

Dex's smirk only made my situation worse. It didn't matter that I was still mad at him for his evasiveness and mood last night; I wanted him…badly. I'd waited so long to feel his body against mine—in mine —again that I couldn't think about much else. Did that make me pathetic after all he'd done? Probably, but not even my suspicions that he still wasn't telling the truth, or at least not all of it, mattered. It was as if my soul was linked to his, and the thought of leaving him physically hurt.

Dex touched my cheek. "What just put that look on your face?"

I pulled back a bit. "Nothing." My denial was empty, and we both knew it.

His smile turned sly. He stepped forward, his body crowding mine, and he walked into me, forcing me backwards until the wall stopped my progress. I could have pushed back, but I didn't want to. His hands slapped against the rough walls of the tunnel, either side of my head.

"That's not true. But it's okay, Angel. You'll tell me when you're ready. Until then, I need to give you something else to think about." He smiled right before he slanted his mouth over mine, kissing me until my head spun. My fingers grasped those leather-clad hips, digging in and pulling him against me. When he came up for air, we were both breathless. He leaned his forehead against mine and grinned.

"You test my self-control so much. Do you know that?"

I gave a sassy shrug, pretending he didn't do the same to me.

"I try." I leaned up and pecked him on the lips while palming the bulge in his trousers. "But don't we have a gateway to find?" Dipping under his large arm, I swayed my hips, walking further into the tunnel he'd led me down. I bit my lip to hold my grin when he cursed. His footsteps were hurried, only slowing when he caught up with me.

"Which way?" I asked when the passageway split into two.

He stepped close enough that his body heat seeped into me. "That way is to the ocean." He inhaled. "Can you smell the salt?" He didn't mention the stench of death that floated on the breeze.

"Yes."

"I think this one leads to the dungeons."

It didn't escape my notice that he offered no comment on the stink of unwashed bodies, urine, and fear that came from that one. I shuddered, my stomach churning. Had I really forgotten that the man I shared my bed and body with, who was such a passionate and considerate lover, had locked away hundreds of magickers in a bid to hide his secret; a secret I'd kept for him last night when I'd sat for hours with the sickly queen.

Tension simmered between us, and I refused to look at him. I couldn't. For a while, I'd forgotten about his part in the genocide of mortal magickers. He wasn't even mortal, so what gave him the right to be judge and executioner? He was appeasing the princes only because he needed to be in this castle to find a way home, for him—and me. I swallowed hard. Their plight was partly my fault.

"This is the one we need to explore." His words were tight.

I watched as he stalked away down the third tunnel. Was I seriously going to help him rather than run down that other tunnel and set those poor people free? The need to help them was almost overwhelming.

"You can't help them, Lia. Their fate is already sealed. If you try, you'll make yourself a target for the princes. They'll figure out you're the one they seek, and every mage hound in this kingdom will be sent to hunt you down."

Hating that he was right, I followed him. We walked deeper and deeper into the rock, the tunnel winding down into the earth. It was so cold my fingers went numb, but at least it was dry. Dex could see in the dark, but I couldn't. My magic felt weak, but Dex had warned me it would. There was still enough for a spark to light the torch I'd brought with me. I held it high, its light making the shadows dance. At one point, I stumbled, sure I'd seen the appearance of wings and horns among those flickering shapes. A moment later, it was gone.

Dex reached back, his palm landing on my stomach and halting my progress. "Can you feel that?"

I rubbed my arms. Despite wearing a leather jacket, thick leather trousers, and boots, goosebumps erupted over my skin. There was a charged energy in the air, something that tugged at the magic locked inside me, drawing it away.

"Y-yes," I whispered, unwilling to tell him I suddenly felt far weaker, even light-headed.

"Extinguish your torch," he commanded in a whisper.

Stealthy and light-footed for a man his size, he crept forward into the darkness.

I followed though I couldn't see much with the lights extinguished. Yet, it wasn't necessary to see to *feel* the malevolence in the air. It was like a heavy blanket, making it difficult to breathe. My heart pounded, and my palms were slick with sweat. I was…scared. Gods, I couldn't remember the last time I'd felt fear like this. Before I could stop myself, my fingers clawed at Dex's back, grabbing the little amount of give in his leather armour. His double-headed axe sat squarely between his shoulder blades. I could see its shadow in the minuscule light glowing further down the tunnel.

My fingers tightened. He was my anchor here in the darkness. I used the feel of his muscles shifting against my fingers to ground myself and concentrated on keeping my feet moving and my legs from collapsing.

He stopped, reached around, and touched my grasping fingers. "We've found it. The gate I've been searching for all these years. It's here, right under this castle all this time, just like I thought."

I released his jacket and gripped his fingers, just for a moment, before pulling back. This wasn't me. I was stronger than this.

"It's okay, Angel, that fear is an enchantment. Its whole purpose is to send people running from the gate." He pulled his axe, the blade glinting in the strange bluish light. He moved forward with stealthy footsteps until we were at the end of the tunnel. He indicated I should stand on the other side.

With my back against the rock, I took a deep breath and glanced at Dex. The light illuminated the gorgeous planes of his face, distracting me from any residual fear. My breath stuttered. Being with him again had been my fantasy for so long. Now he was back, and I had no idea where that left me, especially knowing he was involved in killing innocent magickers.

He gave me a sexy little smile. "I don't know what's going through that beautiful mind of yours, but head in the game, Lia. If anything comes through that gate, you need to run. You hear me? You are their purpose, so if they sense you, they will not stop. I'll fight for as long as I can, but neither of us has our magic at full strength down here. If they catch you, you'll be dragged back to the Nether and taken to their King."

We peered around the rock into what looked like a cavern. Weak light illuminated the space, casting dancing shadows over the walls and ceiling. Dex smiled as he called those shadows to him and whispered in a language I didn't understand.

His green eyes pierced mine. "You stay here. And remember what I said, if demons break through, you run. Fast. You hear me? No heroics. Too much depends on you. If I'd known for sure it was an active gate, I'd have made you stay behind."

I snorted. "Made me stay behind. As if."

He glared right back. "If it keeps you safe, I'll tie you to your gods-damned bed. Don't think I won't."

It might be wrong that his threat made me hot while we were so close to danger, but I couldn't deny my reaction. Besides, I wasn't about to admit it to him. "Like to see you try," I hissed.

He grinned and winked. "Deal." That levity disappeared quickly, though. "Seriously, Lia, if they're already using this gate, don't stay and fight—run."

I gave a reluctant nod. If this turned to shit, I'd have no choice; my magic had never felt weaker.

Dex stepped into the cavern. Ignoring his order to stay back I followed. He shook his head but didn't say anything. Pausing, he inhaled sharply and studied the ground. Runes were etched into the rock under our feet.

"That's why my magic was suppressed. Those runes blocked it. Now that I've stepped over the threshold, my magic is back." He grinned and pulled the darkness into him.

I blinked. He looked so powerful. In comparison, my magic seemed to be getting weaker. Beads of sweat rolled down my temples.

He caught me under my arms as I stumbled. "You're weak. Shit. Why didn't you tell me? Either the Heart or the dark side of the Veil is draining you. It's pulling your magic through the gate." He cursed, his attention flickering to the glow of light that arched in the air. I couldn't see anything beyond that glow. He sheathed his weapon. "This is what I feared; the darkness is consuming your light. You're connected to the light side of the Veil, and the dark side can sense that —so can the Heart. It's feeding on you. Come on." He swung me into his arms and strode away from the cavern. "We're leaving. I'll come back alone."

"No." I didn't want him to go through the gate alone. "What if the King's waiting for you on the other side?"

He snarled and pulled me close. "Then he'll die. For now, we are leaving. I won't put you at risk." His lips brushed my forehead, his eyes glinting in the darkness. "You're too precious."

My breath caught at the conviction in his words. Shaking and weaker than I'd ever felt, I rested my head on his shoulder, but I knew I was a burden to carry through the darkness. I patted his shoulder. "Put me down. I can walk."

He ignored me.

"Dex, put me down," I insisted.

"No." His jaw was set at a stubborn angle, and though part of me hated appearing weak like this, another part wanted to stay exactly where I was, safe and warm in his arms.

"I can walk..." I repeated.

"No, you can't. Stop trying to bullshit me, Lia. I can feel how weak you are. I'll get us back to the castle, and then you feed—on me."

I swallowed at the deep wave of need that ran through me. Feeding from him had been erotic, and coupled with thoughts of his naked body thrusting against mine only hours ago, I couldn't wait to get back. I *was* starving, but not for food. For him. It was as though he'd become my sustenance, and I didn't need anything else.

He remained silent as we passed the intersection of the tunnels and headed back up to the surface. He took the steep steps with an ease that belied how many there were. I kept my attention on his face, loving the excuse to drink him in.

"If you keep looking at me like that, we won't make it back to the castle before I make you feed on me..."

Unable to resist, I levered myself up and trailed my nose up the column of his neck, inhaling the scent of man, sweat, leather and something uniquely him. That deep midnight scent that always sent my mind reeling.

"Dex..." I whispered his name, my insides clenching with hunger and raging lust. I squirmed in his arms. I had no idea what was happening to me, only that I needed him so badly I would surely die if he didn't give me what I craved. I kissed his jaw, fighting against his hold until I'd managed to move so my legs were wrapped around his waist, and I could drag my lips over his skin and fill my mouth with his taste.

"Fuck, Lia, what are you doing to me?"

I had no idea what had put that breathless and desperate sound in his voice, but I loved it. I slammed my mouth over his and kissed him, devoured him like he'd devoured me. Our tongues duelled, our teeth clashed, and I rocked my pelvis against his rock-hard abs. My magic writhed, pulling his shadow closer.

I was vaguely aware of my back hitting the rock wall of the steps as he twisted us. He pushed his weight against me, and I gripped his soft hair, holding him in place. I was crazy with need.

"Fuck me, right now, demon," I demanded, knowing nothing else would do. I didn't care that we were in a stairwell or that it was dusty and covered in cobwebs. I pulled harder at his shadows. An urgent growl escaped him, making me clench my thighs tighter, driving me crazy as I worked my moist centre against him.

It wasn't enough.

Frustration made me grip harder onto his hair and pull his head back. His eyes glinted red for a split second, and then it was gone, replaced with deep-glowing jade and huge black pupils that seemed to see right into my soul.

"More," I demanded.

A smug smile curled his lips, and he pulled me off the wall; this time, his shadows wrapped around my hands, yanking them from his hair and binding them around his neck.

"Careful what you demand, Angel."

I smirked right back, my apex slick with need. "Why?"

"Because I'm about to give it to you."

"Good." I undulated against him until I found my hips locked still. I screeched with frustration.

"I'll give you what you crave, sweetheart, but you must feed first." He met my eyes. "Take your fill of my magic, Angel."

I glared at him, my nostrils flaring. I had no idea what had come over me. All I knew was I needed him like I needed my next breath, and I'd do anything to get him. I wound my magic through his with an urgency that made me snarl. And I fed, pulling more and more energy from him.

He rumbled low in his throat. "I'm getting us back to your room. Keep feeding."

I didn't even acknowledge him since there was no way I was stopping.

His breathing came in deep pants, and by the time he hit the top step, we were kissing desperately. He kicked the hidden door to my room open, pushed the tapestry to the side with his magic, and strode in, throwing me down on the bed. Before I'd finished bouncing, he had my boots off and my waist ties undone. He made short work of my weapons and yanked my leathers and underwear off.

Cold air caressed my skin right before his hot mouth descended. A cry wrenched from my throat as he dragged his tongue through my folds, stopping at my apex to tease that bundle of nerves. He licked and sucked, groaning like I was the best thing he'd ever tasted.

A hurricane of sensation hit me, and all I could do was hold on. I felt drunk from pulling on his magic; my skin was hot, and fire lit my insides, getting hotter and hotter the more he twirled his talented tongue. I whimpered and panted, but he didn't stop. He held down my writhing hips and feasted until I was begging.

"Dex, please..."

"Feed more," he rumbled before returning to his task.

I had no idea how to concentrate on that when I felt like I was going to explode out of my skin, but I didn't need to. My magic sought out his and gorged itself like he was gorging on me.

I cried out his name over and over, needing to undulate my hips. I fought his hold. He growled but released me, and I moved in a frantic rhythm. All he did was thrust his tongue inside me until I was a mindless mess of urgency.

With a satisfied growl, he replaced his tongue with his fingers, then returned his tongue to my bundle of nerves. My whole body spiralled tighter and tighter. With a scream, I detonated, my spine arching, pleasure locking up my body, and not releasing me from its hold. Sparks exploded behind my eyes, and I felt myself floating. I was totally at his mercy as he licked and swirled his tongue, ripped from reality as I trembled in the aftermath of that all-consuming ecstasy. Slowly, he brought me down from that post-orgasmic high. My limbs turned boneless, my hands resting in his hair as he kissed the inside of my thighs.

I whined when his weight disappeared. "I'm not going far, love," he reassured me.

I forced my eyes open at the sound of metal hitting the floor. He dropped his weapons, one after the other, and there were plenty. He unfastened his vambraces and metal shoulder protectors and ditched his leathers.

Higher Powers, he was the most stunning man I'd ever seen. Broad shoulders, heavily muscled pecs covered in rune tattoos, and dips and valleys across a washboard stomach that sent me into a spiral of lust again. But the intense look of desire in his eyes was what had me reaching for him.

"More."

He didn't speak, just fell over me, catching himself with his hands, his muscles popping impressively before he rocked his pelvis until the tip of his hard length slipped through my folds and found my entrance. With one hard thrust, he sheathed himself in me. In unison, we groaned.

I couldn't keep still, neither could he. His eyes locked onto mine. The look of awe and desire in them must have mirrored mine. I slammed my hips up, meeting him thrust for thrust.

"Fuck, Lia, what are you doing to me..." he murmured, looking almost pained.

I had no idea. But whatever drove this need between us was so intense it scared me. "More. I need more."

Muscles bunching, he flipped us until I was on top, my hands planted on his chest, my fingers gripping him.

"Use me; take what you need."

I did. I flung my head back, thrusting my breasts forward. He took the hint and massaged them roughly, twisting my nipples, which made me whimper as I worked my hips. Soon, it wasn't enough. I tipped my head down, my silver hair falling in a curtain around us. I held his stare as I lifted my hips and slammed down, impaling myself on his steel erection.

We soon found a wild rhythm. Sweat coated us both, our movements frantic.

"That's it, Angel, ride me. Take what you need."

I did, aware I was still absorbing his magic. More. More. I was starved. For him, his body, his magic; I wanted it all. That savage need wasn't something I could control. I just knew if I didn't feed, I'd die.

"Dex," I whispered in a confused yet pleasure-soaked plea. "I need more." It frightened me how much I was taking from him, yet I still felt empty.

Hooded green eyes met mine. He grabbed my hips and held me off him. My hands, flat on his hard chest, supported me as our gaze locked.

His face softened. "It's okay. I've got you. Don't fight it. Just let it happen." His voice turned reverent. "Fate chose us to be together."

I bit my bottom lip. I didn't understand what was happening but nodded, knowing he'd lead me through this, whatever *this* was.

He released me and watched, hungry and so fucking sexy, as I undulated on his steel shaft. His eyes dropped to where he disappeared inside me, and I watched his face as he watched me ride him.

"Damn, Lia, that's the sexiest thing I've ever seen," he growled, grabbing my hips and holding me in place. I didn't fight him, my muscles shaking, my breath seesawing in heavy pants.

"My turn," he snarled. And slammed up into me. Harder and harder, faster and faster, until all I could do was hold on. He pushed me further back, changing the angle so he hit every nerve ending inside me. My body responded immediately, tightening until I moaned at every thrust, chasing another release.

"Give me everything," he demanded, unrelenting in his thrusts until I exploded.

"Dex!" I cried, writhing on him, yanking his shadow inside my chest until I was senseless with pleasure. His rhythm stuttered, and he bellowed, throwing his head back against the pillows, his whole body locking up as spasm after spasm rocked him. Dex coming undone under me was the most amazing sight I'd ever seen. Tendons rose in his neck, and every muscle on his stunning warrior's body stood proud as his flesh pulsed inside me.

I held myself up with my hands on his pecs, locking my elbows as his grip on my hips fell away, and he relaxed, panting heavily, sweat shining on his skin.

My head lolled forward, exhaustion slamming through my every cell. I smiled as he lifted his head and opened his eyes. Blood-red irises glinted.

Horror froze my blood. I blinked rapidly, and they were green and full of softness. I slumped across his chest, and his arms went around me, holding me close. Had I imagined it? I didn't know, but my mind was sluggish, so probably.

That had just been the most intense experience of my life. I had no idea what made me so hungry, so desperate for him, but right then, I didn't care.

"That was…" I kissed the soft skin beneath his ear lobe and nuzzled his neck, inhaling him deeply. There were no words to describe how I felt at that moment. I just knew I didn't want to move.

A deep, exhausted chuckle rumbled from his chest. "It was," he agreed. His hand trailed up my spine, brushing my hair to the side before cupping the back of my head and holding my face into his neck. "Sleep, Angel. I'll make sure nothing harms you."

"'Kay." I wanted to ask what had happened, but my body had other ideas. With Dex still inside me, I drifted into a deep, dreamless sleep.

CHAPTER TWENTY-ONE

ex

My growl was long and low. Snow flurries swirled around Omeron and me, the soft flakes raising goosebumps over my naked chest and arms where they landed and melted. I felt the cold right down to my bones, but for once, I didn't give a shit. My fingers were numb, and my toes stung, but my mind was wrapped in what had happened with Lia. I was still reeling from it. It hadn't just been sex; it had been far more, solidifying the emotions that had been raging through me for years. I wanted to hear Lia's desperate moans as I pushed into her, to feel her magic dance with mine, to know I was the only one who could ease the insatiable hunger that had arisen to fuck and feed. But it was more than just a physical need. She had touched my heart, and it had thawed just a little. I found myself caring about her friends and wanting to please her by letting her spend time with them.

Shit.

I rubbed my face. I wanted her to be—happy. Because if she was happy, then so was I. And that was dangerous. The Demon King would be thrilled to know he could break me by taking her and pulling her apart piece by piece until he destroyed us both.

Omeron swiped his front paw. Gods, I was even too distracted to see his attack coming. Claws, hooked and lethal, sliced open my naked skin, splitting layers of muscle open. Blood oozed from the wounds, running down my chest and soaking into my waistband.

His snarl bared sharp and deadly fangs. Narrowed amber eyes homed in on my shaking hand, and I could see the question in them. He huffed, and in the blink of an eye, the armoured, scaled, four-legged beast with horns was gone. In its place stood my friend, utterly unbothered by his nakedness.

"What the fuck, Dex?" he hissed, rushing forward to help me as I stumbled.

"I'm fine."

"Fine? Aether's teeth, you're weaker than I've ever seen you. You need to feed…"

"No! Not tonight." The thought of taking in another being's energy made my stomach turn. I couldn't feed from Lia, not yet, possibly not for years, or maybe ever, but after what we'd shared, I couldn't face taking another's essence into my body. I laughed at myself. My father would have been disgusted to see his son, one of the most powerful demons in the Nether, reduced to an exhausted shadow of himself by a female. No doubt he would have had me beaten for my weakness.

"Why not?" Omeron questioned, his brow drawn.

I didn't blame him; he'd never seen me like this. And I never refused to feed before. Normally, I had no remorse. I wasn't a 'good' soul, not by mortal standards, and killing was in my nature.

I owed him an explanation. A truthful one.

I'd forced myself away from Lia over an hour ago when all I'd wanted was to stay wrapped around the softness of her body. I'd never invited a lover to share my bed. Sex had always been to fulfil a need. It was something I did because I could. It gave me an extra measure of control over my life, even over the women I fucked. But one thing sex didn't do was blow my mind with emotions or make my heart want to pound out of my chest with the need to be close to my partner.

Lia had stomped on my illusion of control. I'd been a slave to her demands. All I'd wanted was to give her everything she needed and more. I swallowed hard. I still did. And it scared me shitless. I'd never felt such intense emotions or connections before. Even leaving Lia years ago hadn't been as difficult as leaving her alone in her bed this morning.

She had been in a deep sleep when I'd carefully slipped out of bed. Her body kept luring me in, the urge to take her again making me shake. Still hard as rock, I'd dressed in my battle armour and walked away.

Omeron had just been returning to the castle with Dala when we'd passed in the courtyard. I hadn't even acknowledged them, having been too focused on controlling my overwhelming desire to go back to Lia.

Keeping a few feet distant, my beta had followed as I rode from the castle and out through the city gates. I'd needed to think, and he'd respected that. He'd echoed my movements, silently dismounted from his horse when I did and disrobed as I took off my armour and shirt. The cold had grounded me, as had the pain of his strikes.

Lia had almost drained me to unconsciousness after she'd demanded we go a third time, wrapping her power with mine until I'd followed my instincts and given her access to the part of my soul that held my power. She'd wound my magic through her soul, and immediately, a sense of rightness had sunk into my flesh and bones. I'd never experienced anything like it before.

Yet my angel had not stopped feeding even when she was sleeping. She'd consumed me almost to the point of insensibility, and I was helpless to stop her.

I sank to my backside in the snow, uncaring about the wetness seeping into my leathers. My wounds continued to bleed, not healing as usual.

"I'm just not…" I shook my head, unable to believe I was saying this: me—King of the Haldaag race. "I'm not…ready to take demon souls inside me." I closed my eyes. My anger that Lia had refused to feed on another's soul seemed cruel now that I found myself repulsed by it. I rubbed my face. She was right. I wasn't just a liar. I *was* a hypocrite, too.

"Not ready? What the fuck does that mean? You're a Shadow Demon! In hundreds of Heart cycles, I've never seen you like this. You have to feed!" Omeron snapped.

"No!" I snarled, panting hard enough my hot breath formed small clouds of air in the cold. With a conscious effort, I softened my voice. My friend was only worried about me, and I didn't blame him. He was right. I'd never been like this.

"Lia she..." I met his eyes. "Had a feeding frenzy...She bonded my magic to her."

"Oh, shit. And you survived?" Omeron's eyes widened incredulously.

I smirked and chuckled tiredly. "I did."

Omeron sank down beside me, utterly unconcerned with the ice meeting his naked skin. I envied his total resistance to such cold. Especially right then, when my buttocks were practically numb. My natural resistance to the cold had completely deserted me.

"How did you survive without accessing the Veil?"

I grinned but collapsed back in the snow. "I have no idea..." Snow fluttered down, landing on my stomach and melting. "Maybe her needs are weakened in this world, away from the Heart."

Omeron grunted. "Maybe. But your shadow is weaker, too. Or maybe you have more of a power reservoir than you realise, perhaps even greater than your father had?"

"Maybe," I mumbled, echoing him.

I might not have experienced a feeding frenzy before; not many demons ever had. But like all of my kind, I knew they existed. And not just that. My mother and father had been the only ones, for hundreds of Heart cycles, to survive it.

My mother had likened her sudden hunger for the power and body of one male to being starved of life itself. She said it had happened with no warning. It was as if her magic had been drained from her until she was as weak as a newborn, and she became ravenous. Once the Heart had sensed the Angel's magic was mature, that she had been at her zenith, it had started to feed, pulling sustenance from her. Only a Shadow Demon could help her replenish what the Heart had taken, feeding her from the dark side of the Veil as she took from the light. Once bonded to that Shadow Demon, she'd had to feed regularly for her magic to flourish. The cycle of life depended on the balance between the Heart, the Angel, and the Veil.

My father had fed my mother, and in turn, she had fed the Heart—until he had realised the power he would have over the whole of the Netherworld if he could control her. From all over the Nether kingdoms, demons bowed to him. They revered him as king because he demanded it—all except Haldaag. The Alpha I'd killed had refused to bow. The war for the border between the Aether kingdom and Haldaag was one of the oldest wars in the history of the Netherworld.

When my mother and I had escaped into their territory, the Alpha had seen it as an opportunity to end us and cause his enemy great pain. He didn't know my father would have killed us anyway.

I blinked snowflakes from my eyelashes.

I'd learnt at a young age that matched and mated in magic didn't necessarily mean matched in love or soul-bonded.

Omeron sat quietly for a few minutes, clearly shocked. I didn't blame him. If an Angel fed without her partner having access to the dark side of the Veil, it could kill him. I did have access from this realm, but only partially. It would take me days to replenish my power.

Lia had always fed on the light side of the Veil, but she no longer could. She needed to be by my side to feed because as soon as we returned to the Nether, the Heart would drain her as surely as the snowflakes melted on my skin. Even feeding on demon souls was no longer an option. I had to get her to Haldaag, where I could protect her, where I had an army of loyal Barg who would help me fight the Demon King when he discovered she was in the Nether.

She had no idea her insatiable need to absorb my darkness was one of the only ways to keep me weak. Yet, if I couldn't keep up with her demands for magic, if I wasn't strong enough to feed her, she could die. That meant the Heart and Veil would have to wait until another Angel was born. The Higher Powers had always come through and sent another Angel in time to keep the Heart strong. But they couldn't predict what would happen to that Angel as she grew, just as they couldn't stop my father from spiriting her away from the Nether. If they abandoned us and chose not to gift us another Angel, all life in both worlds would perish.

And once the Heart and Veil were gone, all who died would never be reborn. All life would cease to exist.

I pushed upright. "We have to find a way home, Ome. If we don't, Lia could die because I can't give her the power she needs. And there will be nothing I can do about it. " I glanced at him. "We found the gate yesterday. I think that's what triggered her zenith."

Omeron's eyes widened, a grin curling his lips. "That's great! When do we leave?"

I shook my head. "I'm sorry, my friend. The gate is out. I sensed our enemy waiting on the other side. The king knows it's there, only there are runes protecting it. Someone from this side enchanted it. Without the right incantation, he can't use it, which means he can't come through. But it also means we can't get back that way."

Omeron stood and began dressing, not bothering to dry his skin. He swiped my shirt and leather jacket off my saddle. "Get dressed, General, we're going hunting."

I scowled. "I've told you I will not feed off a demon. Not yet...I need time."

"Not to feed. We need a portal demon. And to find one, we need someone with elemental magic. If Hentus is who you say, then we might still have a chance of getting home."

I stared at him for a moment, then a slow smile curled my lips. He grinned when he realised I'd caught on. Portal demons were rare, but they couldn't resist the lure and chaos of elemental fire. That kind of magic was like dangling jewels in front of a thief and expecting him to walk away. An elemental fire summoner was one of the only mortals who could entice a portal demon out of hiding and into this world. And Hentus would likely know where to find one.

I met his gaze. "We need to destroy that doorway before we leave. The weaker the Veil becomes, the more likely the doorway will open itself."

"We do. But we need a plan first." He mounted, and I followed.

"We'll visit the Vipers first and then head back to the castle. Hentus once had a reputation for being the most deadly magicker in Pa'dur's Army. But he hasn't used his skills for many years."

"How quickly does he need to remember those skills?" Omeron's voice held an ominous quality. He would use any means necessary to ensure Hentus's compliance, but I had no wish to hurt the man who'd offered shelter to Lia and me, regardless of where that shelter had been or the kind of casteless life it had resulted in.

"I'll give him three days. Today, I'll tell him to connect with his old contacts. Tomorrow, he gets to think about it and realise he has no choice, and the day after, he'll tell us where to find a fire summoner who can entice the portal demon."

Omeron guided his horse towards Tetris. "What if he refuses?"

Hentus wasn't a friend. I didn't know how to define what he was to me, but he *had* kept me updated about Lia's safety after I'd left. He cared for Lia, and she cared for him. That said, I didn't trust him. He was cunning and well-prepared, and he'd survived against all odds. I gave a grim smile. He also knew I'd rip his head off if he did anything to put Lia at risk.

"He won't refuse. If he doesn't come through for us after I've explained Lia's life depends on it, he dies."

CHAPTER TWENTY-TWO

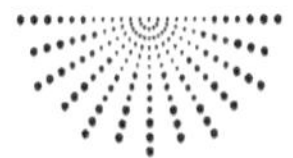

ia

The man being served tea in the armchair by the fire relaxed like he owned the place. Which, I supposed, he did. The servant trembled, almost spilling tea onto the tray. The poor girl was pale and clearly petrified of the prince.

Haruin watched her with a detached expression, but his eyes glinted. I'd spent my life studying people. He tried to hide it, but I recognised the satisfaction her fear gave him. My hackles rose. Polite or not, he was dangerous.

"I don't know what time the General will return," I tried again, not so subtly, to get rid of him. He'd ignored my previous comments and ordered godsdamned tea instead.

He gave a tight smile. "So you said. There is no need to repeat your words; I am neither deaf nor an imbecile."

My belly clenched, and I had to grit my teeth to avoid snapping back at him. "I wasn't suggesting either of those things." *No, you're an arrogant hogsack who enjoys playing power games with young women. I* couldn't help but wonder who else he bullied. The young maid scurried out the door, snagging it shut behind her.

I weighed up my unwelcome visitor, assessing the threat he posed to me. Haruin was tall and rangy. He was afflicted with an illness that made him look as pale as the corpses floating in the harbour. He walked with the help of a cane and struggled for breath. Even walking to the armchair had left him breathless.

He was weak.

I could get behind him and slit his throat in an instant.

He fixed me with a cold stare, his voice icy. "I wasn't suggesting either of those things, *Sire,* my prince, or my liege. One of those forms of address will do nicely. Omit them again, *magicker,* and I will see it as a sign of disrespect and have you thrown in the dungeons to rot with your brethren—or I'll execute you." He crossed his legs, the expensive material of his clothes whispering, the leather of his highly polished boots shining. "Contrary to what the General may think, you are my prisoner, not his. If I want you to grovel at my feet, then you will."

My eyes narrowed. His. Not his brother's, the crown prince? Interesting. Was there a power struggle between the two? It didn't matter. I didn't even care if he locked me in the dungeons. I'd escape. If he tried to kill me, I'd jump on the Aether and run. One thing I wouldn't do is grovel at his feet or anyone else's,

"No, *sire,* I won't."

Dark delight lit his face as if he'd wanted that reaction. It sent alarm bells peeling in my brain.

"Dala, isn't it? The friend you brought with you into my home?"

My blood ran cold. I fixed my stare on him, not trying to hide the wrath in my gaze.

"She leaves here every night with the General's guard dog, Omeron, does she not? They go to fight the Nether creatures that plague our city. Something the General assured me you would be doing, in addition to finding the magicker who is enticing them here. You have been doing neither. If you and your friend are to remain within the safety of my home, you will become useful and find me what I'm looking for. That magicker is mine. You have five days."

I didn't speak. My magic was locked tightly away, but my fingers twitched over my thighs where my daggers normally sat. I wanted badly to kill him, but it wasn't lost on me that, yet again, he'd referred to this castle as his. It made me wonder how much the Mad Prince knew about his brother's actions—and aspirations. Perhaps Haruin was as mad as his brother; maybe he was even worse.

He picked up his teacup with long, elegant fingers, and took a measured sip. As he swallowed, his gaze slowly devoured my body, lingering on the swell of my breasts before resting back on my face. A shudder of disgust rippled through me. I'd seen that kind of lust in men's eyes before. He wanted me, yet he hated that he did. That made him dangerous, the sort of man who would hurt a woman because he hated the power they held over his desire—over him. Normally, I'd show him exactly how repulsed I was, but his threat against Dala was crystal clear.

He smiled tightly. "You are a beautiful woman, magicker. It's a pity you have such tainted blood. Yet I still find myself intrigued by you." He cocked his head. "I can see why the General keeps you sequestered in his house. Now, to show me that you take your friend's well-being seriously, you will kneel at my feet."

He snapped his fingers and pointed to the rug by his foot.

Fury slammed through me. I had to exhale through my nostrils, gritting my teeth to stop my magic devouring him. I'd never killed another mortal with it, but I'd make an exception for him.

Sweat beaded on my forehead. Since Dex had rocked my world the night before, I'd been struggling to keep my magic within the confines of my control. I still had a voracious need to suck his magic into my own—to hunt him down and ride us into lust-filled oblivion.

Yesterday was a blur. I remembered that the doorway we'd found had tugged on something deep within me, and before I knew it, my legs had buckled, and my soul had felt empty. As soon as Dex touched me, that feeling had settled, only to be replaced by a consuming hunger I couldn't control. I'd pulled at his magic, instinctively knowing he was the answer, that he could help me.

I frowned and rubbed my chest, where my heart ached. I'd never felt anything like the need or pleasure I'd shared with Dex. It had changed everything for me. Because now I knew I couldn't leave him behind. If Dex were lying when he said he'd be by my side, if he betrayed me again, I knew it would break me. I needed his words to be true. This feeling in my chest, the hunger that still simmered in my blood, it wouldn't go. It hadn't been sated even when I'd awoken this morning, and it was getting worse. I craved to touch him again like last night, to feel his demanding fingers on my skin, his talented tongue stroking every sensitive inch of my body, the steel of his erection spearing my swollen core...

Despite the heat and lust coursing through me, I stood frozen to the spot. Kneeling for this evil fucker wasn't going to happen. Dala would kick my arse herself if I did. She would never want me to subjugate myself to anyone for her.

My nostrils flared. If I didn't, she, and without a doubt, Dex, would suffer for my defiance.

I could escape with Dala. She'd be asleep in Omeron's room on the other side of the house, but could I really leave Dex to face whatever punishment this bastard would inflict on him if I ran? Dex would be blamed for bringing a magicker he couldn't control into the castle. Some would say it was poetic justice for all those he'd helped execute. I shook my head. Even knowing that, I couldn't let him be hurt because of me.

The air between the sickly prince and me crackled. Haruin took another drink of his tea as if unbothered by it. In his eyes, though, the promise of violence lingered.

I swallowed, my heart pounding, my palms slick with sweat. Lifting my chin and gritting my teeth hard enough they creaked, I took one step forward. The lives of my best friend and my lover were worth my dignity. I'd get it back—somehow. I exhaled, shoving my magic as far inside as I could. Lover seemed such a weak word for what Dex was to me. I didn't have a perfect word to explain it. But I wouldn't let him suffer, or die because of me.

Haruin watched with malicious satisfaction as I stood in front of him. It took every bit of self-control I had not to kill him. It would be so easy to spear him through with my magic and send his soul to wander, lost in the Aether.

His eyes glinted, and he smiled, showing perfect white teeth. "Kneel."

My nostrils flared. Humiliation flushed my cheeks as I dropped to my knees. He contemplated me silently for a moment while my whole body was locked tight, wanting to launch myself at him but knowing I couldn't.

His head tilted. "Now, is that for your friend—or the General my brother listens to far too closely?"

I glared at him, respect be damned.

He smirked—and stood, looming over me with his groin at my eye level. It was a deliberate move, done to cause me more humiliation. But I wouldn't let it. He chuckled when I didn't cringe back. Nor did I look up at him. He could only take my dignity if I allowed it. Picking up his cane, he walked to the door, hesitating with his hand on the brass door knob, his breath wheezing.

"Remember, five days. You bring me the whereabouts of the magicker who is dragging these Angel-forsaken creatures into my city, or you, your friend, and the General will die."

He pulled the study door open, and I saw the same maid waiting by the front door with his cloak and hat. She met my eyes and immediately looked away, but not before I saw the pity on her face. My cheeks burned with shame. I'd given in, and even though I knew why I'd done it, it still smarted.

The prince walked into the hallway, his boots clicking almost as loudly as his cane as it hit the tiles. His back was to me, so I took the opportunity to jump to my feet. As I did, a vast shadow walked in the front door. I felt his energy brush my own immediately. Tears burned my eyes but I blinked them away. If Dex saw me upset, even if most of it was unreleased anger, he'd do something stupid. He'd brought me here to protect me, and that was before we'd become lovers.

My heart rate kicked up, and my magic thrashed to get to my bonded. I swallowed and wiped at my eyes. Everything about Dex screamed of dominance and power. No matter if the sickly man standing before him were a prince, he'd kill him for his threats, maybe even just for upsetting me. Gods, I'd seen him kill in the blink of an eye when I'd been younger. He was lethal and utterly cold when it came to my safety. He always had been. Why hadn't I seen that before?

I bit my top lip. Because I'd chosen to forget everything he'd done for me, and instead, I'd held onto my anger. Despite that knowledge, I wasn't the only one who needed protection. He did, too.

He glanced at me, and I gave him what I hoped was a convincing smile. The skin puckering of the bridge of his nose was the only sign that I had failed.

"Prince Haruin, why do you honour us with your visit?" he asked, his voice cool and calm but magic, as turbulent as the winter wind, swirled beneath the surface of his skin. So close to him, I could feel it, even if he couldn't free it. Hunger flooded me. I fisted my hands, desperately trying to control my craving as desire pulsed through me.

"Oh, I came to personally invite you and the magicker to the winter solstice ball."

Dex looked nonplussed. "A ball?" I would have laughed at his horrified expression if it hadn't been such a dangerous situation,.

"Yes, General, a ball."

His jaw tightened, his posture stiff. "I was...unaware of such an event."

I doubted Dex would ever want to attend a gathering with the pompous elite of the mortal world, one where he didn't belong. I couldn't begin to fathom why the princes wanted to celebrate such a day of worship when the city and the rest of Tetron were in such chaos.

"That's because you aren't aware of everything that happens in this castle. You are here to lead our army, and have access to our resources to do that. You and that army are a weapon against the creatures of the Nether and the magickers that plague our city. You are required to be at the ball for appearances. You will parade that *thing* around to ensure the heads of the castes are reassured that we are doing all we can to stop the invasion of this city."

"We are too busy for balls," Dex shot back coldly.

My spine stiffened. Hadn't he worked out how dangerous this sickly man was?

"You *will* attend, General. It isn't a request. My brother and I wish to see you there." His eyes flicked to me. "With her. Dress her in something revealing so I know there are no weapons on her. Make sure she has silver cuffs around her wrists to contain her magic."

"She has no active magic. She can merely sense it."

Haruin sniffed. "Like one of the hounds."

Dex's fists clenched.

Haruin glanced at me and smirked. "Well, she *has* shown me she can be as obedient as one of those bitches. She'll not fight when it comes to those orders." He turned to me. "Will you?"

Dex's face became darker, but he remained silent.

"In fact."

My stomach flipped when he looked at me, an evil glint in his eyes.

"Come here, magicker."

A muscle in Dex's jaw clenched, his spine snapping straight.

Dread pulled at my heart, but I kept my chin up as I walked past the maid.

"Show the General what you have learnt."

I fought to contain the fury burning in my chest. I could do this, but somehow, I had to stop Dex from reacting. It was what Haruin wanted. For some reason, he resented Dex, and I wouldn't give the bastard any reason to hurt him. I just needed Dex to stay calm and detached.

Haruin snapped his fingers and pointed to the tiles at his feet.

My face burned, but I had no choice. Haruin's threats weren't empty. I could sense the evil beneath his civilised facade.

Haruin glanced at Dex, but Dex's eyes were on me. I gave a minute shake of my head, pleading with my eyes for him to not react. He unclenched his fists and jaw and raised a condescending eyebrow, but I could see the fury in his eyes.

"Well? Do as your prince commands. Kneel," he clipped.

Relief washed through me. He understood. The only sign of his fury was the energy filling the room. It was like the atmosphere before a thunderstorm, thick and heavily charged.

Haruin didn't seem to notice. His gaze fixed back on me as I dropped to my knees at his feet. He curled his upper lip and looked back at Dex, satisfaction burning in his eyes.

"Train this bitch to follow orders, General. She's clever enough to understand the consequences of not fulfilling her purpose. Be certain you are, too." He brushed some imaginary lint from his shoulder. "You have five days to bring me the one who's luring those monsters here. Fail, and you both die, along with her friend—and yours."

Dex rested his hands on the swords at his hips, his fingers curling around the hilts. He met Haruin's gaze, and even the prince had the sense to step back. Death shone in Dex's gaze, an iciness I'd never seen before. I knew then that, eventually, Haruin would die by Dex's hand.

"My plans will not fail, Prince. They never do."

Haruin swallowed and stepped even further away. He indicated the door and waited while the maid opened it. Snow-laced air blew loose strands of my hair across my face.

"See that they don't. Find me tomorrow, and we'll arrange a time to deal with the prisoners. The ball is in four days. I expect to see you there."

I tensed. Would Dex actually harm those innocents? I didn't understand why he was serving the princes. Even they couldn't stop him if he decided to wipe them out. I just needed time to get Dala to safety first.

I blinked, keeping my gaze on the floor, unwilling to look at Dex's face. The princes were not the best rulers, but who would take their place if he killed them? It would start a civil war, maybe even leave the way open for an attack by another kingdom. I thought of Mari and her brother. Did all power corrupt those who held it?

"Get up," Dex ground out, reaching down to me. I stiffened, expecting to be yanked to my feet. His anger was palpable, yet his grip under my arm was gentle. When I was on my feet, he turned to the maid, who had quietly closed the door.

"Leave us," he commanded.

"Yes, sir." She gave me a small smile, then slipped away.

Sliding his hand down my arm, he entwined his fingers with mine, pulling me behind him towards his study. I'd barely got into the room when he kicked the door shut, let go of my hand, and pressed me so my back was against the door. He leaned his forearms against the door, his breath warm on my face. Tension vibrated from his body.

"You do not kneel for him ever again. Do you hear me?" His voice was hoarse, his magic swirling madly around us. "I don't care whose life he threatens. I will not have you subjugated by the likes of that vile little mortal. You are worth far more than his pathetic soul will ever be…"

Heat slammed through me at his wrath on my behalf. Beautiful jade eyes flashed with a level of protectiveness that made my belly flutter. In truth, I loved it. No point in denying it. I'd always loved how he took care of me. And now my feelings for him were far more profound and a hundred times more complicated, especially after yesterday.

I wanted him—badly. Grabbing his shoulders, I levered myself up, wrapping my legs around his waist and slamming my lips against his before he could get another word out. If I'd had any reservations about his feelings for me, they were eradicated by his outrage on my behalf.

He greeted my seeking tongue, groaning and kissing me back with a desperation that matched mine. I wound my arms around his neck. My body and magic were hungry for everything he could give me. But I held back. He'd looked tired when he'd walked in. Thankfully, Haruin hadn't noticed, but I had. My chest tightened at the realisation that I'd weakened him, yet I was as ravenous now as I'd been before, and I wasn't sure I could stop myself from taking more of his power if I kept touching him.

I wouldn't hurt him.

Shaking my head, I tried to climb off, but he just gripped me harder.

I cupped his face. "Dex, we need to stop. I fed too much last night, and I've hurt you."

His dark eyes held my gaze. "No, you didn't. But you're right; we do need to stop and talk about what just happened."

My face burned with shame. Being submissive, especially to a bigot like that vile prince, wasn't something I'd ever wanted him to see. I kept my eyes trained on the wall over his shoulder. "He threatened you and Dala." That was all the explanation I needed to give, but I added. "If you'd killed him we might not have gotten out of here before the mage hounds sensed us."

"Fuck," he grated out, his jaw muscles popping.

Gentle fingers raised my chin.

"Look at me."

I did. Fury glinted in his eyes, but I knew it wasn't aimed at me.

"We'll have to do as he asks. I need more time to figure out a way back to the Nether for us all. "But believe me, Lia, once we have a way home, nothing will keep him safe."

"Us all?"

He released a sigh. "Yes. Omeron is not from this world, and some of my best warriors are here too. They keep to the shadows and go where I go, but very few people notice them."

"They stick to the shadows? Like you?"

He smiled a little. "They do. They're loyal and would never leave me behind, so I will not leave them. We all go home, or none of us do."

I nodded, my heart warming at his words. "So? A non-dress then?"

Dex's jaw clenched hard enough that I thought his teeth might break.

I gripped his shoulders. "Hey, it's okay. I'll wear whatever I have to. Just…don't let anyone touch me. Especially that evil shit."

A growl rolled up his throat. "Never. I don't care if it leaves this kingdom without a ruler or if Escalon sends an army after me. Haruin will not lay a finger on you—on any of us. I'll end him and consume his soul if he tries."

Relief made me shake. I wasn't ashamed of my body, but wearing dresses had never been my thing, and wearing something small enough to prove I wasn't carrying weapons made me shudder. How many pairs of eyes would be on me?

"Dex? What he said about containing my magic. You won't really do that, will you?" I hated the quiver in my voice, but the thought of being without my power and the safety it offered was terrifying. It would be hard to do if I kept feeding from Dex but I'd manage somehow. "I'll hide it. I promise. I'll do anything else you ask, but I can't…"

He blinked slowly. "I'm sure we can find another way to hide your magic," he whispered, but I wondered if his words sounded as hollow to him as they did to me. "Right now, you need to feed. I can feel how hungry you are."

He was right, and part of me knew he was deflecting my plea, but being this close to him was like torture. I was starving for the power only he could give me, though I still held back, searching his face. Would he really lock my magic away?

"Sweetheart, I'll only do it if I can sense your magic on the day. Because if I can sense it, then the mage hounds will as well. It will put you at risk."

I nodded, swallowing hard. "Then you won't have to. I'll hide it. I just won't feed…"

"No, you have to feed. Otherwise you'll be too weak to fight, to protect yourself in a room full of sycophants if something goes wrong."

I chewed my lip. Surely, it would be better if I didn't feed… But I was so weak, so hungry, not just for his magic, but for him. I chewed my lip, trying to decide on the right thing to do. His eyes narrowed, and cursing under his breath, he decided for me, pushing his magic against every part of my body.

"Take it," he growled against my lips before claiming my mouth.

Aether, help me, I did. My defences fell, and his strength poured into me. His fingers grabbed my backside and ground me down onto the impressive erection that made itself known under the thickness of his leather trousers. I whimpered into his mouth as he rubbed me against him, the friction sending bolts of pleasure from my slick centre to the rest of my body. My insides began to clench. Swallowing my whimper, he pressed against me, holding me to him.

I welcomed his firm hold, my fingers digging into his shoulders. I didn't care about the hardness of the door behind my back or that anyone could walk right in. Nothing mattered but Dex.

I moaned as he held me in place with his weight, moving his large, calloused hands to my face to take control of our kiss, positioning my head where he wanted it. I let him. When I felt like I was high and floating on his power, his touch grounded me. His skin was hot as I mirrored his hold and took his face in my hands, but I happily let him lead our kiss. Breathless, I whimpered, needing to get closer to him, but he pulled back, gently nipping my lower lip.

We both panted for air, and I forced myself to release his magic. I already felt stronger, but it wasn't enough—it would never be.

"Lia, It's okay. Take what you need. You won't hurt me."

I shook my head.

He kissed me softly, just a brush of his lips. "You have to. Trust me. You won't hurt me. Please. Do it for me."

I winced yet nodded. With that softness in his voice, I'd do anything for him. He moaned as I caressed his magic with mine, enticing it inside me where I began to absorb it.

"Who do you belong to?" There was an urgent edge to his voice.

I bit my bottom lip, hesitating. I belonged to Dex; I always had. Everything about me wanted to be with him, no matter what he'd done, but admitting that made me vulnerable. A darkness came over his face, his body locking up, and gods forgive me if I didn't hold my breath in anticipation.

"Mine, Zahlia, you're fucking mine. You don't belong to that weak arsehole prince or his mad brother. And you sure as fuck don't belong to the Demon King. You're mine. Mine to feed. Mine to protect. Mine to fuck."

My gaze locked onto his, needing precisely the same reassurance he did. "Who do *you* belong to, Dexalion? Because this body, heart, and soul remain mine until yours belong to me."

A guttural growl rumbled up his throat, his eyes more red than green now, and I saw the demon side of him that he always kept hidden. There was obviously more to him than he'd ever shared, yet I found I didn't care about that. I just needed the same promise from him as he wanted from me. That he was mine, that he wouldn't leave me.

Shadow encompassed us.

A feral grin stretched his mouth.

"I do belong to you, Angel. I always have. My body. My heart. My whole fucking soul. It all belongs to you."

I groaned as he undulated his hips again and again, moving against me and ramping up my pleasure.

"Tell me who you belong to, Lia." It was a hoarse command.

My eyes fluttered, my breathing harsh, moaning at each powerful roll of his hips.

"Tell me!" he demanded, harsher this time.

My eyelids snapped open. I snarled, digging my fingernails into his thick biceps. "You. Gods, Dex, you. Always."

He muttered a curse and kissed me, his mouth feasting on mine. Our tongues duelled, while we kept our eyes on each other. I couldn't get enough of him. My heart squeezed, and my breath caught in my throat. I never would. That certainty scared me, but I'd work through it. My fear of being deserted and having everyone I loved leave me wouldn't stop me being with him. He'd told me he was mine. I swallowed against my dry throat. And I had always been his. I always would be.

"I want you in my bed, Angel. I want to worship this body, take my time, and erase that fucker from your mind, even if it's only for a little while."

I nodded, unable to look away from him. Reluctantly, I released my hold on his magic. He pulled back, his lips curved in a soft smile. He searched my face, then he leaned in, and kissed me so tenderly my heart squeezed.

That soft smile stayed in place. "Don't worry, you can feed more later. First, I'm going to take care of you. Wrap your arms and legs around me."

My muscles shook, and I had no desire to protest, not when it meant I could stay close to him. He opened the door and cool air fanned us. In the distance I heard a door and Dala's voice, but I couldn't move. No, that wasn't quite right. I didn't want to. I was hungry, turned on, and exhausted from—I had no idea.

"What you got there, General?" It was Dala's voice, curious but with a hint of warning, too.

"I'm fine," I mumbled against Dex's neck.

"I can't see you through all that shadow shit, so you'd better fucking be, lady, or I'll chop his balls off when I see him again."

I chuckled against Dex's skin, still unwilling to move. I kissed his neck and inhaled deeply, sighing when his hand left my back and cupped my head, holding me to him.

Another door clicked, and then I heard water running.

Giving a satisfied grunt at its temperature, he walked us into it, clothes and all. I murmured with contentment, the warmth heavenly. Showers were not something anyone in the Slopes owned or had access to. And our poor excuse for a bath was a bowl of cold water or the ocean.

Dex carefully lowered my legs. I leaned against him as he pulled off his jacket and shirt. My hands explored the bumps and ridges of his muscular back and down the curve of his spine to the perfect globes of his arse. Silently, he undressed us both and then washed every part of my skin, the lavender-smelling soap relaxing me as much as his touch. I still couldn't stop touching him. My hands seemed to have a life of their own. I began to kiss his chest, my hands smoothing around his hips to explore where his erection grew long and hard between us.

"Lia…" he breathed as I pulled away enough to have room to cup his heavy balls and slide my hand up and down, working his length. "You need to rest before we feed."

I shook my head. "No, what I need is you."

The strong column of his throat bobbed, and with a grunt of surrender, thrust his hips into my grip. He met my gaze with dark eyes. "Fuck, I can't refuse you anything," he whispered, looking almost desperate.

He spun me in his arms and moved my hands, placing my palms against the shower wall. His hands brushed down my spine, sliding over my wet skin until his fingers curled around my hips, grabbing and pulling them backwards, giving him access to my body.

We both groaned as he slid straight into my swollen flesh.

"Dex…" I whispered, overwhelmed by my craving for him and the pleasure only he could give me.

"I know, Angel. Trust me. I have you and am not letting you go ever again. I'll never let anyone hurt you."

His promise wrapped around my heart just as his magic had done. I straightened, arching my spine so he could fold his arms around me.

Then, with one hand, he gently turned my head, seeking out my mouth, kissing me like he never wanted to stop. He began moving languidly until I rolled my hips, urging him to thrust harder and faster. He refused, the warm water caressing us as he made love to me slowly and thoroughly, not upping his pace until his talented fingers had teased two orgasms from my exhausted body.

CHAPTER TWENTY-THREE

ia

Slowly, I lifted back the covers. Dex was spooning me from behind, his large arms caging me in. While I could, I revelled in feeling safe, protected, and, quite possibly, loved. Something I'd rarely felt. And only when Dex was close. My eyes burned, and I squeezed them shut. I had no time for tears.

Inch by inch, I freed myself from his hold and slipped out of bed. Silently, I pulled on a nightgown. Shadows danced around me protectively, and I swore it felt like Dex was standing behind me. Goosebumps erupted on my arms as if he were running his fingers down them, and I was convinced I felt his lips brush my cheek.

I peered over my shoulder, but he slept on, his face and body relaxed. The usual rigid set to his jaw wasn't there. Sleep definitely made his expression softer, and the angular planes of his face almost beautiful. It was so hard to curb my desire to climb back into bed and sink into his warmth. I clenched my fists. I couldn't. I needed more information on him, the Nether, and who or what I was.

Besides, Dex couldn't be angry. He'd left me with no choice but to do my own research.

I blew him a kiss, jumping when I felt a brush of softness against the back of my neck. Again, he had yet to stir. Standing transfixed, I took in the glorious view of his beautifully sculpted body. Protectiveness tightened my chest. He was vulnerable like this. It most likely was why he didn't sleep much. I rubbed a hand over my heart, hating that I had already taken too much magic from him, exhausting him into a deep slumber. I hated leaving him like this, but I wanted to see Mari again.

Finding the gate also meant Dex would soon take us to the Nether. But being in a new world where I had no idea how anything worked made me more than uncomfortable—I'd never admit it to Dex, but I was scared. I'd never left Tetris. Sure, it was a shithole, but at least I knew the dangers here.

"Sleep well," I whispered with one last look at his face before slipping out of the door. I stepped into the Aether, zipping along the corridors, past the guards, through doors and walls, and right into the library.

I smiled. Mari was already there. Her wavy blond hair fell forward, brushing the dark oak table as she poured over a dusty old tome. I wondered again how she got there without being seen, but I assumed she'd tell me when she was ready. Magic was dangerous in this kingdom, and trust had to be earned.

"Hey," I greeted.

She tensed and looked up, only relaxing when she saw it was me.

I hid my shock at her appearance. Her skin was so pale it was almost translucent, and the whites of her eyes had a purple tinge. Even her lips looked tainted.

She smiled tiredly.

"Hi, Zahlia." She might look ill, but her eyes sparkled with excitement. "Look," she said, spinning the book and pointing at an ink drawing of an enormous demon with red eyes, curled horns and black bat-like wings. "This is the Demon King."

"Ugh, ugly bugger, isn't he?" He wasn't, not at all; imposing, terrifying, powerful, and stunning, but not ugly. It just seemed a fitting response. I lifted my eyebrows expectantly.

She rolled her eyes. "Depends on your perception of beauty. That aside, I know why he's sending demons here." She clapped her hands, and I had to grin, even though the reminder that I was being hunted by the powerful Netherworld King made me sweat. Mari was good and kind. I could feel it, but I still wasn't sure I could completely trust her with everything I knew, so I'd not shared my suspicions about what my magic was or that Dex had it too, only that I was looking for a cure for the Veil.

"Good—I guess." I sat down next to her. The sweet smell I associated with her illness seemed worse tonight, and my heart ached for my friend. She deserved better than to die as a prisoner in this castle. Her husband might love her, but that love was toxic and controlling.

"It is," she agreed, halting my thoughts. "The Demon King is always a Shadow Demon, and to have ultimate control of the Nether kingdoms, he needs to be bound to the Angel of Aether. Look." She pointed to a beautifully drawn picture of a goddess pulling darkness from the demon. He, in turn, had a hand outstretched to what looked like a dark curtain of mist.

"It says that once he's bound, they work together to balance darkness and light. Ultimately, if the Angel doesn't feed from the darkness to balance her light, the Heart will drain her—or she will begin to burn so brightly she'll destroy everything." Her voice dropped to a whisper. "And if the Angel is no more, the Heart cannot function. If the Heart is weak, the Veil cannot replenish...." She looked up at me. "Shit," she murmured, her voice hoarse. "Have we found the reason for all this? Is the Angel dead? Or is the Heart?"

I swallowed thinking of Dex's mother. Her death had been the beginning of the end for the Veil. I had to get back to the Nether and fix this. My heart raced at the thought of what all this meant. I wiped my sweaty palms on my nightgown and peered at the page, my heart slamming against my ribs as the reality of what she said came crashing against me.

I squeezed my eyes shut and rubbed my chest. Dex was here inside me. His magic wrapped around my heart and soul. I could feel it, that sense of him touching me all the time. I smiled. He'd told me. He'd explained it all, but it just now made sense. I stared at the picture.

Except Dex wasn't the Demon King.

My heart fractured a little. That meant the Aether would die unless I found the Demon King and became his. Because I knew now, without any doubt, that I was an Angel—the only being alive who could prevent the destruction of both worlds. A tear trickled down my cheek. Dex had always called me his Angel. I'd always been that to him.

He'd always known what I was.

What my destiny is.

Only now, I knew it wasn't to be by his side.

My destiny was the Demon King. Tears burned my eyes, my heart aching with the knowledge of what I needed to do.

To fix the Veil between our worlds, I had to leave Dex behind.

The Slopes were more crowded than ever, the faces of those around us full of hopelessness. People jostled to get where they wanted to be or just stepped on those who had fallen to the ground and were too weak or ill to move. Shouts came from the nearby harbour as warrior caste guards held back a desperate mob from breaking through their lines and ransacking the supply ship that had been brave enough, or stupid enough, to dock.

I gritted my teeth as bodies fell, people screamed and yelled, and blood spilled. It was carnage.

"Fucking upper caste elites," I mumbled, knowing the supplies that had just been unloaded from the Medallion Isles clipper were going straight to the castle to be distributed to them. I shuddered. Since Dex had taken me there, I'd accepted the delicious food and safe shelter he'd offered, which, by default, had been granted by the very princes who condoned this behaviour.

"Don't do that! You won't survive unless you take what's offered," snapped Dala, her face dark and her eyes glittering. She gestured with her chin at the rioting people. "And finding a way to the Nether is a priority if you can help stop this."

I swallowed the bitter taste in my mouth and nodded. Knowing she was right didn't make me feel any better about the senseless death I was witnessing.

"For now, we need to speak to Hentus. If the Queen…"

"Shh!" I whispered viciously.

"Sorry," Dala mouthed.

I'd told her everything: how Dex had found me, where we were truly from, even about my midnight trysts with the sickly Queen. I'd shared that I thought Hentus might know the Queen but not who I thought she was to him. If Dala and I got caught, I didn't want Dala to suffer for keeping that secret. And she would because she was so loyal. No, Mari's and Hentus's secret would be on me alone.

We wound through the crowded streets and alleys until we reached the Vipers' nest. Hiding among the crowd, we watched the building for a while. Rivals of the Vipers rarely came right to the nest, but it wasn't impossible now everything had gone to shit, and gang boundaries weren't respected any more. It was survival of the fittest. That meant war on all fronts.

I saw familiar faces guarding the street. Angus leaned against a wall near the front door. His axe was held loosely in his hand, resting down his thigh on the wall side where it was less obvious. His eyes darted around, watching the alleys and the people. His eyes briefly rested on us. The only sign he'd seen us was a slight shake of his head.

I smiled to myself. He'd just warned us that it wasn't safe to approach—yet.

I stiffened as Garret stepped from the rotting front door. Two of his cronies followed him as he pulled up his hood and walked into the crowds.

Dala and I waited patiently. Time ticked by. Eventually, another of the Vipers came to relieve Angus. He met my eyes and nodded. Dala and I covered our heads with our hoods and pulled scarves over our faces. We were unrecognisable in the new leather armour and cloaks Dex had given us as we weaved our way through the crowds, watching closely for any threats.

Silently, Angus held open the door, and we followed him into the gloom. There was no lighting except what came through the dirty, broken window panes. Our boots clicked on the bare wooden floorboards, echoing around the empty house.

Angus gestured into the room I knew Hentus used as an office of sorts.

Hentus sat at a desk, a look of concentration on his face as he studied a crudely drawn map. Edge peered over his shoulder, his hands on the desk supporting his bulk. Both men looked up, their bodies tensing. Weapons were pulled, and their eyes narrowed as Angus shut the door behind us.

I lowered my hood and pulled off my scarf, and both men relaxed. I grinned.

"You can put them away. If I wanted to kill you, you'd be dead already," I quipped, raising one brow.

Edge grinned back. Hentus, as always, was more reserved, but his eyes warmed.

"Zahlia. I wondered how long it would take before you came back."

My smile slipped a bit. "I'm not here to stay, Hent. Things are...complicated."

"I'll say," quipped Dala, smirking while cleaning her nails with a small knife. I shot her a warning look.

Edge watched her, suspicion written all over his face. I didn't blame him. She looked as badass as she indeed was in her new outfit with the scythes Omeron had gifted her strapped to her waist. Dala grinned and kissed the air between them without so much as pausing with her little knife.

Angus chuckled from where he leaned against the wall near the door.

"S'alright, old man, if D wanted you dead, you already would be. You can trust them both."

Edge grunted, nodded at me, and stepped away from Hentus. It was clear he would still protect his friend's back, regardless of our brief history. It was a good feeling to know he watched over my friends. I wondered at that level of loyalty after what had happened between Hentus and him; then again, even if I were angry with her, I'd always remain loyal to Dala.

Hentus studied me, his eyes narrowed. He interlaced his fingers and rested them on the desk in front of him. I tried not to look as uncomfortable as I felt. He had a way of analysing me that always made me squirm. His mouth ticked up a bit at one corner, and his eyes glinted with rare humour.

"So, he's grown some balls and finally told you, hasn't he?"

I blinked, my brows drawing down. Did he already know about Dex's origins? About mine?

"Told me what?"

"How he feels. That boy threatened me on pain of death to keep him updated about your well-being after he fucked you and left, all those years ago." His grin widened as my cheeks flamed.

"You knew?" I squeaked.

"Of course, I know everything that happens on my turf, kiddo. You should know that by now. I knew you loved him. I just hoped it would fade over time for both of you. It's why I moved our nest when I heard he was returning. I wanted to give you time to run if you wanted to before he found you."

His eyes narrowed on my shocked face.

He shrugged. "But you didn't. Otherwise you would have left the night he found you on that rooftop."

I blinked and shook my head. "You knew about that, too? All this time, you knew how I felt about him, and you didn't tell me who he was, where he'd gone, or what he was fucking doing?" My voice rose until I was almost shouting. Anger slammed through me, along with a heavy dose of betrayal. Magic danced at my fingertips.

"I did." Hentus eyed the light dancing around my fingertips.

I didn't bother to hide it. The princes already knew I had magic; they just didn't know how much. I was already their prisoner, and if I didn't give up what they wanted, meaning me, in the next four days, I was dead anyway. A real case of damned if you do, damned if you don't.

"He didn't want you to follow him. Whether it was a conscious decision or not, you chose to stay here to wait for him. You could have left this shithole city anytime. But you didn't."

My nostrils flared, though I let my magic settle. Edge released a breath. I glanced at him as he carefully watched me. "Relax," I muttered. "I won't hurt the cagey old bastard." I plopped myself in one of the chairs opposite Hentus. "Okay, I'll admit you're right. I could have left. I didn't, though not for the reasons you think. I stayed to find my parents' killer. And that's the only reason."

Hentus smirked and nodded. "Of course, if that's what you want to tell yourself."

I scowled. "It is."

Hentus carefully folded the map away and pocketed it, but my curiosity was piqued. Obviously, he didn't want Dala or me to see what had appeared to be the sea and cliffs around Tetris.

"So why are you here? Dexalion wouldn't let you out of his sight, especially not now. So you've run from him. He'll hand me my arse if he finds you here, so this better be good."

"Nice to see you too," I snarked. "And I doubt anyone can hand you your arse." Except, I suspected Dex and maybe Omeron, but I didn't say that. "And what do you mean, especially not now?"

His knowing words irritated me. I leaned forward in my chair and gripped the table, a scowl on my face. I was fed up with the people around me knowing things I didn't. The swollen skin between my legs ached as I moved, reminding me that no matter where I went or for what purpose, Dex was with me, both his magic and the seed he'd left behind in my body. The thought made me squirm even more, but I hadn't come here just to talk about Dex...

"Zahlia, I can sense his magic *in* you...You've bonded him to you, haven't you."

Dala's sharp intake of breath was my only clue she was shocked by that revelation. She was right; I should have told her myself, but I had no idea how I'd even done it. I needed time to process the new feeling of completeness that warmed my chest. Feeling Dex's presence so deeply attached to my soul was both disconcerting and comforting.

I'd intended to talk to Dala about it, but this visit wasn't planned. Dex and Omeron had left this morning to meet the princes. I knew they were going to discuss the fate of the magickers. That knowledge had made me so fucking angry that I couldn't just stay behind and wait for their return. Even the library didn't hold the same appeal as usual, not without Mari.

"I think so. I-uh-I don't know what that means, but I feel him…" I placed my hand over my heart. "Here."

Hentus nodded. "I sensed the power in him the moment I found you both on that street, hiding in the filth and rain. Yours I didn't feel until you were older."

"How do you know about magic?" Maybe his answer would lead us to the reason I'd come here.

Hentus sat back and peeled off his shirt. He dropped the linen bundle at his feet. A Viper tattoo curled around his right bicep and forearm arm, its tail winding around his hand until it finished by coiling around his middle finger. I gaped as it came alive, moving and slithering across his heavily muscled chest until it wound around his neck, and lifted its wide head away from Hentus's body to stare me directly in the eyes. It hissed, revealing long fangs.

"Meet the real viper." He gently kissed her as she bumped that scaled head into his jaw, demanding attention. "She's with me always. She tells me about any magic that is nearby. You often used to ask how I defeated my enemies." He ran a finger reverently over her head. "When I release her, they die within seconds. Even those from the Netherworld."

I couldn't tear my eyes from the snake writhing over his body. "Is this your magic, Hent? Is this what made you the most feared and respected general in your brother's army?"

Within seconds, the viper was wrapped around my neck, her fangs perilously close to my jugular.

Dala threw the knife she'd been toying with. Edge lifted his axe to block the blade and vaulted over the table. Lightening quick for a man of his bulk, he spun, securing Dala in a headlock. Angus swore loudly from behind me, clearly wondering what had just happened.

"What do you know?" Hentus barked sharply.

I raised my hands placatingly. I could dissolve his magical viper without a thought, but I didn't want to. I wasn't here to fight with Hentus; I wanted his help—to get Mari out of the castle.

"Only what I've worked out."

It suddenly dawned on me what Dex had held over Hentus the day he took me.

"Dex didn't tell me a thing. I met someone. Someone who told me stories of her childhood, of the uncle she loved far more than her father, how that uncle went missing when her brother took control of their kingdom and murdered their father."

Hentus paled and opened his hand. The snake slid back through the air until it wrapped around Hentus and appeared to seep into his skin, becoming no more than a tattoo.

"Marianna?" he breathed. "You've seen her? Is she well? Is she happy?"

Edge let go of Dala, who promptly spun and smashed her fist into Edge's jaw, sending him staggering backwards. "Touch me like that again, and you'd better end me because I won't be so forgiving next time."

Edge didn't laugh off her warning; instead, he nodded and bowed slightly. "Noted. But I will protect my prince until my dying day."

My heart lurched, my breath catching. "So it's true? But how? Marianne said you'd disappeared when her brother took control, but you were already living here with the Vipers…"

Hentus cocked his head. "Members of any royal family are notoriously at risk from assassination from all directions. Andras, my nephew, was always an ambitious little shit. He played people against one another all the time. He was a master manipulator by the time he was eight. I saw through his well-behaved, sweet little prince act years before anyone realised what he was really like." He stroked his fingers over the viper tattoo. It seemed to shimmer before settling once again.

"I knew he'd try and kill off his family eventually or pay someone else to do it. He sent assassins after me several times over the years. Each time, I'd get rid of them." His face darkened. "Seeing his spite turned to disappointment every time I came home satisfied me to no end. But because I don't believe in having only one option for survival, I built a secret life here in Tetris. Edge was with me when word came that Andras had killed my brother and his own mother and taken the throne."

"But why didn't you return? At least try to find Mari?" I shook my head. "She's so unhappy, Hentus."

He swiped his shirt from the floor and put it back on, his expression dark and forbidding, though his eyes were anything but, guilt shone in them.

"I tried to get back into the palace, but he'd blocked all the tunnels I knew of. He was waiting for us at every one we tried. It was a trap. Edge and I barely escaped with our lives, and all of my men died. After that epic failure, I returned here to plan another way to get Mari, but I learnt that she was betrothed to the crown prince of Tetron. I knew Andras wouldn't hurt her, not if he wanted the alliance between Pa'dur and Tetron, so I stayed hidden, intending to free her from the confines of her royal marriage once she arrived in Tetris."

"So what happened? She's been here for years." I didn't want to sound accusatory, but that's how it came out. Hentus was powerful. He had access to magic that was as vicious and deadly as he was, but he'd left his niece, someone who loved him dearly and had believed he would come back for her, alone, to be used as a commodity.

"The Mad Prince took her everywhere with him. Even to what was the front line on the moors. And if he wasn't by her side, his brother was. There were always dozens of guards around her. It was impossible even to get a glimpse of her, let alone speak with her. She was never permitted to hold an audience or leave the castle without them. And I believed she was safer there, away from her brother." His jaw tightened. "Besides, I've heard that the Mad Prince dotes on her. If that's true, why would she leave him?"

I scoffed. "He dotes on her so much that she's a prisoner in what should be her home. She's not even allowed out of her rooms alone; she's kept hidden away, told what to eat, what to drink, when to speak..."

"So, how have you spoken with her?"

"I met her in the castle library. She goes there sometimes in the early hours of the morning."

"How does she get there if she isn't allowed to leave her room and is constantly guarded?"

"I don't really know. All she'll tell me is that she waits until her husband is sleeping, then sneaks past her guards. She says the library is the only solace she has in her life."

Hentus nodded. "She has magic, though I don't know what shape that took as she grew. I haven't seen her for so long." His voice shook a bit. It was unsettling to see the man who'd always seemed hewn from granite at a loss for words, and showing the same emotions the rest of us did. His eyes met mine.

"But she's well? The prince doesn't hurt her, does he?" He no longer sounded sure.

I shook my head. "Not physically. At least, I've seen nothing that would lead me to believe he does, but…" I paused and took a fortifying breath. This was going to be more complicated than I'd thought.

"What?" His brows dipped.

"Mari…well…she's sick. Very sick."

His hands fisted. "What do you mean?"

"She's dying," I breathed, hating that I was bringing him news that would hurt.

He stared at me, his face dark. Silence fell as everyone processed what I'd said.

"No!" he yelled, picking up his chair and smashing it into the wall. His rage was a palpable thing, stealing the air from the room. His viper slithered around his bare forearm, looking agitated and hissing.

"Hentus!" yelled Edge, wrapping his big arms around his friend. "Don't do this to yourself. Just—don't. None of this is your fault. Andras stopped you getting to her, but we can do it this time. We can rescue her and bring her back to you."

I inhaled shakily. I'd never seen Hentus lose his cool like that. He definitely loved Mari enough that he was devastated by the news that she was dying. We all remained quiet, though I couldn't relax. Not until Hentus nodded and tapped his friend's forearm, signalling he was calm enough to be released. He briefly closed his eyes before looking at me.

"Mari..." He coughed to clear his hoarse voice. "Mari, she isn't my niece, she's my daughter..."

"Oh shit..." breathed Dala.

I mirrored her. "Your daughter? But..."

Hentus held up his hand. "I had an affair with my brother's queen. Well, more like one night of passion. We both agreed it was something that would never happen again. Nine months later, Marianna was born. I knew she was mine and could never leave her alone like I should have. I have no idea if my brother suspected, but he was always too busy with matters of state to pay much attention to his family. Andras grew up a cunning, greedy, and coldhearted bastard, just like his father, and I didn't want that for Mari, so I spent time with her whenever I was home. I ensured the best guards were by her side to keep her safe and fixed it so she would have the best and wisest tutors in the kingdom. The hardest part was knowing that she was always at risk, that I might be forced to leave her behind one day."

"You never intended to fight for the throne, even if Andras took it from his father, did you." It was more a statement than a question. It was written all over his face.

He shook his head, a faraway look in his eyes. "I didn't want it. Not the responsibility or the restrictions of leading a kingdom. My brother was a cold-hearted man whose sole purpose in life was to amass more and more power, land and riches. The people of Pa'dur were insignificant to him so long as they followed his rules and worshipped the ground he walked on."

"You knew his son was just like him and that he'd come after you when he eventually killed his father?"

Hentus nodded. "That's right. I was a threat to him. I led the armies, and he knew I had powerful magic. He just didn't know what it was. I started preparing to leave. Disappearing with Mari was more important to me than the people of the kingdom, my wealth, my men —all of it. Setting up the Vipers took time and effort. Lots of effort. I had to establish myself here. That meant getting rid of the last uncasted gang leader and dealing with the fallout. I was on my way back to Pa'dur with my battalion when some of them turned on me. We," he nodded at Edge, "made it look like I had died when they attacked." His eyes hardened. "I sacrificed good men that night to keep our secret. After my failed attempt to rescue Mari, we left Pa'dur behind and started our new lives here. I've been here ever since. Even if he suspects I'm alive, among the casteless dregs of society in another kingdom is not somewhere my nephew would think to look for me."

He rubbed his face with one hand. "I've hoped to see Mari every day since she was brought here, and I've been working on a way to get her out of that castle." He cocked his head, his eyes contemplative. "Perhaps you are it."

My heart sank, and I shook my head because I knew what he wanted. "Hentus, I can't get you into the castle. I'm really sorry. There's too much security, and the mage hounds patrol every inch of the castle and grounds. If I used magic, they'd sense us."

He nodded, his face carefully neutral. "I understand." He met Edge's gaze. The other man nodded. "We've found another way in." Taking the map from Edge, he smoothed it out over the table. Charcoal lines made up what I recognised as the coastline, and in the centre was Tetris. The castle loomed over the ocean, but there was a dark circle under the water line at the base of the cliffs.

"What's this?" I asked, peering more closely.

Dala did the same. "A cave?" she queried.

Hentus stooped, picking up the broken bits of his chair. At least it wouldn't get wasted. They'd burn it to help keep the reapers away.

"No, Angus has been down there." He looked at Angus expectantly.

Angus shrugged. "It ain't no cave; well, not much of one. It's only accessible at low tide and is hidden by this jutting bit of rock." He jammed his meaty fingertip on the map. "It's a tunnel. I've explored as far as here..."

My heart lurched. Three crosses marked the page, side by side. The tunnels beneath Dex's house.

"Where do they go?" I asked innocently, not sure yet how much I wanted to share. So far, Dex had kept silent about the gate, and I didn't know how I felt about it, not since it had almost sucked the life from me. Would we return to the Nether that way if he couldn't find another way home? I shuddered, rubbing my arms. There was malevolence lingering on the other side of the gate that scared me. The

Demon King might be my destiny, but neither Dex nor I would risk leaving the gate intact for him to have free rein to move between worlds. I wondered if the evil around it was why reapers and demons stayed away from the castle.

I peered at the map again. If I could get Hentus into the tunnels, I could guide him away from the gate and maybe even help get Mari out of the castle. My heart squeezed. Hentus was Mari's father. That was huge. I understood better than most how losing your parents changed you, but her own brother had murdered them. She must have feared for her own life every day after. The Mad Prince had never harmed her physically, and she sounded fond of him, but she was sure it was Haruin who was somehow persuading Escalon to behave as he did, including keeping her locked away. My eyes strayed back to Hentus. Yet, no matter the affection she had for her husband, she had someone who truly did love her. She deserved to know that.

"I can get you into the castle. I think I've seen these tunnels before —from the inside. I know where they go." I jabbed my finger on the parchment. "This one goes to the dungeons, though I've never been through it." My nose wrinkled. "It stank worse than the harbour. This one goes to a large empty cave. There are no other exits from there that I could see when I explored. This one goes to my bedroom in the General's quarters." The twisted truth slipped easily off my tongue. There was no way I could risk them going down the wrong tunnel and finding the gate. Their safety wasn't worth it.

"What do you think they were used for?" Dala asked, peering closely at the map.

I shrugged. "Who knows? Maybe for when the castle and dungeons were built to get rid of rock or something?"

Hentus grunted. "It doesn't matter. What matters is we can get in that way." He looked right at me, lines etching his face. "Will she listen? Will she leave her husband behind?"

His questions were curt, but I understood why. Mari meant far more to him than I'd ever believed. And she'd been a prisoner for years. First of her brother, then of her husband. She had no idea that her 'uncle' was even alive, let alone that he had tried to free her before or that he'd been trying to find a way to get to her for years. I honestly had no clue if she was open to leaving her life behind again. She was a Queen and had been lavished with materialistic things since she was born. I glanced around. And no matter how much Hentus loved her, his life was full of violence and poverty.

"I think she'll hear you out, but I can't say whether she'll leave with you. Despite what her husband has done, in his fucked up way, he's trying to protect her, and she cares for him."

Hentus frowned. "He's treated her no better than a whore, locking her away and not letting her see or speak to others. Even palace courtesans in Pa'dur are granted freedom of movement and access to the harem where they can seek the company of others."

I pressed my lips together. It was pointless to voice my suspicions that Haruin pulled Escalon's strings. "There's something else—something odd about Mari."

"What?" Hentus asked.

"That's just it. I don't know how to explain it. She looks unwell, but it doesn't look like a decline that's..." I searched for the right word. "Natural."

Hentus shook his head. "I don't understand. What are you saying?"

"That's just it. I don't know. She told me she was dying, and I could smell death on her, but when I was near her, my magic behaved strangely. It recoiled, and it's never done that with anyone or anything else. The last time I saw her, the whites of her eyes had an odd purple tinge. So did her lips."

Hentus sat back, his fingers brushing over the coiled viper. He glanced at Edge, who shrugged.

"It's possible," Edge said, his face twisted in consideration.

"What is?" I asked.

"Some poisons can discolour the eyes, lips, teeth, and even skin. Were her teeth or her skin tainted, too?"

I shook my head. "I'm not sure; it's quite dark in the library; even the castle is short on burning oil. Besides, I didn't think to look. Why would anyone want to poison her? No one benefits from her death."

Hentus stood and began pacing. "I don't know, but I'll find out." Under his shirt, the viper slithered, the outline of its body rising and disappearing in a disconcerting rhythm while Hentus's eyes turned an eerie green, his pupils elongating. "And they will die...fucking painfully."

I swallowed hard. This was why Hentus had never conceded control of the Slopes to another. He was a powerful magicker who knew how to hide his gift. He was dangerous without the viper, but with it, he was almost indestructible.

"In two days, there's a ball in the castle. Dex and I have been ordered to be there." I didn't go into how I was to be paraded around as a possession of the princes. Hentus didn't need to know. My face blanked even as my heart rate spiked at the prospect of being on display like that, but I knew Dex would keep his word. I'd be safe. "But if you follow this tunnel..." I traced my finger along the map where Angus had drawn the line of the tunnel. "It will lead you to some steps. Take them. They lead up directly into my room in the General's quarters. A tapestry covers the door so I can leave it ajar."

"Doesn't the General have staff who could uncover it?" asked Edge.

I shook my head. "No, Dex doesn't trust anyone enough for them to wander the house at any hour. They're permitted to clean in the early morning only while he is out doing..." I frowned, unsure what Dex did every morning when he left the house. "Generally things."

I ignored Angus's snort of amusement.

"The rest of the day, they're around to serve meals should he require them. Other than that, they're confined to the kitchen and the servants' quarters. They'll not defy him."

Silence.

Dex had always been my protector, my friend, and now my lover, but my friends all knew he would punish, if not kill, anyone who ignored his commands, especially if it invaded his privacy.

"Wait in my room. I have no idea how long it will be before I can escape that ball, especially if the princes put more guards on me, but somehow I'll get away. And I'll find a way to get word to Mari. Maybe I can bring her to my room or transport you somewhere to see her. She's always well-guarded but manages to get away in the early hours."

Hentus flashed me a considering look. "How do you both manage to move around the castle unseen?" he asked.

Should I tell him? I loved Hentus, but that didn't mean I fully trusted him. I wanted to believe Hentus wouldn't betray me, but I wasn't sure. I didn't know the prince of Pa'dur—at all. Like Dex, he'd hidden his identity all these years, though granted, for different reasons. I sighed. Secrets. It was sad that we all needed them.

"The mage hounds patrol the corridors of the castle interior, but I know their schedule and can easily miss them. They've never sensed me yet, so I don't see why that should change." I glanced at Hentus, and made a snap decision to trust him with at least a little of the truth. "My magic helps me move quicker than sight. I'll only be able to take one of you at a time, though."

"That's fine," Hentus quickly interjected.

"No, it's not," Edge argued, a stubborn set to his jaw.

A smile made my lips twitch. No one questioned Hentus—ever.

Hentus couldn't hide his irritation. "Listen, my friend, I'm happy you're back in my life, but you are no longer my personal guard. You haven't been for years. Not since you left with the woman we both loved."

Edge snarled. "Yes, I am back. And I never reneged on my oath to protect you. Even if I had and didn't consider you my prince any longer, you're still my friend. That means I'll watch your back when you can't watch your own. Besides, Arma will kick my arse out of the Aether when I die if I allow anything to happen to you. She loved you. Now, stop being a stubborn bastard and accept I'll be going in first in case there are any traps." My eyes met his. "No offence."

I bit my lip to stop my smile from spreading. Hentus looked so uncomfortable at his friend's declarations it was comical. "None taken."

Edge nodded. "Good. 'Cause it wouldn't make any difference."

Now, I did grin. "Of course not," I conceded gracefully.

He grinned back.

"Okay, Hent, so I'll take Edge in first, and if everything looks safe, I'll come back for you."

"What happens then?" asked Dala, flipping her knife in a steady, repetitive move.

"I have no idea," I admitted. "It all depends on how Mari reacts to seeing her uncle again."

Hentus jutted his chin. "Father," he declared.

"Okay, but you might not want to lead with that," I cautioned, standing from where I perched on the edge of the table.

"I know. But before I leave, she will know what she is to me, and she will know that I've never forgotten about her or think that I abandoned her to a cold, loveless marriage, one no better than a prison."

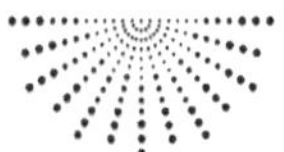

ex

Drowning in self-loathing for planning an execution of unarmed innocents wasn't a new experience, but this was the first time I wondered if I could go through with our usual plan.

Omeron strode alongside me as we walked through the stinking gloom of the dungeons. "You have no choice, you know that."

Behind us, the metal door clanged shut, echoing coldly through the darkness. I tried not to flinch.

"One life," Omeron whispered. "One to save one hundred." His voice was reasonable; the commander who stayed calm and objective even under emotional pressure.

"I know. It doesn't make this whole fucked up situation right, though."

He said nothing. That in itself spoke volumes.

With each step, we walked further away from the large cave used to imprison those unfortunate mortals born with latent magic in their veins. Magic that they had no concept of and, therefore, couldn't hide from the mage hounds. The metal door that imprisoned them was solid silver. Centuries ago, the Tetron King had commissioned it so that any magickers caught disobeying the law by using magic were imprisoned behind its neutralising effects. Not even my magic could break through it.

By the time we'd made our way past the desperate inmates housed in the cells and up to the guardhouse, my jaw ached from clenching so hard. The young guards on duty snapped their spines straight at my entry. Their eyes widened, making them appear even younger. Haruin and Escalon had left the dungeons before us, along with their personal guards, and I doubted these warrior caste trainees had ever been so close to their princes or their general.

"At ease," I barked as I walked out into the saline-soaked air of the training ground.

I inhaled deeply, hoping this was the last time I'd ever have to execute any innocent magickers. Even if Omeron was right, and one life for a hundred was worth it, it still sucked. I was a warrior, not an executioner.

Suddenly, I was desperate to feel Lia's soft skin under my palms and her magic dance with mine. I hadn't fully recovered from her feeding frenzy. My body felt weaker than it should, but as soon as darkness fell, I would replenish from the Veil and the demons that invaded this world. I needed to be strong enough to protect her as well as feed her magic with mine. The constant tugging as she pulled gently on our bond had been both distracting and reassuring. We were connected, and even if I couldn't be by her side every moment, I could feel where she was.

"The ball is in two days. As soon as Lia and I have shown our faces for long enough, we need to get out of the city and secure a portal demon," I said.

Omeron's face was grim, his body tense, yet his movements were still powerful and fluid enough that only I would notice. "Then I'll call in the others. We'll be ready. Will you and Zahlia?"

"We will. Be back for the execution, my friend. It'll look suspicious if you're not. Once it's done, we'll be on a tight schedule to deal with the other magickers, destroy the gate, and get Lia back to the Nether and within the protection of Haldaag before the Demon King finds out."

"I understand. Your warriors will be waiting, sire."

For once, I didn't berate him for using my title. Soon, I wouldn't need to pretend. The time for half-truths and lies would be over.

My friend's lips pressed tightly together before he inhaled deeply, his nostrils flaring. "I have one request. Will you protect Dala in my absence?"

Any amusement I once had at my friend's expense when he lusted after a female was nowhere in sight. His feelings for the Riou warrior were true and deep, just as mine were for Lia. He would only make them known to her once he'd asked his father's permission to bond with her. That was just Barg tradition. I had no idea what my friend would do if his father didn't agree that Dala was a suitable match. But I knew what *I* would do.

I nodded at my friend; further words weren't necessary. Just as it wasn't necessary for him to request she be allowed to join us in the Nether. Both Lia and Omeron needed Dala.

On the way back to my quarters, I nodded at the soldiers on duty. All were warrior caste members, though many were barely more than boys. Thousands of older, more experienced warriors had died for their king out on the moors, which had left our ranks depleted. He'd ordered his army out there only weeks before I'd joined his ranks. For years, the demons and reapers had been contained—until Lia's magic had matured, and she had started taking from the Veil to replenish her power. It had been an innocent move on her part but one that had broadcast her whereabouts to the reapers, putting her in more danger. She had marked herself and weakened the Veil over the city. It was why I'd conceded defeat and persuaded Escalon that the city needed us.

Lia had become my world, which meant I had to get her out of the city. Haruin's threats weren't empty. He'd come for us and our friends if we weren't at that ball. I wasn't worried about Omeron; he could take care of himself, especially with the rest of our pack behind him, but I *was* worried about Dala—and Lia. My Angel was fierce, but Haruin was far more cunning than I'd ever suspected. I ground my teeth. I'd have to hide the strength of her magic from all the guards and hounds at the ball. I hated that I'd have to, especially as she'd begged me not to, and I hoped she'd forgive me, but we needed to get out of the city with our friends before the princes realised we'd left. To do that, I needed to make sure her magic was undetectable. Once we were out of the castle, now that Lia's magic was at full strength, we could combine our power and call a portal demon. We just needed the time and space to do it.

I'd hoped for enough time to break the enchantment around the gate, but even if I did, it would leave the way open for Baladon to invade this world. It was a miracle the princes hadn't found the gate, particularly since they were still so obsessed with finding the magicker who had killed their mother. I frowned. It was also strange that they hadn't found the tunnels and secret passages beneath the castle—especially after that night.

It wasn't just that night that had solidified their hate for magickers, it had been ingrained from birth, and in their family history. Past Tetron kings had condemned magic, and the princes had grown up learning to despise it. It was ironic that their mother had been a demon, and they had no clue. She was a portal demon who'd taken advantage of her access to this world and the Nether. How would they feel if they knew they had latent magic in their veins? Their mother had somehow found a way to hide her magic. I had no idea how, but I damned well needed to find out because however she'd done it, she'd managed to hide that gateway from me, too. She'd also done something to deter the Nether creatures from attacking the castle and its inhabitants. It was almost as if they couldn't stand the energy her enchantment threw out.

Perhaps some of the tomes Lia and Mari studied had the answer? Gods knew they'd found out more than I'd expected, and that was only on the nights when I silently watched them from the shadows. I liked to give Lia a sense of freedom, of being able to escape me, but one day, she would know and accept that I would never leave her side. For now, I only watched her at night when it was easier to summon my shadows, and there were no mage hounds around.

My footsteps quickened. I needed to reassure myself that she was safe and well and didn't need anything. She could go into another feeding frenzy without notice. Heat flushed my skin, and it was all I could do not to jog back to my house. I sped up, praying to the Higher Powers that she was fine and I'd just find her being fitted for a ball gown.

Grimacing, I prepared myself for the onslaught of vitriol I was sure to receive. Ball gown was pushing the description. The design was more a scrap of silky fabric, which left very little to the imagination from what the baroness of the trade caste had explained to me. The baroness was the pinnacle of power among the nobles of the trade castes. Below her were the lords and ladies who ran their specific trade caste. The lord she'd chosen to help me with Lia's outfit was a twisted little man who regularly served the castle, supplying all of their outfits. I didn't like the smarmy little prick. But then again, I didn't need to. He had one job to do, and if he even looked the wrong way at my Angel, I'd snap his scrawny neck.

Irrational as it may be, my chest tightened at the thought of him looking at Lia's body. Maybe I should have insisted on a female seamstress for the job. Not that I could protect Lia from all the leering glances she would get at the ball.

Haruin had ordered her to wear an outfit 'revealing' enough that she couldn't hide weapons. My fists tightened. The memory of the lust in his eyes when he'd commanded her to kneel made me want to break something, namely his neck. I wasn't stupid. He would get a kick out of humiliating her and parading her in front of his nobles. It would show him as merciful and able to control one of the only magickers in Tetron who could use their gift yet be allowed to live.

My fingers curled into fists. He had no idea Zahlia was far more powerful than any mortal could ever be. She just had to learn how to command her power.

I pushed open the heavy front door. As I did so, Lia's voice reached me. Raised, tight, and full of fury. Taking a breath, I stopped to listen, my grimace very real. I could do this. She was my bonded. I smirked as she railed at the obsequious little tailor.

"Are you kidding me? I will not parade around in this excuse for a dress! For a start, I don't wear dresses! Ever! And no matter how many stitches you put in it, it is still just a scrap of material!"

"If you allow me to pin it, it will fit better."

"Touch me again, and I swear I'll chop your bloody hand off!"

I snorted a laugh even as my chest warmed. There was no hiding the pride on my face as I entered my study to find Lia standing on some kind of box, with the tailor on his knees before her, trying to pin what was indeed a scrap of material to the right length. My smile widened at the frustration on his face. Lia was standing up for herself, and he obviously wasn't used to his clients questioning his advice. Yet there was little we could do about Haruin's orders for her dress. And in truth, it wasn't the tailor's fault.

In the far corner, my maid smiled broadly, her eyes sparkling with mirth. Until she saw me and dropped her gaze, wiping her face of any expression. It had been easy to see the respect in it as she watched Lia. I wasn't sure how I felt about that. I'd never given her or any of my other staff a second thought, but maybe I should have. They could watch over Lia when I wasn't there…

Lia's head snapped up as I walked in, her face relaxing from a dark frown into a bright smile. I didn't miss the relief in her eyes, either.

"Dex!" she breathed but didn't move off the box.

"Hey, Angel. You wouldn't be giving this upstanding member of the nobility a hard time, now would you?"

She rolled her eyes, but her beautiful smile remained in place.

"Well, that's a stupid question when you see what she's supposed to wear." Dala scowled at me from where she lounged on the sofa, her knee over the arm and her foot swinging back and forth as she cleaned her nails with a dagger. I hid my grin. That seemed to be a favourite pastime of hers. It also meant she had a weapon handy should she need one.

Taking my time, I studied the scrap of material, my lust soaring at the sight of Lia's generous breasts framed by the lilac silk. The material met around the back of her neck and was sewn together at her waist before falling in one thin panel down to her ankles. The long slits on either side revealed the smooth length of her thighs and her knee-high boots.

The stink of the tailor's fear filled my nostrils as I inspected my mate's outfit, then slowly turned my gaze on him. Many mortals had trembled and begged for mercy from my gaze alone, especially when it was clear they had incurred my wrath. Yet the tailor had done his job. There was certainly nowhere to hide a weapon in the scrap of material.

"You may leave."

"B-but, sir, there is the hem to finish."

I glared at him.

"Y-your right. I-I can return for the dress tomorrow and s-still have it finished in time."

I waved him away. "No need. I'll have it delivered to your work-shop tonight." I looked at the maid. "You, what's your name?"

Her attention snapped to my face. "Irene, sir."

Thankfully, she didn't stutter or shy away from me. I nodded. "Very good. Irene, you'll return in three hours and take the dress to this man." I glared back down at the tailor, still on his knees. "Give her your details and leave."

"Y-yes, sir," he stuttered before crawling away from us. He didn't stand until he was halfway across the room.

Lia raised a brow at me, but I just raised one right back. I didn't care if the mortal male walked or crawled from the room. Only that he left. My magic was pushing to reach Lia, but I kept it under tight control while Irene was in the room. So did Lia. She didn't reveal her internal struggle to hide her magic, if indeed there was one.

"Um, where shall I collect the dress from?" Irene asked, looking pleased as the tailor practically ran out of the front door.

"Oh, right here. I'm about to divest my lady of it," I answered without looking away from Lia. "Now leave us. All of you." I growled the last order at Dala.

Her sigh was loud. It irritated me, but then I saw the smirk Lia aimed at her, and my irritation turned to amusement.

"She'll find you later, Dala." I looked at the warrior my friend intended to pursue as his Queen. Even if she didn't know it, that's what she would eventually become—a Queen and my closest friend's beloved. Because of that, and because she was more than loyal to my

Angel, I would treat her with the respect she deserved. "Omeron is on a mission for me. He's asked that I keep you safe, so no leaving the castle grounds tonight."

She straightened into a sitting position. "But what about the creatures? We should be out there, saving lives, not sitting here behind closed doors while innocent people die."

"The mission he's on will help us to end this devastation. On both sides of the Veil." I shot her a pointed look. "Please give Omeron the respect he deserves and stay within the walls of the castle. He's never asked me for anything before. I hope you realise the enormity of his request."

Her mouth opened and shut, her wide eyes searching out Lia before returning to me. For once, it seemed she was stuck for words. My lips twitched into a smile.

"Well, he should have warned me first," she muttered, walking up to a grinning Lia.

"Dala, you know he couldn't, not when he had to leave on this mission without warning." Lia's tone was calming and utterly reasonable. Her slim fingers held Dala's hands.

"Maybe," Dala groused before letting go and striding across the room, her footsteps muffled by the thick rug.

"Close the door on your way out, Dala."

Lia's smile widened as Dala muttered something about having better things to do than listen to us go at it like moor bunnies.

The door clicked shut.

A split second later, I stood in front of Lia. Her gasp hit me in my gut, as did her scent. It was enough for the worry that coiled in my belly to loosen.

Taking my time, I allowed my gaze to drink her in. Desire shot through me as she snagged her lower lip between her teeth. Damn, if she knew the power she had over me, any command she issued right then, I'd follow without question. I tore my attention from her mouth, taking in the swell of her breasts and the inviting strip of skin between them that the barely-there material revealed. My gut tightened. Her skin was laid bare from her cleavage right down to her navel. I had to take a breath to control the lust that slammed through me. In the hundreds of Heart cycles I'd lived, no female had ever affected me like Lia.

I glanced at my large desk, contemplating what it would be like to lean her over it and slip into her sweet, hot tightness. My fingers wrapped around her throat, sliding up to grip her jaw, tilting her head and guiding her lips to mine. I swallowed her moans of pleasure as I kissed her deeply, my whole body burning with need. Nipping her plump lower lip, I pulled away enough so I could look at her. Her nipples peaked under my gaze, her breathing ticking up. Before I embarrassed myself completely by losing control, I glanced down the length of her body.

"You are stunning." Too stunning. I hated that she had to be on display. Grinding my teeth, I contemplated all the ways I could kill Haruin before the ball. If we were in the Nether, he'd already be dead. Lia was my bonded, and I should be able to protect her from him...

A warm hand on my cheek forced me to refocus.

"Dex? It's okay. This means nothing. He thinks it will keep him safe, but I *am* a weapon; we both know that."

I exhaled heavily as guilt crushed my chest. But I would follow through on my plan because it would keep her safe from the mage hounds and the demons when we ran from the palace. "You'll be wearing silver. You know that Haruin wants your magic neutralised so he can parade you around like a dangerous dog. Leashed and muzzled."

A wicked smile graced her lips. "But maybe my fangs are sharp enough to bite right through that muzzle."

My teeth hurt from clenching them so hard. She'd never had her magic trapped. It was an experience I wished she could avoid—but it was necessary for her safety. I forced myself to take a step back.

"Hey," she said softly, reaching out so her fingertips brushed over my clenched jaw muscles. "It's okay. You'll put the metal on me because you have to. I understand you don't want to, but you can remove it straight away afterwards."

My magic thrummed around us, my spine locking tight and my fists curling and uncurling. It was harder this time—to lie. "Fine. It comes off immediately after the damned ball. I'll accessorise your outfit with silver, but if Haruin dares click his fingers at you, bids you kneel, or dares to humiliate you in front of those cowards that are supposed to lead the castes of this city, I will eat his fucking soul, and damn the consequences to this kingdom."

Her pupils swallowed her irises. Damn, she liked the aggressive and possessive tone in my voice. That only turned me on more. Knowing she felt like that was a relief because that's how protective I felt, and it would never change. I loved Zahlia. I always had. I know that love made me vulnerable and gave my enemies someone to use against me, but it didn't change anything.

My heart squeezed. Even though I'd declared her mine and that I belonged to her, I wasn't sure she'd feel the same way once she knew everything. My secrets would likely destroy us. And if she broke our bond, it would destroy me, but it would be her choice. I would never imprison her like my father did to my mother. When we were home, I'd confess my sins. Perhaps she would forgive me. Until then, I needed to protect my heart and keep the depth of that love to myself.

Lia wound her arms around my neck and her legs around my waist. I held her against me and gave her absolute reign over my body. Magic ripped open my leathers. I didn't care. I could replace them in the blink of an eye. My shirt followed until it hung loose from my shoulders, baring the muscles of my chest and stomach.

"Off," she mumbled against my lips.

I smiled. Supporting her with one hand under her firm buttocks, I pulled off my shirt and then fingered the material of the dress that had ridden up around her waist. "This needs to come off too."

The scrap of silky material slipped easily over her head, and I dropped it to the floor, leaving her utterly naked. Sweet and lust-filled, the scent of her desire hit me like the bouquet of a fine wine. I grumbled low in my chest, thirsty as fuck.

"Mine."

The word was out before I could stop it. Lia was strong and independent, but I felt the shudder that rippled through her at my declaration. Satisfaction lanced me, especially when I dragged her hips down from my waist to rub the steel of my erection against her apex, leaving a slick trail of her desire down my abs.

She glanced down at my trousers.

"Off," she demanded again, kissing me hard, undulating her hips until I couldn't think straight. I grunted but couldn't stop touching her long enough to undress.

"Lia, Angel, please, stop moving or I can't."

She bit my lip, growling low in her throat, her hands gripping my hair, tightening to the point of discomfort. That, and the nip of pain on the soft skin of my lip, had a pleasured groan rumbling from my chest as she took what she wanted.

I loved it. Her confidence. Her need. Her taste. The feel of her soft, demanding lips against mine. All of it.

A moment later, cool air brushed my skin.

I blinked. She'd used her magic to disperse my remaining clothes. That show of power and control only turned me on more.

Iridescent flames lit her eyes.

"Beautiful," I murmured.

"Now fuck me—hard," she demanded.

I gripped her hips, controlling myself long enough not to shove forward and hurt her. She mewled in protest as I held her still.

"Shh, not going to hurt you." And I slid my cock through the slickness of her folds. Again. Again.

She was whimpering, and my balls were so tight they ached by the time my control snapped Notching myself at her entrance, I pushed into her tight, soft heat. No matter that it nearly shattered my self-control, I held still, only part way in, giving her time to adjust. But Lia didn't want that. My grip loosened on her hips, and she growled, lifting herself and slamming down until I was balls deep inside her.

"Gods," I groaned, tipping my head back as she engulfed me. "So tight. So hot."

She panted. "Move, Dex, please. Need you so bad…"

So I did. I lost myself in the pleasure of our bond. This wasn't fucking, not for me. My whole existence had shifted. She was the centre of my universe, and I'd kill anyone who tried to take her from me. Hell, I'd burn every fucking world in existence for her.

ia

Watching Dex sleep was fast becoming one of my favourite things to do. After we'd finished in the study, he'd carried me up to his room. We'd both been sated, but when my stomach rumbled, he'd ignored my attempt to cling to his body like a limpet and deposited me in the shower while he organised some food. That done, he'd joined me.

Liquid warmth flowed through my limbs. Not only had he insisted on washing every inch of my skin, but he'd dropped to his knees to pay special attention to certain parts of my body before sliding his fingers inside me. When I'd moaned his name, he'd looked up at me and smiled. The sexy bastard had known exactly what he was doing. My chest heaved at the memory. I'd given in, moving my hips and begging him to put his mouth on me. He had. And it had been utter bliss.

My internal muscles clenched. Aether's balls, I was always so turned on around him. I'd thought having him would dampen my need, but I wanted him more than ever. I groaned quietly. If Mari weren't waiting in the library for me, I'd wake him up with gentle touches until he was moaning, his erection rock hard, and then slide down onto his impressive length. He'd wake up with his mind and body full of me and only me.

I ran a hand over my face. If I didn't get out of this bed, I never would.

His magic tugged on my heart, maybe in protest that I was leaving his side; I didn't know. Shadows lingered across the room, turning dark enough the moonlight was nearly hidden from the window.

"Hey," I whispered to them. *"Don't fret. Keep him safe for me, and I'll return soon."*

They shimmered and swirled around me, touching my skin with the softest of caresses before settling back near Dex. I wondered why he didn't wake up when I left his side. I watched him for a moment, but nothing suggested he was pretending to sleep. His breathing was even, and his body relaxed. Warmth filled my chest. It was all I could do to leave him there. He was my anchor, my other half, and I believed him when he said he would never leave me again.

My fingers curled into fists. *But you'll have to leave him; you know it, and something tells me he knows it, too.* Tears burned my eyes. Leaving him would break me, especially if I had to give myself over to the control of the Demon King. *You don't have to,* my magic whispered. I rubbed my chest over my heart. Dex's magic, *Dex* was always with me now. A stray tear rolled down my cheek. Would I have to break our bond so the Demon King could make me his? I had no idea how to do that. The thought of losing our connection terrified me. I knew without a shadow of a doubt that he wouldn't let me go without a fight. Yet, if I didn't let him go and make him believe I didn't want him, the Aether would die, and along with it, all living things.

The cycle of life had to continue. And I was part of it. It was time I accepted my fate.

Mari sat at our little desk, the light from a candle illuminating the gold highlights in her hair. A small book sat before her, but she wasn't reading it. She looked troubled, her lips pressed into a tight line.

My heart pounded. Telling her about Hentus filled me with anxiety. There was no guarantee she would want to see him. Would she blame him for leaving her? Especially as she went cold and distant when she talked of her time as her brother's prisoner. It said something that even the restrictions of her marriage didn't elicit that kind of response.

"Hey." Venturing closer, I sat down next to her. She gave me a tight smile in return. "What's wrong?" Hesitantly, I reached out, wanting to give her any measure of comfort I could. Her fingers were cold under mine, her face drawn, and her expression hollow. Unable to prevent it, I gasped. Her eyes were even more discoloured, her lips a deep purple. Dark veins spidered out from her lips, stark against her translucent skin.

My stomach sank. "Oh, my gods...."

She gave me a watery smile. "Gods indeed. Or perhaps not." She twirled the book, turning it so that I could read the title.

My heart skipped a beat. "The apothecary guide to tinctures & cures?"

Mari nodded. A purple-stained tear fell from the corner of one eye. Perhaps it was terrible of me, but I knew this was a way into the conversation about Hentus. He knew about poisons...

"You think someone is poisoning you?" My question was tentative.

"I do..." She coughed to clear her throat. "I do," she said, her voice stronger. "Escalon."

My heart flipped, and my brows drew down. "But why would he do that? He dotes on you..."

"Does he?" she snapped, her gaze meeting mine. Hurt swam in the depths of her eyes. For all his over protectiveness, I knew Mari cared for Escalon. She'd thought his concerns genuine, that he loved her, even if he didn't show it in the way our society said he should. But did he truly? I didn't know the Mad Prince, only that he'd gained that moniker because of how he treated his Queen. The whole of Tetron knew he went to extremes to keep his wife locked away and safe.

"What makes you think you're being poisoned?" I asked gently, even though it was what I believed, especially after speaking to Hentus.

She sighed and sat back, crossing her arms over her chest. "I've wondered for a while. The castle physicians never answer my questions about what's killing me; they never speak except to tell me what to do as they poke and prod." She took a shaky breath, her trembling fingers gripping mine. "As soon as we'd eaten dinner tonight, my eyes changed. This..." She circled her face with her hand. "Became worse immediately, and I felt like all my energy was being drained. Escalon just stared at me. He looked...angry. Or maybe scared." She shook her head. "I don't know. But he didn't hang around. He just grabbed his wine glass and left." She looked down at her hands. "I've suspected for a while that I am not dying from a rare illness, but I wasn't sure until today." Another tear dripped from her eyes. "Why would he do such a thing, Lia?" A small sob escaped her. "He's always been protective, or at least that's what I thought. Perhaps he never wanted to marry me, and keeping me from seeing anyone else wasn't to keep me safe but to stop anyone else from figuring out what he was doing to me."

I quickly rose and hugged her. "I honestly can't answer that. I expect the only one who can is Escalon. Just..." I took a deep breath. "Don't say anything yet. You aren't alone, Mari. You have far more people in your corner than you know, and they're fighting for you. They want you back."

She swallowed hard and pulled away enough to look at my face.

"What do you mean?"

Without letting go of her hands, I dragged my chair closer with my foot and sat down.

"Okay, so you told me about your uncle? Hentassian, wasn't it?"

She nodded, her brow furrowed. "Yes, but what's he got to do with anything? Andras told me he died."

Biting my top lip, I met her gaze. "He's alive, Mari. Your brother didn't manage to kill him."

Eyes lined with tears, she shook her head. "No. He wouldn't just leave. He'd have come back for me," she whispered.

I held her hands. "He didn't leave you, and he did try to rescue you.

He'd always suspected Andras would betray your father, and knew you were both at risk. He spent years setting up a new identity here in Tetris. It was for you, Mari. He was going to bring you with him to get you away from your brother."

Her face hardened. "But he didn't, did he? He left me. And I was kept a prisoner then used as a bargaining chip to foster ongoing peace with Tetron."

"Mari, he really did try to get into the palace. But Andras was waiting. Hentus and his friend Edge barely escaped with their lives."

Maria's eyes widened. "Edge? He's alive, too?"

"He is. You knew him, too?"

It was good to see the start of a smile on her lips instead of utter disbelief and shock. "He was my uncle's shadow. Always there to protect his back."

I smiled back. "Well, I think they took a break from each other. Something about a woman," I told her dryly.

Mari smiled wider. "That figures. I heard stories when I was young about how they always had women following them around." She huffed a soft laugh. "I never understood why women wanted to run around after men."

I rolled my eyes. "Power and strength are definitely aphrodisiacs. I've just met Edge, so I can't say, but Hentus has never been short of female attention."

Mari stared at me, pulling her hands from mine and twisting her fingers together. "Is he really alive?"

"He really is. He's been looking for a way to get to you for years. He knows you're here, and he also knows about your life being threatened."

"How does he know that?"

"Because I was worried about you. I suspected you were being poisoned when I saw that purple tinge in your eyes. I couldn't think of any illness that would do that."

Mari took a deep breath. "So what now? I know Escalon is possessive, but I never believed he'd hurt me…"

She looked so despondent that I didn't want to hurt her further by confirming I thought it was Escalon, too. I had no idea why he would do it other than he wasn't rational when it came to Mari. Instead, I tried to think about other possibilities. "Maybe it isn't him. Maybe someone else is doing it. Who prepares your food and drink?"

Mari's shoulders rose and fell, her brows twisted in thought. "I honestly have no idea who sorts out my food. It comes from the castle kitchens, as far as I know. Any drinks I ask for, too. But Escalon always brings my medicine every night. That's why I think it's him."

I agreed, but I could also see how much that thought hurt her. "Maybe it isn't. Maybe someone else prepares it, and he just brings it in."

"Maybe." But her voice broke, tears rolling down her cheeks, the wetness leaving a shining violet trail.

It hurt to see my friend so upset. Not in any stories of her past had she sounded as broken as she looked now. I wished I could give her some words of reassurance, but I had nothing. Her decline in health may have looked natural for the past years, but clearly, enough of the poison had built up in her system for it to show. That meant whoever was doing it wasn't concerned about others noticing. "Either way, you have to refuse to take it."

"But how? I can't pretend to take it or refuse, not when someone watches over me even when he isn't by my side." Her hands twisted in her lap. "I-I think they'd force it down my throat if I refused."

I sat back, my nostrils flaring, hating that she felt so threatened. "I don't know. We'll work something out. Besides, we don't know for sure if your medicine *is* laced with poison."

Mari's shoulders rolled forward like the weight of the world rested on them.

"The only way to truly know is to refuse to eat or drink. Then whoever's doing it will know I suspect and might finish the job."

She was right. This whole situation was impossible. My friend leaned back in her chair and rubbed her stomach.

"Are you okay?" That was such a stupid question. Of course, she wasn't okay.

Her eyes closed. "I just feel so sick all the time."

"I'm sorry," I said quietly. Then, an idea struck me. "Do you have access to a bathroom?"

"Yes."

"So drink water from there. Are you alone in your room during the day?"

She shook her head, and my heart sank at her lack of privacy. "No, if Escalon has to hold court, he sends in one of my ladies in waiting, plus a guard stands on the inside of the door as well as the outside."

I bit my top lip. "Okay, so when your meals arrive, you need to fake sickness. Say the smell of food makes you nauseous. That will get you out of eating, at least for the next day." I leant forward, needing to know she believed me. "Hentus really is alive, Mari. He's found a way into the castle. Will you agree to meet him? Please?"

A kind of yearning crossed her face, but she bit her lip, remaining quiet, pushed it away and straightened her spine.

"I understand you're unsure, but just give him a chance. Please?"

Her lips pressed together, but she nodded. "I will, but I'm done letting the men in my life manipulate me. If Hentus wants to get me out of this castle, I'll gladly accept his help, but I'll not be forced into another life against my will. Make sure he knows that before he comes here because if he plans to control me, use me, or sell me on, he'll regret it." Her fierce eyes met mine, glowing with a strange light that made my breath catch in my throat, and a bubble of pride burst in my chest. She snapped her fingers, and a tiny spark shot into the air. Understanding dawned. She had magic. Enough that if she wanted to fight her way out, she could. It wouldn't be as easy as accepting help, and there was a high possibility that she could die. But if fighting her way out was her only option, I knew she'd do it.

"I stayed because, despite his strange way of showing it, I believed Escalon loved me." She coughed to clear her thick voice. "But no matter how much I love him, I can't stay here. I honestly thought I was sick. Whether it's him or someone else poisoning me, I need to leave." Her eyes met mine. "Maybe Hentus can help me find an antidote?"

I nodded and met her eyes. "I'm sure he will. If you have magic, why haven't you left before?"

She smiled sadly. "Escalon wasn't my only reason to stay. Where would I go? I have no money, and no one to help me. I've never lived outside the walls of a palace. I don't know how to get anywhere or even who to find to arrange it." She raised her chin and set her jaw. "But if I have to, if it's a choice between dying and surviving on my own, I'll learn how to survive. I can do it," she said, determination in every word.

I smiled. "I've no doubt about that. But you won't have to. Hentus has his faults. He's a hard and cold man, except to those he loves. And believe me when I say he loves you. He'll protect you with his life."

She studied my face as if trying to weigh the truth in my words. I didn't blame her. Once she left the castle, she'd be vulnerable to so many; there were sure to be enemies of the crown, not to mention her brother and every other predator looking to ransom or sell a valuable commodity like her.

"I hope you're right."

"Me too." And that was the truth. "If you meet me here tomorrow night after the ball, I can use my magic to get us to my room. I've told him to wait there."

"Okay." Her voice was quiet and weary.

"When did you last have some fresh air?" I asked gently.

She shook her head. "I-I can't even remember. But there's a beautiful rose garden under my living room window. It makes me happy to see it, even if I can't walk there. Perhaps we could go see what it looks like in the moonlight?" she asked with a watery smile.

I stood and held out my hand. Mari was so very different from Dala, but she was still a warrior in her own way. She had survived being manipulated, sold as a bargaining chip, and locked in a gilded prison. No matter the scars all of that had left, it was time for her to spread her wings and go where she willed.

Her cold hand held mine as I walked us through the library to the big window. There was no sign of the mage hounds, and for once I was grateful that Dex sent them away from the castle every night. Mari peered down at the ground, a small line on the bridge of her nose.

"Do you trust me?" I asked with a smile.

"I do."

My chest warmed at her answer. "Then, once we're outside, lead us to the garden."

Her eyes widened as I stepped into the Veil and gracefully moved us through the window, floating to the ground.

Her eyes were huge. "Higher Powers, that was amazing."

I smiled. "Thank you, but let's go before the mage hounds return."

Stealthily, we made our way to the small rose garden and sat on a small bench, watching the clouds pass in front of the moon, lost in our thoughts, until I felt Mari shaking badly.

"You're freezing. Why don't you go in?" I suggested, worried about her.

She nodded, her face ghostly in the moonlight.

"Do you want me to take you back to your room?" I asked.

She shook her head. "No, it's fine." She stood, then leant down, wrapping her arms around me.

"I'll see you tomorrow," she said before making her way to the glass doors of the living area she shared with Escalon. I watched curiously. They were locked. All the doors were at night. Mari clicked her fingers, and light sparked. The lock snapped open. She looked over her shoulder, smiled and disappeared into the darkness of the castle.

I huffed a chuckle. At least she could get out of this castle if she decided not to go with Hentus. Pollen tickled my nose, the scent of winter roses delicate and soothing. I sighed. Their scent was definitely better than the smell of the Slopes. It was beautiful, sitting in the fresh air with the moon shining above, casting silver light over the world, yet I shivered.

Staring at the moon had seemed peaceful with Mari at my side. Now, it felt lonely. A sudden cold penetrated right into my bones. I glanced around, the hairs on my neck rising. My belly tightened, and my body trembled, my heart racing. What the fuck? I'd never been afraid of the dark; it had always been my solace, especially as it reminded me of Dex. Yet I searched the shadows, instinct telling me something was wrong. I stood, ready to jump on the Veil, when something caught my eye.

Out of the darkest shadows stepped a man. I immediately snatched a dagger from my thigh. Jumping into the Veil wasn't an option, not when he would see me. He lifted his hands in supplication.

I inhaled sharply. He was stunningly beautiful, especially with the way moonlight danced over his flawless skin. The blue-black hair resting over his shoulders gleamed like silk in the soft glow, and his stunning silver-grey gaze captured mine, looking right into my soul.

Dex was handsome in a ruggedly appealing way. His power and strength, the aura of raw danger that surrounded him, had always intrigued me, never scared me. This man was the opposite. Tall and sleekly muscled, he also screamed of danger, yet I didn't want to go near him. Under my wide-eyed scrutiny, his full lips curved into a rueful smile.

"I apologise for scaring you."

His voice made my heart pound harder. All I could do was stare at him. My voice dried up, and even the fingers around my weapon relaxed as I stared at his enchanting face. Without conscious thought, I took a step towards him. It was like he had a string attached to me and was winding it around his wrist, drawing me closer. Part of me was happy to let him. Only, along with that draw came a deep sense of wrongness.

I shook my head to clear it. What was I doing? No matter how stunning, this man was a stranger. I forced myself to take a step back. His brows rose. I took another step away.

He smiled reassuringly, yet my gut told me it was false.

"It's okay. I'm not here to hurt you. I'm a guest of the prince's. For the ball."

When I just looked at him, he seemed to take that as encouragement to continue talking.

"I was taking a walk to see this incredible moon." He didn't even look up, his eyes staying focused on me. "It's so large here and so bright. We don't have moons like this at home."

"Where's home?" I managed to croak.

"Oh, a long way from here." His piercing gaze still ensnared mine. "It's called Cimeria. Have you heard of it?" He narrowed his eyes, and I sensed that I somehow should.

There was something familiar about the name but, unable to place it, I shook my head.

"Pity."

The vicious cold was making me shake. I'd dressed for the library, not outside, and my shirt and soft trousers were not made for a Tetron winter.

His smile widened. "A quiet one, aren't you?" he said almost gently.

"Not usually," I mumbled, instinct telling me this man was far more than the sleek courtier he appeared to be.

His face lit up. "You do speak! Well, at least tell me your name?"

I swallowed. Was that a good idea? I couldn't see that it was dangerous for him to know my name. "Zahlia."

His head tilted forward, his brows raised slightly like he expected more. He took a step towards me. I took one back, unwilling to let him get closer. He had a strange effect on me, and I didn't like it.

"Well, Zahlia, it's been lovely to meet you. When I came to see this beautiful moon, I didn't know I'd meet an even more beautiful woman. I'm presuming you're a guest of the princes if you're allowed to wander the castle at night like this, so I look forward to seeing you at the ball. Now, I must get back inside. This cold is bitter."

His gaze dropped to where my nipples had pebbled, pushing against the soft fabric of my shirt. Going outside hadn't been on my agenda, so I hadn't bothered with a breast band. My face flamed, but I resisted the urge to cross my arms over my chest. His lips twitched like he knew that's exactly what I wanted to do, yet he took a step back.

"Goodnight, Zahlia. I'll see you very soon."

Once he'd disappeared into the shadows, I released a huge breath and resheathed my dagger. I rubbed my hands over my face, suddenly exhausted. All I wanted was to slip back beneath the sheets with Dex and hold him tight. I hadn't told him of Mari and Hentus, but I would after the ball. He had enough on his mind.

I stepped onto the Veil, taking comfort in the shimmering light. Despite its power warming me, there was a sense of dread in my heart that I just couldn't shake. It made me desperate to get back to Dex. I needed his arms around me as much as I needed to hold him.

CHAPTER TWENTY-SIX

ex

Once my shadows reassured me that Lia had reached the library and was safe with Mari, I pulled them back and allowed myself the luxury of sleep. Lia had been meeting the young queen regularly, and I was party to many of their discussions thanks to my shadows, but I'd started to give them privacy when I knew they would stay within the safety of the library. I'd never had a conscience when it came to spying with my shadows, but with Lia, it was different.

Omeron's boots made very little sound on the stone floors. He'd barely spoken since he'd arrived at my study this morning. "You ready for this?"

"Yes," I clipped, not ready at all. It was always the same when it came to the mortal magickers. Killing any of them made me sick, no matter how many lives I'd taken or souls I'd consumed over my lifetime. War and death were my calling, but against my enemies, not against people who could no more threaten me than they could use their magic.

Omeron walked alongside me, the atmosphere between us heavy. He didn't like our role in this deception any more than I did, but we had to keep the princes off our backs just a little longer.

We stepped outside, walking with purpose, our boots crunching over the freshly fallen snow. I frowned. When Lia had slipped into bed and into my arms, she had smelt of fresh air, not books and that unique musty smell the library had. She'd been cold enough that I wondered if she'd been outside, but before I could ask, she'd kissed me. All I could think about then was how her soft breasts pressed against my chest, how smooth her skin was under my hands, and how I wanted to hear her moans of pleasure. I scowled, rubbing a hand over my face. Damn, I could barely go a few minutes without thinking of her and how perfect she was. I fixed a stern look on my face as I threw open the door to the guard room.

"Sir!"

"Sir!"

The guards snapped to attention, saluting me. I nodded and waited. One scurried forward and opened the door to the cells.

"The princes will arrive shortly. Inform them we are here," I said as I stepped through the doorway, grabbed a lantern from the wall and descended the stone steps. My foot hit the bottom one, and Omeron stepped down beside me a second later. Without the lantern, it would be pitch black. I didn't need its light to see. Omeron didn't either. He and our warriors were made for hunting in the darkest reaches of the underworld, but the lantern gave us some semblance of weakness, of mortality.

There was noise from the guardroom above.

We exchanged a look. "Let's go. I want to speak with the leader of the magickers before the princes arrive."

Omeron's face was grim, but he nodded. The lantern flickered out, and we stepped into my shadows. Seconds later, we stood outside the heavy silver door that imprisoned the mortals. Pulling a key from under my breastplate, I hardened my heart and unlocked it. The clatter of the lock echoed, and a moment later, the stench of terror tainted the air. As old and used to death as I was, it was a familiar smell. The whole underground level of the castle reeked of it. Inside this cave, it thickened the air until it was difficult to breathe.

The man I sought waited near the door, his jaw clenched and a determined look on his face. He was no more than skin and bone, his ragged and soiled clothes hanging off him. He'd already earned my respect for his sacrifice, and I would reward him for it—eventually. I didn't bother with polite greetings. We'd already met, and he knew what was to happen.

"They're coming. It's time."

His throat bobbed, his fingers curling into fists, but he nodded. I wondered if he would change his mind, but then he turned to the others.

"You know what's going to happen. None of you will try to stop it."

"No, you can't do this, Kendrick," begged a woman who stepped forward and clung to his arm. He touched her face, such love in his eyes that even I had to swallow down my rage and self-loathing at what I was about to do.

"Yes, my love, I do. I'll do whatever it takes to save the rest of these people. So will you."

The woman nodded, and they stared into each other's eyes.

Omeron took the lantern from my hand and tipped it until the small channel of burning oil that circled the cave caught fire. As more sconces burned, light illuminated the magickers huddled at the back of the cave. Whimpering and murmurs started in earnest when those flames illuminated the warriors Omeron and I had already positioned around the cave. They had arrived from the shadows wearing the Tetron army uniform but none of them belonged to the princes. I looked each one in the eye and nodded a greeting. One by one, they lowered their gaze in respect before watching the crowd again.

Even through the stench of panic, I sensed the approach of the two princes and their personal guards. I nodded at the two nearest warriors, and they took up a position outside the great silver door.

The mortal man, Kendrick, stood stoically with his wife clinging to his hand. He met my gaze and raised his chin. "You will honour your promise, or when I am reborn, I will hunt you to the ends of this world and the Nether. I will never stop, not until you are dead and gone with no soul to be reborn."

I almost smiled. No mortal or lesser demon could kill me, no matter how vengeful. Kendrick was physically weak, but he was a brave man who deserved every bit of respect I could show him. Knowing I had time, I placed my hand on my heart and flickered into my demon form. Screams started somewhere in the crowd, the stench of piss strong in the air, but Kendrick held my fiery gaze. I bowed my head.

"I will honour my promise as you have pledged to serve me."

His throat bobbed again, and he disengaged his arm from the woman's grip.

"Step away," he encouraged.

She did, wringing her hands, her attention solely on him as if committing every inch of his face to memory.

"Kneel!" I bellowed just as Escalon marched into the cave, Haruin close behind. All of the prisoners dropped to their knees.

The two brothers stopped on either side of me, our usual position for this charade. Omeron stood against the wall, watching my back. Escalon eyed the kneeling magickers with a blank face, yet something like pity shone in his eyes. He swallowed hard before turning to look at Haruin, his gaze, once again hard, his jaw set.

"The mage hounds scented magic on every single one of them?" he asked his brother.

Haruin cocked his head. "Do you doubt me, brother?" His voice was etched with warning.

Escalon turned away, gazing at the cowering people, looking at each one like he wanted to commit their faces to memory. "No."

The Mad Prince glanced at me, his mouth flattened into a thin line. His face was more gaunt than usual, and he looked exhausted. Tension simmered between the brothers. Then again, Escalon could never stomach watching these deaths. He and Haruin only ever observed the first magicker die, then left.

Cowards.

I held back my snarl and stood quietly, the obedient general awaiting orders.

Escalon remained stiff, staring at the whimpering prisoners who knelt before him. He'd never hesitated like this before. Shit. Now was not the time to develop a conscience. I needed the princes to leave, but I didn't let my frustration show, aware of Haruin's gaze bouncing between his brother and me.

The silence stretched.

"Problem, brother?" Haruin enquired softly.

Escalon didn't answer, though I heard his teeth creak, his jaw muscles popping. I kept my eyes on the bowed heads of the prisoners, but my shadows saw it, the smirk on Haruin's mouth, as if he were enjoying his brother's discomfort.

Escalon spun and faced Haruin, his eyes flashing and his nostrils flared. I bit back my surprise at the hate that burned in his gaze. Escalon didn't so much as look at me, and neither did Haruin. I took a slow step back, wondering at the loathing between them.

Haruin cocked his head, a slow, evil grin baring his white teeth. "Careful, brother. Remember, control is key, especially when you have an ill wife who needs you. Only the Higher Powers know how quickly she could deteriorate...."

I frowned at the warning in his tone. There was obviously something else going on between them. Escalon leaned forward, his rage thickening the air. He was physically imposing, unlike his younger, sickly brother, and could easily settle whatever their dispute might be with physical strength.

My eyes narrowed, another possibility crossing my mind. Maybe it wasn't about the two of them. I thought about the queen, how ill she looked, and how she'd told Lia she was dying. Before I could sort out my thoughts, Escalon straightened, his whole body tense.

He turned to me. "Kill them all." His breathing remained fast, his fists clenched.

This was not a man who wanted to exact such justice.

Haruin patted his back, and I saw the flash of murderous intent in Escalon's eyes before he stepped out of his brother's reach. "I am going to my Queen," he barked. "Do not follow me."

"Wouldn't dream of it, brother." Haruin waited for a beat and then added. "I have already had her medication delivered."

Escalon's steps faltered before he strode out, not even bothering to wait for the first magicker to die.

"Well," murmured Haruin. "I guess my brother has lost his taste for revenge. General." He raised his brows and looked pointedly at the prisoners.

I was acutely aware of Omeron at my back. Escalon's footsteps faded. There was far more going on between the princes than I understood, but I didn't need to; I just needed to refrain from wiping them off the face of this world for another few hours, and then I would be back home, walking through the halls of Haldaag's castle with my queen by my side.

Keeping my movements fluid and expression blank, I stepped up to Kendrick. He lifted his head and bravely met my stare. Sobbing started behind me. His wife. I blocked out the sound. This needed to happen. Without another word, I lifted my heavy axe and swung it down with all my strength.

A second later, a wave of agony slammed into me as if my heart was being ripped out. My legs nearly buckled, and only sheer force of will kept me standing.

"A clean execution, General. More than someone like him deserves," Haruin snarled from behind me.

I didn't turn. I couldn't. Not when I'd locked my knees to keep them from collapsing. His presence receded from my back. The ringing in my ears settled, but I could only hear quiet sobbing. I looked down. Kendrick's dead eyes looked at nothing. I staggered, and a strong arm came around me.

"What the fuck, Dex?" hissed Omeron, helping me to the wall where I leaned, trying to get my bearings.

"I-I..." My whole body started to shake. I had no idea what was happening, but there was no time to waste; we had to finish this.

"Close the door, Omeron. We need to deal with these people."

"No, *we* don't. I do. You need to get yourself together and call Kendrick to you. The men and I will do what needs to be done."

I could only nod. My gaze fell on Kendrick. Closing my eyes, I forced myself to move into the darkness. I searched and searched until

I found him. Without waiting, I pulled Kendrick's soul into the dark side of the Veil, but I didn't feed off him. I had a promise to keep.

CHAPTER TWENTY-SEVEN

ia

Saline spray misted my face. I wiped at it with the back of my hand, annoyed when more dripped into my eyes, making them sting. Dala and I stood in the cave mouth, holding up a flickering ball of light I'd formed with my magic and watched the small boat thrash up and down in the churning waves. It was so rough I wondered how Angus had ever managed to get into the tunnels alone.

Angus laughed and threw me a rope. "Come on, Zah. Haul us in." He must have seen my face because he flashed me a wink. "I have all kinds of talents," he yelled over the boom of the waves.

I shook my head and laughed. "I don't want to know."

His grin widened, his grey eyes sparkling with humour. "Who says I'd show you anyway?"

"Bet you'd show me, though, wouldn't you, big boy?" quipped Dala, smirking.

We both knew he'd always been sweet on her. Angus rolled his eyes.

"Concentrate," snapped Hentus, throwing another rope up to Dala.

I laughed, though I understood the tightness around Hentus's mouth and jaw. He was about to meet his daughter for the first time in years, and Mari had no idea she could break Hentus without even trying.

A vicious swell hit the small boat. I clenched my teeth and held tight to the rope, glad for the leather gloves I wore. There were a few rocks past the entrance to the tunnel that thankfully broke the worst of the waves. Nevertheless, it was damned dangerous. By the time Hentus, Edge, and Angus scrambled out of the boat, we were soaked to the skin and shivering.

"Did you see any guards or lookouts up on the cliff?" I asked.

Edge peered out at the rain-laced darkness. "No, it's far too dark for them to see a small boat like ours, but something feels off."

"Like what?" asked Hentus, frowning at his friend

Edge shrugged before studying the shadows of the cave beyond the small ball of light I'd formed. "Not sure. Like there's someone out there—or in here..."

Hentus studied the darkness, then met my gaze. "Be on your guard. Edge has a knack for sensing anything unusual."

I nodded. "Is that your magic?"

Edge shrugged. "Some of it. My magic's not as powerful as Hent's, but it's proved useful over the years."

Hentus smacked him on the shoulder. "It has, my friend."

I had a feeling there was more to Edge's magic, but it wasn't the time to pry. They should probably know about the drain on their magic, too. Just not why. "Be careful with your magic down here. This place—the castle, it seems to mess with it."

"What do you mean?" asked Angus.

I shuddered. "It dampens it somehow. It's a horrible feeling."

Hentus and Edge nodded. "Good to be warned."

With Angus's help, Dala and I hauled the boat out of the water while Edge explored deeper into the cave. Hentus waited for us. I peered out over the ocean, goosebumps rising on my damp skin. Was Edge right? I thought he might be since I couldn't shake the feeling that something awful was about to happen.

"This way," instructed Dala, leading the way into the tunnels at the back of the cave. I willed the small ball of light to follow them. Bringing up the rear, I suddenly spun. Something was watching me. I was sure of it. Was it Dex? I peered back at the mouth of the cave and the shadows that now swamped it as my light moved forward with the others.

"Dex?" I whispered.

Nothing. I shivered even more. A light flickered on the horizon like the lantern on a ship. My heart thumped, and I blinked to clear my sea-soaked vision, but it had disappeared. I stood watching the dark sky, starting when a hand landed on my shoulder.

"You okay?" asked Angus, his voice low, his body coiled and ready to fight.

I swallowed. Maybe I'd been mistaken. Movement caught my eye, and I stared at the shadows. Once again, they were still. Empty. I huffed a quiet laugh.

"Yeah, it's Edge. He spooked me."

"Spooked you? Damn, Zah, that's not like you. You've been lording it in this bloody castle too long. You're going soft. You never used to see things that went bump in the dark."

That was before I knew the Demon King was after me, and there was a gate to the Netherworld under my feet, ready to suck magic from me.

"Hey," I thumped his massive arm. "I'm not going soft."

He laughed. "Yeah? Maybe not, but it took that uneasy look off your face."

I smiled. "Come on. Let's catch up with the others."

He nodded and though he was smiling, moved quicker than he should over the slippery rock surface. The darkness closed in behind me, and I was sure I heard the soft snort of an animal's breath before we entered the tunnel.

"Which way?" asked Hentus.

We stood at the intersection of the tunnels. One led to my bedroom, the other to the dungeons. My blood ran cold. Pained and desperate whimpers echoed down that tunnel. That sense of dread from earlier returned, twisting in my gut.

Hentus met my gaze, his own hard and cold. "Don't go there, Zahlia. No matter what's happening, you can't help those people."

"How do you know that? You don't know what's going on any more than I do."

Edge blocked my path. "He's right. Don't go down there." He met my eyes. "You'll get hurt." His statement was quiet, almost sorrowful like he knew what would happen if I did..

"Listen to him, Zah. He's never wrong. How do you think I lived so long as the brother of one of the most hated rulers in Pa'dur's history? How do you think I survived Andras's betrayal?" Hentus took a step towards me, his face pleading. "His *feelings* aren't frequent, but when they come, he's usually right."

No matter that I believed him, I couldn't ignore those poor people.

"I know you need to get to Mari." I nodded towards the tunnel that led to my room. I hadn't shared my change in plans with Hentus, but Mari and I had decided it was safer for her to wait in my room than to transport Hentus through the castle. She was confident she could escape her guards and move through the corridors undetected, and I didn't doubt her. I worried that she was too unwell to wait for us, but something was pulling me down this tunnel towards the dungeons. My stomach churned. Part of me knew what I'd find, and though I didn't understand it, I knew I had to see if I was right. I prayed I was wrong, and it wasn't Dex causing those sounds of pure terror and agony.

"Don't go down that tunnel. There's nothing there but a dead end." I pointed at the one that led to the gate. The darkness pulsed, tugging at my magic. I shuddered, never wanting to feel that voracious hunger strip me of every bit of energy ever again. "Just follow this one. It will lead you to the stairs that will take you to my room. Dex isn't in the house tonight and has no house staff who might discover you as long as you stay in my room. Either Mari will be there by now, or she'll find you." I met Hentus's gaze. "Don't hurt her, Hent. If she doesn't want to leave with you after the ball, that's her choice. She may need some time..."

"I know." His gaze went to the tunnel behind me. "Why?"

He didn't need to ask any more than that. It was too unlike me to completely ignore his warnings.

"Because if Dex isn't the man I hope he is—then I need to know." I released a shaky breath. "The magickers are in that dungeon. I-I need to know that he hasn't hurt them."

Hentus cocked his head. "But he isn't a man, is he, Zahlia? He's far more. You can't push the morals of our world onto him. If he's set on a course of action, there's always a reason behind it. You know that better than anyone."

I swallowed. Did I? I'd started to trust him, to believe his words. "But murdering innocent people?"

Hentus raised his brows. "All of us in this tunnel have spilt innocent blood at one time or another, Zahlia. Don't be a hypocrite."

Anger burned through me, not to mention a heavy dose of guilt. "Not on this scale, Hentus. And never because someone else told me to kill."

His smile was bitter, his eyes far too sharp. "You sure about that, sweetheart? It was me who sent you out night after night to thieve. It was me that expected you to kill…"

No matter how much I wanted to deny it, he was right.

"Morals are all well and good, but life is never black and white; there are always shades of grey," he said before he turned away, disappearing into the pitch black.

Dala stepped up to my side. "I'm not leaving you."

I nodded, glad she was with me.

The small ball of light I controlled above our heads was only just bright enough to illuminate our progress. The stench of fear, unwashed bodies, and excrement filled the small space. I'd seen plenty of depravity in my life, but the thought that Dex ordered this kind of treatment of innocent people made me ill.

Eventually, we were forced to stoop low and then crawl on our hands and knees. As the voices got louder, our space became barely big enough to shuffle forward on our bellies. I doused my magic and wriggled along like a snake, uncaring of the rips in my clothes or the cuts and grazes on my skin.

My stomach sank when I realised the tunnel was a dead end,

though right in front of my face was a small opening, slightly larger than my head. It was big enough for me to peer down into the large cave and see all the frightened people kneeling, their heads bowed.

My breath caught. Opposite me stood Dex. His face was hewn from granite, his dark eyes utterly cold. Escalon stood just in front of him, glaring at the prisoners. It wasn't hate I saw on his face, but pity, even guilt. He closed his eyes and locked his spine before turning back to Dex. It was then I saw Haruin. His expression turned my blood cold. He said something to his brother, but even though I strained my ears, I couldn't hear. Escalon hesitated. His back was to me, so I had no idea if he answered his brother before he walked away. From my position opposite the open door, I saw him slump against the wall of the dungeons. Perhaps there were no guards in the hallway, or if there were, he didn't care if they saw that show of emotion from him.

Haruin barked something at Dex. Dex kept his eyes on the prisoners, his whole body radiating tension, and I held my breath. Would he end Haruin? My heart sank when he strode forward until he loomed over one of the prisoners. The man's face was accepting but not weak, not pleading.

"No," I whispered. I couldn't tear my gaze from his face as he lifted the axe.

Don't do it. Please... I silently begged him.

The blade swung, and my heart shattered.

CHAPTER TWENTY-EIGHT

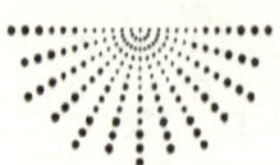

ia

A wave of dizziness hit me. *Why? Why would he do this?* I still had no idea, but it sickened me to suspect he'd gone through with this because of me, because he needed more time to get us out of this world. Haruin was cruel enough to threaten Dex the same way he threatened me. If he'd refused to end that poor man, we'd probably not even make it to the ball, let alone escape this castle. Neither would Omeron or Dala. My chest squeezed as I realised that Dex himself had just given me a reason to break our bond.

To save this world, I had to bond with the King of Demons, and I couldn't do that if I was already bonded to Dex. Tears flooded my eyes at what I had to do. Especially knowing Dex had bowed to Haruin and Escalon to protect me and give him time to get us to the Nether.

Using instinct to guide me. I yanked at the ribbons of magic I'd wrapped through my heart and magic. This was a gamble. Not only was it dangerous, but the thought of feeding from anyone other than

Dex made me shudder. I could magically starve if this went wrong and the Demon King didn't find me in time.

The world tilted, and pain ripped at every fibre of my being, but I kept pulling and tearing. When the roaring in my ears faded a little, I heard the sobs and whimpers from the other prisoners.

"Hey! Zahlia!Talk to me, what's wrong?" Dala shook my shoulder.

A choked sob escaped me. I hated lying to my best friend, but I had to. If she discovered my plan, she'd stop me, and I couldn't let that happen. "He did it. He killed an innocent, unarmed man. I can't..." There was no time to wallow in the pain of breaking our bond, so I shoved it away. I felt hollow, like a huge part of me had disappeared along with our bond.

Dala let her hand drop from my shoulder. "Come on, we need to get out of here."

I vigorously shook my head, wishing the waves of nausea away. "No, I can't leave them. He'll kill them all."

"And what are we supposed to do against all of those guards?" Dala studied the room. "There's at least ten, plus Omeron and Dex. Not to mention this solid stone wall in the way."

I swallowed and wiped at my face and nose. I could fall apart later. A glance back into the cave confirmed Dala was right, but I couldn't leave those people to be killed by Dexalion. Surely, he'd find a way out of this and spare them.

Dex leaned on the far wall as if trying to prop himself up. He rubbed his chest, his face ashen. Even from where I hid, I could see his throat work and his eyes briefly close. I bit my lip, using the pain to focus, instead of falling apart at how much this was hurting us both.

"You go if you want Dala. I've at least got to try and save those people. To reason with him."

"Lia, I know you're angry, but listen to me. How the hell are you going to get them out? We can't even get into the godsdamned cave!"

"Yes, we can." My light seared the shadows away.

"No! No!" Dala pinned my arms to my sides, her eyes glaring into mine. "If you go in there now, we'll both die, and they will still kill all those people. We can't win against all of them." She peered into the cave. Omeron's voice was loud as he issued commands. I felt her stiffen. No matter what she said, I knew she'd developed feelings for Dex's second-in-command.

"I'm sorry, Dala." And I honestly was. My lies were going to affect her future as much as my own.

Her smile was full of venom and promise, which only made me feel worse. "Don't be, my beautiful friend. I was never meant for a relationship or love."

Her brows drew down, and I craned my neck to follow her gaze. We exchanged a look.

"Okay, now I'm completely confused," she whispered.

Dex had straightened from the wall, and though he was still pale, it was the anguish on his face as he spoke with Omeron that pulled the pieces of my heart apart again. I forced myself to look away, guilt heavy in my chest. I shifted my body to see the silver door to the cell, but it was closed. Thankfully, Haruin had completely disappeared. In the opposite corner, another doorway in the rock was open. I frowned, sure it hadn't been there before. The prisoners were being ushered through it.

My heart sank. "Oh my gods, he's taking them somewhere else. Do you think he's going to kill them and throw their bodies in the sea?"

Dala stretched her neck to better see through the hole and shook her head. "But there was no other exit."

I pointed. "There is now."

"Lia, it doesn't matter; we've got to leave. They can't be helped right now, but you can save yourself and still give Mari and Hentus a chance. You've just got to hide your magic until after the ball. Then we can go with Hentus and leave all this behind. Hell, maybe we could actually leave this shitty city, maybe even get on the next ship to the Medallion Isles."

Dala didn't know about the silver I had to wear at the ball, and it wasn't the time to tell her. I looked back into the cave. The prisoners were gone, along with the silent guards. Dex was standing tall again, though his face was still pinched. By his legs stood a giant, scaled hound. My breath caught. Bigger than a mage hound and covered in scaly thick skin, with horns than curled from the side of its skull, I'd never seen anything like it. It silently watched me. After a moment, it huffed and looked up at Dex, who shook his head.

"No, leave them. Go after the others."

The hound trotted forward, aiming a snarl in our direction before it trotted out of the door. Omeron strode across the room and shut the extra door. Dex's shadows brushed across its surface, and it disappeared. I couldn't hold back my gasp. Even the man's beheaded corpse had gone.

Dex faced our hiding place, though his shoulders were stooped. I wanted to cower, but I didn't. I hated myself for what I'd done, yet I knew I had no choice.

A fine sheen of sweat covered Dex's upper lip. "We need to talk, Angel."

Dala curled her upper lip. "No, don't, Zahlia. We need to get back to the others."

I shook my head. "No, he can find me anywhere, and I won't put you all at risk. We need to buy time. Then, once Mari, you, and the others are safe, I'll get away from him." And I would, just not to my friends. I would be escaping to somewhere far more dangerous.

She clenched her jaw, then nodded.

I gave her fingers a squeeze. "Good, then go. Get the others out tonight, and I will play this game with him and the princes until after the ball. Dex won't harm me, Dala. He needs me if he wants his world to survive."

It hurt to think I'd be going to the Nether without him. But neither he nor Dala needed to know my actual plan. Lying to them both would be hard, but I'd do it to stop our worlds, and them, from dying. Dala's nostrils flared but she didn't argue. She knew it was pointless to run. There was nowhere to go. Thank the goddess I hadn't shared my suspicions about Marianne with Dex. Pulling my magic to me was hard work, but I pushed onto the Veil and stepped through the rock and into the cave.

"Why?" Dex asked as soon as he saw me, hurt twisting his features.

I swallowed and plastered an angry look on my face. He had to believe my disgust was genuine. "Are you for real? You just murdered an innocent man for possessing less magic than you have in your little finger, and you ask me why?"

He shook his head. "No, you don't understand. You're killing me, Angel."

"You're such a fucking liar, Dex. Nothing I do could ever hurt you like you just did me."

A loud warning rumble filled the air. Omeron snarled his predatory gaze fixed on me.

"That's enough!" Dex barked at him. "Stay out of this, or leave."

Omeron shifted his glare from me to Dex but stood way off to the side.

I ignored him. "Why did you do it, Dex?"

"Because that man agreed to it."

My eyes widened, hating that I couldn't ask why or tell Dex I believed him. Instead, I shook my head. "No, he damn well didn't! I watched the whole thing. He didn't say a word."

Dex heaved a sigh, lifting his hand. I narrowed my eyes, my heart racing as I saw his fingers tremble. He never trembled. He was the strongest person I knew.

Oh gods, what had I done? I wanted to throw myself at him and make sure he was okay—but I couldn't.

"Sweetheart, it isn't what you think. He sacrificed himself…"

Strong. Stay strong…

"Bullshit! Just stop, Dex! I thought you'd changed…that you wouldn't be so…evil." A small, choked sob escaped my throat. I hated that he thought my sorrow was for that unarmed man and not the pain I'd inflicted on him by breaking our bond.

"So you tore our bond apart?" he whispered.

Omeron swore. I didn't take my eyes off Dex. I couldn't because he looked so broken. I'd never hated myself as much as I did then.

"You don't know what you've done," he croaked and fell to his knees. "Angel, please, just listen to me; let me explain."

No matter my resolve, I couldn't stop myself from running forward and kneeling down in front of him. I placed my hands on his shoulders to prevent him tipping from forward. My next words sliced at my already torn heart.

"I can't, Dex. How can I trust anything you ever say to me? You killed someone because the princes ordered it. I don't understand why you would do such a thing. Are you so scared of what they could do to you?"

"No, not them."

He looked at me then. I gasped, tears pricking my eyes. Sorrow swam in his eyes, pain etched on his face. His large hand cupped my cheek.

"I'm so sorry, Angel. I'd hoped you'd trust me enough."

I frowned. "Enough for what?"

"To let me put these on you without a fight."

Before I could utter another word, something clamped down on my wrist, my arm was yanked behind my back. I instinctively went to strike my attacker with my free hand, but Dex caught my wrist.

"Please, don't fight this."

Another click of silver. There was no pain. I thought I felt hollow from breaking our bond, but this was a whole new level of emptiness. Gasping, I sagged forward, tears pricking my eyes.

Dex climbed to his feet and stared down at me, his face devastated.

"This is only temporary. I'll explain everything once we're back in Haldaag, then all my actions will make sense. I'll remove the silver when you're safe."

I should have known he'd do something like this. He'd said so many times he'd do anything to keep me safe. "Fuck you." I managed to croak, keeping up my pretence of fury, but even my voice was weak. Covering most of my forearms, thick silver bands gleamed.

Omeron watched me warily as he clipped two more around my thighs.

I looked back at Dex, tears blurring my vision. We were hurting each other so much. A little sob escaped me. I had no other choice.

He reached out a trembling finger.

"Don't you fucking touch me," I hissed, injecting venom into my words.

He paled but nodded. "This isn't what I wanted, Lia."

"Really? Me either. Why don't you take them off?"

He attempted to smile, but it didn't work. "And let you have enough magic to try and kill me? No, I don't think so."

"But you can't be killed. Can you, Dex? Or is that a lie, too?"

He remained quiet.

My heart sank, but I forced a bitter laugh. "It is, isn't it? You can die. Well, don't worry, I'll figure out how and put you out of your misery."

"Only you could, Angel."

"Like I said, take these off, and I'll gladly end you."

He hauled me to my feet. "'Fraid not. I'll not explain my actions to you right now because you're not in the frame of mind to listen, but there is an explanation for all of this. We just need to get through that ball and keep the princes off our backs. Then we'll summon a portal demon to get us back to the Nether."

"If you can summon a portal demon, why haven't you done it before?"

"Because I can't do it by myself. I need your help."

I shook my head and laughed in his face. "Silver, you arsehole. I can't access my magic."

"I'll take some of it off after the ball. You'll be able to access enough to do what we need. I just need you to stay calm until then." He took hold of my arm, not painfully but firmly enough to walk me to the door. "It isn't just our lives that rely on the portal, Angel. So, you *will* help me."

"What? You're threatening my friends now, too? You're no better than that smarmy, weakling prince, are you!"

For a moment, he looked confused. "Friends? What?" Then he blinked slowly and released a breath. "Yes, that's right, Angel. You need to behave and do as I tell you, or one by one, your friends will die until we have our portal. Now walk."

Omeron walked behind us as Dex took my arm and marched me through the darkness, up the steps and out through the guard house. I had no strength to fight him. Besides, if the demons couldn't get to me in this castle, I'd never be able to action my plan. I needed to get into the city and find them there, or if that didn't work, let Dex take me back to the Nether. Once I was there, I'd escape and search out the Demon King.

My breath caught when I saw a sheen of sweat on his skin. I didn't imagine that tremor in his grip, either. I looked away, the emptiness in my soul consuming me to the point I could no longer think of anything else. I stumbled several times, and even though I tried to shake off the hand that held me, Dex's hold was firm and unwavering.

We didn't exchange any more words. I was too exhausted. Too broken by the loss of my magic, of what I'd done to Dex, and what I still had to do.

When we reached his house, he guided me up the stairs, yet turned away from my room. "You'll get ready in my room."

"No."

He sighed, his face shrouded in shadow. "You will. Omeron, find Dala. Ensure she is contained and kept out of trouble until it's time for us to leave."

"Don't you hurt her, you bastard," I hissed, though I knew he wouldn't. Or at least, I was mostly sure he wouldn't.

"Then cooperate, Lia, and I promise nothing will happen to her. We just have to get through this fucking ball, and then I'll explain everything. If you still want to kill me, I'll let you."

Why would I want to do that? "What? There are more lies to confess?" I scoffed.

He just stared at me. Then his throat bobbed.

"Oh, my gods, there are." I looked away from him, unable to comprehend what was really going on with him. I'd known him most of my life, yet he was still a total stranger. The worst thing was, if my plan worked, he'd become my enemy.

CHAPTER TWENTY-NINE

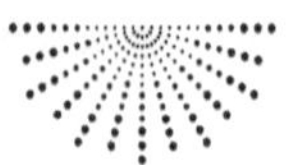

ex

"Hold still," I growled.

"Fuck you."

I hated the underlying tone of defeat in Lia's voice, but I didn't let it show. I lowered the scrap of material that was her dress. "Lia, please just put the dress on. The alternative is to go naked." I laid the dress on the bed.

Lia's eyes widened, and she bit her lip. "You wouldn't," she whispered, her voice shaking.

I clenched my jaw, stared unwaveringly at her, and lied. "I would. There's more at stake here than your dignity, or even the lives of your friends. If you don't return to the Nether, our worlds will die." I didn't add that I was running out of time myself. Since Lia had severed our bond, the dark side of the Veil had shunned me. I couldn't feed.

I knew a rejected bond could kill, but I'd always believed I would have a chance to explain my actions to Lia before we even tried to bond. I hadn't counted on her reaching a feeding frenzy before we were even back in the Nether. Now, I'd die if I couldn't fix this mess between us. If she was unbonded and I removed the silver, the Heart would suck her dry when we returned home.

I squared my shoulders. I'd hoped she'd let me explain about the man I'd killed. Instead, she'd believed the worst of me, so I'd given up, knowing it would be easier to explain when she'd calmed a little and we were safe. Her throat moved as she swallowed hard and studied me with her cerulean eyes. I didn't allow my remorse to show. Let her think me cruel enough to kill her friends if it would get her to behave herself. We had precious little time to get to the ball.

Lia pressed her lips together. "Pass it to me." She held out her hand.

I picked up the scrap of fabric, straightening out the silk.

"I can do it!" she snapped.

Our fingers brushed, and a bolt of electricity zapped up my arm, right into my belly. I'd always been drawn to her fierceness, but since our bond had been severed, my whole being was desperate to touch her. I couldn't and wouldn't accept that she would throw me away so easily, but now wasn't the time to show her how much she needed me or how much I needed her. I willed my desire to settle as she dropped the dressing gown she wore from her shoulders, letting it fall to the floor, leaving her standing utterly naked and magnificent in front of me.

It wasn't defeat on her face anymore but a challenge. Her eyes flashed, and her chin lifted.

Fuck, she was testing my self-control.

My magic thrashed to escape my hold, my breathing ragged.

She smiled, but it wasn't warm. "That's what I thought. You wouldn't make me go naked."

I took a step forward.

Her defiance slipped a bit. "Touch me, and I will fight you until one of us dies."

I grimaced. "Have you forgotten, Lia? I can't die." I stepped forward, unable to resist. "And we both know if I touch you, you'll be mine within seconds. You won't fight me."

She huffed, but her pupils widened. "I will fight. With every fibre of my being."

I cocked my head. She would. But she wouldn't win. "At first, maybe. But you'd end up begging for my touch, for my body to destroy yours." I dared to step close enough that there was barely any space between us. Her body heat mingled with mine, and she was forced to tilt back her head to maintain eye contact. "Because deep down, you know I belong to you, Angel. Our destiny is written in the stars of this world and our own. And even though you've severed our bond, I won't let you go." I inhaled deeply and allowed a small, arrogant smile to stretch my lips. "And you don't want me to."

She swayed forward, her lips brushing mine. I had to bite down on my moan as lust blasted through me. Her fingers grabbed and rubbed at the steel length of flesh pushing against the ties of my dress uniform trousers. My mind went blank. Her touch was dangerous to me. She had power over me like no other in existence. Her mouth slanted over mine, and I groaned as her tongue pushed between my lips. My breathing turned harsh, my heart hammering.

"Lia," I whispered hoarsely as her hand moved up and down in a fast, hard rhythm that made my head spin and my balls tighten. My magic thrashed to get to her, and I was a second away from letting it, from begging her to let me back in so I could touch her body and soul⋯and *feed*. I was ravenous and weaker than I'd ever been. Higher Powers, I was about to climax in my trousers like a teenage boy. I'd lost this fight, and I knew it. I was ready to beg when she pulled away, leaving me hanging.

It took me seconds to pull my head back together, at which time Lia had grabbed the dress and slipped it over her naked body.

I panted, struggling to regain control of my body and the lust raging through my blood. I throbbed, twitching as her eyes dropped to the bulge in my trousers.

"Just remember who has power over whom, Dexalion." She lifted her arms, the silver cuffs I'd fixed on her creamy skin gleaming sickeningly. "These only contain my magic, not me."

I opened my mouth to tell her how glad I was, but before I could speak, there was a knock at the door. I took a deep breath, trying to regain some of my equilibrium. She'd used my feelings to prove that she still had power, even without magic. It left me cold to think she hated me for what she'd witnessed. She truly believed I'd kill an unarmed, innocent man for no reason. Then again, I hadn't given her a reason to believe anything else. Part of me was convinced that even when she knew why I'd murdered him, she wouldn't forgive me for the other things I'd done.

I gave her a small smile. "My body's reaction to you changes nothing. We still have a ball to attend, a gate to destroy, and two worlds to save."

Another more insistent knock rattled the door.

"Dex?" Omeron barked.

Stepping away from her didn't lessen the ball of need that simmered in my soul. I stuck my shaking hands in my jacket pockets and hardened my face.

"Come in."

Omeron walked in, looking resplendent in his dress armour.

"Where's Dala?" Lia snapped.

Omeron faced her and bowed his head. Respectful, even in the face of her contempt. "She is safe and well."

"That isn't what I asked."

Omeron nodded. "I know. Please don't worry about your friend. If everything else goes as it should, Dala will remain safe and well."

Lia swallowed hard. "I will kill you both if there is so much as a scratch on her."

Omeron actually looked affronted. I hid my smile. Lia had no idea that Omeron would rather gouge his own eyes out than hurt Dala, but the threat to her safety was needed to accomplish what we had to do tonight. He exchanged a quick glance with me.

"There is no scratch on her flawless skin, nor will there ever be by my hand—unless you don't cooperate tonight." He actually managed to growl the last few words. I had to give him credit for his acting skills. I raised my eyebrows behind Lia's back. Omeron didn't react.

"Lia, we need to finish your outfit and go."

She glared at me but nodded.

"Turn to face Omeron."

She did, without any resistance. It hurt my heart that she thought we'd hurt Dala, but tonight would be much easier to get through with her compliance.

"Lift your arms, Angel."

"Don't call me that anymore," she hissed. Her voice shook, but she did as I asked.

At least she couldn't see the hurt on my face. Thank the Higher Powers. My fingers worked quickly, sliding the silk rope belt, intertwined with silver thread, around her to hold the silk panels to her slim waist. I picked up the strappy sandals that the tailor had picked to go with the excuse of a dress. They weren't much more than soles with leather ties attached. I knelt in front of her, not daring to look into her face. She had no undergarments on, the bare side panels of the dress showing her naked skin. I gritted my teeth, hating that this was necessary, but Haruin had ordered her outfit to show she was not armed and her magic was neutralised.

I'd already vowed that Haruin would die, but I chanted that promise to myself as I took one of Lia's perfect feet and wrapped the leather ties around her ankle and calf. Still not looking at her, I did the same for her other foot. I felt Omeron's gaze on me as I stood. A wave of dizziness hit, but I locked my knees and faced him.

"Let's go."

His eyes narrowed, but he nodded.

"Lia, we just need to get through tonight. Be polite to those who approach you, and only engage with Haruin if you have no choice. Omeron will shadow you if you get separated from me. I will not allow anyone to harm you. Nor will I allow you to escape. Remember that."

She sneered. "Really? You won't let anyone hurt me? Yet you're prepared to hurt my friends. How about if they humiliate me? Will that incur your wrath?" She swallowed as if her next words cost her. "You're the biggest hypocrite I've ever met. Perhaps *I'll* whisper words of condemnation about *your* treachery, *your* magic to the Mad Prince."

It cost me, but I sent a wave of magic around her, squeezing her arms tight to her sides. She snarled back at me but was helpless in my hold. "You won't if you want Dala to remain in the land of the living. Omeron might not want to hurt her, but I will do whatever I must." I blew out a breath. Remaining calm around her was difficult, but she had to believe I would follow through on my threats. "Remember all the innocent lives that will be saved by you returning to the Nether by my side."

She blinked. "I do. But I don't have to be by your side to save everyone, do I, Dexalion?"

Dread hit me. "What do you mean? Yes, you do."

She shook her head and walked to the door. I let her go, cold spreading through my chest. Did she know? Had she worked out that I wasn't the only one who could feed her? Not now that our bond was broken.

Music filled the air. In other circumstances, it would fill me with joy. Tonight, I barely heard it. I smiled politely, danced with the wives of caste lords and spoke with the husbands and lovers of caste ladies. I conversed politely with the elite of Tetron's society, all the while sickened by their ignorance of the plight of Tetron's people.

After three hours of dancing and insipid conversation, I'd had all I could stomach. I set my sights on where Lia stood compliantly by Haruin. Mari had pushed her way to Lia's side and would not be moved. She was the only reason the prince still lived. She had her arm linked through Lia's, and for once, I was thankful for Escalon's attentiveness to his queen's needs. She wanted to 'get to know' the magicker her husband had allowed to live in the castle. I hid a smile at Haruin's expression. He looked like he'd sucked on a lemon.

Mari carried on regardless, chattering away about inane things, ignoring her husband's urging to return to her room and rest.

He sighed and tried again. "But you are exhausted, dearest."

Mari made a dismissive gesture. "Nonsense, my love. I rarely have the opportunity to dance and enjoy company like this. Especially female company. You and your brother are the only ones I ever talk to. Allow me this night, my love." She met his eyes and fluttered her eyelashes endearingly. If it hadn't been for the dire circumstances of tonight and the knowledge of what I must do next, I would have smiled at her manipulation of him.

I bowed low. "Queen Marianne. It's a pleasure to see you. But may I steal the magicker from your side?"

"Why?" Haruin's question was sharp, suspicious.

"Prince Haruin." I greeted him politely and respectfully, even if I felt anything but respectful to the bastard who wanted Lia paraded around little more than naked. "I have reports of magic used in the East of the city. It is the magicker's role to track it."

He barely held in a snarl. "Use the mage hounds tonight. She's here at my command…"

Mari gasped as Lia tensed, her gaze dropping to the floor. But not before I saw the tears lining her eyes. She'd been paraded around, ridiculed and leered at by so many people I was ready to rip someone's head from their shoulders. Particularly Haruin's. In the corner of my vision, Mari placed her hand on Escalon's forearm. I cast a quick glance their way and didn't miss the pleading look she gave him. Escalon's brows dipped, and he squared his shoulders, standing tall and strong.

"Actually, brother, she's here on mine. And I wish her to spend more time with my wife."

Escalon turned his back on Haruin and faced me. I hid my surprise at him standing up to his brother.

"General, please accompany my wife and the magicker while they take a stroll on the balcony. When my queen is done, you may steal your charge away." His brown eyes met mine, for once not clouded with worry but clear and hard.

Holding his gaze, I nodded. He had an agenda, yet I had no idea what it was. Not knowing was dangerous, but if it got Lia away from Haruin without me murdering him, I'd readily agree. It also gave us the perfect opportunity to leave.

"Good." Escalon nodded and met his wife's gaze. Something passed between them. Mari gave him a blinding smile before Escalon leaned down and brushed a gentle kiss on her cheek.

Haruin's eyes narrowed on my face as if he was silently

commanding me not to obey Escalon's command. And that's what it had been, a command. I purposefully ignored the younger prince.

Escalon looked back at me. "General. I should appreciate you keeping my wife safe while I say my farewells to the other guests." He moved his gaze to Haruin, whose face was a mask of pleasant humour, but his eyes? They were full of a hatred so cold it made even me shudder.

"Shall we mingle, brother?" Escalon asked, seemingly oblivious. Yet, part of me wondered how ignorant the Mad Prince actually was. There was something in his face that I'd never seen before. Determination. But for what, I wasn't sure.

Given no choice, Haruin gave a jerky nod. Wrath that was nothing short of a promise of death shone in his eyes. I held his gaze with one of my own. My time serving him and his brother was very nearly done. Showing him my true self was tempting, but I held back. Getting to the Netherworld was my goal. These mortal princes would soon be a part of my past, nothing more.

Mari smiled up at her husband, her eyes huge. She squeezed Lia's hand and then stood on her tiptoes and kissed Escalon's cheek. "Thank you," she whispered.

"You're welcome, my love. Enjoy your walk. I'll find you soon."

Escalon and Haruin walked away, soon sucked into the crowd of preening Tetron elite.

"Come on, let's get out of here," Mari whispered urgently in Lia's ear.

Shame hit me as Lia just nodded, not lifting her gaze from the highly polished floor. She'd been talked about and studied like a prize mare for hours, and I hadn't stopped it. I'd watched closely and had tasked Omeron with her safety, so I knew no one had touched her, but being stared at and talked about for hours on end had taken its toll. I just hoped that Mari's presence had curbed the worst of it.

Keeping Lia's magic contained until we could leave this castle was the safest thing for us all because I knew once I released it, her magic would fly, and she would aim it straight at me. Anyone around us would become collateral damage, and she'd hate herself for that.

I walked ahead of them and pushed open the door to the balcony.

They breezed through arm in arm. It was cold enough outside that there wasn't anyone else on the balcony.

Lia shivered, her nipples peeking under the ridiculously sparse scrap of silk. Her gaze met mine, and a blush stained her cheeks as she crossed her arms over her breasts, hiding them from me. Biting down on a growl, I removed my jacket and placed it around her shoulders.

"This is nearly over, Angel," I said, my voice gravelly.

Her eyes lifted to mine, sorrow on her beautiful face. "I know."

There was something in her voice that worried me. Resignation, maybe? I'd only meant our time in this world, hiding who we were, was nearly over. In truth, our journey together had only just begun. Bond or not, she was mine, yet once we got to the Nether, there would be a whole new chapter of pain and mistrust, one that I wrote years ago.

We walked along the balcony, pausing in the shadows. I peered over the edge and noted that the guards were where they should be.

"Keep going." I gestured to the far end of the walkway where the shadows were darkest, and there was a door into the far end of the ballroom hidden from most guests by the large curtains.

"I need to get to Lia's room," Mari said urgently.

"Mari..." Lia warned.

Mari's eyes widened. "What? He doesn't know? Why haven't you told him?"

Lia's gaze flicked to me, her cheeks flushing guiltily. "Because...he can't be trusted."

I had no idea what they were talking about, but I needed to get to the gate to destroy it, and I wasn't leaving Lia here.

"My queen, I really do need to take Lia with me. Visiting Lia's room will be best left for another evening."

Mari raised her brows, the very picture of a haughty queen. She turned to Lia. "Do you want to go with him? Or come with me?"

Lia's nostrils flared, but she nodded as she took hold of Mari's hands and kissed her cheek. "You have been an amazing friend to me, Mari. Now, it's time for you to get your life back. I have to go with him, and you have to follow your own path. It's time." She turned to me. "We can take Mari to my room, can't we? To make sure she's safe? We have to go that way to reach the gate."

So Hentus had found a way in at long last. "We do." I studied Mari's face and felt a sense of pride that these two strong women had worked out that Hentus was the one who could save the young queen, not her overbearing husband. Although I was no longer sure that Escalon was as mad as he was perceived, nor was I as certain of his bond with his brother. Something was happening between the princes, but whatever it was, it wasn't my concern, so I pushed those thoughts aside. "You know Hentus is your uncle?" I asked.

Lia's eyes narrowed, not giving Mari a chance to answer. "You knew. That's why he didn't fight you when you came for me. You threatened to expose him, didn't you? That's how you got him to let me go without any trouble."

"That's right."

She gulped. "You really are a cold-hearted bastard."

I leaned in close. "Am I? Who do you think whispered from the shadows to urge Mari to the library so you two could meet?"

Mari gasped, but Lia cringed, remaining silent.

"That's right, Angel. I know who Hentus is and that Mari is his niece. I owe Hentus for everything he did for us when you were young, and seeing how ill Marianne was when I returned from the moors made me realise that he would never meet her unless I intervened. Escalon's love is destructive, and Mari needs to get out of this Aether-forsaken castle before it kills her."

"Escalon is not the one poisoning me, I'm sure of it," Mari said.

Lia took her friend's hand. "How do you know that?"

Mari bit her lip. "I just do. He wouldn't. He wants to save me..." Her words faded as she bit her bottom lip.

I didn't know what Mari and Escalon had planned, but I had an idea, and it changed nothing, we needed to go. Even if I *was* right, there was no need to let it interfere with destroying the gate and summoning a portal.

"We must go before your husband suspects you are missing. He'll set his guards on us and shut down the castle."

Mari's eyes flickered, and her lips thinned, but she just nodded.

We slipped through the isolated doorway and out of the ballroom into the servant's corridor. The staff stopped in surprise, bowing their heads to their queen, but we didn't slow our pace, nor did we run.

"Is Dala coming with us?" Lia half-whispered as we marched through the corridors, me nodding at the guards who stood watch near the doorways to my quarters.

I nodded. Now that we'd finished with that farce of a ball, I could give her the truth, or at least some of it. "Yes. I wouldn't really expect you to leave her behind any more than I'd expect her to stay here alone. She'd find her own way to the Nether." Neither would I separate Omeron from the female he knew was his mate, not in a million heart cycles.

"She would," Lia whispered, her voice catching.

If Mari was surprised to hear us discuss the world beyond the Veil, she didn't show it. Then again, she had her own issues consuming her thoughts.

We reached the entrance to my house. I nodded at the guards and ushered Lia and Mari through. As soon as the door closed, I turned the lock. "Let's go."

I urged the two women up the stairs, our footsteps muffled by the old carpet. As we passed my room, I halted them. Without speaking, they understood, followed me in and waited just inside the door. I didn't bother with my armour; there was no time. I quickly strapped my sword down my back, called my axe from the shadows and fixed it to my waist, and fastened a heavy baldric across my chest, ensuring the knives and daggers it contained were secure.

Lia's gaze lingered on the weapons across my chest, and I couldn't help but wonder if she was planning which one she'd use to end me. I cocked a brow at her. She lowered her eyes and turned her back, crossing her arms over her chest. I glared at that damned stupid dress and wondered if we had time for her to change. It had taken longer than I'd wanted to return here, so I didn't want to risk it. At least my jacket covered her and offered some protection.

My magic was weak, but I felt better with my weapons secured to my body. Wiping the sweat off my brow, I swallowed against my dry throat. Weak. I was too weak. But I wouldn't ask Lia to renew our bond until we were home and she knew everything.

Lia's eyes narrowed, and she studied me closely, but I ignored her unspoken question and indicated we should leave. We walked quickly to her room, and I couldn't sense anything amiss until we reached the door. There were multiple people in there.

"Wait," I hissed as Lia reached for the door handle.

She scowled but withdrew her hand. "Why?"

With my brows raised, I moved forward, and she was forced to step sideways as I opened the door. "Do you know for certain who's behind this door?"

Her nostrils flared, but she stayed silent.

Inside, the room was dark. I quickly scoured the corners for threats. Thankfully, there were no surprises. "You can come out," I said.

"About damned time," muttered Hentus, stepping out from behind the curtains. "We've been here too long."

Angus almost fell out of the old oak wardrobe, another big man behind him. I huffed a laugh. "Seriously? You two actually fit in there together?"

Angus scowled, but the large warrior behind him laughed and slapped Angus's back. "We do. Good and cosy, though, wasn't it, boyo? I enjoyed it, anyway. Happy to repeat it anytime, sweetheart." He winked at the younger man, whose cheeks flushed pink.

"Piss off, old man," he snapped, which only widened my grin.

Hentus snorted. "Enough, Edge, now's not the time."

I studied the warrior. I already knew Edge was Hentus's personal guard. That they'd grown up together and fought side by side—until a woman, and perhaps the lifestyle Hentus had chosen, had come between them.

Hentus walked over to Mari. Her smile was genuine as she flung her arms around him, and for the first time ever, I saw Hentus hug someone. His eyes briefly closed before he kissed the top of her head.

"You're safe now, but we need to get out of here. Once the Mad Prince realises you're gone, all hell will break loose."

"He's not mad! He-he cares about me," Mari hissed, her face falling as her voice petered out.

Hentus cocked his head, disbelief etching the hard planes of his face. "If not him, then who do you think is poisoning you?"

Mari looked at Lia, who gave her a reassuring smile. "I-I don't know," Mari said. She swallowed hard. "His brother?"

Hentus cocked his head, slight lines on the bridge of his nose. "Why would that pathetic weakling take so long to kill you? If he wanted the crown, he'd end you swiftly, along with his brother."

Lia frowned but remained quiet. She held Mari's hand and squeezed it. A silent show of support.

Mari lifted her chin. "I don't know, but I'm going to find out who and why. Right now, we have to leave. Like you said, he'll search for me."

"She's right; you need to leave, and we need to get to where we're going," I said, unhooking the axe from my waist. I didn't expect any of Escalon's forces to know there was an entrance to the tunnels from this room, but I had discovered another entrance to the cave where the gate was. The small steel door had been enchanted to hide it, though it couldn't hide from my shadows. My fingers tightened on the handle of my weapon. My magic was weak, and my body lacked its usual strength, but I could still fight with physical weapons, especially since I needed my remaining magic to destroy the gate.

Angus and Edge eyed my dual-headed axe with appreciation. I lifted it. "It was made by the Onta." I grinned wickedly. "A caste of demons who have their own island kingdom, far from Aethris."

"Aethris?" Angus frowned and looked at Lia like she'd explain what I was talking about. Her face remained stoic. "Where's Aethris?" he asked when she continued her silence.

"In the Netherworld." And I walked to Lia, taking her other hand. She shook me off and disengaged her hand from Mari's. I watched as she went to her dressing table, opened a drawer, and pulled out a locket on a chain. My heart stumbled. Inside was a moonflower, the one I'd given her when she was young. I'd carried it with me for years as a reminder of my mother and had wanted Lia to have it. It had never withered or lost its ethereal glow. Even the sight of it made my eyes burn. Lia clutched it in her fist, her eyes meeting mine.

Without another word, she slipped it on. I couldn't speak. She'd kept it. That last link I'd had to my mother. Not only that, she'd had it preserved in a piece of jewellery. My throat was too thick to speak, so I took up one of the torches I'd stored in Lia's room and lit it from the sconce on her wall. I held it out to Hentus. He shot me a look and leaned down to pick up his own. "I didn't intend to fumble my way back in the dark, Dexalion. I found my own."

I forced a smirk and nodded. "Of course you did."

Handing the torch to Lia, I lit the other one and led the way into the tunnels. I'd need to take the silver from Lia's body to call the portal demon, but I couldn't risk it yet. As much as I wanted to be by her side, she'd made it perfectly clear how she felt about me. Confused thoughts swirled in my head. She'd broken our bond and spent all night barely talking to me, but she'd purposely made sure she didn't leave the flower I'd given her behind. I couldn't think too deeply about what that meant right then; I had a job to do. I'd ask her when we were safe.

Carefully, we descended into the tunnels. The only sounds were the flames of the flickering torch and our footsteps as we walked. There was no sign of anyone else, and we travelled unhindered. Omeron was gathering our remaining men and would meet us near the gate. I'd spent hours searching for another door in the cave and had eventually been rewarded by the steel door. My blood had run cold when I realised it had been locked and disguised with a demon enchantment. Not a powerful one, but one that no one in this castle should know or be able to use. I wondered if the queen had enchanted it before she died. Maybe this was the first time anyone else used it.

After I'd found Lia, I'd spent years trying to find a gate back home. I knew they existed because demons had always escaped our world. All I'd needed to do was find one, and I could have gotten Lia home when she was a little girl. Instead, I'd failed, and everything had started to unravel. I'd felt the presence of another demon when I'd tracked a mark to the castle and had come here to find out how it had gotten into this world. I wanted access to the portal or gate it had used, so I asked.

She'd refused.

We cautiously made our way along the old tunnel, the scent of the sea thickening the air. We reached the intersection in the tunnels. My stomach turned. The smell of excrement and piss remained, but the fear had gone.

Lia studied the tunnel that went to the dungeons before her heavy stare turned to me. The accusation behind it was hard to ignore. Not wanting to incur any further wrath, my grasp was gentle as I pulled her to a halt. "This is us," I said to the others.

Hentus nodded. "Look after her, demon. Hurt her, and no matter your strength, we'll hunt you down and end you."

I gave him a nod of understanding, and didn't doubt he would try.

For the second time that night, I saw Hentus hug someone. Lia held him tightly before giving Angus a hug. I stiffened as the big guy encircled her with his arms. Even though I'd known him as long as Lia had, jealousy seared my chest, and I wanted to knock his hands away. I tensed but stayed back, allowing her to say her goodbyes.

"Bye," rumbled Angus. "Wherever you're going, give 'em hell."

She smiled, though it didn't reach her eyes. "I will. Stay safe, big guy."

"Always," he said, giving her one more hug before they stepped away from each other.

She walked up to Edge and stood on her tiptoes to kiss his cheek. "Been nice meeting you, Edge. Good luck to those beautiful girls. Make sure Kayla hides her magic. She doesn't want to be discovered and end up here."

"Don't worry," said Mari before I could growl a response. "I can help them now."

Edge looked at her and raised his brows.

Mari shrugged. "I've been hiding my magic most of my life. If I can do it, I can show your little girl how to do it as well. Until such time as magickers no longer need to."

I wished I could tell Lia what happened to those people so she would look at me with something other than mistrust and condemnation.

"You're taking her to the Nether to become the Angel and fix the Veil," Mari stated, looking at me.

I debated lying, but what was the point? I nodded. "That's the idea, yes," I agreed, not surprised they'd figured out how Lia fitted into the cycle of life, not just for the Nether, but for this world too.

"Then I wish you luck. Both of you," she whispered, worry ghosting over her features.

"We'll be fine," Lia said quietly and hugged Mari. "Good luck," she whispered in her friend's ear before she stepped closer to my side, pulling my jacket tightly around her. It was little protection against the icy air of the tunnels, but it was better than her bare skin.

"Good luck, Zahlia," Mari whispered, tears lining her eyes before she looked at me. "Promise you'll keep her safe," she pleaded.

That was an easy vow to make. "I promise with every piece of my shadowed heart, I will do my best to keep her safe."

Lia blinked rapidly but didn't look at me and kept her lips pressed tightly shut.

Taking Hentus's hand, Mari turned and walked away from us.

"Come," I commanded, holding out my hand.

To my surprise, Lia took it.

"Yes, let's get this over with; then we can both do what we need to do to fix this mess."

I tried not to listen to the finality in her tone. But my heart sank. No matter what had really happened to those magickers, earning her forgiveness was becoming less and less likely.

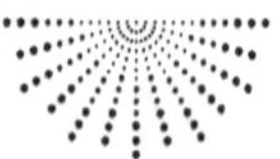

ia

Shivers racked me. The breeze down the tunnel was frigid and relent-less. I caught hold of Dex's jacket. It drowned me, but I did the buttons up and clutched at it, thankful for the protection against the cold and indignity of my exposed flesh. I inhaled deeply, almost groaning when Dex's midnight scent filled my nose. It might be wrong after what I'd done, but it made me feel closer to him. I could at least pretend that I wasn't lying to him. I blinked my tears away, trying to bury the consuming loss I'd felt since I'd severed his magic from me.

I could do this. I could let him free my magic. Because summoning a portal demon would get Dex and me to the Nether. Once there, I'd leave him in the dirt and search out the Demon King. I'd do whatever it took to save our worlds. And I'd do it without the man I'd relied on since I was a little girl. I shook my head, remembering Hentus's words. Dex wasn't a man. He was a demon. A powerful one with his own agenda that I didn't understand—yet. There was a reason he'd killed that magicker and taken the others elsewhere. I was sure of it. But I didn't have time to figure it out.

Dwelling on my situation with Dex was too painful, so I distracted myself with thoughts of my friends. I was glad things were going well between Mari and Hentus. At least my friend would be safe from whatever poison had been used on her. She'd looked a little better at the ball tonight, which had been reassuring. Perhaps she'd found a way to avoid any food and drink supplied by the kitchens after all.

"Where's Dala?" I asked as we trudged deeper into the tunnel.

Dex didn't look at me, just moved forward into the inky blackness, the torch flames flickering, casting eerie silhouettes.

"She's with Omeron and my men. They'll meet us at the gate."

I didn't speak, but relief barrelled through me. Then it registered what he said. "You found another entrance." I wasn't really asking a question. If Dala and Omeron were going to meet us in the cave and they weren't coming this way, there had to be another entrance.

He took my hand. "I did. Hold onto me. From here, the darkness is our friend."

"You could always get these damned cuffs off me. Then I could use the Veil to see," I said, forgetting for a moment that my magic would be drained down here.

"I'm sorry, Lia, it's safer if they stay. If I release your magic so close to the gate, the Heart will drain you again." He paused, searching my face. "And without me to feed from, you won't survive."

I shook my head. "I've survived on what I could take from the Veil all these years. I can do it again."

He shook his head, his dark eyes gleaming before he looked away. "You can't, Angel. Remember? Now your magic is awakened, you'll need to be connected to both sides of the Veil, or eventually, you'll wither and die."

My heart sank, but I shook my head, my chin jutting forward. "I will not wither or die. Nor will I bond with your magic again. I'll find another way."

Dex snarled, dropping the torch. Red flames flickered in his eyes. My heart slammed against my ribs as he walked up to me. His big body crowded me, not stopping until my back was against the wall. He placed his hands on either side of my head, caging me in.

"Let me make myself perfectly clear." He leaned his head down until his lips almost brushed mine, his warm breath and closeness making my head spin. "I will end anyone else you try to bond with." His lips brushed mine, and my breath caught, desire pooling between my legs. My palms flattened on his chest, yet with no magic, I had no strength to push him away. Who was I kidding? I didn't want to. I didn't really loathe him. Maybe he was a liar and a hypocrite and had killed innocent people, yet my body responded to him like it was under a spell. I wanted him. Badly. And I fucking hated that I was weak enough to crave his touch, his lips against mine, devouring me in the way only he could. The last time we'd been together, it had felt more like making love than just sex, and I missed that closeness. But it was useless. We would never be together like that again.

Hardening my heart was the only way I could force words out of my mouth. "I'm not yours, Dex. I never was, and I never will be."

His forefinger trailed down my cheek so tenderly, my eyes stung.

"You are, sweetheart. And no matter what you do, I will always be yours." His mouth slanted over mine. What I had to do, what he'd done, or how much we'd lied to each other; I knew he was right. My heart would always be his, even if I would ultimately have to give my body to someone else.

His warm lips devoured mine, his tongue slipping inside my welcoming mouth. His groan rumbled into my bones, his fingers tangling in my hair, angling my head. Our kiss was hot and heavy and desperate. The world fell away, and all that existed was the feel of his mouth and tongue owning mine.

Until he pulled away.

But only enough that he could talk. His chest heaved, heavy breaths fanning my mouth. He pressed his forehead against mine and closed his eyes. It was intimate and heartbreaking because, despite our chemistry, nothing between us had changed.

"We should go," I whispered, proud that my voice didn't break with the sobs I was holding in.

"We should," he agreed.

The torch flickered out, and without my magic, I was effectively blind. Dex took my hand. Ironically, I had no choice but to trust him as he led me through solid darkness towards a powerful gate that had almost killed me the last time I was near it. I gripped his hand tighter as I stumbled.

"Okay?" he whispered. My lack of sight didn't stop me from feeling the heavy weight of his gaze. He must be looking back over his shoulder.

I nodded, knowing he could see me.

I hadn't asked how he planned to destroy the gate. My knowledge of magic was limited, and knowing how to break apart a doorway to the Nether was beyond me. If it involved blowing anything up, I could only hope that Mari and the others were far away and safe.

The air became stale and thick, heavy with that otherworldly feel. It was almost as if even the sea breeze couldn't find its way into this tunnel. The enchantment had to be something ancient and powerful to linger so thickly in the air.

"Wait," Dex commanded.

I did, halting my footsteps immediately. He pulled my hand from his, but just when I thought he would leave me in the dark, he guided my hand to his lower back.

"What's wrong?" I whispered.

His muscles tensed. "Something doesn't feel right."

"Then we should leave."

"We will. But this gate is a risk to the people of this world. If the Demon King solves the enchantment, he could send an army through it and destroy this world. If he gets through, he could also hunt us down before we have a chance to call a portal demon."

Knowing he was right, I held my tongue.

His fingers tightened around mine, making me grab onto him. "Hold on to me."

Dex slowly moved forward, then stilled. I guessed he was studying the darkness of the cave beyond. Gods, I missed my magic. With it, the darkness had never been a hindrance.

"Aren't your shadows spying for you?"

"They are," he murmured, remaining utterly still. "But they have been silent all night. That worries me."

Goosebumps rose on my skin. He never admitted to being worried. Gently, he pulled my grasp from his shirt.

"Something is very wrong, my shadows never go silent. Stay here. Omeron will arrive soon. When he does, I'll send him to you." He released a steady breath, and a second later, his hand cupped my chin. "I need to destroy that gate, and quickly. We'll join our magic and summon the portal demon when it's done. If something happens to me, Omeron and my warriors are sworn to get you to Haldaag. They'll protect you from the Demon King."

I flinched. That was exactly the opposite of what I needed, but I nodded, and his thumb brushed over my lips.

"I know you don't trust me, and I am sorry for every lie I've told and every action that has led you to hate me. But it will all make sense soon."

His lips brushed mine, and I gasped at the unexpected contact. At the same time, he pushed the handle of a dagger into my empty fingers, and then he was gone. I blinked, not sure what to make of his words or his kiss. I just wished I could tell him I didn't hate him, not at all.

Shrinking down on my haunches and pushing my back against the hard stone, I listened. There was no sound as if the darkness itself swallowed it.

I waited, gripping my dagger, my body winding tighter and tighter. Dex was right. There was nowhere to run from the Demon King. The only thing that could save everyone, was if I ran towards him. A flash of light and shouts came from far down the tunnel, away from the cave.

My heart missed a beat. "Mari," I whispered.

I was torn. I could fumble my way back and make sure my friends were safe or stay in case Dex needed help. The decision was taken out of my hands. An explosion slammed me against the wall, knocking me on my backside. Pain detonated through my skull as my head bounced off the rock, stunning me. I blinked furiously, trying to get my bearings.

"Dex?" I moaned, rolling onto my side. "Dex!" I shouted louder this time.

There was no answer, but the blanket of darkness had lifted. It was chaos. Shouts, snarls, and the clash of weapons rang in my ears. I blinked furiously, trying to understand what was happening. The gate was ablaze with silver flames.

A silhouette stepped through it.

"No…" I whispered as it solidified into a tall, muscular demon, its black armour gleaming. I forced my body to move. I had to help Dex. Another warrior—and another—stepped into the cave. There was a loud, bone-chilling snarl from behind me. A massive shadow with glowing yellow eyes sprinted past. Its skin was spiked along the back of its neck, scales shining like armour over the rest of its body. Horns curled up from behind its ears, and its jaws were massive, easily big enough to bite off a man's head.

I froze as more ran past, the dagger falling from my lax fingers, my brain fumbling for an explanation. They hadn't come through the gate, they'd come from behind me. That meant all of these huge creatures were already in this world. I fumbled along the ground for my dagger. The silver flames burning around the gate cast shadows, making it difficult to see my weapon. I cursed Dex for fixing the gleaming silver bands around my limbs. I'd never wished harder for my magic. My hand desperately searched the stone floor as one of the huge hounds stalked over to me.

"Shit. Shit. Shit," I mumbled, not sure if they were friend or foe.

It stopped about four feet from me but didn't attack. Instead, in one fluid movement, it stood on its back legs, its shape morphing into that of a man.

"Here," he said and swiped my dagger off the ground, handing it to me, handle first.

"Omeron?" I gasped.

"Yes."

"Oh my gods, where's Dala?" I couldn't process that I'd just seen him turn from a beast into a man. I was more worried about my friend.

"She's following," Omeron said, turning so he could see the battle. More and more demons flooded from the gate. My chest squeezed. I didn't understand what was happening but knew I needed to help Dex.

"The gate. How do we destroy it?"

"You can't. Not without your magic."

"Then get these fucking things off me!" I yelled.

"No. If I do, the Heart will drain your magic and kill you."

"No, I-I have to help Dex."

"The best way to help him is to stay alive..."

"I'm here! What did I miss?" snapped a voice from the darkness of the tunnel.

"Dala!" I flung my arms around my friend.

"Hey. You okay?"

"Yes, but all these demons mean the Demon King has found a way to use the gate. We need to stop them and help Dex destroy it before they overwhelm us."

An evil smile stretched Dala's lips, her skin and head gleaming as darkly as Omeron's in the flickering light. "Just like old times, then?"

"No, because I don't have magic," I snapped, glaring at Omeron.

"Free her," Dala demanded, staring at the big warrior.

"No. My Barg and I will handle this. You will both stay here and if we are overwhelmed, you will run." His eyes flashed yellow, his focus totally on Dala.

She sneered, stepping up until she was nose-to- nose with him. "No," she echoed his answer.

I rolled my eyes. We didn't have time for a standoff.

"What are Barg?" I asked instead.

"Me," he said simply, and in the blink of an eye, he became the huge hound I'd seen before. He leapt into the fray and ripped out a throat before I could process how quickly he'd moved.

Coils of darkness wrapped around the next two demons who stepped through the gate. The darkness sucked the life from them until they shrivelled into nothing.

"Dex!"

Still no answer, but I knew it was him. I could feel him, his wrath, his presence. Even without magic, my skin prickled with the energy filling the cave.

Another blast of power smashed Dala and me against the wall.

Demons and hounds fought, snarls and the clash of metal filling the cave, the air thick with the coppery smell of blood.

More and more demons entered the cave.

"Fuck me!" I whispered, fear skittering down my spine. We were completely outnumbered. I looked down the tunnel. We could run. I shook my head and snarled. Not only was there nowhere to go, it wasn't in my nature.

"We have to fight."

Dala grinned. "I thought you'd never ask." She already had a sword in one hand and a dagger in her other. She grinned and shrugged. "I've got my own hidden in my clothes, but he didn't know so he gave me weapons to protect myself."

I scowled. "That's not fair, I only got this!" I held up the small dagger Dex had given me.

"Here," she said with a wide grin, and threw the sword hilt first before pulling another long dagger from a sheath on her waist. She favoured working with an equal-sized weapon in each hand and loved fighting with the Riou daggers she owned. "Let's go and save their arses, even if they don't deserve it."

I nodded, afraid for Dex, no matter that he was more powerful than anyone I'd ever known. We ran forward through the shadows that were trying to smother the silver flames.

Dex was fighting four demons. They circled him warily. He grinned, confidence oozing from him. Yet, I saw the light sheen of sweat gleaming against his paler-than-normal skin.

"I've got the left!" I shouted, stamping down my concern for him.

"Right," yelled Dala.

And we both leapt.

The demon didn't see me coming before my sword had half-severed his neck. Relief poured through me when blood spurted, glad they were mortal when they came through the gate. I tried to catch onto his soul to throw it back through the gate, but I couldn't sense anything. My eyes filled. Now wasn't the time to get upset about my lack of magic. I needed to focus. Another wave of demons entered the cave.

I struck and defended, twirled and jabbed until I was shaking.

Dex used ribbons of magic and ripped the heads off his opponents. With a roar, he sucked in the demons' souls. Except nothing happened. He couldn't take them in, no matter how hard he tried. His eyes widened and flew to mine. Red flecks glowed in their depths, but they were dull. Dread curled in my belly. Why couldn't he feed?

I had no time to ask or think about the answer because more shouts and snarls came from the doorway.

"Oh shit!" Dala yelled, sprinting towards me and standing by my side, sword at the ready. I couldn't believe what I was seeing. More demons stepped into our world, and by their sides came the biggest mage hounds I'd ever seen.

One launched towards us, its focus on me. Instinct drove me. I raised my hand to blast it away with magic. Nothing happened. Just as it went for my neck, I had the presence of mind to shove my dagger up. It slid right into its flesh, but I had no chance to see if my strike killed it because it was ripped backwards, not by shadow, but by Dex's grip on the back of its neck. He roared and lifted it in the air with one hand, driving his other fist through its chest and ripping out its heart. He flung the animal away and strode to my side.

I stared up at him open-mouthed.

"You were supposed to stay safe," he growled, his voice guttural and deep.

"You're…you're…you have…."

I stared at the enormous horns curling from the side of his head and the huge bat-like wings that flared behind his massive shoulders. His skin glowed red, and his shadows eddied around him like living things. He grinned, exposing a row of sharp teeth.

At a loss for words, I shook my head as I looked up at his nearly eight-foot frame.

"What's wrong, my love? Cat got your tongue?"

I vigorously shook my head. "No…gods, you're beautiful…" I breathed, the words tumbling out before I could stop them. And he was. I'd never seen anyone like him. He looked like a powerful god, all rippling muscles and wrath. Yet he seemed taken aback by my compliment, and his face softened as he looked at me.

"Thank you, Ang..." He looked down. His eyes widened, and his mouth dropped open.

"No!" I gaped at the coils of shadow penetrating his chest, shoulders and stomach. Blood spurted from his mouth as he rasped my name.

Then he was gone. Pulled backwards and lifted in the air.

"Dex!" I yelled, sprinting towards him until more ribbons of shadow slithered out of the gate and wrapped around my middle, legs, and arms. It squeezed tight enough to pin my wrists to my sides, forcing me to drop my weapons as it lifted me in the air.

"No!" Dex roared, blood spraying from his mouth and down his chest as he thrashed and fought.

Demons formed a wall in front of us, blocking Omeron and his Barg.

"Lia!" yelled Dala, but she couldn't reach me no matter how hard she fought. In front of the wall of demons, the huge mage hounds snapped and fought, holding my friends near the tunnel entrance. In the distance, other voices yelled, and I heard more shouting but couldn't see a thing as the curtain of shadow thickened. I heard Omeron's furious bellow as he tried to reach his friend but couldn't.

The flames around the gate shimmered so brightly that I was forced to close my eyes. When I opened them, a beautiful man stood below me. His black hair gleamed, and his sleek body was covered in dark armour that was as beautiful as it was intimidating. His silver eyes studied me with a coldness that belied the smile curling his full lips.

My eyes widened. This demon exuded danger and power, and I knew exactly who it was. "Baladon?" I whispered, shaking my head in disbelief. How had I not seen it before?

He lowered me until I was almost standing in front of him. "You know who I really am? Interesting."

"You keep your hands off her!" roared Dex.

Baladon looked over his shoulder, his face dark. Turning fully, he cocked his head, then, brought Dex down to eye level using the shadows under his command.

"Dexalion—the traitor prince. After all these years, you're finally mine. Eternity is such a long time for me to enjoy torturing you."

My heart lurched. "No!" I whispered, my gaze darting to Dex's ashen face.

Baladon glanced back, his eyes studying me intently before his smile stretched into a grin. "Really, Dexalion? Now, that's just cruel. You made her fall in love with you?"

"I'll fucking end you if you hurt her," Dex panted, though his voice was weak.

The King of Demons laughed. "Tell me, does she know the truth?"

"She knows what I am," Dex hissed, blood trickling from his mouth.

Baladon cocked his head. "Really?"

He drew me closer and lowered me until I stood beside him, but his shadows didn't release me, and his attention remained on Dex. "But what about all the other lies and half-truths you have fed her?" He crossed his arms over his chest, a bitter sneer curling his lips. "You forget how many Heart cycles I've known you. There are other things besides what you are that she needs to know before she makes her choice. Aren't there, Dexalion?"

Dex stilled his fight against the shadow. Whether it was Baladon's words or because he was too weak to fight anymore, I didn't know.

"What are you talking about?" Dex asked, his throat bobbing and his eyes flicking to me before he coughed violently.

I wriggled against my bonds.

Baladon looked at me, his humour gone. All of a sudden, the bonds disappeared completely. "He has lied to you, Zahlia."

I shuffled my feet to get my balance. There was little point in trying to run. Baladon was obviously as powerful as Dex. I bit my lip. Dex hadn't used his shadow as much as I'd expected him to in the battle. Was he right? Had I made him weak by severing our bond? Baladon watched me closely. Perhaps he thought I *would* run. Well, he didn't know me. At all. I would never flee from a fight, and certainly not when someone I cared about was in danger. I cocked my head and met Baladon's gaze.

"He isn't the only one, though, is he? You told me you were a guest of the prince's for the ball."

Baladon grinned, ignoring the wet sound of Dex's breathing.

"Oh, but I am. It wasn't a lie. I just didn't quite make it to the ball-room." He turned to the gate.

I gasped when Haruin stepped through. He didn't look stooped or weak. He didn't limp or wheeze. He looked tall, solid and completely well. He smirked at me.

"He didn't lie, magicker. He is my guest. And now you are his."

Haruin turned to Dex. "It's good to see you put in your place…"

"Now, now, Haruin. Let me explain some things to Zahlia before you steal all my fun."

Haruin scowled but nodded, his eyes on Dex. He completely ignored me. I was insignificant to him. Whatever this was, it had to do with Dex, not me.

"Zahlia?" Baladon held out his hand.

I looked at it, then at Dex.

"There are things about this demon you need to know. He's a liar and a murderer. If you go with him, your life and the lives of everyone you love will be at stake. If you come with me, I will ensure you get everything you need to save both our worlds."

"You could be lying too," I pointed out.

His face was grave. "Yes, I could, but I'm not. Once you know the truth, you can make up your mind. If you want to stay with him, I'll not stop you, but know we will become enemies." His gaze met mine. "Do you want the Demon King as an enemy, Angel of Aether?"

I swallowed hard. My decision to search him out had already been made, but I cocked my head and gave him my best arrogant smile. "I haven't decided yet. But, let me promise you; you do not want me as *your* enemy. So whatever you tell me now had better be the truth, or I'll wipe you from existence."

He laughed, a deep, rich sound that vibrated into my bones. "I like you already, Angel."

Dex snarled. "Don't call her that. You don't deserve her."

"And you do?" snapped Baladon, more of his shadow wrapping around Dex and squeezing. Pain etched Dex's face, but he didn't drop his eyes from Baladon's.

"Let me tell you all about the traitor prince," Baladon said to me. "He killed the Demon King—our father before he ran like the coward he is."

I blinked. "You're brothers?"

Baladon snarled. "Yes. For what our blood connection is worth. Or at least half-brothers. Our father is the same. Our mothers are not. Dexalion's mother was a leech. A parasite that sucked the life from my father whenever she could. All she did was take."

"She did not!" bellowed Dex before coughs racked his body, blood speckling his chin. "That bastard starved her. He beat her and abused her, then went back to his queen!"

Baladon's eyes burned red. "That's right! His queen! My mother! The woman he loved and who loved him! You killed him. You took him from us, and she has lived with a broken heart ever since!"

Spears of shadow slammed Dex against the cave wall. Haruin inhaled, his eyes gleaming, a smirk on his thin lips. Dex hung limply, but his eyes met mine. Pleading.

My heart skipped a beat. He'd never looked at me like that. I hated this. All I wanted was to help him, but if I did, my chance with the Demon King was over. So was my opportunity to heal this world.

Baladon turned to me. "Even though this traitor hid in his stinking lair in Haldaag for Heart cycles, his spies fed him information. He discovered my father had found the next Angel of Aether. You were born in the kingdom of Myrkis. My father ordered you to be protected and kept safe, and the Demon King has always had an accord with the king and queen of the mortal realm. He knew it would be safer for you here than in the Netherworld. He knew Dexalion would be searching for you so that he could take the Netherworld throne for his own. It's all he's ever wanted."

Dex shook his head. "You lying bastard," he croaked.

Baladon bared sharp teeth. "That's rich coming from you." He looked back at me. "My father paid your parents to raise you here…"

"That's a lie…" spat Dex.

Baladon glared at him. "Is it? Then why did you hunt them down and kill them?"

I gasped, my eyes wide. "No…" I shook my head, trying to process, yet unwilling to believe it was true. "No...No. That person had red eyes. And he was huge..." I couldn't speak as it hit me. Dex was a demon. He could change his shape and appearance. He'd already admitted the boy I grew up with was a lie.

Dex's gaze implored me. "Lia, please...they weren't your parents. They, *he*, my father, he stole you from your real parents..."

"Shut up!" I ground out, panting heavily as tears tipped down my cheeks. How could he? More lies... "You killed them? It was you? All this time?" I was going to be sick. I leaned forward, taking huge gulping breaths as the world spun. Giving him the benefit of the doubt with the magickers was one thing, but this?

A hand landed on my back, rubbing in calming circles. "I'm afraid it's true, Zahlia. He killed your parents because he wanted you for himself."

"It's not true, Lia. They weren't your parents."

"Stop," I said, shaking my head at Dex. It was impossible to sort truth from lies. I needed time to think. "I can't deal with any more of your lies right now. It doesn't matter if they were my birth parents or not. They were the only parents I knew. And you killed them." I closed my eyes against gruesome memories. "You sliced them open, then spent the next ten years of my life lying to me." It was clear what I had to do. Baladon needed to believe I was totally on his side, yet out of both of these powerful brothers, despite everything, I knew who I trusted more. It didn't matter, not when the survival of two worlds depended on my success. With my dagger in my hand, I stepped forward, and thrust it into Dex's chest. Thank the Aether, it wouldn't kill him so long as he didn't bleed out before his warriors could reach him, but Baladon would believe I meant it to. I hoped Dex would forgive me, just as he had begged for my forgiveness. The agony in his eyes, on his face, was blurred by my tears. "You lied! Every. Damned. Day. You deserve every bit of pain you're suffering. You *bastard*."

I stepped away, ignoring the anguished bellows of Omeron and the other Barg, who howled, separated from Baladon's troops by a wall of shadow. Dala stared at me, but not even the horror on her face could stop this from happening. I met her eyes, willing her to understand.

Haruin smiled, his eyes glittering. "If I could, I'd kill him myself, magicker. He came to the castle years ago. He was the one who murdered my mother."

I looked at his evil face but couldn't find it in me to speak. His words didn't surprise me, but I couldn't feel anything other than guilt at my actions. None of this felt right. If Dex was telling the truth, I was aligning myself with a king who would treat me as little more than a slave. But what choice did I have? The tome had been clear. The Angel of Aether had to be bound to the Demon King to give both worlds a chance at survival. Numbness spread through my whole body, and my heart shut down.

Haruin stepped closer to Dex, studying his pale face and devastated expression. Dex didn't look at him, he was still focused on me, mouthing a word I would never forget.

"Sorry..."

Acknowledging him, letting him know I believed him would be a mistake. He had to let me go.

Haruin grabbed Dex's hair and yanked his head back, but looked at me. "He wanted to know where the gate was so he could get you home after he killed your parents. He killed my mother because she wouldn't tell him. I followed them the night he threatened her and tortured her. No matter what magic he used or how he hurt her, she still wouldn't tell him. This gate has been in my family for over a thousand years. The mage hounds were a gift from Baladon's father to the ancient ancestors of our family as a reward for protecting the gate."

"Why do you hate magic so much, then?" I managed to ask, though all I wanted to do was chop his damned fingers off for touching Dex like that.

"Because my mother knew magickers could destroy the gate if they learnt how to wield their power, and she always wanted a way back to the Nether. Destroying the gate would end our ties, and my families power. Now I don't have to worry." He nodded at Baladon, whose eyes glinted darkly, his expression blank as he nodded back. "The King and I have...an understanding. That understanding means I will rule this world; Baladon will rule his own. The gate will remain, but all magickers here will be hunted down and executed by the army of mage hounds and demons I now have."

My heart ached, my stomach roiling. "You can't kill all of them. There are too many…."

Haruin flashed a cold smile. "Oh, I can, and I will." He faced the Demon King. "Especially now that the Demon King recognises my power and right to conquer this world."

There was a sneer in his tone, but Baladon merely nodded, his face expressionless.

The Demon King turned to me, dismissing Haruin, and held out his hand.

"Well? You are the Angel of Aether. You have a choice: stay here and watch your world die, or come with me and save both worlds. I will not force your hand."

I blinked the tears from my eyes. There was no choice, and something told me he knew it. Dex had lied, killed, threatened, and cheated to keep me in the dark. And now he'd neutralised my magic. Despite all that, I believed he had his reasons. The trouble was, it didn't make any difference.

"If I come with you, I want these off." I held up my arms. Even covered in blood, the silver bands glinted.

"No! Lia, don't. Please. He's lying…"

I spun around, settling my face into a mask of anger, part of me wanting to hurt him for all the lies he'd told, part of me hating that I had to do this. "No! You're the liar, Dexalion. You! No one else!" Ignoring his bubbling breaths and the blood trickling from his wounds and lips was so hard. I had to believe he would survive. Beyond the curtain of shadow, Omeron glared at me, the promise of vengeance in his eyes. At his side, Dala pleaded silently, shaking her head.

"Don't go," she mouthed, her eyes wide.

I turned away from her. She was better off here, in this world, with Dex and Omeron. She was strong. She'd survive. If I cured the Veil. I forced my gaze to meet Baladon's. "I choose to go with you. I want to save the Veil."

Baladon smiled gravely and held out his hand. "Good. A whole new world awaits you, Angel."

"No!" bellowed Dex.

"Quiet, traitor!" Baladon hissed. "You have become weak in this world. You are no match for me. I don't want you anywhere near my Angel, so I will forego my right to avenge my father's death by taking into my world to torture you, instead, I leave you to rot in this magicless world." He slammed Dex into the wall before throwing him through the shadow curtain towards Omeron.

My whole body tensed as Dex's head cracked against the wall. Bile flooded my throat as he fell to the floor, his head rolling enough that I saw the concave shape of his skull. Blood oozed from the stab wound, forming a pool under his inert body. Omeron's roar covered my sob, and Baladon's hand tightened on mine as he stepped through the gate, pulling me behind him. All of the Demon King's warriors followed.

There was a painful tug at my soul as we passed through the light side of the Veil before Baladon continued through the dark side. Both sides of the Veil were ethereal and almost non-existent.

Beyond the gate was a world of darkness so black I could barely see. I found myself clutched in Baladon's grip as he walked the short distance over a rocky surface to several four legged creatures hooked up to what looked like a dark carriage.

"Come, let me take you home. You can rest and process all that has happened in comfort and safety."

The carriage bounced and rocked as we climbed in, but the inside was plush and comfortable. I had no energy to appreciate the deep red velvet seats or warmth. Sinking into the soft seat, I closed my eyes against the pain in my heart, wishing I could switch off my emotions. Turning away from the Demon King I stared out of the window even thought there was nothing but blackness outside.

Fear, and pain at what I'd done, crushed me until I could barely breathe. Even the oppressive silence in the carriage, and the weight of Baladon's gaze couldn't turn my thoughts from the memory of my blade slicing through Dex's flesh. My fists clenched. I just wanted to go back, to change everything, but I couldn't. I closed my eyes exhausted, and slipped into oblivion.

CHAPTER THIRTY-ONE

ex

I roared, the agony that swamped my body nothing compared to the feel of my heart shattering into a million tiny pieces. Through a haze of pain and helplessness, I watched the other half of my soul walk away.

As she stepped through the darkness, holding onto Baladon as if he were her lifeline, Haruin stepped up. Behind him, soldiers poured into the cave from the steel doorway. They weren't demons, but neither were they fully human.

He grinned, his eyes flashing with a vicious light. "Attack! Spare none. Show no mercy!" His manic gaze landed on me. "Bring him to me!"

The blank-faced, blank-eyed soldiers moved forward. There was no sound, no rage—nothing.

"Fuck, they're bespelled," muttered Omeron.

I coughed, blood filling my mouth. I spat it out. I was immortal, but my head was foggy and painful enough that I knew my skull was crushed, and this amount of blood loss would render me useless until I could access enough magic to heal. Which meant I'd never heal, not without my bond to Lia. I swallowed the coppery thickness in my mouth, trying to curb my fear, and closed my eyes against the flashing lights in my vision. The dagger Lia had shoved in my chest couldn't kill me, but severing my magic eventually would. I didn't blame her, not when she had no idea how magical bonds worked. None of this was her fault. If I'd been honest with her from the beginning, maybe things would be different now.

I met my friend's gaze. "You have to leave. They outnumber us."

Bodies littered the ground, some of them my loyal Barg who had lived in this world, protecting and serving me from a distance. My heart squeezed in anguish. I'd failed them. I'd failed their families. Most of all. I'd failed my Angel.

Omeron's gaze darted between Dala and me. He grabbed Dala's arm. "You have to go."

"No! I will not. I have to get through that gate and find my friend."

Before she'd finished speaking, the gate burst into silver flames and burned hot and bright.

Haruin's eyes widened before he cursed loudly. He tore his gaze from the gate and stormed towards us, chanting. Hatred shone in his eyes as the air exploded, sending us all flying into the nearest wall.

Agony swamped me again, and my spine cracked, sending a white-hot blast of pain down my legs before I hit the ground. Omeron landed beside me. He had changed mid-air, and his armoured scales saved him from the worst of the blast. He shook and staggered to his paws. It was then I saw Dala underneath him. He'd protected her from the worst of the blast. Her eyes were closed, and blood trailed from her temple.

"Get her out of here! Quickly!" I hissed at him.

He bared his teeth, but we both knew I was done. My strength was used up, my body broken.

Omeron howled. Other Barg limped towards us through the dust and rubble. The gate was gone, but Haruin had somehow shielded his soldiers from the blast. And they were coming. I wouldn't sacrifice any more of my men.

"You will all leave. Right now."

I pushed all of the Alpha strength and magic I had left into that command, gritting my teeth against the need to pass out.

Omeron snarled and snapped at the air, but he changed back. Naked, he scooped Dala from the ground. He looked down at me.

I shook my head. "There's no point trying to save me, Ome. I'm dead without her."

"Not yet, you're not," he growled.

I smiled weakly. "No, but I will be eventually."

He snarled. "Do not give up, my King. We'll find a way. He'll use her and lie to her like your father did to your mother. Are you going to allow that?"

I swallowed against the lump in my throat, and for the first time since my mother died, tears burned my eyes.

"You have to get her back," Omeron insisted.

I nodded if only to get him to leave. "We will. For now, you'll leave me here and find somewhere to recover." I thought of my mother's words and my promise to her. Omeron was right. I had to get Lia back and at least make sure she was safe and bonded to a demon who Could protect her before I died.

"Go." My order was absolute.

Omeron nodded, but I knew he would return.

The dust and smoke cleared, and I saw the blank-faced warriors stalking my way. Haruin watched with a manic grin on his face.

My magic was but a flicker. I could heal my spine or use what was left to take down some of these soldiers. I quickly shoved it into my spine to knit my bones. No matter my other injuries, at least I could fight longer and give the others a chance to escape.

Haruin's grin widened as if he knew what I planned, though he didn't move, merely stood there with his arms folded over his chest. How had I ever thought him crippled or weak? He'd lied far more effectively than I ever had.

I staggered to my feet and pulled the sword still hanging down my back. My arms shook, and my legs wobbled. Pain hammered my skull threatening to overwhelm me, but I wouldn't show it. Hoisting my weapon, I struck, fighting with everything I had left. The first blade that slashed my skin burned like hell. I staggered under the agony of it. My eyes widened as an arrow thudded into my chest, followed by another and another. The strikes were well placed enough that they incapacitated me.

"Cease!" commanded Haruin.

The soldiers parted. I swayed, but the new blood pouring from me on top of my other wounds was too much. I sagged to my knees. Lifting my chin, I glared at the mortal prince who had bested me.

Haruin smiled and held out his hand. A bow appeared. All I could do was watch as he knocked a silver arrow and pulled back the string.

"You will not die from this. But you will wish you had. My mother deserved better than to be ended by a traitorous bastard like you."

His fingers released the string. The force of the arrow knocked the breath from my lungs. Excruciating pain flooded every part of my body. I tried to swing my sword, but it was too heavy to lift. Another arrow drove into my thigh and another into my other leg. I toppled backwards, a dozen or more arrows embedded in my skin.

"Lia," I managed to whisper. The weapon she'd stabbed me with lay on the ground nearby. *I'm sorry I failed you,* was the only thought in my head as I was hauled up and dragged to Haruin.

His hand cruelly pulled my hair, yanking my head back. Satisfaction burned in his eyes. "I've waited a long time for revenge. Now, you'll have plenty of time to appreciate all the lessons I've studied about torture. My brother wouldn't agree to this, but he no longer matters. The crown will soon be mine, and once Baladon bonds with that magical whore as per our deal, the Veil will heal. The people of Tetron will revere me as their saviour, or they will die, while the general who failed them, and the prince who was so mad he forgot about them, will rot in this dungeon."

He nodded at the men who held me. They dragged me down the dark corridors without thought for the arrows that stuck out of my flesh and snagged on the walls and floors. I ground my teeth together, unwilling to give them the satisfaction of screaming.

After what felt like an eternity of agony, they left me bleeding in the darkness. I prayed with everything I had to the Higher Powers for strength. I would not abandon Lia to the Demon King, nor would I die here in this stinking cell. I was a prince of darkness and shadow. I'd find a way out of this or die trying.

Thank you for reading the beginning of Dex and Lia's story!
Their fight for survival continues in Angel Of Aether.
Please could you take a moment to leave a review on your chosen book platform and Goodreads? Every review makes a difference.
Thank you so much.

Special Editions of the Aether Chronicles with full colour maps, character art, exclusive formatting, under-jacket art, foiled dust jackets, and optional sprayed edges can be purchased from
www.karentomlinson.com/shop

N
W E
S
XERION
AXERIA
AETHER KINGDOM
HEART OF THE AETHER
ERAMIN
AETRIS
ALGARON
WARLORD ENCAMPMENT
HALDAAG KINGDOM
MYRKIS KINGDOM
MYRKIS
HALDAAG CITY
ONYA
NETHERWORLD

CHARACTER AND PRONUNCIATION GUIDE

CHARACTERS

ZAHLIA (Zaa-lee-ah) (Lia) A thief and member of the casteless criminal gang, the Vipers.

DEXALION AZARAAH (Dex-a-lee-on Az-a-raah) Once a member of the Vipers. General of the Tetron army.

DALA (D-ar-la) Close friend to Zahlia. Half Riou (ree-oo) warrior. Member of the Vipers.

OMERON (Oh-mer-ron) (Ome) (Oh-mee) Dexalion's friend and guard.

HENTASIAN NZIRA ALAMAN (HENTUS) (Hen-tus) The Viper. Leader of the Vipers

EDGAR (EDGE) Hentus's right hand man and friend.

KAYLA (Kay-lah) Edge's daughter

DAISY (Day-see) Edge's daughter

ANGUS (Ang-us) Viper. Zahlia's friend.

MARIANNE (MARI) (Marry-anne) Queen of Tetron. Married to Escalon-the Mad Prince.

PRINCE ESCALON (THE MAD PRINCE) (E-s-ca-lon) Heir to the kingdom of Tetron. Married to Marianne. Brother to Haruin.

PRINCE HARUIN (ha-roo-in) Sickly prince. Younger brother of Escalon.

GARRET (Ga-r-et) Viper. Captain of his own Viper faction.

JESS Dexalion's maid.

KENDRICK Mortal accused of having magic.

BALADON (Bal-a-don) Demon King

KING ALAMAN (Al-a-man) Assassinated King of Pa'Dur

ANDRAS (And-ra-s) Usurper of the throne of Pa'dur

THE ANGEL OF AETHER A goddess of souls. She guides all souls to the Heart to be judged.

PLACES

TETRON Southern kingdom in the mortal world. Ruled by Escalon.

TETRIS Capital city of Tetron

PA'DUR Kingdom that borders Tetron

KAMARAT (Kam-ar-rat) Capital city of Pa'dur

MEDALLION ISLES Cluster of tropical islands south of Tetron that trade with the other mortal kingdoms

CIMERIA (Ky-m-ear-ia) Palace in Aetris and home of the Demon King

AETRIS (Eat-ris) Capital city of the Aether Kingdom (Nether World)

AETHER KINGDOM (Ee-th-er) The biggest kingdom in the Nether World and seat of the Demon King

ONTA An island kingdom in the Nether World, renown for producing spectacular weapons.

MYRKIS (Mer-kis) A Nether World Kingdom

HALDAAG (Hal-darg) A kingdom in the Nether World. Land of the Barg.

OTHER INFORMATION

ORM Tetron's currency

PUCHINELLA (pu-ch-in-ella) Heavily spiced savoury pastry delicacy of Tetron

MAGE HOUNDS Large black hounds found only in Tetris and owned only by the royal family, that can scent out magic in mortals.

BARG Shape shifters. Demons who can have humanoid form.

Known as hounds of death. Their heads are as high as a human's. They are scaled with boney exoskeleton and huge horns.

MOONFLOWER (A.K.A The Heart Flower. A flower with magical properties that grows only in the Nether World. Pearlescent flowers with black vines and leaves.

THE HIGHER POWERS The gods who made both the Nether world and the Mortal World.

THE HEART The center of all life in both worlds. A place where souls will go to be reborn into the world it chooses for them

THE VEIL The light of energy from all living things that forms a barrier between both worlds

THE DARK VEIL The power that balances the light of the Veil and gives sustenance to the ANGEL OF AETHER

PORTAL DEMON A demon of the Nether World who can balance the Dark Veil with the Veil enough to form a portal from the Nether World to the Mortal World

REAPERS Demons of the Nether World who search for the energy of souls.

ABOUT THE AUTHOR

Karen Tomlinson is a USA Today Bestselling author of action-packed, spicy romantic fantasy, and paranormal romance books.

Karen writes a mix of M/M, M/F, and M/M/F romance. If you love fierce female leads, morally grey and powerful Alpha heroes, magic, action, battles, bloodshed, hot scenes, and a HEA (happy ever after) then look no further! Come and meet amazing characters who will destroy worlds for those they love.

Like you, Karen adores books and likes nothing better than to lose herself in a spicy romance with]a HEA! She lives in Derbyshire, England, (think Mr. Darcy territory) with her husband, twin girls, and her gorgeous Dalmatian. As well as reading and writing books, she loves keeping fit, walking in the hills with her family, and dancing around with her earbuds in while singing badly!

You can find her books, any special editions, including special edition e-books, & current selling platforms on her website: http://karentomlinson.com

If you want a gorgeous SE of the Aether Chronicles head here: https://www.karentomlinson.com/shop

Find all of Karen's book and their links on:
www.karentomlinson.com/books

The Goddess and The Guardians Series
(M/F High Fantasy)
A Bond of Destiny and Dragons
A Bond of Venom and Magic
(ABOVAM available onAUDIBLE)
A Bond of Blood and Fire
A Bond of Sovereigns and Souls
A Bond of Swords and Sacrifice
The Goddess and the Guardians Boxset

The Eight Kingdoms
(M/F High Fantasy)
Blessed King (Duet #1)
Wiccan Queen (Duet #2)
Emerald Warrior (Standalone)

Shadow Sentinels (M/F Urban Fantasy Shifter Romance)

Beginnings
Wrecked
Ruin
Reign

Shadow Sentinel's world (M/F Standalone Paranormal Shifter Romance)
Alpha Scorned
Broken Alpha

M/M Vampire PNR (Blood Throne World)
Vampire Chained
M/M/F Vampire Urban Fantasy
Blood Throne Series
Coming soon!

The Aether Chronicles (M/F Romantic Dark Fantasy)
Veil Of Souls
Angel Of Aether
King Of Demons

NEVER WANT TO MISS A RELEASE?
Join Karen's newsletter>>
https://www.karentomlinson.com/subscribe